# TO LIVE AGAIN

## AND

# THE SECOND TRIP

## TWO COMPLETE NOVELS

## ROBERT SILVERBERG

OPEN  ROAD

INTEGRATED MEDIA

NEW YORK

*To Live Again* copyright © 1969 by Robert Silverberg
*The Second Trip* copyright © 1972 by Robert Silverberg
*The Second Trip* first appeared as a serial in *Amazing*, July and September, 1971.

ISBN 978-1-4804-4852-0

This edition published in 2013 by Open Road Integrated Media, Inc.
180 Maiden Lane
New York, NY 10038
www.openroadmedia.com

# PRAISE FOR THE WRITING OF ROBERT SILVERBERG

"*Nightwings* is Robert Silverberg at the top of his form, and when Silverberg is at the top of his form, no one is better. A haunting, evocative look at a crumbling Earth of the far future and a human race struggling to survive amidst the ruins, full of memorable characters and images that will long linger in your memory, this is one of the enduring classics of science fiction."
—George R. R. Martin

"What wonders and adventures he has to tell us."
—Ursula K. Le Guin

"No matter if Silverberg is dealing with material that is practically straight fiction, or going way into the future . . . his is the hand of a master of his craft and imagination." —*Los Angeles Times*

"When one contemplates Robert Silverberg it can only be with awe. In terms of excellence he has few peers, if any." —*Locus*

"The John Updike of science fiction."
—*The New York Times Book Review*

"In the field of science fiction, Silverberg occupies a place in the highest echelon. His work is distinguished by elegance of style, intellectual precision, and far-reaching imagination."
—Jack Vance

"One of the very best." —*Publishers Weekly*

"Robert Silverberg is our best . . . Time and time again he has expanded the parameters of science fiction."
—*The Magazine of Fantasy and Science Fiction*

"He is a master." —Robert Jordan

*For Damon and Kate Knight*

# Contents

# TO LIVE AGAIN

There is therefore but one comfort left,
that though it be in the power of the weakest arm to take away life,
it is not in the strongest to deprive us of death:
God would not exempt himself from that;
the misery of immortality in the flesh he undertook not, that was in it immortal.

SIR THOMAS BROWNE: *RELIGIO MEDICI*

# 1

The lamasery rose steeply from the top of the bluff on the Marin County side of the Golden Gate. Feeling a faint cramp in his left calf, John Roditis got out of the car near the toll plaza and, stretching and kicking, looked across the water at the gleaming yellow building, windowless, sleek, ineffably holy as a fountainhead of good karma. It was an extraordinarily warm day. San Francisco had been gripped by an unaccustomed heat wave throughout the four days of Roditis' visit. Hot weather in the psychological sense did not trouble Roditis; he thrived on it, in fact. But when heat came to him not as a function of metaphor but as a blazing golden eye staring from above, he longed to switch on the air conditioner.

There was no way for him to change the outdoor environment to that degree. At least, not yet. Given enough minds in one skull, though, who was to say what limits a man might have?

Roditis gestured at the lamasery. "I hope it's cooler in there, eh?"

"It will be," Charles Noyes said. "The guru is cool."

Roditis scowled at his associate's pun. "Still infested with the antique slang?"

"Not me. It's—Kravchenko." As he spoke the name of the persona who shared his body, Noyes' grin turned to a grimace, and he clung to the polished railing just before him. His long body sagged. His elbows trembled and beat against his ribs. "Damn him! Damn him!" Noyes grunted.

"Have him erased," Roditis suggested.

"You know I can't!"

"When an unruly persona threatens the integrity of the host, he ought to be expelled," said Roditis crisply. "If Kozak made trouble for me I'd throw him out in a minute, and he knows it. Or Walsh. Either of them. I can't afford to have a troublemaker in my head. Can you?"

"Stop it, John."

"I'm just talking common sense."

"Kravchenko doesn't like it. He's giving me a hard time." Noyes' arm came up from the railing in a fitful jerk. "He's fighting me. He's trying to speak."

"You won't be satisfied," said Roditis, "until he goes dybbuk on you. Throws you out of your own body."

"I'd kill him and me both first!"

Roditis scowled. "You're becoming an unstable bastard, you realize it? If I weren't so fond of you I'd let you go. Come on: into the car. Mustn't keep the cool guru waiting, or he'll get hot under the toga. Or whatever he wears." Roditis, chuckling, opened the car door and pulled Noyes away from the railing. There was momentary confusion as Noyes struggled to regain full control of his limbs. Then Roditis thrust his companion into the car, got in beside him, and slammed the door.

"Finish the route as programed," Roditis said to the car.

The generator thrummed and the car backed out of the plaza area, swung around, and headed for the tollbooths. The actuarial sign over the row of booths announced the day's vehicle toll: 83¢. As the car passed through a booth, a brief data interchange took place between the bridge computer and the car's, and Roditis' central bank account was automatically billed for that amount. Onward sped the car over the elderly bridge and toward the yellow shaft of the lamasery just beyond.

Within the cool depths of the car, Roditis flecked perspiration from his corrugated brow and regarded the other man uneasily. He was growing more and more worried about Noyes, who perhaps was becoming a risky liability. It would be a pity to have to let Noyes go, after a relationship that had lasted so long and worked so well.

They had met in college, nineteen years before. Their roles had been reversed then: Noyes was the campus leader, tall and dashing, appropriately Anglo-Saxon, with the fair hair and blue eyes of the highest caste, and seven generations of respectable money behind him, while Roditis, the immigrant shoemaker's son who looked the part, was short, thick-bodied, dark, a scholarship student, a nobody. But Noyes had a gift for dissipating his many assets, Roditis a gift for capitalizing on what little he had. It was an attraction of opposites, instant, permanent. Now Roditis controlled an empire, and Noyes was a cog in that vast wheel. Poor Noyes. He hadn't been able to handle his own wealth, couldn't deal with a fine wife, was even making a mess of his persona transplant. Roditis hated to patronize anyone, but he couldn't help a certain feeling of smugness as he contemplated his own position vis-à-vis Noyes. Sad. Sad.

The car purred to a halt in the gravelly parking oval adjoining the lamasery. The men got out. It seemed to be at least ten degrees hotter on this side of the bridge. Reflected heat from the lamasery's polished sides, Roditis wondered? He looked up, and felt Anton Kozak within him responding affirmatively to the chaste elegance of the architecture. Roditis had become infinitely more aware of esthetic matters since taking on Kozak's persona. It had seemed odd to some that a businessman like Roditis would choose a sonic sculptor for his second transplant, but Roditis knew what he was going toward. He was assembling a portfolio of personae as another man might assemble a portfolio of common stocks—for diversity, and for ultimate high profit.

"Feeling better?" Roditis asked.

"Much," said Noyes.

"Kravchenko is pushed way down?"

"I think so. He's had his exercise for the day."

"If there's more trouble while we're here, ask the guru to help you. He'll run a few simple exorcisms, I'm sure."

Looking pale, Noyes said, "It won't be necessary, John," and they approached the building.

Sensors scanned them. They were expected; the tall Gothic doorway peeled open, admitting them. Within, all was dark, cool, reflective. Roditis caught glimpses of saffron-robed monks scuttling to and fro in the rear arcades. A great deal of money had gone into the building of this lamasery; some of the best families had contributed to the fund. They said that the late Paul Kaufmann had donated over a million dollars fissionable. It was funny to imagine a rich Jew contributing that much money to a Buddhist monastery's construction fund; but, Roditis reminded himself, Kaufmann had not been a terribly orthodox Jew, any more than these monks were terribly orthodox Buddhists. And what had a million dollars more or less mattered to Paul Kaufmann? The crafty old banker had had his motives. Roditis saw a kindred spirit in Kaufmann. He himself had reached wealth too late to aid in this place's construction fund, but now he was here to make amends for that, and for what he thought were much the same motives.

Two shaven-headed monks emerged from inner rooms. They made appropriate pseudo-Buddhist gestures, tracing mandalas in the air, touching cardinal points of their bodies, murmuring gentle welcoming mantras. Roditis, unsmiling, flicked a glance at Noyes. The tall man seemed as awed as though he stood at the threshold of God's throneroom. Once upon a time, Roditis would have envied Noyes his ability to don such a goddam sincere expression of respect, as contrasted to Roditis' own look of impassive, poker-faced piety. But now Roditis was not at all sure whether Noyes was faking anything. In these latter troubled years, old Chuck might well have turned into a believer. Stranger things had happened.

"The guru will be with you shortly," said one of the monks. "Will you remove your worldly coverings and join us in prayer?"

He indicated a room where they might change. Within, Roditis stripped away his sweat-stained clothing and gratefully shucked his shoes. His body, at thirty-seven, was tight-muscled and solid, a compact bullet of flesh still traveling unswervingly on its designed trajectory. Noyes, who was no older, still gave the illusion of lanky grace, but it was only an illusion. Beneath his clothes the tall man was thickening at the paunch, going flabby at thigh and rump. Such weakness of the flesh struck Roditis as a symptom of the decay of the will. He judged men harshly in this respect.

Arrayed now in loose, billowing robe and soft sandals, Roditis said, "It's certainly more comfortable this way. If men were saner they'd dress like this all the time."

"It wouldn't be practicable."

"No," Roditis agreed. "It leads to undue relaxation. A slackening of striving. Are we supposed to wait here for them to come back and get us?"

"I suppose," said Noyes.

The room was bare of furniture, but for the two saddle-backed benches on which they had left their worldly clothes. The walls were of some dark, highly reflective stone, slabs of black marble, perhaps, or possibly onyx. If onyx could be had in such quantities, Roditis thought. There was an inscription in inlaid letters of gold leaf on each wall. The one facing Roditis said:

If so far you have been deaf to the teaching, listen to it now! An overpowering craving will come over you for the sense-experiences which you remember having had in the past, and which through your lack of sense organs you cannot now have. Your desire for rebirth becomes more and more urgent; it becomes a real torment to you. This desire now racks you; you do not, however, experience it for what it is, but feel it as a deep thirst which parches you as you wander along, harassed, among deserts of burning sands. Whenever you try to take some rest, monstrous forms rise up before you. Some have animal heads on human bodies, others are gigantic birds with huge wings and claws. Their howlings and their whips drive you on, and then a hurricane carries you along, with those demonic beings in hot pursuit. Greatly anxious, you will look for a safe place of refuge.

They read it in silence. Roditis said, "That's a lot of gold to waste on such nonsense. Recognize it?"

"The *Bardo Thödol*, of course."

"Yes. The good old Book of the Dead, eh? A hot line of revelation straight from the Himalayas."

Noyes pointed to the inscription on the rear wall. "What do you make of that one?"

Roditis turned, narrowing his eyes. It read:

He who lacketh discrimination, whose mind is unsteady and whose heart is impure, never reacheth the goal, but is born again. But he who hath discrimination, whose mind is steady and whose heart is pure, reacheth the goal, and having reached it is born no more.

A muscle twitched in Roditis' cheek. He said bleakly, "It's pure nirvana-propaganda. Subversion. I thought they didn't try to push that concept in the Western world."

"They can't help allowing a little of the orthodox theory to survive," Noyes said, sounding apologetic.

"Why not? We've adapted all that Oriental foolishness to our own purposes. And our own purposes don't include nirvana at all. To be swallowed up in the cosmic all? To be born no more? That's not our object at all. To live again, that's what we want. Again and again and again. So why do they put that up?"

"They pose as the heirs to Eastern mysticism," said Noyes. "Catering to Western pragmatism. In theory, rebirth is undesirable, freedom from the wheel of existence is the highest goal. Yes?"

"Yes. In theory. Not for me."

A monk entered. "The guru now will see you," he murmured.

Roditis shuffled forward through clouds of incense, his sandals sliding on the smooth stone floor. Over the arch of the door he found another slogan in letters of gold:

11

It is appointed unto man once to die.

Yes, he thought. Once to die: I'll grant that. But many times to be reborn. He felt the warm presence within him of Anton Kozak and Elio Walsh, who lived again because he had chosen their personae from the soul bank. Had they hungered for nirvana's sweet oblivion? Of course not! They had bided their time in cold storage, and now they walked the world again, passengers in a busy, well-stocked, active mind. Roditis would leave nirvana to real Buddhists. He preferred the Westernized version of the creed.

The guru looked like a salesman of motel appliances who had seen the light. Not even his shaven skull and saffron robes could conceal the blunt, earthily American features, the jutting jaw, the prominent lips, the glossy, somewhat hyper-thyroid blue eyes, the domed vault of the forehead. He was squat of physique, even shorter and stockier than Roditis, and was perhaps sixty years old, though it was difficult to be certain of that. The only creases in the holy man's face were those of its youthful geography made deeper: the deep valleys alongside the strong nose. His skull, newly mown, was pink and smooth. It had a curious occipital bulge.

Taking Roditis' hand with his left, Noyes' with his right, the guru offered a blessing and a wish for many lives for them both. Roditis was reassured. He had no interest in being fobbed off to nirvana while reincarnations were available.

"To my study?" the guru suggested.

Hideous Tibetan scrolls defaced the walls. Roditis eyed them with displeasure; within him, Anton Kozak surged with delight, but Elio Walsh, the bluff old philistine, voiced distaste even stronger than Roditis'. There was a desk, and on it a very secular-looking telephone with vision and data-transmitting attachments. Beside the telephone lay a book expensively bound in full morocco. The guru, smiling as he noticed Roditis' interest in the volume, handed it to him.

"A priceless first edition," said the holy man. "Evans-Wentz, the original translation of the *Bardo*, 1927. You won't find many of these about."

Roditis caressed the book. Its cool binding held a sensual appeal for him. Opening it with care, as though he expected pages to spring free of their own will, he eyed the familiar text with its lengthy burden of prefaces, its endless table of contents. He turned to the first section, the *Chikhai Bardo*. "HEREIN LIETH THE SETTING-FACE-TO-FACE TO THE REALITY IN THE INTERMEDIATE STATE: THE GREAT DELIVERANCE BY HEARING WHILE ON THE AFTER-DEATH PLANE, FROM THE PROFOUND DOCTRINE OF THE EMANCIPATING OF THE CONSCIOUSNESS BY MEDITATION UPON THE PEACEFUL AND WRATHFUL DEITIES."

Nonsense, Roditis knew, and Elio Walsh echoed the sharp judgment while Kozak registered mild annoyance. On a different level of his mind Roditis admitted that it was useful nonsense, in its way. How mumbo-jumbo from the icy plateaus of the yak country could be a guide to American man was a complex matter, but so it had befallen, and Roditis, comforted by his multiple personality, was flexible enough to accept and reject in the same moment.

"It's a beautiful volume," he said.

"A gift from Paul Kaufmann," the guru replied. "One of his many kindnesses to our establishment. His loss is truly a great one."

"Luckily, only temporary," Roditis pointed out. "It can't be long before a transplant of his persona will be awarded."

"Quite soon, now, I understand."

"Oh?" Roditis lurched tensely forward. "What do you know about that?"

The guru looked startled at Roditis' eagerness. "Why, nothing official. But he has been dead several months now. The family period of mourning is over. Surely they have processed the applicants for Kaufmann's persona by now, and a decision soon will come. So I assume. I have not been told anything."

Relaxing, Roditis saw Noyes' quick glower of disapproval. He knew he had acted in bad form, blurting like that. Too damned bad. Noyes had nicer manners; but Noyes wasn't hungry for Paul Kaufmann's persona. Sometimes there was a strategic advantage to a seemingly accidental tipping of your hand. Let the guru know what he wanted. It couldn't hurt.

Roditis said, "Kaufmann was a great man and a great banker. I don't know which aspect of him I admire more."

"For us his greatnesses were combined. He favored us with many donations and sometimes with his presence at our rites. Shall we pray?"

A couple of sandaled monks had slipped into the room. Roditis heard the soft chanting of the great mantra: *"Om mani padme hum."* Beside him Noyes' voice took it up. Roditis, too, unselfconsciously began to repeat the catchphrase. They said it was the essence of all happiness, prosperity, and knowledge, and the great means of liberation. *Om.* The liberation they talked about was one Roditis did not seek: nirvana, oblivion. *Marti.* No one sought that, really, except possibly in places like India, where rebirth meant yet another breaking on the wheel of karma. *Padme. Hum. Om.* Who wanted liberation from existence? First a man wanted nourishment, and then strength, and then power, and then long life. And then rebirth so he could savor the cycle once more. *Om mani padme hum.* Roditis participated in the chant but not in any wish that the chant be fulfilled, and he suspected that of those about him only Noyes might seriously feel otherwise. *Om.*

The religious interlude was over.

It was time to talk business.

His voice tougher, less ethereal now, the guru said, "I'm glad you took the trouble to visit us, Mr. Roditis. Some men a whole lot less important than you can't be bothered to pay a personal call even on their own philanthropies."

Roditis shrugged. "I've been curious about this place for a long time. And since I had to be in San Francisco anyway—"

"Was it a successful trip?"

"Very. We closed the contracts for the entire Telegraph Hill redevelopment. Five years from now there'll be a hundred-story tower on top of that hill, the biggest thing that's been put up anywhere since '96. It'll be the Pacific headquarters of Roditis Securities."

"I look forward to blessing the site," said the guru.

"Naturally. Naturally."

"In our humble way we have our own building program here, Mr. Roditis. Would you care to view our grounds?"

They stepped through an irising gate of burnished beryllium steel and entered a broad spade-shaped garden several hundred yards deep. The rear was planted in blue flowers, delphinium, lupine, convolvulus, several others of varying heights, surmounted by a massive wistaria whose tentacles reached in all directions. Cascades of flowers dangled from the many limbs of the wistaria. Closer by were humbler flowers, and it dawned slowly on Roditis that the entire garden was laid out in the shape of some vast mandala, circles within circles, an esoteric significance of the highest degree of solemn phoniness. The thought came from Kozak;

Roditis himself had not perceived the pattern. Beyond the garden lay rocky, uncleared land sloping down the hillside.

"There is to be our refectory," said the guru. "Here, the library. On the far side, overlooking the bridge, we anticipate building a guidance center for the uninformed. And just here to our left we will establish a soul bank."

"Your own soul bank?"

"For storing the personae of the chapter members. Obviously we can't allow our own people's personae to be thrown into the general bank. We must remain in control of each incarnation. So we propose to establish a complete Scheffing-process installation here and carry out every stage of rebirth."

"That'll cost you a fortune!" Roditis said.

"Exactly."

Noyes said, "When do you expect to build it?"

"Within the next several years. It depends on our receipt of funds, of course. We have the basic equipment for a pilot plant now. We've already had a fine contribution from the estate of Paul Kaufmann. And I understand his young nephew Mark is planning to match it."

"Mark. Yes." Roditis sucked his belly in sharply at the painful mention of his enemy. "He would. A very generous man, Mark Kaufmann."

"A generous family," said the guru.

"Quite. Quite. They all recognize the obligation of the wealthy to repay the society that has treated them so well. As do I," Roditis said a moment later. "As do I." Noyes looked pained. Roditis kicked pebbles at his ankle. A rich man does not need to be subtle, he told himself, except where subtlety pays.

They received the full tour. They were handed rare Tibetan manuscripts, prayer wheels, and associated sacred artifacts. They

visited the young lamas in their chambers. They received sam-
ples of the lamasery's publications, its painstaking theological
substructure for the modern materialistic cult of rebirth. Noyes
fidgeted, but Roditis calmly followed the guru about, asking questions, nodding in frequent response, showing utter concentration
and complete patience. The shadows lengthened. Twilight was
creeping across the continent. The guru made no request for a
contribution; Roditis offered none. At the end, they were back in
the guru's own chamber for farewells.

"May you attain your heart's desire," said the guru, "whatever
it may be. I'm right to assume that a man of your station has some
unfulfilled desires, even now?"

Roditis laughed. "Many."

"I have no doubt that some of them will be gratified shortly."

"That's kind of you," said Roditis. "I'm grateful for your sparing us so much of your time today. The visit was fascinating."

"Our pleasure," said the guru.

A youthful lama with a bony face took them to the room where
they had left their clothing. They dressed and departed from the
lamasery in silence. Noyes seemed to have a powerful headache.
Probably good old Jim Kravchenko was hammering on the inside
of Noyes' skull again.

They got into the car.

"In the morning," said Roditis, "transfer a million dollars
fissionable to their account."

"That much?"

"Kaufmann gave them a million and then some, didn't he? Can
I afford to do less?"

"You're not Kaufmann," Noyes pointed out.

"Not yet," said Roditis.

# 2

Risa Kaufmann was sixteen years old: old enough for her first persona transplant. She had come of age, so far as the Scheffing process was concerned, three months earlier, in January. But that had been the time of old Paul's death, and it was bad taste for her to bring up the matter of the transplant just then. Now things were quieter. The black armbands had gone into the drawer; the rabbis had stopped bothering them; family life had reverted to normal. Talk of transplants was very much in the air. Everybody in the family was worried about who was going to get old Paul. They didn't speak about it much in front of her, because they still assumed she was a child, but she knew what was up. Her father was sizzling with fear that John Roditis would get Paul. That would be a funny one, Risa thought. It would serve everybody right for being so rude to the little Greek. But of course Risa knew that her father would fight like a demon to keep Paul Kaufmann's persona from finding its way into Roditis' mind. She giggled at the thought. Touching a shoulder stud, she caused her gown to drop away, and, naked, she stepped out on the terrace of the apartment.

A thousand feet below, traffic madly swirled and bustled. But up here on the ninety-fifth floor everything was serene. The April air was cool, fresh, pure. The slanting sunlight of midmorning glanced across her body. She stretched, extended her arms, sucked breath deep. The view down to the street did not dizzy her even when she leaned far out. She wondered how some passerby would react if he stared up and saw the face and bare breasts of Risa Kaufmann hovering over the edge of a terrace. But no one ever did look up, and anyway they couldn't see anything from down there. Nor was there any other building in the area tall enough so that she was visible from it. She could stand out here nude as much as she liked, in perfect privacy. She half hoped someone *would* see her, though. A passing copter pilot, cruising low, doing a loop-the-loop as he spied the slinky naked girl on the balcony.

Risa laughed. This building belonged to the Paul Kaufmann estate. Once they got the will straightened out, title would pass to her father, Paul's nephew and chief heir. And one day, Risa thought, this building will be mine.

She let her unbound hair stream free in the morning breeze.

She was a tall girl, close to six feet tall, with a slim, agile body, dark hair, dark, sparkling eyes, and what she liked to think of as a Semitic nose. It pleased her to pretend she was a Yemenite Jew, a lively daughter of the desert, descendant in a straight line from the stock of Abraham and Sarah. Certainly she looked like some Bedouin princess; but the sad genetic truth was that the Kaufmann line could be traced back to twentieth-century London, to nineteenth-century Stuttgart, to eighteenth-century Kiev, and then became lost in nameless Russian peasantry. She clung to her tribal fantasy anyway. She began to touch her toes, rapidly, not bending her knees. Hup. Hup. Hup. She could do it a hundred times, if she had to. Her small breasts bobbled and jiggled as she moved down, up, down, up. Risa was profoundly glad she hadn't sprouted a pair of meaty udders, even though bosoms were becoming fashionable again lately. She went in a good deal for nudity in her costume, and small girlish breasts were more pleasing to the eye, she thought, than full heavy ones. Of course, she might get bigger later on, but she didn't think so. She hadn't grown much, in height or bust or anything else, since she had turned fourteen. Hup. Hup. She lay down on the terrace, cool tile against her back and buttocks, and lashed her heels through the air.

It might be interesting, she thought, to find out what it was like to be bosomy. To know what it is to carry all that meat below your clavicles. Risa made a mental note to request some top-heavy breasty wench when she applied for her first persona transplant. By checking through the memories she inherited, she'd get a notion of what voluptuousness was like without the bother of gaining all that nasty weight.

When will I get the transplant, though?

That was the frustrating part. At sixteen she was medically old enough for the Scheffing process, but not legally competent to apply for it. She needed her father's consent. It had been simpler last year when Risa decided it was time for her to part with her virginity; she merely took the next rocket to Cannes, picked out a likely stud, and surrendered. But they'd throw her out of the soul bank, Kaufmann or not, if she walked in without the proper consent form.

She looked over her shoulder and saw figures moving on the far side of the sliding glass door between the living room and the terrace. Risa got to her feet. Her father was coming toward her. His girl friend, the Italian bitch, Elena Volterra, was with him. Smiling, Risa lounged against the wall of the terrace and waited for them to come out to her.

Her father was wearing some sort of sprayon business suit, very chic, very shiny. His long black hair was slicked down across his skull in a style that highlighted the savage cragginess of his features, the hard thrust of the cheekbones, the vulpine chin, the corvine nose. Somehow he managed to be handsome, Mark did, despite the collection of outcroppings and bladed planes that was his face. Risa was desperately in love with him, and they both knew it, of course. And hid the fact, as they must. His eyes barely flickered over his daughter's angular nakedness.

"Looking to visit the hospital?" he asked. "April's too early in the season for sunbathing in this latitude."

"It's warm enough out here, Mark," she said sullenly.

"Put something on."

"Why should I if I'm not cold?"

"All right," Mark said. "Don't. But I don't have to talk to you, either. Not while you're bare."

"How bourgeois of you, Mark. Since when have you enforced the nudity taboo?"

"This has nothing to do with taboos, Risa. Simply with your health. Now and then I have to take some sort of interest in your physical welfare, don't I? And—"

"Very well," Risa said. "We'll talk inside."

Defiantly naked, she sauntered past them, through the glass door, and slung herself down in the abstract webfoam cradle near the great screen-window, wrapping her hands about an upraised knee. Her eyes passed from her father to Elena, who was clearly annoyed by the interchange. Good. Let her stew. Elena had the sort of body Risa had been thinking about a short while back. Fleshy.

Indeed. Full hips, solid thighs, high, bulky breasts. And always dressed to display her assets. Risa didn't envy her father's mistress her figure. Usually Elena kept herself cosseted with stays and braces so that the flesh made its intended effect; but it was easy for Risa to summon the memory of that beach party last year when they had all been swimming naked, and poor Elena had jiggled and bounced so dreadfully. A body like that was designed for the nakedness of the bed, or the semibareness of formal dress, but not for casual out-door nudity. Risa asked herself if, should Elena die tomorrow, she would request her persona on a transplant. She doubted it. It would be a pleasantly spiteful thing to do to Elena, but Risa didn't think she cared to have the woman in her mind, even as a temporary.

Mark and Elena came in from the terrace. Risa chuckled. She had won that round by a dozen points. Her father had come up here with Elena because he knew it annoyed her to see the two of them together, but he had found her nude, which annoyed him because it awakened the nasty Electra thing in him and humiliated him before Elena, so he had made a fuss about her catching pneu-monia in the cold outdoors. Whereupon she had come obediently inside, but remained nude, compounding the effect of rebellion and provocation. Mark was smiling too; he knew that he'd been beaten by an expert, and he couldn't help being proud of her.

His apartment was a floor below hers. She had left a message for him, asking that he come up and see her when he came home for lunch.

She said, "I wanted this to be a private conference, Mark."

"You can talk in front of Elena. She's practically a member of the family."

"That's odd. I didn't see her at Uncle Paul's funeral."

Mark winced. Risa chalked up another cluster of points. She was really sharp this morning. Elena was fuming!

Huskily, Elena said, "If this is a family conference and I'm intruding—"

"I'd just like to talk to my father a little while," Risa said. "If it's all right with the two of you. I hate to come between you, but—"

Mark shrugged a dismissal. Elena snorted in a way that made the pounds of flesh above her neckline ripple and dance. Wig-wagging her hips, she stalked from the apartment.

"*Now* will you put something on?" Mark asked.

"Does my body make you that uncomfortable, Mark?"

"Risa, it's been a difficult morning, and—"

"Yes. Yes, all right." She knew when it was time to cash in her winnings. She picked up a robe, wrapped it about herself, and politely offered her father a tray of drinks. He chose one capsule and pressed it to his arm. Risa did not hesitate to select a golden liqueur herself, administering it expertly and shivering a little as the ultrasonic spray drove the delicious fluid into her bloodstream. She eyed her father carefully. He was tense, wary; this Roditis thing had him worried, no doubt. Or perhaps it was merely the complexity of unraveling Uncle Paul's will that keyed him up.

She said, "I think you know what I want to ask you about."

"Summer vacation on Mars?"

"No."

"You need money?"

"Of course not."

"Then—"

"*You* know."

He scowled. "Your transplant?"

"My transplant," Risa agreed. "I'm well past sixteen. Uncle Paul's funeral is out of the way. I'd like to sign up. Can I have your consent?"

"What's your hurry, Risa? You've got a whole lifetime to add new personae."

"I'd like to begin. How old were you when *you* got your first?"

"Twenty," Mark told her. "And it was a mistake. I had to have it erased. We were incompatible. Can you imagine it, Risa, despite all the testing and matching I took on the persona of an ardent anti-Semite? And of course he woke up and found himself in a circumcised body and nearly went berserk."

"How did you pick him?"

"He was a man I had admired. An architect, one of the great builders. I wanted his planning skills. But I had to take his lunacy with his greatness, don't you see, and after three months of sheer hell for both of us I had him erased. It was several years before I dared apply for another transplant."

"That must have been unfortunate for you," Risa said. "But it's getting off the subject. I'm old enough for a transplant. It's unreasonable of you to deny your consent. It isn't as if we can't afford it, or as if I'm unstable, or anything like that. You just don't want to let me, and I can't understand why."

"Because you're so young! Look, Risa, sixteen is also the minimum legal age for getting married, but if you came to me and said you wanted to—"

"But I haven't. A transplant isn't a marriage."

"It's far more intimate than a marriage," Mark said. "Believe me. You won't merely be sharing a bed. You'll be sharing your brain, Risa, and you can't comprehend how intimate that is."

"I *want* to comprehend it," she said. "That's the whole point. I'm hungry for it, Mark. It's time I found out, time I shared my life a little, time I began to experience. And there you stand like Moses saying no."

"I honestly think you're too young."

Her eyes flashed. "I'll translate that for you, dearest. You want me to stay too young, because that way you stay young too. So long as I remain a little girl in your estimation, your whole time scheme stays fixed. If I'm eight years old, you're thirty-two, and you'd like to be thirty-two. But I'm past sixteen, Mark. And you won't see forty again. I can't make you accept the second, but I wish you'd stop denying the first."

"All your cruelty is exposed today, Risa."

"I feel like going naked today. Physically and emotionally. I won't hide anything." Languidly Risa selected a second drink for herself; then, as an afterthought, she offered her father the tray. As she pressed the capsule's snout to her pale skin she said, "Will you sign my consent form or won't you?"

"Let's put it off till July, shall we? The market's so unsettled these days—"

"The market is always unsettled, and in any event it has nothing to do with my getting a transplant. Today is April 11. Unless you give in, I'm going to bear an illegitimate child on or about next January 11."

Mark gasped. "You're pregnant?"

"No. But I will be, three hours from now, unless you sign the form. If I can't experience a transplant, I'll experience a pregnancy. And a scandal."

"You devil!"

She was afraid she might have pushed her father too far. This was a raw threat, after all, and Mark didn't usually respond kindly to threats. But she had calculated all this quite nicely, figuring in a factor of his appreciation for her inherited ruthlessness. She saw a smile clawing at the edges of his mouth and knew she had won. Mark was silent a long moment. She waited, graciously allowing him to come to terms with his defeat.

At length he said, "Where's the form?"

"By an odd coincidence—"

She handed it to him. He scanned the printed sheet without reading it and brusquely scrawled his signature at the bottom. "Don't have any babies just yet, Risa."

"I never intended to. Unless you called my bluff, of course. Then I would have had to go through with it. I'd much rather have a transplant. Honestly."

"Get it, then. How did I raise such a witch?"

"It's all in the genes, darling. I was bred for this." She put the precious paper away, and they stood up. She went to him. Her arms slid round his neck; she pressed her smooth cheek to his. He was no more than an inch taller than she was. He embraced her, tensely, and she brushed her lips against his and felt him tremble with what she knew was suppressed desire. She released him. Softly she whispered her thanks.

He went out.

Risa laughed and clapped her hands. Her robe went whirling to the floor and she capered naked on the thick wine-red carpet. Pivoting, she came face to face with the portrait of Paul Kaufmann that hung over the mantel. Portraits of Uncle Paul were standard items of furniture in any home inhabited by a Kaufmann; Risa had not objected to adding him to her décor, because, naturally, she had loved the grand old fox nearly as deeply as she loved his nephew, her father. The portrait was a solido, done a couple of years back on the occasion of Paul's seventieth birthday. His long, well-fleshed face looked down out of a rich, flowing background of green and bronze; Risa peered at the hooded gray eyes, the thin lips, the close-cropped hair rising to the widow's peak, the lengthy nose with its blunted tip. It was a Kaufmann face, a face of power.

She winked at Uncle Paul.

It seemed to her that Uncle Paul winked back.


Mark Kaufmann took the dropshaft one floor to his own apartment, emerged in the private vestibule, put his thumb to the doorseal, and entered. From the vestibule, the apartment spread out along three radial paths. To his, left were the rooms in which he had installed his business equipment; to his right were his living quarters; straight ahead, directly below his daughter's smaller apartment, lay the spacious living room, dining room, and library in which he entertained. Kaufmann spent much of his time in his Manhattan apartment, though he had many homes elsewhere, at least one on each of the seven continents and several offplanet. At each, he could summon a facsimile of the comforts he enjoyed here. But these twelve rooms on East 118th Street comprised the center of his organization, and often he did not leave the building for days at a time.

He walked briskly into the library. Elena stood by the fireplace, beneath the brooding, malevolent portrait of the late Uncle Paul. She looked displeased.

"I'm sorry," Kaufmann told her. "Risa was simply in a bitchy mood, and she took it out on you."

"Why does she hate me so much?"

"Because you're not her mother, I suppose."

"Don't be a fool, Mark. She'd hate me even more if I *were* her mother. She hates me because I've come between herself and you, that's all."

"Don't say that, Elena."

"It's true, though. That child is monstrous!"

Kaufmann sighed. "No. She isn't a child, as she's just finished explaining to me in great detail. And she's not even monstrous. She's just an apt pupil of the family business techniques. In a way, I'm terribly pleased with her."

Elena regarded him coldly. "What a terrible tragedy for you that she's your own daughter, isn't it? She'd make a wonderful wife for you in a few years, when she's ripe. Or a mistress. But incest is not one of the family business techniques."

"Elena—"

"I have a suggestion," Elena purred. "Have Risa killed and transplant her persona to me. That way you can enjoy both of us in one body, quite lawfully, gaining the benefit of my physical advantages joined to the sharp personality you seem to find so endearing in her."

Kaufmann closed his eyes a moment. He often wondered how it had happened that he had surrounded himself with women who had such well-developed gifts of cruelty. Steadier for his pause, he ignored Elena's thrust and said simply, "Will you excuse me? I have some calls to make."

"Where do we eat lunch? You talked yesterday about Florida House for clams and squid."

"We'll eat here," said Kaufmann. "Have Florida House send over whatever you'd like to have. I won't be able to go out until later. Business."

"*Business!* Another ten millions to make before nightfall!"

"Excuse me," he said.

He left Elena arrayed like a fashionable piece of sculpture in the library and made his way to his office. He touched the door-seal, full palm here, not merely thumb. The thick tawny oaken door, inset with twining filaments of security devices, yielded to him, an obedient wife that would surrender only to the right caress. Within, Kaufmann consulted the stock ticker the way an uneasy medieval might have searched for answers in the sortes of Virgil, or perhaps in a random stab into the Talmud. The market was off six points; the utilities averages were up, finance steady, interworld transport a little shaky. Kaufmann's fingers tapped the console as he executed two swift trades for ritualistic purposes. He closed out at 94 a thousand shares of Metropolitan Power purchased that morning at 89%, and an instant later accepted a realized loss of half a point on a lot of eight hundred Königin Mines. The net effect on his central credit balance was inconsequential, but Kaufmann had learned the therapeutic value of making small trades in times of stress from his uncle, long ago.

Next he switched on the neutron flux scanner with which he monitored Risa's apartment. There was little of the voyeur in his psychological makeup; he merely regarded it as good sense to keep an eye on his increasingly more unruly daughter. Especially when, as today, she had blackmailed him into giving his consent to a transplant by the elegantly simple method of threatening to get pregnant. Now that she had voiced the notion, he knew he had to guard against it. He was well aware of Risa's sexual adventures of the past year, and had no objections to them, but a pregnancy was beyond the scope of the acceptable.

He watched her for a few moments.

She was naked again, rushing about the apartment, getting ready to go out. No doubt to make the preliminary arrangements for her transplant. Kaufmann allowed himself the pleasure of admiring her coltish grace, her long-limbed sleekness. Then he switched the scanner over to record and let it run; it would monitor her apartment so long as he wished.

Swinging around to his desk, he activated the telephone.

"I want my daughter traced wherever she goes today," he said. "I expect her to visit the soul bank, and don't interfere with that, but tell me where she goes afterwards. Especially if she goes to any of her friends. Male friends. No, no interceptions; just surveillance."

He suspected he was being overcautious. Nevertheless, he would have her watched, at least today. If necessary, he'd order surreptitious external contraceptive measures as an extra precaution. Risa could sleep around all she liked, but he had no intention of allowing her to get more than a few days into any premarital pregnancies just yet.

Kaufmann said to the telephone, "Get me Francesco Santoliquido."

It took more than a minute. Even Mark Kaufmann had to be patient about getting a call through to Santoliquido, who was not merely an important man, as chief administrator of the soul bank, but also a very busy one. Whole light-years of secretarial barricades had to be penetrated before Santoliquido could discover who was calling and was able to free himself long enough to respond.

Then the amiable face blossomed on the screen. Santoliquido was about fifty, ruddy of skin, white-haired, with a large, commanding oval face. He was a man of considerable wealth who had entered the bureaucracy out of a sense of mission.

"Yes, Mark?"

"Frank, I wanted you to know that my daughter will soon be on her way down to your bank to pick out a persona."

"You broke down, then!"

"Let's say Risa broke me down."

Santoliquido shook with pleasant laughter. "Well, she's a strong-willed girl. Strong enough to handle a transplant, I'd say. What shall I give her? A Mother Superior? A lady banker?"

"On the contrary," said Kaufmann. "Someone softly feminine, to balance all the aggression in her. Someone who died young, quite sadly, after a life of suffering for love. Preferably a girl of an opposite physical type, too, less athletic, less masculine of build. You follow?"

"Certainly. And what if Risa isn't interested in a persona of those specifications?"

"I think she will be, Frank. But if she isn't, give her what she wants, I suppose. I'll leave the final decisions up to the two of you."

"You'll have to," said Santoliquido. His eyes regarded Kaufmann with some amusement. "You know, Mark, you were supposed to come to the bank yourself this month. You haven't been recorded in nearly a year."

"I've been so damned busy. Paul's death, and everything—"

"Yes, I know. But you shouldn't neglect the semiannual recording. A man of your stature—you owe it to the world, to the future inheritors of your persona, to keep yourself up to date, to etch all the new experiences into the record—"

"All right: You sound like a recruiter."

"I am, Mark. We've been expecting you for weeks."

"What if I come tomorrow, then? I wouldn't want to be there today. If I ran into Risa, she'd think her horrible old father was spying on her."

"True. Tomorrow, then," Santoliquido said. "Is there anything else, Mark?"

"Just one thing." Kaufmann hesitated. "The question of Paul's persona."

"No decision's been taken yet. None. We've had dozens of applicants."

"Roditis among them?"

31

"I couldn't say."

"You *could* say. Maybe you *won't* say, but that's a different thing. I know Roditis is hungry to add Paul to his collection of transplants. I'd merely like to emphasize that such a transplant would be distasteful and offensive not only to the immediate Kaufmann family, but to—"

Santoliquido's ringed hand swept across the screen. "I'm aware of your feelings," he said gently. "However, family wishes cannot be binding upon us. The decisions of the soul bank are made strictly on an impersonal basis, taking into account the stability of the recipient and the merit of his application, and you know very well that we regard it as desirable to go outside the genetic group whenever possible."

"Meaning that you favor giving Paul to Roditis?"

"I said nothing of the kind." Santoliquido's geniality began to ebb. "We're still weighing all applicants."

"I wish I could take Uncle Paul myself, and keep him out of the skull of that—that fishmonger!"

"What about the consanguinity laws?" Santoliquido asked. "Not to mention your uncle's own will? He'll have to go outside the family, Mark. And I suspect we won't be giving him to any Schiffs or Warburgs or Lehmans or Loebs, either. Can we drop the subject, now?"

"I suppose."

Santoliquido smiled again. "I'll see you tomorrow. And then, Saturday, your party, Dominica."

"Yes. Dominica on Saturday."

The screen went dark. Kaufmann felt cross; he had played his hand poorly, making that frontal attack on Santoliquido just now. Risa had upset him, clearly, shaking his tactical faculties. Or was it Roditis? *Roditis. Roditis.* For ten years, now, Kaufmann had watched that grasping little man accumulate first wealth, then power, and then some measure of social prestige. Now the audacious upstart wished to thrust himself deep into the core of a fine old family, making up for his own lack of ancestry by seizing the available persona of the late Paul Kaufmann. Mark scowled. He was less of a snob than he had a right to be, considering who and what he was, but nevertheless the thought of Roditis lying down on a pallet in the soul bank and emerging with Uncle Paul was intolerable to him. He had to be blocked.

Kaufmann's own three personae stirred and squirmed. Ordinarily they were mild, passive, guiding him without making their presence known, but the tensions of this hideous morning were seeping into their place of repose. He put his hands to his forehead. I'm sorry, friends, he told the three captive souls beneath his scalp. We'll all relax on Saturday. I'm genuinely sorry about this.

*Damn* Roditis!

Kaufmann turned back to the ticker. The market was rallying, but now the utilities were weak. He scanned the tape, made a quick velocity projection of Pacific Coast Power, and went five thousand shares short at 43. Moments later it came across the tape on high volume at 45⅜. Not my day, Kaufmann thought, and covered his sale for a rapid loss. Not my day at all.

# 3

Charles Noyes awoke slowly, reluctantly, fighting the return to the waking world. He lay alone in a bed that was just barely long enough for his lanky body. His arms twitched; his eyelids fluttered. Morning was here. Time to rise, time to toil. He fought it.

—Come on, you cowardly bastard, said James Kravchenko within his mind. Wake up!

Noyes moaned. He jammed his eyelids together. "Let me alone."

—Up, up, up! Greet the morning's glow.

"You aren't supposed to talk to me, Kravchenko. You're just supposed to *be* there."

—Look, I didn't ask to be pushed into your brain. Anytime you'd like to let me out, you know where to go.

"You don't mean that. You're only bluffing. You want to stay right where you are, Kravchenko. Until you can take me over entirely, and run me like a puppet."

Kravchenko did not reply. Several minutes passed, and the persona remained silent. Once again Noyes considered getting out of bed, but waited, convinced that Kravchenko would nag him again, and willing to arise only when nagged. But in the continued silence he knew the onus was on him to get their shared body up. He pushed back the covers and disconnected the night monitor.

Beside his bed lay the deadly flask of carniphage. Noyes eyed it tenderly. His first thought upon arising, like his last at night, was of suicide. No. Duicide. When he went, he would take Kravchenko with him. He picked up the flask and cradled it in his hand, stroking it with affection.

Within the fragile container lay a lethal quantity of beta-13 viral DNA, a replicative molecule whose action it was to persuade the cells of the body to release autolytic enzymes, certain acid hydrolases, from the lysosomes or "suicide bags" within themselves. Moments after ingestion, the carniphage created such a cascading wave of autolysis that the body literally fell apart; cell death was general and consecutive, and as each cell in turn succumbed to the flow of fatality, the carniphage devoured it. It was a swift but unusually agonizing way to die, since the body turned to slime from the digestive tract outward, and as much as eight or ten minutes might pass before the nerve centers were no longer able to register the pain of dissolution. But the splendor of the poison lay in its total irreversibility. There was no known antidote, nor even a conceivable one; neither could a stomach pump or any sort of similar device halt the process once it had begun to affect even a few cells. Let that cascade of destruction begin, and the victim was irrevocably doomed. Noyes sometimes thought of it as the Humpty Dumpty effect.

He set the carniphage down.

—Go on, gulp it, why don't you!

"Very funny, Kravchenko."

—I mean it. Do you think you frighten me, waving that suicide juice around? I'll get a new body soon enough, once you're gone. Maybe you'll be right in there with me, when I'm transplanted the second time.

Noyes reached for the flask.

—Just put it to your lips and go crunch. It's easy.

"No, damn you! I'll do it when *I* want to. Not to amuse you!"

It seemed to him that he heard Kravchenko's ghostly laughter. Putting the flask aside again, Noyes shed his nightclothes and began his morning rituals.

*Religious observance.* He reached for the *Bardo.* Untold generations of Episcopalian ancestors whirred like turbines in their New England tombs as the last and least scion of the Noyeses opened the barbarous Tibetan holy book. He turned, as usual, to the *Bardo* of the dying, the early section, before the demons appear, when nirvana is still within reach. In a low voice he read:

O nobly-born, listen. Now thou art experiencing the Radiance of the Clear Light of Pure Reality. Recognize it. O nobly-born, thy present intellect, in real nature void, not formed into anything as regards characteristics or color, naturally void, is the very Reality, the All-Good. Thine own intellect, which is now voidness, yet not to be regarded as the voidness of nothingness, but as being the intellect itself, unobstructed, shining, thrilling, and blissful, is the very consciousness, the All-good Buddha.

*Cleanliness.* He stood in the vibrator field for a minute.

*Nutrition.* He programed an austere breakfast.

*Bodily hygiene.* Grunting a bit, he performed the eleven stretchings and the seven bendings.

He ate. He dressed. The time was ten in the morning. He had returned with Roditis from San Francisco the night before, and he was still living on Pacific Standard Time, which made his awakening even more difficult than it normally was. Activating the screen, Noyes saw that the outer world looked cheerful and sunny, and the sunlight was the yielding light of April, not the harsh winter light that had engulfed this part of the world so long. He lived in a small apartment in the Wallingford district of Greater Hartford, Connecticut, close enough both to Manhattan and to his ancestral Boston. He tried to keep away from Massachusetts, but old compulsions drew him there periodically. One, at least, was external: at Roditis' insistence, the two of them attended their Harvard class reunion each year. That was painful.

Any window into the past was a source of pain. Anything that reminded him of a time when he had been young, with prospects before him: a legal career, a fruitful marriage, a fine home, the joys of tradition. He had flunked out of law school. Flunked out of marriage, too. Today he was a wealthy man, but only because Roditis had picked him up from the junkheap and stuffed money in his pockets, as the price of his soul. Noyes' credit balance was high, but he spent little and lived in a kind of genteel poverty, not out of miserliness but merely because he refused to believe that the largesse Roditis had showered upon him was real.

"Charles! Charles, are you up yet?"

—His master's voice, said Kravchenko slyly.

"I'm here, John," Noyes called into the other room, while sending a subliminal shout of fury at his persona. "I'm coming!"

One entire wall of the sitting room bore a viewscreen that was hooked into Roditis' master communications circuit. No matter where Roditis was, at any station along the territory of his far-flung empire, he could activate that circuit and introduce himself, life-size, three dimensions, into Noyes' apartment. Noyes presented himself before the screen and confronted the blocky figure of his friend and employer. The furniture surrounding Roditis was that of his office in Jersey City: stock tickers, computer banks, data filters, the huge green eye of an analysis machine. Roditis looked wide awake. He said, "Feeling better?"

"Passable, John."

"You were in lousy shape when we got back last night. I was worried about you."

"A night's sleep, that's all I needed."

"The acknowledgment on the lamasery gift just came in. Want to see what the guru's got to say?"

"I suppose."

Roditis gestured. His image shattered and vanished, and for a moment a cloudy blueness filled the screen; then came the sharp snap of a message flake being thrust into a holder, followed by the appearance in Noyes' sitting room of the holy man from San Francisco. Noyes had the illusion that he smelled incense. The guru, all smiles, poured forth a honeyed stream of praise and gratitude for Roditis' generous gift. Noyes sat through it impatiently, wondering why Roditis was bothering to inflict these few minutes of fatuity on him. Of course the guru was going to sound grateful, after having been handed a million dollars; of course he was going to say that Roditis was blessed among men in wisdom, and worthy of many rebirths. Noyes had the uneasy suspicion that Roditis genuinely *believed* what the guru was saying—that he felt it was praise earned through merit, not merely bought for cash. It was something like a sonic sculptor who bribed the *Times* critic to give him a rave, then called up all his friends and proudly read them the glowing review. Not a day passed on which Noyes failed to rediscover the core of naïveté that lay within John Roditis' energetic, shrewd, ruthless spirit.

The guru reached his peroration and vanished from the screen. Roditis returned, beaming.

"What did you think of *that?*"

"Fine, John. Wonderful."

"He really sounded happy about the gift."

"I'm sure he was. It was very handsome."

"Yes," said Roditis. "I'll give him some more, by and by. I'll make them name a whole damn wing of that place after me. The John Roditis Soul Bank for Departed Lamas, or something. Onward and upward, yes? *Om mani padme hum,* fella."

Noyes said nothing. Kravchenko seemed to chuckle; Noyes felt it as a tickling in his frontal lobes.

Then, as though experiencing some inner shifting of gears, Roditis lost his look of jovial self-satisfaction, and a glimmer of strain showed through his carefully abstract expression. He said, "Mark Kaufmann is giving a party Saturday at his Dominica estate."

"He's coming out of mourning, then?"

"Yes. This is the first social thing he's done since old Paul was gathered to repose. It's going to be a big, noisy, expensive affair."

"Are you invited?" Noyes asked.

Roditis looked scornful. "Me? The filthy little *nouveau riche* with delusions of grandeur? No, of course I'm not invited! It's mainly going to be a party for various Kaufmanns and their Jewish banking relatives."

"John, you know you shouldn't use that phrase."

"Why? Does it make me seem a bigot? You know I've got nothing against Jews. Can I help it if the Kaufmanns are related to the other big Jewish bankers?"

"When you say it, somehow, it comes out like a sneer," Noyes dared to tell him.

"Well, I don't mean it as a sneer. You don't sneer at a social and cultural elite. What you hear in my voice isn't anti-Semitism, Charles, it's simple envy without any neurotic irrational manifestations attached. There'll be a mess of Lehmans and Loebs at that party. There won't be any John Roditis. Frank Santoliquido is going to be there, too."

"*He's* not Jewish."

Roditis looked annoyed. "No, dolt, he isn't! But he's important, and he's socially well-placed besides, and Mark Kaufmann is trying to buy his support in this business of the old man's persona. Santoliquido and his girl friend are flying down on Mark's own jet; that's how tight things are getting. And you can bet that Mark is going to spend the whole day letting Santo know how important it is to keep Uncle Paul out of my clutches. That's got to be counteracted somehow. Which is why you're going to go to the party too."

"Me? But I'm not invited!"

"Get yourself invited."

"Impossible, John. Kaufmann knows I'm connected to your organization, and if you're on the dead list, you can bet that I—"

"You're also connected to the Loebs, aren't you?"

"Well, my sister married a Loeb, yes."

"Damn right, she did. Won't she be at the party?"

"I suppose she's been invited, at any rate."

"I know she has. I've got the complete guest list right here. Mr. and Mrs. David Loeb. That's your sister, right?"

"Right."

"Fine. Now, what happens if she phones Kaufmann and says she's in the air over Cuba, say, and she'll be landing in five minutes, and she's happened to bring her kid brother Charlie along for the party. Is Kaufmann going to say no, send the scoundrel home?"

"He'll be furious, John."

"Let him be furious, then. He'll have to maintain decorum, though. It's not the sort of formal party where one extra guest throws the whole thing out of balance, and he can't very well refuse you permission to attend with your sister. You'll be admitted. The worst that'll happen is you'll get a few sour stares from Kaufmann. But socially you'll be among your equals, and everybody else will be glad to see you, and there'll be no hard feelings."

Noyes' fingers began to tremble. Kravchenko scrabbled derisively against the walls of his cranium. Carefully, Noyes reached to his left, out of the range of the sensors relaying his image to Roditis, and scooped a drink capsule from a tray. He activated the capsule and let the fluid flow into his arm. That was better. But not good enough. He felt sick. The idea of muscling his way into a party like this, parlaying his own tattered status and his sister's connections by marriage into Roditis' advantage, chilled and saddened him.

He said, "Assuming I succeed in crashing the party, John, what's the purpose of my going there?"

"Mainly to get next to Santoliquido and work on him."

"About the Paul Kaufmann persona?"

"What else? You can be subtle. You can be indirect. He's going to make up his mind about the transplant any day now. I want it so bad I can taste it, Charles. Do you realize what I could do with Paul Kaufmann inside my head? The doors—that would open for me, the plans I could bring off? And it's all up to Santo. He'll be down there, relaxed, out in the sunshine, drinking too much. And you can work on him. Use the old charm. That's what I pay you for, the old Episcopalian Anglo-Saxon charm. Turn it on!"

"All right," Noyes muttered.

"And even if you don't get anywhere immediately with him, perhaps you can find a plan of action. Some vulnerable spot in his makeup. Some opening wedge that we can get leverage on."

Appalled, Noyes said, "Are you thinking of blackmailing Santo-liquido into approving your request?"

"Now, did I say that? What a terribly crude suggestion, Charles! I expect more finesse from you." Roditis laughed heavily. "Call your sister. Get everything set up. Oh—Charles? How's Jimmy-boy?"

"Kravchenko? I think he's asleep."

"I'm sure he'll appreciate going to the party too. He'll see many of his old friends there. Call your sister, Charles."

The screen darkened.

Noyes looked at the floor. He knelt and dug his fingers into the carpet, trying to steady himself. His head seemed to be splitting into segments.

—Call your sister, Charles. Didn't you hear the man?

"I won't!"

—You'd better. You don't dare defy him.

"It's filthiness! To crash a party so he can use me to suck up to Santoliquido—"

—He wants the old Kaufmann persona, doesn't he? It's his ticket to social respectability. Your job is to help him get what he wants.

"Not at the cost of my integrity."

—You got rid of that a long time ago. Come on, Chuck. He's right: I want to go to that party. At least three of my wives ought to be there. I'd love to see how they're aging.

"I'll kill myself first!"

—If you had the guts, I suppose you would. Pick up the phone. Call your sister.

Noyes heard mocking laughter in his skull.

He returned to the bedroom and eyed the carniphage flask. But, as ever, it was only a dramatic gesture, fooling neither himself nor the demonic persona he harbored. Defeat dragged at his muscles. He seized the phone and jabbed out the numbers. Moments later, his sister's privacy code appeared on the little gray screen. She's taking her morning bath, Noyes thought. He said, "It's me, Gloria, just Charlie. Your womb-mate."

The screen cleared, and the face and shoulders of Gloria Loeb appeared. She wore some sort of flimsy wrap, and her cheeks and forehead were glossy with whatever mystic preparation she favored to keep her complexion eternally young. She was three years older than Noyes, and looked at least a dozen years younger. They had never liked one another. Her marriage to David Loeb had been a stunning social event sixteen years ago, a grandiose blowout, as was appropriate for the union of old New England aristocracy with old Jewish aristocracy. That was the fashionable sort of marriage these days, rapidly creating a tribe of Anglo-Saxon Hebrews whose formidable bloodlines linked them securely to Plantagenets on one hand, Solomon and David on the other, an unbeatable combination. Noyes had become very drunk

43

at his sister's wedding; in a way, his decline and fall had begun that evening, a few weeks after he had turned twenty-one.

She said coolly, "How good to hear from you again, Charles. You look well."

"That's a polite lie. I look terrible, and you can feel free to let me know about it."

Her lips quirked impatiently. "Is something the matter? Are you all right?"

Noyes took a deep breath and said, "I need a tiny favor, Gloria."

# 4

The building housing the soul bank rose in stunning tiers from a broad plaza three superblocks in area. The site had been chosen with an eye toward deliberate ostentation, at Manhattan's southern tip in an area thick with historic associations. Here, Peter Minuit had haggled with Indian braves and bought a world for a handful of beads; here, Pegleg Stuyvesant had tromped in choleric efficiency; Washington had walked these streets, as had J. P. Morgan, Jay Gould, Thomas Edison, Bet-a-Million Gates, Joseph P. Kennedy, Paul Kaufmann, and Helmut Scheffing, along with others. Few traces of that history remained. A block of eighteenth-century buildings had been preserved as a sort of museum; the seventeenth-century New York was gone, as was the nineteenth, and all that survived of the twentieth in this neighborhood were a few scruffy, faded curtain-wall skyscrapers put up by the big banks during the boom of the midcentury, shortly before the panic. Serene, isolated, set apart from its neighbors by thousands of priceless square feet of pink noctilucent tile, rose the glowing shaft of the Scheffing Institute tower: eighty stories, then a setback and forty stories more, and a twenty-story cap tipped with black granite. The tower was easily visible from Brooklyn, from Queens, from Staten Island, from New Jersey, and especially from Jubilisle, the floating pleasure dome in New York Harbor. One looked up from the sins and gaming tables of Jubilisle to see the reassuring bulk of the Scheffing Institute at the edge of land, offering the promise of rebirth beyond rebirth, and it was comforting. The architects had taken all that into account when planning the building.

To the Scheffing Institute that Friday morning came Mark Kaufmann to renew his lease on life. His small hopter landed as programed on the flight deck at the tower's first setback, and waiting guards hustled him inside to see Santoliquido. The morning was cool; he had chosen a thick-fibered tunic that sparkled with dark brown and red highlights.

Francesco Santoliquido's office was deep, high, consciously impressive. In one corner stood a sonic sculpture, the work of Anton Kozak: a beautiful piece, all flowing lines and delicate rhythms, emitting a gentle white hiss that swiftly infiltrated itself into one's consciousness and became rooted there. Kaufmann's pleasure in the lovely work was marred by his awareness that Anton Kozak, who had died nine years ago, had returned to the corporate form as one of the implanted personae of John Roditis.

Santoliquido's desk split obediently and the administrator came through the sections to greet Kaufmann. He was a bulky man, heavier than the fashion prescribed, but he carried himself well. His thick fingers glittered with the rings that betrayed Santoliquido's innocent predisposition toward vanity. At his throat hung a cluster of small beady-eyed crustaceans, violet and green and azure, within a crystal container: products of the mutagenetic art, elaborate little baroques that moved through their prison in an unending stately dance. Santoliquido's shirt was green, his epaulets vermilion. In the blaze of color his white, slicked-back hair took on a compelling vividness.

The two men touched hands. Santoliquido returned to his desk, extended a tray of drinks, took part with Kaufmann in the moment of pleasure. Shafts of sunlight danced across the room. The window, a vaulted arch, was wholly transparent. From where he stood Kaufmann enjoyed a superb view of the harbor, and peering down into gay Jubilisle from this height was like staring into a prismatic image from some unimaginable protonic subuniverse.

"Well," said Santoliquido, "we had the pleasure of your lovely daughter's company here yesterday. She seems hard to please, though. We unrolled our best carpets for her, but there was no deal."

"Not yet. She'll be back."

"Yes, certainly. Next Tuesday. She's choosing among three interesting alternatives."

"I'd like to scan them," said Kaufmann.

"That would be a little irregular."

"I know."

Santoliquido smiled elegantly. Kaufmann had always had a good working relationship with this man; they had participated in several joint ventures, most notably a power scheme in the Antarctic, and always Santoliquido had come out of them with his considerable fortunes considerably enhanced. Reciprocal favors were not impossible.

The pitch of the Kozak piece altered perceptively, growing more definite, more passionate. Once Kaufmann had had several Kozaks. After Roditis had received the sculptor's persona, Kaufmann had found occasions to bestow the works on delighted friends.

Kaufmann said, "Nothing new on Uncle Paul since Wednesday?"

"Nothing new."

"I'd like to see him, too."

"Really?"

"You'll satisfy my curiosity, won't you?" Kaufmann leaned forward at the waist and fingered an amber rubbingstone on Santoliquido's desk. "There's a therapeutic reason. I find it hard to believe that the old man's really dead. You know, he rose above the whole family like such a colossus—"

"So that when you see him taped and carded, you'll finally accept that he's gone?"

"Yes."

"It's not the first time I've heard something like that, Mark." Santoliquido clasped his hands over his belly and laughed. "Paul was quite the titan, wasn't he? I'll admit I ran his persona off myself, after the funeral, just to get some feel for the man. And I was awed. Let me tell you, Mark, I don't awe easily, but I was awed."

"Toying with the idea of taking him on yourself?"

Santoliquido looked displeased, and even the crustaceans at his throat rapidly changed hues, as if somehow attuned to the flavor of his thoughts. "I have no desire whatever to have that terrible old man mixing in my nervous system," said Santoliquido firmly. "And in any event, considering the demand for his persona, it would be a grave breach of trust if I were to appropriate him for my own use. Yes?"

"Of course. Of course."

The look of affability returned. "Anyone who wants your uncle's persona is welcome to it, so far as I care personally. What a powerhouse! He'd overwhelm nine out of ten who took him on."

"Just as he overwhelmed us all in life," said Kaufmann. "He reduced my father to a hollow shell, an errand-boy. Me he had a harder time with, but he gave me twenty years of hell before he'd recognize me as a worthy heir. And the others! Of course, we all loved him. He was simply too dynamic to hate. But when he died, Frank, I felt as though a hand had been removed from my throat."

"I can understand that."

"One more thing. None of us could accept the news, when he had the stroke. I mean, he was still a young man, hardly past seventy. We assumed he'd be around at least fifty more years. But his own vitality must have burned him out."

"He'll be back among us all soon enough," said Santoliquido.

"As a persona, yes. That's not quite the same as having Uncle Paul striding through the rooms booming out orders."

"Time will tell about that. It'll take a strong man to hold him down, Mark."

"You're expecting Paul to take over his host?"

"I'm not expecting anything, officially. I'm merely a bureaucrat, and it's not my business to expect. Come. I'll take you to see your uncle."

"And Risa's three possible personae," Kaufmann reminded him.

"Those too," said Santoliquido.

Kaufmann followed him from the office into a private dropshaft that moved so serenely he was unaware of motion; even the tug of gravity was absent. Here in this monstrous house of death and rebirth Kaufmann always felt ill at ease and badly orientated. He had no real notion of the contents of the infinity of offices on these hundred forty floors, nor did he even know how deep into bedrock the structure extended, what possible maze of stories lay out of sight. Within this too conspicuous edifice were filed the personae of the notable dead, some eighty million of them that had died since the introduction of the Scheffing process as a commercial fact. Yet the storage even of eighty million personae, Kaufmann knew, could be accomplished in modest space. There were many rooms in this building where persona recordings were made, and other rooms in which the transplants took place, but a great deal of the building's volume was unaccountable to him.

He did not know where in the tower Santoliquido had taken him now, whether toward the soaring summit or deep into the bowels. He merely followed, through silent passageways agleam with living light.

The Scheffing Institute was a quasipublic corporation, closely regulated by the Government, its administrators chosen by Congress, its board of directors containing a specified quota of Government appointees. Its schedule of fees and services was subject to Federal supervision. In effect, the Institute was a public utility of death, and rebirth. No common stock was available for purchase; its frequently issued debt securities were offered only to municipal and institutional investors; its profits, which were great, went primarily into renewed research, once amortization payments were made. Important as the Institute was, its existence impinged only marginally on the lives of most of Earth's nine billion people. Merely a minority could afford the costs of escaping oblivion. There was a stiff fee for registration; the fee payable each time one recorded one's persona was not small; a registrant was expected, though not required, to make a new recording at least once every six months. The cost of receiving a persona transplant was formidable—more than the average man could hope to earn in a lifetime. In theory, anyone who had the money and was certifiably stable could receive a new persona each year of his adult life, superimposed above the earlier ones. But in practice most people were content with two or three transplants, if they could afford that many. No one, to Kaufmann's knowledge, had ever taken more than nine. Though he could well afford any number of additional identities himself, he had not applied for a new one in more than a decade. He found three quite enough—not counting the youthful indiscretion that had had to be erased.

It was anything but cheap to erase a persona, also. The Institute turned its profit at every stage of the process.

Kaufmann followed Santoliquido into the vestibule of the main storage vault. It was a long, low-roofed tunnel whose far end was plugged by a security door almost comical in its paranoid massiveness. Through apertures in the glossy blank roof came colored lights of scanners: a blue ray, a green, a turquoise, a pale yellow.

"What are they checking?" Kaufmann asked.

"Everything imaginable. Your blood type's going on tape, your retinal pattern, your DNA-RNA, and several other matters too intimate to mention. If you ever came through here bent on larceny, you'd be picked up within minutes after you left the building."

"What if the scanners get through and find I'm too disreputable to admit?"

"It'll be unpleasant."

Kaufmann envisioned a cage of pressure tape springing from the ceiling and trapping him. Whirling blades slashing him into hamburger. A trapdoor opening to hurl him to limbo. But in fact the colored lights vanished, and with solemn ponderousness the great door began to open. Santoliquido nodded. They stepped out onto the grand concourse of the main storage vault.

It was a room perhaps a thousand feet high and three hundred feet wide from wall to wall. At the very top, far above his head, Kaufmann saw banks of light-globes affixed to the fabric of the building; but only a fraction of that light made its way down to the midlevel on which they stood, and below him were levels of Stygian bleakness. Motes of dust hovered in the vast central cavity of the room. Along the walls were ladders, catwalks, a spiderweb of metal pathways. Staring across the gulf, Kaufmann made out racks of shelves, paneled urns, shadows in the darkness. All this has been done for effect, he told himself. Surely the Institute could afford better lighting, if it wanted it.

"Come," said Santoliquido.

They moved along the tier. Silent figures in white smocks traversed private paths on other levels, and robots with blunt heads rolled on soundless treads from tier to tier, inserting something here, withdrawing there. Santoliquido paused in front of a sealed bank of urns and dialed a computer code. The bank opened. Reaching in, he withdrew a shining coppery casket some six inches wide, four inches long, two inches high.

"In this," he said, "is the persona of Paul Kaufmann."

Kaufmann took it from him and examined it with more awe than he cared to reveal.

"May I open it?"

"Go ahead."

"I don't see how—ah. There." He pressed a projecting lever and the casket's top rose. Within lay a tightly coiled reel of black tape, smaller across than Kaufmann's palm, and a stack of data flakes. "This?" he said. "This is Uncle Paul?"

"His memories. His experiences. His aggressions. His frailties. The women he loved, the men he hated. His business coups. His childhood ailments. The graduation speech; the cramped muscle; the wedding night. All there. This was recorded in December. It takes him from childhood to the edge of the grave."

"Suppose I reached over the balcony and hurled all this down there," Kaufmann said. "The flakes would scatter. The tape would be ruined. That would be the end of Uncle Paul, wouldn't it?"

"Why do you think so?" Santoliquido asked. "Your uncle was here every six months for more than thirty years. We have many replicas on file of what you hold in your hand."

Kaufmann gasped. "You keep the old ones after a re-recording?"

"Naturally. We have an extensive library of your uncle's personae. You have the latest one, the most complete; but if anything happened to it, we could make use of the last but one, which would lack only six months of his life experience. And so on backward. Of course, we always use the most recent recording for transplant purposes. The rest are kept as emergencies, a redundancy control, so to speak."

"I never knew that!"

"We don't make a point of announcing it."

"So you have sixty-odd recordings of Uncle Paul in this building! And a couple of dozen of me! And—"

"Not in this building, necessarily," said Santoliquido. "We have many storage vaults, Mark, well decentralized. We guard against calamities. We have to."

Kaufmann considered that. It had never occurred to him that such surrogate recordings existed, or even that there might be supplementary soul banks elsewhere, but both were logical enough. An implication struck him.

"If there are duplicates," he said slowly, "then it should be possible to transplant one man's persona into more than one recipient at the same time, yes? You could give Uncle Paul to Roditis, and Uncle Paul minus the last six months to someone else, and so on."

"Technically possible. But wholly unethical and unlawful. We keep the reserves as reserves. They've never been used that way and never will." Santoliquido looked agitated at the possibility. "*Never.*"

Kaufmann nodded. The intensity of Santoliquido's reply unsettled him. He closed the casket and handed it back.

"Now do you believe he's dead?" Santoliquido asked.

"Well, of course, I've got no evidence that the tape in this box has anything to do with Uncle Paul."

"Would you like to sample it?"

"Me? Are you proposing a temporary transplant?"

"I'll give you thirty seconds of Uncle Paul," Santoliquido offered. "Just as if you were shopping for a new persona. Then you can decide for yourself whether he's on that tape. Come along. In here."

They entered a cubicle with dark translucent walls. It contained a reclining seat, a console of equipment, a row of jeweled scanners. Santoliquido removed the tape from the box and clipped it into the grips of one of the scanners. He beckoned Kaufmann to the reclining seat.

They were in a sampling booth now. This apparatus was used strictly for checking and testing. What Kaufmann would experience was not in any way a transplant, not even a temporary; Santoliquido was just going to tune him in on the recorded thought waves of his late uncle and let him swim in them for half a minute.

Kaufmann watched, chilled and apprehensive, as Santoliquido adjusted his scanners and placed cold electrodes against his forehead. The plump man looked somber too; he had already tasted this experience, thought Kaufmann, and obviously it had been no pleasure for him. An amber warning light went on. Santoliquido tugged at a knife-switch.

Mark Kaufmann winced as his uncle came flooding into his brain.

It was a torrent, an avalanche, a cascade. Uncle Paul swept through his synapses with violent impact. A tide of raw sensuality came first; then a sudden stab of gastric pain; then a set of precise, instantaneous, all-encompassing calculations for the purchase, lease-back, and depreciation of a four-square-mile area in Shanghai's northern suburbs. On top of that came an overlay of family scheming, a nest of intricate and poisonous interpretations of taut relationships. In the first ten seconds of contact with his uncle's soul, Kaufmann thought his mind would burn out. In the second ten seconds he struggled for equilibrium like a man caught in rough surf and dashed again and again to the sand. In the third ten seconds he found that equilibrium, gaining purchase of sorts and discovering a strength within himself that he had not suspected. He realized that he could meet his dead uncle as an equal. The old man had the advantage of greater age, but not really of greater force; the Kaufmann genes had traveled from uncle to nephew in a knight's move of inheritance, and for all the unshackled power of Paul's furious mind, Mark knew that he could handle it indefinitely, if he had to.

The contact broke.

Kaufmann's eyes opened. He slipped the electrodes free and put his hands to his temples. Phantom calculations danced through his skull—the old man's arbitrage schemes, realty enterprises, testamentary codicils, percentage plans, all whirled together in a wild dance of dollars.

"Well?" Santoliquido asked. "Do you know your uncle better now?"

"The ruthless old bastard!" Kaufmann said in admiration. "The wonderful pirate! What a tragedy that he's gone!"

"He'll be back."

"Yes. Yes." Kaufmann clutched the arms of the chair. "I'd give anything to have him myself," he said in a low voice. "I'm the one best qualified to have him. Paul and I were a superb team, these last few years. Think how much better we'd be, working together in one mind!"

"I hope you're joking, Mark."

"Not really. Paul and I belong together. I know, I know, it's against the law to transplant a persona to so close a relative."

"Don't forget that your uncle directly requested in his will that he not be transplanted to any member of his own family."

"As though he didn't know about the law," said Kaufmann.

"Or as though he expected that someone like you would circumvent it."

Kaufmann flushed. "But what *are* you going to do with him? Give him to Roditis? Put those two together and they'll steal the universe!"

"Roditis can handle your uncle's persona," said Santoliquido. "He's got the strong personality that's necessary. What we must guard against is giving Paul to someone who'll be overwhelmed. The host must always remain in command. Roditis would."

"But he's got no scruples. He's nothing but an unprincipled buccaneer. And Paul was a principled buccaneer. Bring them into harmony and—"

"No decision has been taken," Santoliquido said brusquely. "Do you wish to inspect the three potential personae your daughter has selected?"

"Yes," Kaufmann murmured. "I might as well."

Santoliquido opened an information line and uttered a request. Moments later three persona caskets clattered out of a delivery slot. Santoliquido inserted Paul Kaufmann's casket in the same slot and sent it on its way back to storage. Then, turning, he said, "All these three young women died violently before the age of thirty. All three were quite beautiful, I understand. Risa had certain very specific anatomical and sexual qualifications, which of course we were able to meet, since the range of available personae is so great. To preserve the privacy of the dead, I'll call these three simply X, Y, and Z. Thirty seconds of each should be enough to gratify your curiosity. Have you ever sampled a female persona before, Mark?"

"You know I've never done anything like that."

"Of course. Of course. Well, it's an amusing novelty. I often think our prejudice against transsexual transplants is foolish. If a man could incorporate at least one female persona, or a woman at least one male one, there'd be far less anguish in this world. But I suppose we're not yet ready for that radical a step. And I suppose few people are really eager to allow their personae to come to life in a body of alien sex. Oh, they'd like to try it for a few days, but as for making it permanent—" As he spoke, Santoliquido was deftly inserting one of Risa's choices into the scanning equipment. Once more the electrodes touched Kaufmann's skull. He felt vaguely uncertain about doing this, but then he reflected that his exhibitionistic daughter would certainly not mind his peeking into her personae, and also that he had already spied on his daughter in many matters nearly as intimate.

The apparatus hummed.

"This is X," said Santoliquido. "Killed last year in a power-ski accident at St. Moritz, age twenty-four."

In the thirty seconds that followed, Mark Kaufmann learned a great many surprising things. He discovered what it was like to have breasts; he sampled the sensations of the penetrated instead of those of the penetrator; he felt the ebb and flow of feminine biology impinge on him; he scented a new perfume of flesh; he experienced the texture of his own smooth female body. He also generated an instant and electric dislike for the personality of the unknown X.

Giving him no pause for evaluation, Santoliquido said, "And now Y. Drowned off Macao last summer, age twenty-eight."

More of the same: the slow throb of the flesh, the lazy tremor of vaginality. In his brief contact with the mind of the dead girl, Kaufmann ran imaginary hands over silken imaginary thighs, yawned, stretched, yearned for pleasure. This was a more relaxed spirit than X's; in that first persona there had tingled some disturbing undercurrent, some sort of hunger for an unclear vengeance, while in this girl was merely a generalized appetite for gratification, far less intense, far less vivid. Her recorded soul winked and guttered and was gone.

"Z," said Santoliquido. "Twenty-six years old. Pushed or jumped, eighty stories up."

Pushed, Kaufmann decided, after only an instant of contact with Z. This girl had not had the vitality to commit suicide. She was placid, passive, soft within and without. Now that the novelty of peering into female souls had worn off, Kaufmann found himself swiftly bored by this one. She was a void, a hollowness, and the thirty seconds dragged abysmally.

"You may find yourself slightly impotent tonight," Santoliquido was saying. "I suppose I should have warned you. There's a kind of sexual confusion that sets in after you've done some transsexual sampling. But it wears off in a day or so. How did you find it, being female?"

"Interesting. Not very appealing, though."

"Well, of course, these were young, shallow girls. I could find you female personae that would give you a real jolt of character. But the outward manifestations are unusual, aren't they? You never dreamed it was like that, so different, to belong to the other sex?"

"I'm glad to have had the opportunity. I can't say I'm impressed by any of my daughter's choices."

"Which would you prefer her to take? She's going to pick one, you know."

Kaufmann nodded. "Z was nothing but a cow. Risa would be as bored with her company as I was. Y was neutral, good-natured, most likely fun in bed. And X was utterly hateful. Vicious, nasty, selfish, hardly human. Risa wouldn't want a bitch like that in her head. I suppose that Y is the least of the three evils."

"She's going to pick X," said Santoliquido.

"Did she tell you that?"

"She didn't. But X is the obvious one. She's got the right combination for Risa—strength of character and voluptuousness. Why did you hate her so?"

"I don't know. I can't find any particular reason. Just an absence of sympathy. Looking back, I can't pinpoint any single ugly thought from her, but yet I know I loathed her."

"A pity," said Santoliquido. "From Tuesday on, she'll be living in Risa, unless I miss my guess. Do you want to withdraw your consent for the transplant?"

Kaufmann thought it over. It was within his power to prevent Risa from taking this persona on; but he saw the futility of the attempt at once. If thwarted, Risa would merely apply more pressure, and she was an expert at getting her way. He knew he had to adjust to the changed Risa that would come forth, that it was idle to try to block and control her.

He waved his hand. "Let her do as she likes. But I hope she'll take Y."

"Your hope will be disappointed," said Santoliquido. He looked at his watch. "I'm afraid I must leave you now, Mark. I'll turn you over to a technician who'll see to it that your new persona recording gets made right away. That *is* why you came here today, I'm sure you remember."

"Yes," Kaufmann said dryly. "All this spying was only the appetizer. Now for the main course."

Santoliquido produced a young, earnest technician named Donahy, with black hair so dark it seemed to have purple highlights, and startling, bushy eyebrows slashing across his too white forehead. Kaufmann bade Santoliquido farewell, thanked him for his favors, looked forward to his presence on Dominica the next day.

"If you'll come this way—" said Donahy.

Shortly Kaufmann was out of the storage section of the building and back on familiar ground, in the public area where persona recordings were made. Here there was none of the carefully cultivated gloom of that great central vault. Everything was bright, glowing, radiant; the tiles gleamed, the air had a vibrant tingle. This was the place where one came to purchase one's claim to immortality, and its gaiety mirrored the moods of those wealthy enough and determined enough to preserve their personae for future transplants.

He had been here many times. He had left a trail of recordings stretching back to the youthfully restless, ambitious Mark Kaufmann of twenty. And, he now knew, all those recordings still existed in some remote but accessible archive. A biographer, given the right influence, could trace the unfolding of his development from youth to decisive manhood, stage by stage.

Now the latest Mark Kaufmann would be added to the cache. Since he had been neglectful about reporting to be taped, nearly a full year's experiences were to be incorporated in the file now. It had been a more eventful year than usual, marked by his uncle's death, by his own increasingly complex relationship with his daughter, by several turns of his dealings with Elena Volterra, and now—in the final hours of the record—by this quartet of new experiences, his moment of entry into his uncle's persona and the three samplings of female personae. Those most recent events had left their imprint on him most clearly, and they would now become the potential property of the future recipient of his persona.

"Will you lie down here?" Donahy asked.

Kaufmann reclined. The Scheffing process had two phases—record and transplant—and the recording phase was the essence of simplicity. The sum of a human soul—hopes and strivings, rebuffs, triumphs, pains, pleasures—is nothing more than a series of magnetic impulses, some shadowed by noise, others clear and easily accessible. The beautiful Scheffing process provided instant mechanical duplication of that web of magnetic impulses. A spark leaping across a gap, so to speak: the quick flight of a persona from mind to tape. A lifetime's experience transformed into information that can be transcribed, billions of bits to the square millimeter, on magnetic tape; and then, to play safe and provide an extra dimension of realism, the same information translated and inscribed on data flakes as well. There was nothing to it. A transplant, involving the imprinting of all this material on a living human brain, was much more difficult, requiring special chemical preparation of the recipient.

The telemetering devices went into position. Kaufmann looked up into a tangle of gleaming coils and struts. Sensors checked his physical well-being, monitored the flow of blood through the capillaries of his brain, peered through the irises of his eyes, noted his respiration, digestive processes, tactile responses, and vascular dilation.

"You haven't been with us a while," observed Donahy, making an entry in his dossier.

"No, I haven't. I suppose I've been too busy."

The technician shook his head. "Too busy to preserve your own persona! You must have really been busy, then. You know, you never would forgive yourself if you suddenly woke up as a transplant and found a year-long chunk of your life missing from your package of experience."

"Absolutely right," Kaufmann said. "It's unutterably stupid to neglect this obligation."

"Well, now, at least you'll be up to date again. But we hope you'll come to see us more regularly in the future. Here we go, now—lift your head a little—fine, fine—"

The helmet was in place. Kaufmann waited, seeking as always to determine the precise moment at which his soul leaped from his brain, impressed a replica of itself on the tape, and hurried back into its proper house. But, as ever, the moment was imperceptible. His concentration was broken by the voice of the technician, saying, "There we are, Mr. Kaufmann. Your central will be billed, as usual. Thank you for coming, and I hope we have the pleasure of recording you many more times in years to come."

Kaufmann left the building and entered his hopter. According to the ticker, the market had risen sharply; he had profited not a little while wandering within the maze of the Scheffing Institute. And he had fulfilled his obligation to his future recipient by extending the unique and irreplaceable record of his life. Complete with a trifle of Uncle Paul's persona, and minute slices of the lives of three unknown girls.

Within his mind his own resident personae made their presence felt. They reminded him of other duties of this day, still undone. Planning for the party; a realty closing; a conference in Washington. Busy, busy, busy. But at least his conscience was clear for the moment. And tomorrow he could relax.

# 5

The island of Dominica rises like a great many-humped green beast out of the blue Caribbean, well down the chain of the Antilles. Trade winds blow steadily; a tropic sun keeps watch; the lofty mountainous spine intercepts rainfall and keeps the island constantly moist. Here in this still unspoiled island the Kaufmanns had assembled a lordly estate. Industry had come to most of the neighboring isles of the West Indies, but the rain forests of Dominica remained as green and glistening as in primordial times, and in its humid lowlands the banana plantations spread from stream to stream. The arrangement, a quasi-feudal one, did not greatly please the Dominicans, who hungered for the prosperity experienced by Martinique and St. Lucia and Barbados and the rest. But their island was safe from defilement, whether they willed it or not.

The Kaufmann property lay in the northwest quadrant of the

island, between Point Round and the thriving town of Ports-
mouth. There the family had purchased a series of waterfront
tracts encompassing not only a majestic crescent arc of white
beach, but also a string of the humbler dark beaches of black
volcanic sand. Their holdings ran inland, up the rising slope
of Morne Diablotin, Dominica's highest mountain, and so they
sampled the available environments from the dry shoreline to the
riverine interior to the mysterious cloud forest of the mountain.
It had taken three generations of haggling and title search to put
the estate together, and no one could venture to guess what its
true value might be in a world where such tracts no longer could
be had at all.

Risa liked to think of it as her own property, due to descend
to her in time. In fact that was untrue; the estate belonged com-
munally to the Kaufmann family association. It was administered
on behalf of the family by her father, but that did not put her in
line to inherit it. Each of her many cousins and aunts and uncles
and more distant relatives had a share in the property. But Risa
thought of herself as belonging to the main line of the Kaufmanns,
and since she was her father's only child, she saw herself as the
point of convergence toward which all the family wealth flowed.

It was midday, now: the most dangerous hour under the hostile sun. She stood nude in hip-deep water on the crescent beach,
relaxing before more guests arrived. About a dozen were here
already. Risa and her father had flown down from New York late
the previous night to oversee the preparations for the party. Looking up and down the beach, she eyed the early arrivals. They were
scattered like flotsam on the pink-white sand, sunning, dozing.
Four Kaufmanns, a pair of Lehmans, and a trio of Kinsolvings.
Some of them bare, others—not modest but aware of the esthetics
of ungainliness—covering selected portions of their bodies. Not

one was less than fifteen years her senior. Risa wished her cousins would arrive.

Turning her back to the beach, she waded seaward.

Her body glistened. She had oiled it to protect herself from the sun. Her eyes were lensed against the salt water. She dug her toes into the sandy bottom, kicked forward, and began to swim, cutting a lean swathe through the green, glass-clear water. She liked the touch of it against her breasts and belly. The sunlight made sparkling patterns on the ocean floor, five feet below her. Soon she was past the sandy zone and out above the coral reef that lay a hundred yards off shore. Gnarled, twisted coral heads jutted from the bottom. Fish of a thousand hues danced and played between the stony orange and green slabs. Malevolent black sea urchins twitched their spines hopefully at her. Risa sucked air, dived, plucked a sand dollar from the bottom.

In time she lost interest in the reef. When she swam back to shore, she found that another dozen guests or more had arrived— among them, finally, someone of her own generation. Her cousin Rod Loeb stood at the water's edge: eighteen, brawny, tanned, vain. She knew him well and liked him. He wore only a taut red loinstrap. His eyes passed easily over her slender nakedness as she emerged from the water.

"Just get here?" she asked.

"Half an hour ago. There was hopter trouble at the airport and we were delayed. You're looking good, Risa."

"And you. Let's walk."

They strolled through the slapping surf toward a cluster of jagged, metallic-looking rocks piled at the north end of the beach. Risa felt the noon warmth probing her skin for some vulnerable place to singe and blister; but the molecule-thick coating of cream protected her. She reveled in her nudity. She broke into a trot, her small breasts barely swaying. If Elena tried to run like this, Risa thought, she'd hit herself in the face with all that swinging meat.

They reached the rocks, neither of them short of breath. The white turrets of barnacles sprouted on the lower surfaces, licked by the waves. Rod said, "I hear you've had a transplant."

"News travels fast if it's reached Majorca already."

"Gossip moves at the speed of light in this family. Is it true?"

"Partly. I've applied for one. Mark gave his consent a few days ago. I went to the soul bank and tried a few personae out, and on Tuesday I'll have the transplant."

"Who'll it be?"

"I'm not sure yet. I'm deciding between some different types. Whichever it is, it'll be a girl who died young and sexy. Maybe even someone you've slept with."

Rod laughed. "Is that incest? If you pick up a persona with a memory of having been to bed with me, I mean?"

"I don't know. I don't care. Is there anything so special about going to bed with you?"

"Try me and see," Rod said. "Without filtering it through a transplant."

She eyed his loinstrap. "Right out here on the beach, or should we go to your cottage?"

"Why not right here?" he asked.

"All right," said Risa. She stretched out on a flat palm of stone, flexed her knees, drew her legs apart. Anyone on the beach could see them from here. She propped her fist against her chin. "Go ahead," she said. "I'm waiting."

"I almost think you're serious," Rod said.

"I am. And you are too, aren't you? That strap doesn't hide much. You want me. You've been hinting about it long enough. So here's your chance. Get on top of me."

His eyes sparkled maliciously. "I wouldn't take advantage of a child."

"Monster! I'm past sixteen."

"Chronologically. But only a child would want to put on a sick exhibition like that in front of everybody. It's tasteless, Risa. If you really want to have sex with me, get up and we'll go somewhere private and I'll oblige you. But just to show everyone that you're old enough to sin a little—"

"Would I be the first to make love at one of these parties?"

"Stop it," he said. He swung himself down beside her and lightly slapped the outside of her left thigh. "Can I change the subject? What do you know about Uncle Paul's transplant? Who's going to get him?"

Disgruntled by his casual disregard of her wanton mood, Risa closed her thighs and said, "How should I know?"

"The story I hear is that he's going to go to John Roditis."

"Not if my father has anything to say about it."

"That would be a blow, wouldn't it?" Rod said. "Roditis is big enough as he is. With Uncle Paul, he'd be a titan. He'd have the business mind of the century."

Risa yawned. She swiveled around, dipping her toes in the water. A gray ghostly crab scuttled along the sand and vanished, digging down with startling swiftness. Risa said, "My father doesn't want Roditis to have Uncle Paul. My father's a good friend of Santoliquido, and Santoliquido decides. See?"

Rod nodded. "You make it sound very open and shut."

"It has to be. Why, if Roditis got Uncle Paul, he'd be able to come to our family gatherings, he'd have a wedge right into our whole group. Wouldn't that be horrible? That nasty, aggressive little man sitting right there on the beach, sipping a drink, making us be polite to him for Uncle Paul's sake? But it won't happen."

"Perhaps. Perhaps not."

"It won't."

"If it isn't going to happen," Rod said, "what's Roditis' private secretary doing here?"

"*Where?*"

"Look," Rod said, pointing.

Risa peered back and saw a group of new arrivals descending to the beach from the cabanas. Leading the way came Elena Volterra, wearing next to nothing, her oiled body agleam, fusion nodes glistening in her skin, her heavy breasts artfully cantilevered into position by a wisp of sprayon support. Beside her, pink and fleshy, walked Francesco Santoliquido. A pace behind them came an attractive couple whom Risa recognized as David and Gloria Loeb, and on Gloria's right was a very tall, very thin, extremely pale and fairhaired man who indeed closely resembled Charles Noyes, a well-known associate of John Roditis.

His appearance on the beach was exciting comment from many quarters. Heads were turning; whispers buzzed. Noyes himself looked ill at ease. He was thickly lathered to protect his skin from the sun, but even so he continually wrinkled his back as if to make sure he was suffering no harm.

"What could *he* be doing here?" Risa muttered.

"Maybe Roditis is here too," said Rod. "Having a little discussion with your father in the main house."

"No. No." Risa looked for Mark Kaufmann and failed to see him. This was impossible, she told herself. Then she recalled: "Noyes is Gloria's brother. He must have just come along for the ride. This doesn't have a thing to do with Roditis."

"Let's hope you're right. But it seems odd, having a Roditis man right in our midst. Like Death at the feast."

"I want to go over and find out more."

"Go ahead," Rod said. "I'm going swimming. I'll get all the gossip from you later."

He sprang from the rocks and hit the water in midstroke, heading outward toward the reef. Risa, disturbed, crossed diagonally to the new little group standing on the sandy crest of the beach at the midpoint of the crescent. She greeted Elena curtly and took Santoliquido's hand. She smiled at David Loeb, a tall, courtly-looking man of about forty-five to whom she was related in some incomprehensible way, and embraced his lean, leggy blonde wife Gloria. Risa had never known either of them very well. Gloria looked tense and somehow irritated; but she turned smoothly and said, "Risa, I don't think you know my brother. Charles Noyes. Risa Kaufmann. Mark's daughter."

"A pleasure," Noyes said. It didn't sound to Risa as though he meant it. His large blue eyes raced in all directions, as if trying to avoid any direct confrontation of her girlish nakedness; then, with an obvious effort, he smiled at her.

"I've heard so much about you from Gloria," Risa lied sweetly. "It must be so exciting to work with Mr. Roditis. Tell me, is he coming to our party too?"

"No, he—ah—won't be here," Noyes said.

"Pity. I'd love to meet him. Will you excuse me?" Risa grinned icily and went jogging across the hot sand, up onto the lawn and into the main house, where the servants were programing the buffet lunch. She looked for her father and found him, as she expected, in the bamboo-paneled study, on the telephone. She could not see the face in the screen. He hung up after a moment and looked at her.

"Do you know who's here?" she asked.

She could tell from his sour, hooded expression that he did.

70

"Yes. Gloria's little surprise package. She should have had better taste than that!"

"Why'd you let him in?"

"He's her guest. I can't refuse him, even if he *is* Roditis' right hand. It's permissible to bring one's brother to a party like this."

"But what does he want here? Spying for Roditis? Trying to soften us up?"

Kaufmann relaxed and allowed himself to laugh. "Why are you so worked up over it, Risa? It's my problem. You go out in the sun and have a good time."

"If I'm a Kaufmann, it's my problem too. We have certain family standards to uphold!"

"They'll be upheld, love. I'll deal with Mr. Noyes."

It was a dismissal. Mark still refused to accept her as an adult. He was patting her on the head and telling her to run off and play. Risa's nostrils flared, but she kept her anger unvoiced and quickly left the building, narrowly avoiding tripping over a robot crawler that was polishing the patio floor.

Hands on hips, she stood at the edge of the patio, looking down at the guests. Rod had emerged from the water and was talking to Noyes and the Loebs. Santoliquido and Elena, oddly, were off by themselves near the rocks where Risa had tried to seduce her cousin with so little success. Overhead, three huge brown pelicans wheeled and folded their wings, plummeting into the water to snatch up fish; they had been treated with adrenergic drugs, Risa knew, so they'd stay hungry all afternoon and stage a good show for the guests. Suddenly furious, Risa whirled and ran toward the small cottage, one of thirty behind the main house, where she was staying on this visit. She flung herself down on the bed, sobbing sulkily.

Minutes later the doorscreen announced a visitor. She looked up and saw Rod's image.

"Come in," she called.

The door slid open. He stepped in, sticking his feet into the vibrator to rid them of sand. "I've got the word on Noyes," he said. "He's not here on account of Roditis. He happened to drop in on Gloria and Dave just as they were leaving for the party, and they couldn't get rid of him, so Gloria had to say, sure, get in the hopter with us, and here he is. Your father must be burning."

"I'm not concerned with my father's feelings just now," Risa said thinly. "Or with Noyes. Or with Roditis. They can all go to hell."

"Hey—"

Tears ebbed from her eyes. "And you can go there with them!"

"What's wrong? What did I do?"

"It's what you didn't do," Risa said.

Rod stared at her strangely. His eyes traveled the length of her body as though he had never seen her before. Risa trembled expectantly. It was almost time for lunch. But first—

His eyes met hers. Her gaze was steady. He nodded.

He stepped toward the bed.


Noyes thought his brain would melt under that hellish sun. He recited mantras of self-possession and liberation, dug his toes into the scorching sand, watched the nude and near-nude Kaufmanns, their friends, and relatives, flit by, and wished fervently that he were almost anywhere else. It was bad enough that Roditis had pitchforked him into this gathering where he was so little wanted; he also had to tolerate tropical heat, and that was beyond the call of duty. Would the protective cream really protect him? Or would he be parboiled by nightfall?

He felt Kravchenko's jeers.

—Take it like a man, friend.

"Very amusing. But *you* won't feel the sunburn."

—That's part of the business of being dead. You don't feel the pain, you don't feel the pleasure either. Say, say, say, what's Santoliquido up to?

Noyes looked down the beach. He hadn't noticed it, but his persona had; Santoliquido was deep in conversation with Elena Volterra. And Elena was known to be Mark Kaufmann's mistress. In the midst of his discomfort Noyes analyzed this situation in terms of Roditis' needs. Was Elena at this moment doing a hatchet job on Roditis, filling the soul bank administrator's receptive mind with reasons why the Paul Kaufmann persona should not go to him? Or, contrariwise, was Santoliquido attempting to bring Elena into his orbit while Mark was elsewhere? The first possibility held no promise of leverage, but the second did.

Trying to seem casual about it, Noyes edged toward the distant pair. That Elena was certainly a splendid woman, he thought: all that tawny flesh, so well tanned, so opulent, so nicely displayed. He suspected that Elena might easily look sloppy with her breasts unbound, and that if she gained another five pounds her ampleness would turn to grossness. But as she was, she was quite attractive. And Santoliquido's sensual tastes, Noyes realized, inclined toward women of Elena's sort, Latin and statuesque. It would be quite useful to Roditis' cause if Santo worked himself into some kind of compromising position with Elena this weekend.

He got no closer that a hundred yards—still beyond lip-reading range. Then a robot carrying trays of refreshments rolled across his path, and, as he turned to help himself, Noyes was intercepted by a short, gushing woman with golden eyes and an aggressively jutting chin. "Charles," she said. "I haven't seen you in a thousand years. Come meet my new husband!"

He sorted through foggy family memories. She was an Adams, yes, that was clear, and she had attended his sister's wedding to David Loeb, and he remembered dimly that she had been married for a while to one of the Schiffs. He smiled uncertainly.

"You don't remember me?" she asked.

"It's been a long time—Donna, Donna Adams, is it?"

"Donna's my sister. I'm "Rowena. How could you forget a name like that? You should take your memory drugs more often, Charles. I don't believe I'll ever forget the way you carried on at Gloria's wedding! You—"

"I didn't catch your married name now," Noyes cut in quickly.

"Owens. Yes, you were going to meet my husband. Nathaniel Owens. He's right over here. A most extraordinary man. Can you imagine it, Charles, he carries seven personae! *Seven!*"

But he doesn't carry them very well, Noyes decided a moment later, when he had been introduced to Nathaniel Owens. Owens was burly and barrel-chested, flaunting a thick mat of body hair as though perversely proud of its ugly coarseness, and his square, harsh-planed face looked as though it had been constructed from random components. He was about sixty, Noyes guessed. His eyes were black and not quite focused, and when he spoke his voice soared confusingly through an octave or more before settling on its pitch.

"My wife been telling you a lot of nonsense about us?" Owens demanded truculently.

"Not at all. She simply said you're carrying seven personae."

Owens blinked and twitched. "Damned right I am! You see anything wrong with that?"

"If you can handle the strain—"

"He can handle anything, chum," Owens said in a strangely altered voice, a basso growl. "He's the original *übermensch*. You just have to ask and he'll tell you."

74

Noyes was still attempting to understand why Owens had suddenly spoken of himself in the third person when Owens blurted in a much higher voice, "Shut your goddam mouth!"

"It's your goddam mouth I'm talking through," came the deeper voice.

"*Our* mouth, you sniveling idiot!" It was a third voice, bland, silky. "We're all in this cage together!"

Noyes realized, stunned, that Owens' personae had seized control of the man and were carrying on an argument through his vocal apparatus. Owens himself stood stupefied, long arms dangling at his sides, shoulders lifting and hitching in oddly automatic motions. His eyes rolled. His wife, seeing what had happened, grabbed a drink from a roboservitor's tray and plunged it, dagger-fashion, against Owens' thick-muscled arm. His twisting facial muscles subsided. He looked abashed.

"Nathaniel hasn't had much sleep lately," Rowena Owens explained to the little group that had gathered. "Sometimes he finds it difficult to exert the proper authority when he's tired. Feeling better now, darling?"

"I'm all right, yes," Owens said. "I'm in full command again." His voice was neutral; he had ceased to twitch.

Noyes stared, stricken with horror. It seemed to him that he saw his own fate mirrored in Owens' eyes. The man's personae had for the moment ejected him from control of his body and had transformed him into a prisoner in his own skull, assailed by dybbuks. Just as James Kravchenko ceaselessly attempted to do to him. Kravchenko had not yet succeeded even in grabbing the power of vocalization; when he spoke, it was still only an inward murmur. But he was trying all the while. It did not soothe Noyes to reflect that he had merely the problem of keeping one persona under control, while Owens wrestled with a whole team of them.

Owens took Noyes' shocked silence for disapproval, evidently. He said with belligerence, "What's the matter? Don't you believe in Scheffing transplant?"

"Well, I—"

"I know. You're one of the Erasure people. You feel it's all an evil, sinister manifestation of cultural decay, and you want all the personae rubbed out. Right? And here I stand with seven of them under my roof, and to you I'm the embodiment of Satan. Right? Right?"

"It isn't that way at all," Noyes murmured.

"As a matter of fact, my brother isn't part of the Erasure group in the least. Are you, Charles?" Gloria had appeared from somewhere and now stood at Owens' elbow, looking fair and lovely, as much a willowy girl as she had been on her wedding day.

"Of course not," Noyes managed to say. "I've got a persona myself, you know. What gives you the idea I'm against transplant?"

Owens looked mollified. "I suppose I leaped to the conclusion. You know, there are so many of me that I tend to make snap judgments. We assess the evidence as a team, and sometimes we assess it too fast." He thrust out his hand. "Who are you, anyway?"

"Charles Noyes. I'm with Roditis Securities."

"Oh. Yes. Sure." The hand enfolded his. Just as contact was made, Owens twitched again, and a kind of convulsion ran the length of his arm, forcing him to pull his hand back. Noyes watched uncomfortably as the spasm traveled down the entire right side of Owens' body.

Gloria said quickly, "Charles is also an authority on Buddhist reincarnation theory. He and Mr. Roditis have just returned from a pilgrimage to the lamasery in San Francisco. He—"

"You believe in that crap?" Owens asked.

Noyes faltered, astonished by the hairy man's capacity for starting trouble. Rowena Owens bit her lip. As quietly as he could, Noyes said, "I think the teachings form a valuable guide to existence in a world where reincarnation is a practical fact. We must know the art of dying if we're to master the art of living."

"I say it's crap," Owens repeated loudly. "It's an artificial movement grafted onto a materialistic society for reasons of guilt. Those of us who take part in the transplant program are set apart from ordinary humanity, from the clods, if you like, and because in effect we've become immortal we need to console ourselves with a new religion. So we've borrowed this prayer-wheel garbage from the Himalayas, only we've turned it upside down, since in its original form it's inapplicable to our society. It—"

"You sound a little like Mr. Roditis now," Noyes began. "He—"

"Let me finish! The whole idea of the Buddhists is to break the chain of incarnations and go off to nirvana, isn't it? Born no more? And our whole idea is to grab as many incarnations as possible, down through the centuries. For us, good karma leads to rebirth. Is that Buddhism? That's a perversion of Buddhism! I know. I've got a guru right here inside me, one of the best, a real theologian. Murtaugh, from the Baltimore group. You know of him?"

Awed, Noyes said, "Why, of course. He wrote *The Art of Right Dying.*"

"And he died right himself, and I got him! So you better not argue theology with me. I've got it straight from the source, Noyes. *Om mani padme hum.* And I know how cynical the entire movement is. I've got collective karma." Owens twitched again. He was losing control once more. "I tell you, only a tired persona wants off the wheel of sangsara. The rest of us hunger to go round and round and round again. We—" A scabrous obscenity slipped

77

from Owens' lips. He paused, astonished, and hammered his fist against his left cheekbone. He trembled.

It was sickening to watch him being pulled apart this way.

Recovering, Owens said, "Sometimes it's difficult to hang on to the reins."

"Why did you set such a challenge for yourself?" Noyes asked. "Seven transplants—"

"Actually, only four transplants," Owens said. "Murtaugh's persona brought two transplants of his own along, and one of my others already had one. Three hitchhikers, four transplants. Quite a crowd. Quite. A. Crowd."

Noyes understood. Such hitchhikers were known as secondary personae: those that existed as part of the recording of someone subsequently transplanted to another person. The problem of the secondary personae was becoming acute, now that the Scheffing process was more than a generation old. Everyone who carried a persona in addition to his own now handed it on when he was recorded, and some of these crowded minds were being picked up by recipients. In another few years, virtually every transplant would bring the recipient two or three secondary personae for each primary one. Then every transplant would create a babbling mob within the brain, even though the secondary personae were much less vivid than primaries.

There were ways around it, Noyes knew. The simplest was to accept as a transplant only a persona with no secondaries attached, as he had done. Kravchenko had not gone in for the Scheffing process until quite recently, and the recording of him that had been on file at his death had been made before the transplant, so it included no trace of Kravchenko's inherited persona. But of course that method soon would be impossible, since everyone took a transplant young these days, and incorporated the persona in his earliest records.

Another way was to have any secondaries deleted from the persona before adopting it. The erased secondaries thus went back into the soul bank and could be rerecorded as primaries for new recipients. Noyes preferred that idea. However, personae meant prestige, and multiple personae meant multiple prestige. People nowadays seemed to want to clutter their minds. When one took on a transplant, one desired to take that persona's whole package of secondaries, thus getting the full benefit of the transplanted soul in all its complexity.

Which was fine if one could handle it, Noyes thought. But it would be instructive for each potential transplantee to spend five minutes with Nathaniel Owens and find out what it was like to be too greedy.

"—it might be better if none of this transplanting business had ever begun," David Loeb was saying. "And no, I don't believe in erasure either. I've got my personae too. But still—"

"It's our salvation. It's our hope of immortality." That was Owens, speaking in one of his milder voices. "I've recorded myself with this entire tribe of passengers, and I look forward to my next turn on the cycle, in another body, when—"

"Nat! Your arm!" Rowena yelped.

As he spoke, his left arm had reached out in seeming independence of his body to seize Gloria Loeb's thigh. Gloria winced as the stubby fingers dug in. Owens blurted something apologetic, but did not let go. David Loeb and Noyes went to the rescue simultaneously; Noyes grasped Owens' wrist, and his brother-in-law pried at Owens' fingers. The hand came away. Purpling blotches appeared on Gloria's pale flesh.

Owens did not seem to comprehend what he had done. There was a long moment of silence while this group of well-bred people struggled to find a well-bred way of covering the gaffe. Owens solved the problem himself. He said hoarsely, "I think I better go swimming now. Work off this charge of energy and get everything in order."

He ran down toward the water, a lumbering, clumsily powerful figure, stumbling once as some subsidiary persona fought him for control even while he ran. But he managed to hit the water in a smooth dive. Head down, arms pinwheeling, he swam like a torpedo out to the reef.

Noyes closed his eyes. The sun suddenly seemed immense over his head, a great molten ball, dripping flame. Within him Kravchenko sounded his silent mocking laughter.

—Take a good look, Charlie. That's what I'm going to do to you one of these days. I don't need six pals to push you aside. I'll do it myself.

Noyes turned away from the others. In order to speak directly to Kravchenko he had to vocalize his words, and he did not want anyone aware that he was talking to himself. He murmured, "You won't get away with it. The instant you start trouble I'll kill both of us, Kravchenko."

—Ah. The carniphage threat again. Where's the flask, Charlie? In your swimsuit?

"Let me alone."

—Why don't we go over and talk to Elena? *There's* a woman! You're hungry for her, and I'll sit back and watch. I knew her when I was carnate. She wasn't Kaufmann's mistress then. Elena and I can reminisce. Put me in control, Charlie, and I'll seduce her for you.

"Stop it!"

—That would be a good deal for both of us. I'll make Elena, and your body will enjoy the fun.

Noyes shivered. Instead of threatening, Kravchenko now

sought to tempt; but the goal was the same. It might happen at any time: the persona winning command of the shared body, even a countererasure that would wipe Noyes out entirely and leave Kravchenko in undisputed possession, a dybbuk. That was the true rebirth: to take over your host, to have a body of your own again, to walk in the world, freely sampling the sensory intake. Noyes was determined not to have Kravchenko victimize him in that way.

The sun was turning into a flask of carniphage.

Reach up, Noyes thought. Grab it, bite on it. Show him a thing or two.

Trails of sweat ran down his body. He felt his skin puckering and blistering, his bones beginning to melt into rubber. People looked at him worriedly as he swayed-Smiling, bowing, Noyes grinned at his sister, at Elena, at Rowena Owens. I'm all right. Perfectly all right. Maybe a touch of the sun, but nothing serious, quite all right, no need for fear.

Someone screamed.

Noyes thought at first that they were screaming about him, that in his weakened state he had collapsed or split apart or melted or seized the sun. But no, he was still on his feet, and no one was looking at him. They were all pointing toward the water. With colossal effort he swung himself around to see what the matter was.

"He's out of control!" Rowena Owens cried. "Help him, somebody, help him!"

Noyes saw that Nathaniel Owens had reached the reef, swimming to that patch of brownish coral a hundred yards off shore that lay just beneath the surface and broke it to jut up in several places. And there, the warring, incompatible personae within him had rebelled. Now Owens thrashed and leaped about on the reef like a hooked tarpon, flying from the water, smashing down on the razor-keen coral, kicking his legs in the air, vanishing from sight for a moment, then erupting again to crash into another part of the reef. Already long red gashes streaked his skin. Again and again he flung himself at the reef, now mounting one strip of it and doing a wild, frenzied dance along its upper rim.

"He'll cut himself to bits," David Loeb said.

"And the blood in the water—there'll be sharks soon," Santoliquido observed.

Within Noyes, Kravchenko laughed.

—See? See? Just wait!

"No," Noyes whispered. "You'll never do that to me!"

Risa Kaufmann broke from the group. She had been standing silently by, visibly disturbed by Owens' irrational behavior, and now, a tanned nude streak, she ran lithely across the beach, entered the water, and sped toward the reef, swimming nearly submerged, now breaking the water with a kicking ankle, now with an upturned buttock, now a shoulderblade. She reached Owens. He stood upright in water only a few feet deep, readying himself for another lunatic dash against the reef. Deep-hued blood welled steadily through the coarse mat of hair on his body. Risa clambered up beside him, caught him, spun him around, gripped him tightly. The contact of her bell-like little breasts against his hairy fleshiness seemed revolting. But, with brisk efficiency, the girl propelled the dazed, bleeding man away from the coral knives of the reef and drew him into the clear green water closer to shore. He was safe. A cheer went up.

In that same instant Noyes felt the heavens explode and the sun fall at his feet. He snatched it up and devoured it, and as the hallucination overwhelmed him he plunged to the ground, jerking and yammering, seized by an uncontrollable attack. The world grew dark. His limbs lashed the ground. Kravchenko howled in pleasure.

He felt warmth against him. Tender female flesh.

"Easy, easy, easy. You'll be all right."

Elena Volterra was cradling him. He pillowed his head against the ripe, lush mounds of her breasts and sobbed.

"Give him air," a voice said.

Noyes closed and opened his eyes several times. He clung to Elena desperately. "My name's Kravchenko," he said. "James Kravchenko."

"Kravchenko is dead," Elena told him. "You're Charles Noyes."

"Yes. Yes. Charles Noyes. Kravchenko's dead."

"Rest now," Elena whispered. "Easy, easy, easy."

"Rest. I am Charles Noyes. Yes."

"You'll feel better in a little while."

A cool ultrasonic snout touched his arm. Not a drink but an anesthetic, Noyes realized. He saw the Buddha-Heruka, with three heads, six hands, and four feet firmly postured, the right face being white, the left red, the central dark-brown; the body emitting flames of radiance; the nine eyes widely opened; the eyebrows quivering like lightning; the protruding teeth glistening and set over one another. "I am Charles Noyes," Noyes said.

—Give Elena a great big kiss for me.

Noyes' eyes closed. He felt no more pain.

# 6

It was Tuesday morning. Risa entered Francesco Santoliquido's office and stood just within the door. He was busy, using a data machine with his left hand while tapping out computer instructions with his right.

At length he looked up and said, "There she is. Our little heroine. Come in, come in, sit down."

"You got a good tan this weekend," Risa observed.

"There's nothing like the tropical sun. It was a splendid party, Risa. My congratulations to you and your father. Of course, there were some unusual events—"

"They've taken Owens to the therapy satellite. He'll be there a month, floating in nullgrav until he's healthy."

Santoliquido scowled. "Sad, very sad. But nullgrav's not the therapy for him. He's a candidate for erasure."

"I didn't think you used that word here!"

"I'm not speaking in the political sense," said Santoliquido. "Strictly the medical. That man's got more than he can handle under his skull."

"Much more." Risa was flattered that busy Santoliquido would take the time to discuss Owens' problems with her. It was a tacit recognition that she was now an adult. She said, "Is there any provision in the law for mandatory erasure?"

"Well, yes, when the presence of the persona threatens the security and integrity of the host."

"Certainly that's true here."

Santoliquido's eyes twinkled. "But Nat Owens has influence. I'd hesitate to ship him off for erasure against his will. We'll see how he feels when he gets back from his float. Possibly we can get him to give up two or three of the least compatible personae, the ones at war with one another."

Solemnly Risa said, "That would be best. It was scary, out on the reef. Big strips of skin hanging loose on him, and he didn't even seem to know what he was doing, just hurling himself against that sharp coral again and again."

"It was brave of you to rescue him."

She giggled. "I didn't stop to think. Maybe if I had, I wouldn't have done anything. But it just seemed like the right thing to do. I mean, I knew I could get out there and pull him away from the reef, and so I went and did it, and then there was time to be nervous afterward. Especially when I came ashore and found the other man having a fit too, Charles Noyes—"

"It was a wild moment," Santoliquido agreed. "Noyes has been in stasis these last two days, hasn't he?"

"I think they let him out. He's calm again."

"Tell me, Risa. Now that you've seen two men run wild at once, because they found their transplants too difficult to control, have you changed your mind at all about your own transplant?"

"Of course not," she said instantly. "Oh, I admit I've been a little uneasy, but I wouldn't be here unless I meant to go through with it. What happened to them isn't any concern of mine. Owens was asking for trouble when he took on that mob of personae. And Noyes is an unstable character, they tell me. I'm ready."

"Good girl." Santoliquido pressed a buzzer. "We'll get going, then. You've chosen the persona you want?"

"Yes."

"Tandy Cushing?"

"How did you know that?"

"I knew," said Santoliquido. "Ask your father. I predicted the choice you'd make." He opened his desk, came through it, took her by the hand, and lifted her to her feet. "I won't be seeing you again as you are now, Risa. You'll leave my office as Risa Kaufmann, but the next time we meet, you'll be Risa plus Tandy. I hope you find it an enriching experience."

"I know I will," she said.

Heir lips brushed his. She liked him; he was so much like a jolly uncle to her. Though of course she knew it was a mistake to take a patronizing attitude toward a man as powerful as Francesco Santoliquido. He was so kind to her only because she was Mark Kaufmann's daughter, and it was rash to forget it.

A black-smocked technician appeared at the office door. "This way, please, Miss Kaufmann."

She waved goodby to Santoliquido.

Here we go, she thought. Hello, Tandy Cushing!

She followed the technician toward the transplant room. It was a long trip, spanning many levels of the building, and tension grew within her as the moment drew near. She eased her fears by studying the technician. He was young, hardly any older than her cousin Rod, and he seemed plainly in awe of her. It was his job to deal with the rich and mighty, to pump new personae into their receptive brains, but Risa suspected that he himself left this palace of wonders each night to return to some dismal little hovel, full of cockroaches and squalling babies, where he waited tensely for the next day's excursion into fantasy. How brutal it must be to live in the real world, she thought, earning perhaps a thousand dollars fissionable a month, never able to afford anything, and faced with the terrible knowledge that after death comes . . . nothing!

"We go in here," said the technician.

"What's your name?" Risa asked.

"Leonards, Miss Kaufmann."

"Is that a first name or a last?"

"Last."

Last. No doubt he had a first name too, but wasn't supposed to give it. He was merely a piece of walking equipment. Leonards. He was good-looking, in his own worried way, too pale, pinch lines already forming between his eyebrows, but tall and sturdily built. Are you married yet, Leonards? Where do you live? What are your dreams and ambitions? Isn't it frustrating for you to work in the soul bank and never have any hope of receiving a transplant yourself, or of being recorded? Wouldn't you like enough money so you could put your persona on file, Leonards? Suppose I had your account credited with half a million dollars fissionable. Would that be enough? I'd never miss it. I'd tell Mark I gave it to charity. Your life would be altogether different. Or how would you like to meet me when this is over, Leonards, and go to bed with me? Would that please you, sleeping with a Kaufmann? I'm good, too. Ask Rod Loeb. Ask a lot of people. I'm young, but I learn fast.

Together they entered the booth.

She kept her face rigid, masklike, hiding her thoughts from the young man. It would never do for him to know what she had been thinking. He might get upset and bungle the transplant somehow. Let him stay calm and cool at least until the work is done. Afterwards, maybe, I'll have a little fun with him.

The transplant room was a rectangular cubicle, perhaps nine feet by twelve, warm, well lit. It had windows along two walls, one facing the outer corridor, one looking into an inner access room that was part of the spine of the building. Risa saw a couch, a computer terminal, and a cluster of gleaming equipment.

Opaquing the hall window, Leonards said, "Please lie down. Make yourself comfortable."

"Shall I remove my clothing?" Risa asked.

Her hands went to the discard stud. Leonards' facial muscles rippled in shock at the mere suggestion that she was willing to disrobe before him, and it was a moment before he recovered his poise and said, "That won't be necessary. Kick off your shoes, if you like."

She stretched out, shoeless. Leonards grasped a bronze knob and a mass of equipment swung free of the wall. He drew it toward her. "This is a diagnostat," he told her. "We simply wish to check your physical condition before we proceed with the transplant. It's important that your health and body tone be at the top of their cycle. This part just takes a minute-there." The diagnostat hummed and clicked and was silent. Leonards pressed an eject stud. A copper-colored capsule dropped out, and he flipped it into a transfer hatch that would take it to some scanning instrument within the building's computer bank. He looked more nervous than she was. After a moment, a light went on in the access room, and through a slot in the wall came a yellow slip. Risa craned her neck but could not see what it said.

"You're in fine shape," Leonards reported. "Where did you get those skin abrasions, though?"

"In the West Indies on Saturday. A man was in trouble on a coral reef and I pulled him free and got cut up a little. They're healing fast."

"In any case, there's no effect on your receptivity to the transplant. Now, I suppose you're familiar with the Scheffing process, but I know you want to keep up with me on each phase of the transplant, so I'm likely to tell you a few things you already know. For example, the first step is the drug treatment, to enhance your memory receptivity. We inject a nucleic acid booster, coupled with one of the mnemonic drugs. A mnemonic drug—"

"Am I getting picrotoxin or one of the pentylenetetrazol derivatives?" Risa asked.

Leonards looked shaken. "You've been doing some homework!"

"Which do I get?"

"It'll be the pentylene," he said. "We get better response curves on it with women under thirty. Picrotoxin blocks presynaptic inhibition, and some of the others block postsynaptic inhibition, but pentylenetetrazol doesn't interfere with either. It excites the nervous system by decreasing neuronal recovery time, without reference to inhibitory pathways. Thus it prevents memory decay and significantly increases the response latencies. Still following me?"

"Yes," Risa lied. She was damned if she'd let his deliberately accelerated flow of gibberish upset her. "The result is to make me more receptive to the imprint from the recording. All right. I'm ready whenever you are."

He produced a thick, stubby, phallic-looking ultrasonic injector. While he fumbled with the dial settings Risa casually disengaged her tunic, baring the lower part of her body to the groin. Leonards was slow to notice, but when he finally looked at her he was so rattled he nearly dropped the injector.

Staring rigidly at her chin, he said, "Why did you uncover yourself?"

"I understood that the injection was given in the upper part of the thigh."

"No."

"In the backside, then?" She grinned kittenishly and rolled over.

"The arm will do."

She pouted. "Well, all right."

He was sweating and flushed. She figured she had paid him back well enough for that burst of postsynaptic inhibitions and response latencies. Chastely she covered herself again, not wanting him to jab the injector into the wrong place while he was so shaken. He took a deep breath and put the snout to her arm. There was an ultrasonic whirr.

"We allow one hour for the nucleic acid booster to reach the brain. By then the mnemonic drug will have already taken effect. I'll leave you to relax until the next phase can begin. Perhaps you'd like to look through this information leaflet."

He made his escape from the transplant room, looking visibly relieved.

Risa sprawled on the couch and examined the booklet.

SOME FACTS ABOUT THE SCHEFFING PROCESS, it was headed. She glanced through it without interest. It told her things she already knew: how her brain was prepared for the persona to come, how the recordings were made, how transplants were effected. Toward the back was some material of more direct importance: tips on making the transition after your first transplant.

*You will have complete access to the memories and life experiences of your imprinted persona,* the booklet told her. *As with your own memories, some of the experiences you receive will be blurred or distorted and not immediately retrievable. During the period of adjustment you may feel occasional confusions of identity, particularly if the new persona was noted for strength of character in its previous carnate existence. THIS SHOULD NOT BE CAUSE FOR ALARM. After a few days you will establish a satisfactory working relationship with the persona. Your new companion will enhance and support your responses to your environment. You will have the advantage of extra perspective and an additional set of life experiences on which to base your judgments. Think of the persona as a guest, a friend, a partner. It is the most intimate possible human relationship, and represents the finest accomplishment of our era.*

A few pages on, Risa found information on how to communicate directly with the persona. At any time, she could simply reach into the pool of experience and memory that was being transplanted to her brain, and haul out whatever was useful to her immediate situation. But if she wanted to speak to the persona, to address her as an individual, she would have to talk out loud. At least at first, though the booklet said it was possible after a while to talk to the persona via the interior neural channels. Meanwhile the persona, having no other communication access, was able to key herself right into the brain and make her thoughts known.

Did a persona have thoughts, Risa wondered?

A persona was nothing but a set of memories. It didn't have real existence. You couldn't see a persona, any more than you could see an abstract concept. And the persona was dead, a closed account with all totals drawn. How could a transplanted persona think and react and have things to say?

Judging by the behavior of adults she had observed, a persona was not dead at all—merely suspended from the time of recording to the time of transplant. Then, jacked into the nervous system of its host, it could perceive and respond as if literally reincarnated. That was the whole point of the Scheffing process. It assured the participants everlasting life, with occasional interruptions between transplants. At the same time it provided the living with the benefit of the experiences of the dead. Nothing was lost, except the souls of the poor fish like Leonards who never took part in the rebirth game at all. That was ninety percent of mankind, at present. But did they matter?

As her final hour of independence ticked away, Risa inevitably began to wonder if she really wanted to go through with this enterprise.

No doubt everyone wonders about that, waiting for it to begin, she told herself. At least the first time.

And of course it would be eerie, carting about someone else's soul in her head. Risa was accustomed to privacy when she wanted it. An only child, wealthy enough to isolate herself from the world, never called upon to share anything with anyone—and now she'd have to make room in her head for Tandy Cushing. Strange, strange, strange! Yet appealing, too. She had been alone so long. In a world where everyone she knew carried two or three personae, Risa felt pallid and childlike in her solitude. Now she would be like the others. In one bound she'd shed the last vestiges of immaturity. Merely sleeping around hadn't brought her far enough into the adult world, but this transplant would, especially with worldly, sophisticated Tandy Cushing like an older sister inside her mind.

As the booklet pointed out, it was irrational to fear or mistrust the persona. The persona wasn't going to get any charge out of snooping on you, any more than you could snoop on yourself. The persona would *be* you, and herself as well, a joined identity. Risa's mind whirled a little at that concept. She thought she understood it, but of course she knew she did not, could not. No one who did not have a persona already transplanted could really comprehend what it was like. This was a new thing in the world, a fundamental break with the human condition. No longer were people walled up alone in their own skulls. They could have company.

What if she didn't care for Tandy Cushing's company?

Cast her out like a demon. That could be done, for a price. Her own father had had a persona erased when he was young. Of course, a lot of people preferred to suffer along with their personae even when incompatibility was obvious. Just the way, Risa thought, people will stick with a hopeless marriage, or fight to prevent the amputation of a diseased limb, purely because they can't bring themselves to give up anything that has been part of themselves, no matter how much harm it's doing them.

Look at that Owens man, for example. Driven twitchy by all his personae, and yet he brags about them.

Or Charles Noyes. Right there on the beach, he had almost been engulfed and ejected by his own persona. Why didn't he stop in for an erasure? Did he like to live dangerously, knowing that he might get kicked out of his mind at any moment?

Suppose Tandy tries that with me?

It happened, Risa knew. It was a bit improper to speak of it, but she was aware that powerful personae sometimes overwhelmed and destroyed weak hosts, and took possession of their bodies. Dybbuks, they were called, after some medieval myth. According to the law, a dybbuk who had completely vanquished his host was a murderer, and subject to mandatory erasure. But most of them were too clever to fall into that trap. They continued to use the name of the dead host, keeping their dybbukhood a secret. Someone like James Kravchenko, if he finally succeeded in countererasing Charles Noyes, would probably go on calling himself Noyes for his own safety, and nobody might ever be the wiser.

Risa shuddered. Tandy, will you try to be a dybbuk?

Very strong individuals went in for such things. Waking up in a stranger's brain, they found it intolerable to be relegated to the status of a mere persona. So they pushed the host out and took over. Essentially, they lived again, body and soul, real rebirth, if they got away with it.

Tandy was a strong individual, Risa knew.

But so am I. So am I. If I were in Tandy's place, I'd try to take over. But I'm in my place, and I won't let her win if she tries anything like that.

The door opened. Leonards returned, carrying the oblong metal box that contained the persona of Tandy Cushing.

"How do you feel?" he asked.

"Fine. Impatient."

"I'm supposed to ask you if you'd like to cancel at this point."

"Don't be silly."

"Well, then. Here we go. I want to check to see how well the drug has worked."

"I haven't felt anything," Risa said.

"You shouldn't." He wheeled the diagnostat over and ran a test on her. When the report came, he nodded and smiled encouragingly. "You're in maximum recept now."

"That sounds dirty."

"Does it?" he asked, embarrassed again. He leaned toward her and slipped a cool metal band around her forehead. "This isn't for the transplant," he said. "It's merely to let you sample the persona. We take every precaution against an error. You've got to tell me that this persona is actually the one you've requested."

"Go ahead," Risa said.

This part was familiar. He activated the sampler and Risa found herself once more in contact with Tandy Cushing. The memories were unchanged. After perhaps half a minute, Leonards disconnected the sampler.

"Yes," said Risa. "You've got the right one."

"Please sign this release, then."

Risa grinned and thumbed the thermoplastic. Leonards dropped the sheet in the access hopper.

"Lie back," he said. "Relax. Here we go on the actual transplant."

Panic seized her. Leonards was a step ahead of her, though, efficiently shackling her wrists and ankles to the couch, and telling her in a low, soothing tone, "We do this for your own safety, you understand. Some people find it a big impact and start thrashing around. You'll be all right."

She was stiff with fear, and that surprised her. Forcing a laugh, she looked down at her spreadeagled body and said, "How do I know you're not going to torture me? Or rape me? This is a good position for a rape, isn't it, Leonards?"

His laughter was even more forced than hers.

He was in motion, never pausing, adjusting electrodes,

manipulating scanners, balancing switches. Risa thought about the booklet she had read. Odd: it had been completely secular. No mantras, none of the Tibetan stuff, not even a quotation from the Book of the Dead. Nothing about sangsara or nirvana, the cycle of karma, all the other fashionable words people tagged to the Scheffing process. She realized the fundamental truth of something Nathaniel Owens had said on the beach Saturday at Dominica: the whole religious part of the rebirth business was external. It came after the fact, a moral justification, a dodge, a blind. The work of the Scheffing Institute went on serenely in a spiritual vacuum, and the mumbo-jumbo of the rebirth religion had no place within this building.

"Look up, please," the technician said. "Open your eyes wide."

Twin spears of white light stabbed at her pupils.

She could not close her eyes. She was frozen, immobile, penetrated by those sharp beams of brightness. It seemed to her that she heard a voice intone, "Now thou art experiencing the Radiance of the Clear Light of Pure Reality. Recognize it. O nobly-born, thy present intellect, in real nature void, not formed into anything as regards characteristics or color, naturally void, is the very Reality, the All-Good."

She had summoned out of memory the words to welcome the newly dead into death. Surrender to the Clear Light and attain nirvana. Yes. Yes. So her words were directed to the persona of Tandy Cushing, emerging from that spinning reel of tape, but what she offered Tandy was not oblivion but rebirth. Yes. Yes. Now and at the hour of our birth. Come on, Tandy. I'm ready for you.

If only the light wasn't in my eyes!

Time ceased. Eons passed between heartbeats. Risa could feel the blood creeping along her veins and arteries, impelled by the last spasm and not yet at its destination. She could not see. She could not hear.

The tension broke, and she heard a stranger's voice whispering in her skull.

—Where am I? What happened?

"Hello, Tandy. Welcome aboard."

—Did I die?

"Yes."

—When? How? Why?

"I don't know. I'm Risa Kaufmann. I'm your host."

—I know who you are. I just want to know how I got here. How long have I been dead?

"Since last August," said Risa. "You were killed in a power-ski accident at St. Moritz."

—That's impossible! I'm an expert skier. And I had every safety device! I'm not dead! I'm not!

"Sorry, Tandy. You must be."

—I can't remember anything past June.

"That's when you made your last recording. Two months before you were killed."

—Stop saying that!

"If you're not dead, what are you doing in my mind?"

—There's been a mistake. They can transplant a persona even when the donor's still alive. Sometimes they slip up.

"No, Tandy. Get used to it."

—It isn't easy.

"I'll bet it isn't. But you've got no choice."

—If it's a mistake?

"Even if it is, that doesn't affect you. Assuming Tandy Cushing is still walking around alive somewhere, you're still where you are. A persona in my skull. You aren't Tandy, you're just an identity of Tandy's memories up to the day she recorded you. Well, now you're off the shelf and in a body again. You're lucky, I'd say. And in any case Tandy *is* dead. You're all that's left of her."

There was silence within. The persona was digesting all that.

Risa, too, made adjustments. She still lay shackled. The light had gone out, and she could not tell if Leonards was still in the room. Cautiously, gingerly, she made contact with the persona at a variety of points. She picked up a memory of her late body, tall, dark-haired, with high, firm, heavy breasts. A man's hand ran lightly over those breasts, hefting them, savoring their bulk. His fingertip flicked across her nipples. So that was what it was like, Risa thought. You're less aware of them than I expected. Suddenly she darted back along Tandy's timeline and was eleven years old, staring in a mirror at her budding little chest and frowning. And then, coming forward five years, Risa saw Tandy soaring on personnel jets eighty yards above the Sahara, a strong, dark-haired man beside her as they flew.

I have never done that, Risa thought. Yet I know what it's like. I am Tandy!

She did not go deeper. There was time to explore the depths of the persona later. For Risa the world was suddenly tinged with wonder, all objects taking on new hues, extra dimensions. She saw through four eyes, and she had never seen such colors before, such greens and reds and yellows, nor had she tasted wine so sweet, scented flowers so pungent.

"Tandy?" she said. "How is it now?"

—Better. So you're a Kaufmann?

"Yes. Lucky you."

—Why did you pick me?

"You seemed interesting."

—You're very young for this.

"I'm past sixteen, you know."

—Yes, I know. But I was twenty-four, and I hadn't had my first persona yet.

"Don't you wish you had?"

—I was waiting until I was twenty-five.

"I never wait," Risa said. "Not for anything."

—I see that. We've got so much to talk about.

"We've got all the time in the world. You'll be with me forever, Tandy."

—Forever?

"Of course. The next time I record myself, your persona will be added to mine. Someday I'll need rebirth, and you'll be going along to the next carnate with me."

—People can get awfully bored with each other like that.

"*We* won't," Risa said. "I promise you, we won't."

The shackles dropped away. Risa sat up, feeling a little shaky. Leonards was eyeing her hesitantly.

"You've made a good adjustment," he said.

"Is that so? Fine."

"How does it go?"

"I'm very pleased," said Risa. "What happens now?"

"We take you to a rest booth. You can lie down, relax, get to know your persona. After an hour you can leave the building."

"You've been very kind, Leonards."

"Thank you."

"Maybe we can get together after hours."

He looked smitten with confusion. "I'm afraid—that is—I mean to say—"

"All right. Take me to the rest booth."

She lay down on a comfortable webfoam cradle, closed her eyes, sent her mind roaming through the treasury of Tandy Cushing's experiences. Risa felt faintly uncomfortable, seeing the older girl so nakedly exposed. But she told herself that she had every right to explore that material. At this very instant, wasn't Tandy peering into her own soul? By definition they now were one person. They would share everything.

Risa felt no regrets. Her fears had evaporated. She felt only tremendous relief, for she had accepted a transplant and it was good.

She smiled. She said softly to Tandy, "I'll record the two of us in a week or two. Just to be on the safe side."

—Good. And then I want you to help me find out how I really died.

# 7

"Come to Jubilisle!" The barker called. "Games, thrills, pleasure! Three bucks fish, the round trip! Jubilisle, Jubilisle, Jubilisle!" And globes of living light drifted free over Battery Park, soft indigo bursts tipped with yellow, reinforcing the shouted message with subtler pleas, many-hued whispers, *Jubilisle, Jubilisle, Jubilisle . . .*

It was night. The hydrofoil ferry waited at the pier. Crowds shouldered past, hustling toward it, people in rough, low-caste clothes, some of them even waving cash in their fists. Watchful quaestors stood by, ready to make arrests if the mob got out of hand. Charles Noyes experienced a sudden dizzying spasm of resistance. Everything about this outing repelled him all at once: the shouts of the barker, the faces of the people rushing past him, the too sleek hull of the waiting ferry, the quaestors. He turned to the handsome woman at his side.

"Let's not go," he begged. "I'll take you somewhere else, Elena."

"But you promised!"

"Can't I change my mind?"

"I've wanted to go to Jubilisle for months. Mark won't take me. And now you—"

Sweat rolled down his face. "I've only been out of stasis for a few days. The noise, the tumult—it's upsetting me."

She looked at him, wounded. "Before you say yes, now it's no. That's your name, isn't it? No-yes? Don't disappoint me like this, Charles!"

—Pull yourself together, man, came Kravchenko's voice. She won't like it if you back out.

"Ferry leaving now for Jubilisle," roared the barker. "Hurry, hurry, hurry! Thrills! Games! Pleasure! Three bucks fish, that's all it costs!"

Elena silently pleaded. She looked radiantly beautiful, her opulent body sheathed in glittering scales of some dark green material that followed every contour of her majestic thighs and breasts and buttocks. Her black, glossy hair tumbled to her bare shoulders. In this crowd she stood out so vividly that even the jostling plebs stepped back in automatic deference. Noyes peered into the dark, large, soft eyes. He observed the small, flawless nose, the full, shining lips.

Kravchenko obligingly sent one of his own choice memories bubbling up from the storehouse: Elena nude in Kravchenko's bachelor apartment in Rome, sprawled on a divan like a Venus by Titian, one hand coyly resting on the plump *mons*, the eyes beckoning, the breasts heaving, the dark-hued nipples erect, the firm flesh tense and taut with anticipation.

—You'll never get anywhere with her if you let her down now, pal. It's now or never, and she holds grudges.

"All right," Noyes said. "I won't go back on my word. Jubilisle for us, Elena!"

"I'm so glad, Charles."

He slid his arm around her waist. The scales of her gown pricked his skin. He felt the roll of meat at her hip. Sweeping her forward, he joined the flow of pleasure-seekers rushing aboard the ferry. A robot ticket-vendor held out a hand as though expecting Noyes to put cash in it. Noyes shook his head and offered his thumb instead. The robot, adapting smoothly and without comment, rang up the credit transfer, billing Noyes' account for six dollars, and the barrier dropped, admitting them to the ferry. Minutes later they were speeding across New York Harbor toward the pleasure dome. Ahead lay the bright glow of Jubilisle; behind rose the majestic black-capped somberness of the Scheffing Institute tower, with the rest of the Lower Manhattan skyline behind it. Noyes looked from island to tower. Those who could not buy rebirth at one could purchase distraction at the other.

He and Elena found a place at the rail for the ten-minute journey to the anchored artificial island. She stood close to him. The warmth of her body on this cool spring evening was welcome, and the fragrance of her perfume helped obliterate the rank stench of the mob all about them. She had been kind to him last week at Dominica, when he had had that awful convulsion at Kaufmann's beach party; a touch of the sun, she said, deftly concealing the truth, which was that he had suffered a sudden and nearly successful rebellion by Kravchenko. She was kind, yes. Tender, almost motherly, though she was several years younger than he was. That vast bosom of hers, he thought. It makes her seem the mother of us all.

But his interest in her was not at all filial. He had Kravchenko's testimony that Elena was seducible, and her own willingness to make herself available for this night on the town backed him up. Furthermore, she was Kaufmann's mistress and probably Santo- liquido's as well, so that it enhanced Noyes' own sense of self to be out with her. Lastly, Roditis approved. In the final analysis, what mattered to Noyes was how well or how poorly each of his actions served the interests of John Roditis, and in squiring Elena Volterra to Jubilisle he was in a position to serve Roditis handsomely.

Elena said, "I imagined you came here often. Isn't Jubilisle one of Roditis' properties?"

"Yes, of course. One of his most successful. But I don't think I've been here more than three times in the ten years it's been open."

"Don't you like amusement parks?"

"There are amusements and amusements," Noyes said. He lowered his voice. "It happens that Jubilisle is designed mainly to please plebs. I'm not being snobbish when I tell you that; it's the truth. That's why we put it here, right in the shadow of the Scheff- ing building, so these people could look up and see the tower and think deep thoughts about rebirth. Which, since they can't have it unless they've got lots of money, will inspire them to gamble heavily here, making John Roditis a little wealthier."

"Very clever." Elena glanced around. "Now that you mention it, I see that we're a trifle out of place here. Most of them were pay- ing *cash* to get aboard."

"You noticed that."

"It fascinated me. I don't think I've ever touched cash myself, not even once. I wouldn't recognize a bill if I found it in the street. Why do they bother?"

"They like the feel of money," Noyes said. "The central computer balance is a little impersonal for them. Here—I always carry a bill with me, just for luck. Would you like to see it?"

He slipped his wallet out and found his hundred-dollar bill. It was a slender plastic card which bore the atom symbol, a serial number, the Arabic numeral *100* in black type, and the inscription, *The Bank of the United States Government has on deposit One Hundred Dollars Fissionable Material as security for this note. Legal Tender.* Elena studied the bill as though it might be a mounted butterfly from another planet. "Fascinating," she said at last, handing it back. "Can you get me one?"

"Of course," he said.

He took her by the hand and led her across the deck to a refreshment stand where an automatic servitor was dispensing soft drinks. When the scanner beam flashed in his direction Noyes said, "Give me a hundred-dollar bill." He put his thumb to the charge plate. A bill popped through the slot and he handed it gravely to Elena, who examined it a moment, grinned dazzlingly, and slipped the little card into the deep valley between her breasts. Onlookers gaped in astonishment.

"Thank you," she said, as they returned to the rail. "I'll treasure this little souvenir."

"You'll certainly keep it warm," Noyes said, and they both laughed.

The ferry was nearing Jubilisle's approach slip, now. The great arching dome of the pleasure island rose precipitously before them, topped with a layer of living light that pulsed from one end of the spectrum to the other. A hundred acres of area, six separate levels, the capacity to amuse half a million people at once—that was Jubilisle, and Noyes could not deny it was an impressive sight. Even Elena looked moved.

"Roditis owns it all?" she asked in a whisper.

"Through a nominee corporation, yes. I helped plan the financing soon after I joined his organization. It was his first great coup."

"It must have cost *billions!*"

"It did. And of course Roditis didn't have that kind of money yet, so we had to juggle. He pledged everything as collateral. Paul Kaufmann was willing to put up a construction loan of two billion, but he wanted a fifty-percent equity. Roditis said no. Kaufmann was so astonished he lent the two billion anyway. At ten percent, but he lent it. And Roditis kept the full equity. He owns the place outright. The last debenture was paid off in January. He's thinking of arranging a mortgage, now. Say, about seven billion, from a consortium of banks, and using the money to finance Jubilisle Canton and Jubilisle Rio. Eventually he'll have a dozen of them on every continent. Am I boring you with all this money talk?"

"Not at all," Elena said. She did look genuinely enthralled. "I'm very much interested. Roditis must be a terribly exciting man. I'd love to meet him."

"You never have?"

"Never. We just haven't crossed paths. You know, I spend so much of my time with Mark, and Mark is so hostile to Roditis."

"Yes. Yes, of course."

"But I think one day I will happen to meet Roditis. And he and I will both find the meeting rewarding."

"Powerful men intrigue you, eh, Elena?"

"Why not?"

"Mark Kaufmann—Santoliquido—"

She looked startled. "Santo and I are just good friends."

"Is that all?" He saw the color rising in her cheeks. Laughing, he said, "*Very* good friends, I imagine."

"What are you getting at?"

"Nothing. Nothing."

The ferry was at rest. The gangways extruded themselves and the crowd started ashore. Noyes and Elena let the flow carry them along.

A brilliant directory board in at least six colors confronted them. Twenty feet high, thirty feet wide, the board provided a detailed map of Jubilisle's offerings. Noyes paused to study it, but Elena tugged him along. "Let's just wander," she said. "One level's as good as another."

"That's not true. They're aimed for different sectors of the population."

"What does that matter? We're slumming tonight!"

He shrugged and yielded, and they stepped aboard the moving ramp leading to Level D. Noyes was hazily familiar with the structure of Jubilisle from his past visits; he recalled that the island was cunningly laid out in a series of mazes and dead ends, so that the bemused visitor might roam for hours without arriving at any clear knowledge of how much remained to be seen. The intention was to prod the clientele into realizing that it was impossible to see more than a small fraction of Jubilisle on any one visit, and thus one must return again and again.

The island was devised to offer something to every economic stratum, from those who lived off government credit to those who could afford a dozen persona transplants. Generally, the pull of Jubilisle was stronger in the lower middle brackets, those people who could not afford to traffic in the Scheffing process but who had enough disposable income to part with some here. There was no admission charge at Jubilisle; Roditis made his money partly from the ferry ride, but mainly from the income of the booths and concessions. Noyes had seen the analysis: each visitor spent some fifteen dollars fissionable per trip, on which Roditis' net profit was about thirty-five percent. With half a million visitors at any one time, and perhaps three or four million on a busy Saturday night between sunset and dawn, it was easy to see the source of Roditis' affluence. Jubilisle had competitors now, of course, but it was the first of its kind, and the most successful. The powerful Kaufmann interests, having missed their chance to gain an equity investment in the original Jubilisle, had not deigned to open an imitation, much to Roditis' pleasure. Officially, it was because they had no desire to pander to the debauched tastes of the ignorant, but Noyes thought it was more likely the Kaufmanns stayed out of the pleasure-island business out of fear that they would not meet Roditis' level of success.

The inner core of the island provided the highest-priced delights. Those who came specifically to gamble large sums, to purchase costly sexual experiences, or to indulge in the illicit sensory stimulations of forbidden drugs, generally proceeded by a direct route to that area of Jubilisle. But Noyes had come merely as a casual sightseer, as had Elena, and they moved without plan down the glowing halls and galleries and chambers.

At a gambling pavilion, close to the perimeter of the island, the rhythms of exploding atoms determined the payoffs. A barker claimed that the process was completely random and so must be utterly honest. "Everyone stands an equal chance, folks. I don't mind telling you that some games favor the house, but not here, not here, not here! Step right up . . ."

"Can that be so?" Elena asked. "A truly random game of chance?"

"Maybe so," Noyes told her. "Notice that it's on the outside of the island. If people win steadily here, they're encouraged to try the games within. Which are not quite so impartial."

"But Roditis must lose money on this, even so."

Noyes shook his head. "Not if it's truly random. He'll break even, and all he'll lose is his overhead, which isn't consequential. Call it a promotional loss. Let's try it?"

"All right."

They stepped up. You could pay cash, and most did, but of course Elena had no cash except the souvenir nestling between her breasts, and Noyes thumbed the plate to establish a gambling balance for her. The game was intricate; he scarcely understood its workings himself, and those about him must be wholly baffled by it. In the center of the platform lay what purported to be a block of polonium, flanked by a comically ornate gamma detector; an array of tubes and pipettes emerged from it, filled with scintillating colored fluids. A turquoise fluorescence paid off at 3 to 1; carmine yielded 5 to 1; a yellow streak in the ebony fluid produced a 10 to 1 payoff. The barker chanted rhythmically; the polonium atoms disgorged their component particles; the lights lit and went out. The crowd pressed close. A bell rang and a certificate dropped from a hopper.

"You've won ten dollars," Noyes said.

"Glorious! I want to play again!"

"There's much else to see," he reminded her.

They moved on. At a fortune-telling booth a spectral hooded figure predicted long fife for them both, and numerous children. Then, looking Noyes over cunningly, the prophet added, "You will have many rebirths." Noyes tapped the plate and added a dollar to the soothsayer's credit balance.

"How did he know we were recorded?" Elena asked.

"He guessed. He saw how well-dressed we were and figured we were wealthy, and if we were wealthy we must be on file with the Scheffing people. In any case, it's flattery to wish us rebirths, even if we're not in the class that lives again."

"Perhaps he recognized us," Elena suggested.

"I doubt it."

"I'd like a mask, in any case."

Many of the fairgoers were masked, particularly the women. Girls bare to the hips tripped along, cloaked only by striped dominoes. At Elena's insistence Noyes took her to a masking booth and purchased a concealment for her: a dark band of pseudoliving glass that took possession of her face in a kind of caress, slipping snake-like into place from ear to ear. They laughed. She pulled him close and kissed him fleetingly on the lips. "Buy a mask yourself," she said.

He did. Hidden now from the stares of the curious, they moved through the gallery, taking a dropshaft to the one below on a sudden whim. Noyes felt buoyant, relaxed. Within him Kravchenko was dormant for once, and Elena, warm and exciting on his arm, seemed to promise eventual ecstasies. The evening was going well after a poor start. The giddiness of Jubilisle had broken through his habitual melancholy. Yet there was always the *memento mori* not far below the surface; they paused in a closed arcade to embrace, and Noyes drew Elena so tightly against him that the soft mound of her left breast felt the impress of the flask of lethal carniphage that he carried always with him. When they separated, she touched the bruised place tenderly and said, "You hurt me. Something in your pocket—"

"I'm sorry. I didn't realize you'd feel it."

"What do you have there, a gravity bomb?"

"Just a flask of carniphage," he told her pleasantly. "In case a suicidal mood hits me."

Of course she did not believe that, and so she showered a silvery cascade of laughter over him.

A flamboyant sign declared: WELCOME TO THE HOUSE OF HALF-LIFE.

"What's this?" she asked. "More radioactive games?"

"I have no idea. Shall we go in?"

They entered. A fee of a dollar fissionable was extracted from each of them. Swiftly they discovered that the House of Half-Life, despite its name, did not traffic in neutrons and alpha particles; the half-fife offered here was biological, hybrid creatures raised from fused cell nuclei. Behind an electrified barrier stunted beings shuffled around, while a preprogramed speaker recited their identities. "Here we have mouse and cat, folks, one of the most popular hybrids. And this is dog and tiger, believe it if you can! Next you see snake and frog."

The hybrid animals bore little resemblance to any of their supposed ancestors. They tended to be neutral, unspecialized in form, evolutionary prototypes lacking in clear characteristics. Most were less than two feet in length, moving about on small uncertain legs. The dog-tiger had patches of gray fur. The snake-frog was squat and glistening, with pulsating pouches of flesh. "Man and mouse, ladies and gentlemen, man and mouse!" came the disembodied voice. "You think the Scheffing people work miracles? What of this? Infect them with the Sendai virus, blend the nuclei in a centrifuge, toss in a dash of nucleic acid, yes, yes, man and mouse!" A dozen distorted things, neither mouse nor man, moved into the arena. Their eyes were pink and beady, their hands were claws, they could not walk erect. Elena stared in rigid attention.

A shill sidled up to them, proffering a handful of explosive darts. He said silkily, "You look like expensive folk out for a night's fun. Would you like to kill some of the hybrids? A hundred bucks fish a dart."

"Sorry," Noyes said. "No, thanks."

"Try your aim. Some folk your class come back often. We've got a room in back, lots of hybrids to throw at. They aren't rare, really."

"Shall we?" Elena asked him.

Noyes looked at her in amazement. Her eyes were gleaming.

Kravchenko awakened and offered a warning:

—Don't refuse her anything if you're smart.

Sighing, Noyes gave in. They went to the back room. He lowered his credit balance by five hundred dollars fissionable and Elena took a cluster of darts in her delicate hand. On a platform before them, half a dozen pitiful bluish things, half squirrel, half otter, moved in ragged circles. They were slow, awkward animals with lengthy hairless tails and large flippered feet.

Elena aimed and threw. Her breasts quivered beneath the covering of green scales; her arm moved jerkily, a stiff throw from the elbow. To Noyes' relief, she missed, and missed also on the second and third casts, the darts landing and igniting in quick incandescent puffs. But on the fourth she struck one of the hapless hybrids at the base of its twisted spine, and the odor of singed fur drifted toward them. When the smoke cleared Noyes saw the remnants of the creature. Elena looked exhilarated; a deep crimson flush appeared beneath her dark, tawny skin, making her appear disturbingly more sensual than before. She handed him the remaining dart. He thrust it back at her.

"Go on," she cried. "Throw it! It's fun!"

"To *kill*?"

"Those things come out of test tubes. They're not really alive. They're better off dead." She joggled his arm. The nearness of her perspiring flesh maddened him. "Throw it!"

Desperately Noyes hurled the dart. It cleared the platform by ten feet and smashed harmlessly against the backdrop. Then he seized her by the hand and pulled her through a side exit. Up ahead, a cocktail lounge could be seen, and they entered it.

"Don't you care for hunting?" Elena asked him.

"Not really. But hunting is sport. There's nothing sporting about throwing darts at mutated monstrosities."

She laughed. The tip of her tongue flicked out. "There was a grand hunt in Italy six years ago. We chased partridges across the campana south of Rome. You must have a memory of it."

"I?"

"Jim Kravchenko was there. If he's truly your persona, you have the memory."

Kravchenko promptly thrust the memory up into view. A misty October morning; the shattered remains of a Roman aqueduct gaunt against the gray sky; handsomely dressed young men and women, riding power carts, pursuing the terrified birds across the rolling plain. Laughter, the occasional burst of needlefire, the squawk of the prey, the autumn fragrances. Elena beside him, looking a trifle slimmer, chastely garbed in hunting attire, wielding her needlegun to deadly effect and hissing with delight each time she registered a kill. Then, afterward, the tang of iced champagne, the pleasure of spicy foods imported from the outworlds, the easy flow of light conversation in a palazzo at the edge of the city. And Elena in his arms, still clad in her hunting clothes, the pleated skirt pulled up, the white thighs exposed, the hips thrusting, thrusting . . .

"Yes," Noyes gasped. "I remember now."

"You must have many interesting memories. Jim and I were quite fond of one another."

"I haven't done much checking," said Noyes. "Somehow it seems unfair. It overbalances our relationship, Elena. I mean, I carry intimate recollections of you, so you have few secrets from me, but you have no such insight into me."

She looked startled. "Why do we take on personae if not to gain advantage? I don't understand you, Charles. If in your mind you hold Jim's memories of me, why not enjoy them?"

—Because you're a damned masochist, Kravchenko suggested.

Noyes winced. To Elena he said, "You're right. I'm being foolish."

He searched the archive Kravchenko had brought with him into his mind. He was lying, in a way, for he had already done a good deal of peering at Elena's relationship with Kravchenko. He knew that they had been lovers for about two years, on and off, nothing serious on either side. Kravchenko had many women, and, Noyes gathered, Elena rarely confined her attentions to one man at a time. Within his mind was Elena's entire repertory of passion; he had merely to sort it out and study it.

Elena said, "I find it hard to believe that Jim's really dead. He was such an exciting man. Do you and he get along well?"

"No."

"So I've understood. Why is that? Why did you select him, if there were incompatibilities?"

Noyes ordered drinks for them. "We came from the same general background," he explained. "I was playing it cautious when I picked a persona. I could have had a financier, a university professor, a starman. Instead I chose a rich playboy, because I was just a rich playboy myself, and I wanted more of the same. Well, I got it. He gives me no peace."

"You don't have to keep a persona you don't like," she said.

"I know. Perhaps one day I'll ask for erasure and start all over."

—That'll be the day, Charlie-boy.

"It might be best for both of you," said Elena. "It would give Jim a second chance too. Is he your only persona?"

"Yes. I didn't think I ought to risk another."

"Possibly a second one would have calmed him a little."

"Possibly. What about you, Elena? You're such a mystery woman. How many personae are you carrying?"

"Four," she said coolly.

He was dumbstruck. He had calculated her for one, or perhaps two personae, no more. Few women undertook four. But Noyes realized he had made the mistake of assuming that because she was beautiful, she must also be of limited intellect. Evidently Elena could handle four personae, since she spoke clearly, with no signs of internal conflict.

"One secondary, three primaries," she amplified. "It's an amusing group. We get along well. I took on the first ten years ago, the last only in November. I may add others. I've talked to Santoliquido about a possible new transplant."

"Someone in particular?"

"No," Elena said. "Not yet. That is, if I can't have Paul Kaufmann—"

Noyes sputtered. "You want him too?"

"I'm merely joking. They haven't legalized transsexual imprinting, have they? But I imagine it would be fun to have him. I know Mark would be astounded. Mark worshiped that terrible old man. Strong as he is, Mark never could withstand his uncle's wishes in anything. And if I walked into the house one day and opened my mouth and spoke to him with the words of Paul Kaufmann—" Elena giggled. "A delightful picture. It calls for another drink."

Noyes found it difficult to see the humor in it. He summoned the drinks; then, slowly, he said, "Do you have any idea who's really going to get the Paul Kaufmann persona?"

"How should I know?"

"You spent time with Santoliquido at Mark's party."

"I don't discuss Santoliquido's administrative decisions at parties," Elena said. "Why do you ask? Are you thinking of applying?"

"For Paul Kaufmann? He'd burn me out in ten minutes. But John Roditis is interested."

"*Interested* isn't the right word, from what I hear. *Desperate* is more appropriate."

"Desperate, then. It's no secret. Roditis feels he's qualified to handle a potent persona like Paul Kaufmann, and he also believes that the two of them acting together can have much to offer society. The two greatest business minds of the century, blended into a dynamic team. Honestly. I think so, too. I profoundly wish Roditis would be granted the persona."

"Do you know who else wants Paul?" Elena asked.

"Who?"

"His nephew Mark."

"That's impossible! A transplant within the family—"

"Illegal, I know. Mark knows it too. He has no hope of actually getting the transplant. But he has business ambitions too, and they'd be well served if he had the use of his uncle's experiences. Besides, he's eager to keep the old man out of Roditis' possession."

"Why does Mark hate Roditis so much?"

"He regards him as an upstart. It's quite simple, Charles. The Kaufmanns are aristocrats by birth. They have ancestry. As do you. As do I. As does Santo. We have more than wealth; we have pedigrees back into the twentieth century, even to the earlier centuries. Roditis can tell you his father's name, but that's all. Now, with a Kaufmann persona, he'd have social access to our group, access that he can't buy with all his billions. Mark is determined not to let Roditis force his way in. He regards it as blasphemy for a man like that to have his uncle's persona."

"We were all upstarts once," Noyes pointed out. "Take the Kaufmann line back far enough and you find peasants. Go back farther and you find apes."

Elena's laughter tinkled across the lounge. "Of course, of course! But it's the distance between the peasant and the banker that marks the social prestige. Your Roditis is too close. Perhaps his great-grandchildren will rule society, but Mark won't tolerate it now."

"Mark can't have his uncle's persona. He'd be wise to give in gracefully and let Roditis have it. Bury the hatchet, forge a mighty alliance of wealth."

"That's not how Mark operates," said Elena.

"He could. Elena, I'd be grateful if you'd suggest that to him. Point out the advantages of combining with Roditis instead of battling him."

"You want me to serve as a go-between, passing Roditis' messages?"

He colored. "You put it very bluntly."

"We are on the island of truth, Charles. This is what you want from me, is it not? To push Roditis' case with Mark?"

"Yes."

"And perhaps even to talk to Santo?"

"Yes."

"Is there anything else you want from me, Charles?"

He could barely look at her. The carniphage flask throbbed against his breastbone. He felt bitterly ashamed that she would humiliate him before Kravchenko this way. But he had asked for it.

"There's one more thing I want," he said.

"Name it."

He touched the warmth of her shoulder. "An hour with you in the bedchambers of the inner level."

"Certainly," she said, as though he had asked her to tell him the correct time.

They left the cocktail lounge and passed through a hall of gaudy nightmare fantasies, and crossed an arena in which the products of teratogenetic surgery performed a grotesque dance, and rose on a circular ladder leading beyond a pool of slippery cephalopods engaged in a stately ballet, and at length they came to one of the blocs of bedchambers that were scattered at frequent intervals through the galleries of Jubilisle. For fifty dollars he rented an hour's use of a room.

Within, Elena activated a device that cast a kaleidoscopic pattern on the ceiling above the circular bed. Then she disrobed. Beneath the scaly gown she wore only an elastic strip around her hips, and another that bound her breasts, thrusting them upward and close to each other. His hundred-dollar bill was wedged in that deep cleft. She snapped the elastic strips; her massive breasts tumbled free, and the banknote fluttered to the floor. Ignoring it, she faced him, displaying her nudity for his inspection, and without a word arranged herself on the bed.

—Your big moment, Kravchenko told him.

Furiously Noyes dug into the darkest corners of the persona to learn the secrets of unlocking Elena's passion. The information was all there: the proper zones, the proper words, the timing. Kravchenko had most diligently done the research for him years ago.

Noyes joined Elena on the bed. Their bodies met. Their flesh touched and exchanged warmth.

He made the rewarding discovery that she was easily aroused and that she was satisfying in her frenzy. At the climactic moment she dug her heels into the backs of his legs and shivered in authentic ecstasy, but then, amid the stream of wordless syllables of joy that issued from her lips, it seemed to Noyes that he heard her saying, "Jim, Jim, Jim, Jim, *Jim!*"

# 8

John Roditis listened with flickering patience to all that Noyes had to tell him. They sat at the edge of a wide veranda overlooking Roditis' Arizona ranch; before them stretched an infinite acreage of harsh brown turf, tufted here and there by grayish-purple islands of sage. Roditis had been in Arizona all week, supervising the preliminary negotiations for a power project encompassing the region south of Tucson and well over the Mexican border. He had had Noyes fly to him that morning, four days after Noyes' interlude with Elena Volterra.

Noyes said, "Elena will speak to Santoliquido on your behalf. Probably she's spoken to him already."

"Is she his mistress?"

"She's everybody's mistress, sooner or later. Mainly she lives with Mark Kaufmann. But she spends time with Santoliquido too. She's quite intimate with him."

Roditis knotted his thick fingers together and peered past Noyes into the cloudless, harsh blue sky. "Is Kaufmann aware that Santoliquido is trifling with his woman?"

"I imagine so," Noyes said. "Neither of them bothered to conceal it much. And Mark's no fool."

"Has it occurred to you, then, that Kaufmann has deliberately winked at that relationship—so that by lending Santoliquido Elena, he can influence the destination of his uncle's persona?"

"You mean, making Elena the price for Santoliquido's cooperation in keeping Paul Kaufmann out of your clutches, John?"

"Something like that."

Noyes took a deep breath. "I've considered it, yes. But I don't think it's the case. What's going on between Elena and Santoliquido isn't happening at Mark's instigation, any more than Mark had anything to do with what took place between Elena and me. And I believe that Elena will serve your interests in dealing with Santoliquido."

"Why should she?"

"Because I asked her to."

"How much money did she want?"

"Elena's not interested in money," said Noyes. "At least, not in any realistic sense. She's got all she needs, and any time she wants more she can get it from Kaufmann just for the asking. What fascinates her is power. She likes to be close to strong men. She likes to be at the core of intrigue."

"She's not unique in that," Roditis remarked.

"Elena wants to meet you, John. I suspect that she wants to become your mistress. And she knows that the best way to make an impression on you is to help you get the one thing in the universe you most want and can't obtain by yourself, which is Paul Kaufmann's persona. So she'll use her influence with Santoliquido to get it for you, and then she'll try to cash in by throwing herself into your bed."

"It would infuriate Mark Kaufmann if I took away both his woman and his uncle, wouldn't it?" Roditis said quietly.

"It would madden him."

"I'm not sure I want to madden him that much," Roditis said thoughtfully.

"You want the persona, don't you?"

"Of course."

"Elena will help you gain it. What happens after that between the two of you is entirely up to you."

"Why are you so confident that Elena will cooperate?"

"I've explained," Noyes said. Rising, he stepped off the veranda and scuffed at the desert sand beyond its margin. "There's another reason that I haven't mentioned yet."

"Go on."

"Elena knew Jim Kravchenko very well. They were lovers in Italy five or six years ago."

"Yes," Roditis said. "So?"

"Elena was very fond of Kravchenko. She wants to please him, now that she's found him again inside me. She believes that by helping me win status with you, she'll be doing her old friend Kravchenko a good turn."

"That's an intricate line of reasoning, Charles. Kravchenko's dead. If she's reaching through you to him, she can't have a very high opinion of you."

"She doesn't. She hates me. And this is how she shows it."

Roditis spat. "There are times when I wonder why I work so hard to get involved with you society people. You're nothing but beasts, really. You disembowel one another like ballet dancers with tusks, and you find the most complicated possible reasons for doing what you do."

"Inbreeding, perhaps," Noyes suggested.

"Yes, that. And more. Mere money doesn't interest you; your great-grandfathers have made enough for the whole tribe. Mere status is of no importance; you had that before you were old enough to be housebroken. You inherit power and rank. So you turn your lives into a kind of Byzantine intrigue to keep from going crazy with boredom. Rebirth makes it all the more interesting. You can switch back and forth across the generations, opening old wounds, keeping ancient feuds alive, scarring each other, using sex like a dagger." Roditis' eyes glittered. "Let me tell you something, Charles. I'm a *real* Byzantine. I don't practice intrigue for intrigue's own sake. I'm looking to put it to practical ends. And so while the whole bunch of you go on backstabbing and clawing, I'm going to move right in and take everything over. Just the way my ancestors moved in and took over Rome. By and by, the language of the Roman Empire was Greek, remember? That's how a Byzantine works. Watch me."

"I've never stopped watching you, John."

"Good. We'll see about Elena's conference with Santoliquido in a little while. Come take exercise with me, now."

"I'm a little tired, John. The flight from New York—"

"Come take exercise with me," Roditis repeated. "If you kept in shape, you wouldn't be worn out by a little thing like a flight from New York."

They entered the house, passing through corridors lined with smooth white stucco walls, and descended to the cool basement where Roditis had installed a gymnasium. Quietly he adjusted the gravity control to a boost of ten percent. That was unfair to Noyes, but no matter; Roditis had little desire to waste his exercise session by imposing an insufficient challenge on himself. Usually he boosted the pull by twenty percent or more. When things went badly, he had sometimes worked under double grav, straining every fiber, pushing heart and lungs and muscles to their limits for the sake of extending those limits another notch.

Stripping, Roditis said, "Would you like to recite a mantra of exertion, Charles?"

"I'm not sure there is one."

"Give us a pious phrase or two, at any rate. Then get out of your clothes."

Noyes said, "When, by the power of evil karma, misery is being tasted, may the tutelary deities dissipate the misery. When the natural sound of Reality is reverberating like a thousand thunders, may they be transmuted into the sounds of the Six Syllables."

Roditis belched. "*Om mani padme hum.* Excuse me."

"It's all nonsense to you, isn't it, John?"

"Western Buddhism? Well, it has its place. I've studied the arts of right dying, you know. I mean to leave a well-prepared persona for my next carnate trip."

"How will it feel, I wonder, being a passenger in someone else's brain?"

Roditis stared levelly at Noyes. "I won't be a passenger for long, Charles. You must realize that, of course. I play the game to win, all the time. If I can't win through to dybbuk, I don't deserve rebirth."

"I pity the man who picks your persona."

"He'll live comfortably enough. He just won't be supreme in his own body, is all." Roditis laughed boomingly. "All this is sixty, seventy years away, though. Right now we're here for exercise, not speculation on my discorporate existence. *Om mani padme hum.* Wake up, Charles!"

Roditis activated the vertical trampolines. They were two flexible screens, mounted upright about fifteen feet apart and moving in a flagellatory oscillation on their mountings. He stepped between them and jumped diagonally against the left-hand screen, keeping his ankles pressed close together. The screen batted him away, and he pivoted neatly in midair, directing his feet at the other screen, striking it squarely, rebounding, pivoting again. For twenty cycles he let himself be shuttled back and forth between the screens, never once touching the floor despite the enhanced pull of gravity. Then he resisted the elasticity of the screens by tensing his body, and dropped lithely to his feet at his starting point.

"Your turn," he said to Noyes.

"John, I—"

*"Come on!"*

Noyes looked dubious. He stepped between the pulsating screens and leaped. His feet touched the center of the webwork to his left, and the screen hurled him away, slamming him shoulder-first to the floor. He stood up, rubbing himself.

"Again," said Roditis. "You're growing fat, Charles. Sleek-headed, and you sleep o'nights. Let me have men about me with a lean and hungry look."

Noyes leaped again, angrily. As he struck the screen, he flexed his knees, trying hard to achieve the correct propulsive effect that would send him arcing toward the opposite screen. But his feet came in contact with the screen a fraction of a second apart from one another, and he gathered no momentum. Instead he trickled to the floor, striking his cheekbone and the side of his lower lip. He was bruised and bleeding when he arose.

"I'm sorry, John. I'm simply not in shape for this kind of thing, and by the time I get in shape it'll probably kill me," he said thinly.

"I'll make it easier for you."

Roditis seized the gravity control and cranked it to half level. Beneath the floorboards there was a rumbling sound as the straining magnetodynamic field made the adjustment, and shortly Roditis felt the pressure lift.

"Try again," he said.

Noyes moved into position and jumped. In the suddenly lighter gravity, he hit the screen too high, but it made no difference; he was hurled across to the facing screen, landing belly first, bounced back, made another cycle, all the time floundering, kicking his long legs about, waving his arms desperately, like a giant Sancho Panza tossing on his blanket. Roditis watched for more than a minute as Noyes slammed back and forth through the air. Then, feeling irritated and amused all at once, he restored the gravity to normal plus ten, and Noyes dropped heavily to the floor. He was slow to get up this time. His face was reddened and his chest heaved.

"Enough of that," said Roditis mercifully. "Should I call an ambulance, or will you try other exercise?"

Noyes shrugged. Roditis picked up a medicine ball and gently tossed it to him, underarm. Noyes caught it and flipped it back, and for a few minutes they played catch, Roditis surreptitiously stepping up the force of his throws until the heavy ball traveled with considerable velocity. At last Noyes' trembling fingers failed to hold it, and the ball rocketed into the pit of his stomach, rolling away while he gagged and retched. Roditis did not smile.

They played power-shuffleboard, which Noyes found more to

his liking. They swam. They climbed ropes. Roditis took another turn on the trampolines. Then he relented, and they went upstairs to dress. Lunch followed.

Roditis was in a restless, surging mood. His business enterprises were going well; but the one thing that was of highest importance, the Paul Kaufmann project, seemed stalemated and stagnant. He wished he did not need to act through intermediaries in gaining Santoliquido's favor. Especially intermediaries he did not even know, such as this woman Elena Volterra, famous for her beauty and for her promiscuity as well, an unlikely ambassador indeed. He had sent Noyes off to Dominica to make contact with Santoliquido; instead, Noyes had reached this Elena. Perhaps she would serve him well, after all, if Noyes' tortuous reasoning had any merit to it. But Roditis itched to be handling the deal himself. The groundwork had been laid; now was the moment to fly to New York, corner Santoliquido in his den, and make full, formal, and final request for the transplant of the Kaufmann persona. Time was passing. It was unreasonable of Santoliquido to withhold his decision any longer, and Roditis did not know of any other qualified applicant. Possibly Mark Kaufmann had the capacity to handle the persona of his uncle, but Mark was barred by law and the old man's direct wish from taking it. Which leaves only me, thought Roditis.

That afternoon he closed the power transaction with the Mexicans. His computer produced the final specifications for the transmission pylons; the Mexican computer produced the final estimates of allowable cost. There was brief negotiation between the computers, and by three o'clock the contract was ready for signing. Roditis affixed his thumbprint, the chairman of the Mexican Power Authority delivered an eloquent speech in confused English, and substantial quantities of tequila were served.

An hour later, Roditis was eighty thousand feet in the air, bound for New York.

The world had become a strange and infinitely complex place for Risa Kaufmann in the eight days since she had acquired the persona of Tandy Cushing. At a single stroke, her stock of life experiences had been more than doubled; her perceptions of human relationships had become more intense; her attitude toward herself, her father, and the world in general had grown more tolerant. The presence of the persona had provided her with a sense of parallax. She had two viewpoints from which to observe events, and that made a vast difference.

She felt a trifle guilty about her former self's wanton bitchiness. Risa plus Tandy looked upon Risa alone as an insufferable little minx, obsessively self-indulgent, petty, exhibitionistic, with a wide streak of sadism in her makeup. Together, they understood what had created that constellation of undesirable character traits in her: her impatience to erupt into the adult world, which had seemed in no hurry to accept her. Now that she had made that passage safely, it ceased to be important for her to externalize her frustration by tormenting those about her.

Tandy, too, had had her shortcomings. Risa clearly recognized the persona's flaws: laziness, shallowness, lack of discipline. Tandy came from a moneyed family, one of the old New England lines, but it was a family in which no one had done any work in at least five generations. To a Kaufmann such an attitude was abhorrent and almost incomprehensible. Kaufmanns worked. They might flit about the world to a dozen parties a week, they might go off to Venus for a month if the mood took them, they might spend a fortune on clothing or furnishings or illuminated portraits of Uncle Paul or additional personae. Their great wealth entitled them to any luxury they chose, save only the luxury of idleness. Risa's father devoted many hours of his day to business activities that could just as easily be run through hired managers, or even left entirely to the computer services. Risa herself had a keen understanding of the uses of the business cycle, and had every intention of taking her place in the Kaufmann banking hierarchy. But Tandy had no training, no interest in anything but sensuality, no marketable skills. If for some reason the Cushing estate had failed, she would have had no choice but to go into prostitution.

Risa disapproved of Tandy's flightiness. Tandy disapproved of Risa's aggressiveness. They had much to offer one another, by way of countervailing forces.

During their first few days of life together they spent long hours sorting through each other's memory files. Risa withdrew to her apartment for what would have seemed to an outsider as passive meditation, but which was in fact an exciting, vivid, and unending colloquy of the most intimate kind. All in a rush she entered Tandy's backlog of events, the love affairs, the trips, the parties. It was like gaining eight extra years of past in a moment. Tandy, at twenty-four on the date of her final persona recording, had done everything that Risa in her first sixteen years had done, and had gone beyond those first tentative experiments to a full-blown erotic career. Risa had had a few affairs, impulsive, fragmentary, hesitant, the fleeting curiosities of a girl on the edge of womanhood. Tandy had known love, or what she regarded as love, and the record of emotional storm and fervor, of sunrise and sunset, lay accessible to Risa.

She knew now the sensations of lying naked to couple in the Antarctic snows. She tasted strange cocktails in a hotel on the slopes of Everest. She experienced orgasm in free fall. She quarreled with lovers, raked their faces with clawed hands, kissed away the salty tricklings of blood.

Risa sensed that it would not take her very long to exhaust Tandy's stock of incident. Oh, there would always be interesting formative events to return to, yes, and there would always be the useful presence of a second mind within hers, but Risa knew that the present keen stimulation of having Tandy with her would wear off in a year or two, and their relationship would settle into coziness, a marriage that had consumed its passion. Tandy simply did not have the complexity of personality that would permit indefinite mining of her experiences, colorful as those experiences had been. By the time Risa reached Tandy's final age, she would be far beyond the point Tandy had reached at her death.

Then it would be time to add another persona. An older woman, Risa thought. From Tandy she had acquired voluptuousness, a sense of physicality that her own lean body would never provide for her. From the next persona Risa wanted an advanced course in avarice and shrewdness. It would be useful to have the benefit of age to draw upon as she entered the larger world of conflict and achievement.

But that was for the future. For now, Risa had exactly what she wanted.

"You're satisfied?" her father asked her.

Spring sunlight flooded Risa's apartment. She wore an airy gown that might have been made of woven cobwebs. "Very satisfied. It's all I dreamed it would be."

"The change in you is very pronounced."

"A change for the better?"

"I think so," Kaufmann said.

"Then why did you fight me, Mark? Why couldn't you have given your consent when I asked for it the first time?"

He looked sheepish, an expression she had never seen on his face before. "Sometimes I miscalculate too, Risa. It seemed to me you weren't ready. I was wrong. I admit it. You and Tandy are good friends, eh?"

"Extremely."

"What's she like?"

"Very much like me, only eight years older, and much more relaxed about things. With one exception."

"And that is?"

"The manner of her death. Tandy's obsessed with that. She's convinced she was murdered."

"She died in a power-ski accident last summer, didn't she?"

"That's the official verdict," Risa said. "Tandy tells me that it couldn't have happened that way. She was an expert skier, and her equipment had safety devices anyhow."

"Safety devices fail. Does she have any recollection of her last moments?"

"How could she?" Risa laughed. "She recorded her persona two months before she was killed! They don't take recordings of dying girls at the scenes of accidents!"

Mark looked sheepish again. "Stupid of me. But does she have any basis for thinking she was murdered, or is it simply an irrational obsession?"

"Since she's got no evidence, it has to be considered irrational," Risa said. "But she's asked me to do a little checking, and I will."

"Checking? What sort of checking?"

"Detective work. Reconstructing her last day of life. Finding the man she was skiing with."

Frowning, Mark said, "You could get yourself into trouble doing that, Risa. If you like, I'll have a man assigned to—"

"No. I'll handle it, Mark. I'm curious about it too."

It was time to get started on that project, Risa told herself. She had hesitated to make any outward moves, in this week of orientation; but now there was no further reason for waiting. She prodded Tandy for details of her final memories.

"Who would you have gone to St. Moritz with?"

—I'm not sure. Perhaps Claude. Or maybe Stig.

"They were both power-skiers?"

—Yes. And I was seeing both of them last spring. You know that much already.

"Did you have any plans for power-skiing with either of them at St. Moritz?"

—How would I know?

Risa studied Tandy's recollections of her two escorts. Claude Villefranche was a Monegasque, a citizen of that anomalous little Mediterranean principality that so stubbornly retained its sovereignty in a day when such notions were long obsolete. Filtered through Tandy's eyes, he was tall, wide-shouldered, dark, moderately sinister-looking, with a tapering sharp nose and thin, easily scowling lips. He was about thirty, it seemed, athletic, wealthy, a man of strong tastes and a somber, brooding nature.

As for Stig Hollenbeck, the Swede, he was Claude's complement: sunny and open, a slender, lithe man in his late twenties, blond, fair, looking somewhat as Risa imagined Charles Noyes must have looked when younger, though not so tall and lanky. His family had shipbuilding money; Stig himself, like nearly everyone in the late Tandy Cushing's orbit, was a non-worker.

Tandy had been sexually intimate with each of them on many occasions in the last two years of her life. Each had been aware of her interest in the other; neither had shown any flicker of jealousy. There was nothing in Tandy's view of either one that led Risa to think they were capable of murder. Yet Tandy had a powerful conviction that one or the other of them had accompanied her to St. Moritz last August and had chosen to sabotage her equipment with intent to kill.

"I'll look them up and find out if they can tell me anything about your final two months," Risa said. "Which one should I begin with?"

—Stig.

"Why?"

—Because Claude's got such an ominous face. He's the kind of man who *looks* like a murderer. So we ought to begin with the less obvious suspect.

Risa was amused by that. But she humored Tandy; this entire enterprise struck Risa as frivolous, and so there was no point in trying to impose rational judgment on any segment of it. Murder was a rarity in the world Risa knew. Since everyone had a recent persona recording on file, and thus could be said always to be in transition from one carnate existence to the next, it was pointless to risk erasure by committing that crime. If you took life intentionally, your own recordings were destroyed and you were barred forever from participation in the rebirth program. Who would risk such a dread punishment? Why jeopardize one's own eternal life for the sake of bringing a temporary interruption to another's span?

Yet Tandy was convinced she had been murdered, doubtless because she could not accept the notion that some clumsiness of her own had led to her early death in the snows of St. Moritz. Risa dialed the master directory and requested information on the whereabouts of Stig Hollenbeck. To her surprise and relief, it turned out that Stig was currently living on his family estate just outside Stockholm. She placed a call to him the following morning, when it was early evening in Sweden.

His calm, appealing face smiled out of the screen at her, the eyes friendly, a little puzzled. He looked much like Tandy's image of him, though younger and a trifle more lean.

"Yes?"

"I'm Risa Kaufmann. I'd like to talk to you about Tandy Cushing, if I might."

He lowered his eyes. "Tandy, yes. A great tragedy. Were you a friend of hers?"

"I've obtained transplant of her persona."

Hollenbeck's reaction was vivid: a sudden spasm of the muscles of the throat, a lifting of the eyes, a quick and involuntary turning of the head several inches to the left. Risa, watching closely, wondered whether this was the response of a guilty man taken by surprise, or whether, perhaps, he simply was startled by the knowledge that Tandy's persona was at large in the world again and looking at him through Risa's eyes.

At length he said, "I had not heard that she was back."

"Quite recently. Last week. She suggested I get in touch with you. There are questions I'd like to ask."

"Very well. If I can be of any service—"

"Not by phone. May I visit you in Stockholm tomorrow?"

"As you wish. It would be a great pleasure for me to meet—ah—Tandy's new friend. Shall you be coming from America?"

"From New York, yes." As she spoke, Risa requested a timetable over her data line, and discovered there was space available on a flight leaving at nine the following morning. "We could have lunch together," Risa said.

They arranged to meet at the airport. When she stepped

134

through the immigration scanners, he was there, looking pale and rather more fragile than she had imagined. They embraced in the courtly manner prescribed between strangers at their first meeting. As he held her, he peered into her eyes, and it seemed to her that his cold blue eyes were trying to stare through her at the Tandy lurking within. A muscle throbbed in his cheek. Risa doubted that this man had committed murder.

—He's changed, Tandy commented. He looks older, quieter. Almost shy.

"I have reserved a lunch for us," he said to Risa. "My hopter is waiting."

Within minutes they were in a sumptuous building many hundreds of years old that stood at the edge of a lovely park in metropolitan Stockholm. He had arranged for their meal to be served in a private chamber, upstairs, at the inn. At face value, that might seem to be an invitation to a seduction; but Risa sensed that he had no physical interest in her. She was good at detecting the radiations of desire, and there were none forthcoming from him. Evidently he preferred the more robust, fleshy physique of a Tandy. She wondered if he knew Elena Volterra.

A robot servitor brought them cold aquavit and tapering flasks of chilled golden beer. Then a table of delicacies was wheeled into their room, and she followed him about, selecting bits of aromatic herring, snippets of smoked reindeer, lush strips of salmon. A huge window admitted a maximum of sunlight: a scarce commodity at this latitude, and so highly prized.

Tandy fluttered and palpitated within her. It excited her terribly to be in the presence of her former lover. She seemed eager to go to bed with him once more, even vicariously. Without speaking, Risa attempted to communicate to the persona Stig's lack of yearning for her.

As they ate, Stig said, "You wish to ask questions about Tandy?"

"You were very close to her, weren't you?"

He smiled. "Surely you must know that I was."

"Yes. I do. I'm sorry to have voiced the obvious. Can you tell me when you last saw her?"

"Last summer," he said. "Some time before her—death."

"How long before?"

"Let me think. In the spring we were together at Veracruz. April and part of May. Then she returned to Europe, to Monte Carlo and Claude. You know of Claude?"

"Of course."

"Well, then. It must have been at the end of June that I saw her again."

—After I made my last recording, said Tandy.

"Where was this?" Risa asked.

"We met in Lisbon. We traveled together as far as Stockholm, where I had family obligations. She continued on into Suomi—into Finland. I joined her there in mid-July. We journeyed through the arctic regions together, down to Kiev again, and flew to Zurich. In Zurich I left her. Several weeks later she was dead."

"You didn't see her at all after the end of last July?"

"Unhappily, no." He indicated Risa's empty plate. "Shall we proceed to the warm food, or do you wish more fish?"

"I'd like to try some of the other kinds of herring."

"As do I." He grinned, the first sign of warmth she had had from him. They filled fresh plates. At a signal, the robot produced more beer. Risa resisted more aquavit.

"About Tandy—"

"When she left me in Zurich, I understand she met Claude again. They went to St. Moritz." His countenance darkened. "I did not hear of her death until October. I assumed she was still travel-ing with him."

"What can you tell me about her death?"

"This is a wintry subject for such a sunny day."

"Please," Risa said. "It's important for me to know. For—us to know. Don't you see, Tandy has no information about it. Her last recording was made in June. She's trying to reconstruct her final eight weeks, and particularly the events of her—of her death. Can you help?"

"As I say, my information is secondhand. I'm told she was ski-ing with Claude. They were on the high slope, making a rapid descent, one of the long jumps. She was crossing a crevasse, one hundred meters in the air. Suddenly her equipment failed. The gravity repulsors failed to hold. She fell. I understand they did not recover her body until the following week."

Risa felt a quiver of shock. "I hope it was a swift death."

"One can hope so, yes."

They were silent. Risa saw Stig searching her face, and knew that he must still be seeking some way to speak through her, directly to Tandy. But of course it was a grievous breach of eti-quette to address someone's resident persona. One spoke only to the living, not to the merely carnate. Stig could not possibly com-mit a blunder so gross; yet clearly he ached to seize Risa's arms and find himself embracing Tandy.

"I loved her very deeply," he said after a while. "I doubt that she realized it. We were always so elaborately casual, after the approved manner. I would have wanted to have a child by her. I would have wanted to share her life. But I never let her see any of that, and so all we shared was a bed. I regret that."

"Will you be offended if I tell you that Tandy was more aware of your feelings than you thought?" Risa asked.

He smiled faintly. But he did not look convinced.

They scarcely touched the rest of their meal. Afterward, they walked in the garden of the inn, both of them quiet. The indirect conversation between Stig and Tandy had left Risa drained and numb. She had, at least, settled one thing to the satisfaction of herself and the persona within. If Tandy had indeed died through malevolence, Stig Hollenbeck had had nothing to do with it.

At the airport, he said as she dismounted from his hopter, "I wish I could have been of more assistance to you."

"You were extremely helpful. We're both grateful."

"Where will you go now?"

"To see Claude," Risa said. "We didn't know which one of you had been with Tandy at the end, you see. Things are much more clear now. Do you happen to know where I'm likely to find him? By this time I suppose he's over the shock, and willing to talk about the accident."

Stig winced, reacting almost as sharply as he had when Risa had told him she possessed Tandy's persona.

"You do not know?" he asked.

"Know what?"

"Claude is dead too. He died in December, swimming at night on the Great Barrier Reef. He can tell you nothing. Nothing. Unless you can get information from his persona, wherever it may be."

# 9

Francesco Santoliquido said with obviously forced heartiness, "It's good to see you again, John. I'm always delighted when you drop in."

Roditis took the proffered hand. It was soft, warm, not precisely a flabby hand but certainly the hand of a man who welcomed all comforts. The décor of Santoliquido's office did not argue that he had spartan tastes.

"Drink?"

"Certainly, Frank."

They touched ultrasonic snouts to their arms. Santoliquido beamed. "You've kept well, John. Still a demon for exercise, are you?"

"I get only one body to inhabit," said Roditis. "I keep it with respect."

"Naturally." A wary expression crept into Santoliquido's eyes. Roditis suspected that the older man was afraid of him, and he liked that, for Santoliquido was very high in the system of the world, very high indeed. He wondered just what Elena had been saying to Santoliquido about him, and what the response had been.

Roditis said, "The statue looks as splendid as ever."

"The Kozak? Yes. Yes, a masterpiece." Santoliquido chuckled. "Don't think I've forgotten you have Anton Kozak sitting back of your eyes. Has he led you to take up sonic sculpture yet?"

"He tries," said Roditis. "But I know my limitations."

"A wise man."

"I lack the skills of Kozak. I would not defame him by plying his art. His mind cannot drive my muscles."

"Of course not," conceded Santoliquido.

"He is glad to see that piece again. He tells me it's one of his favorites. A brilliant artist, Frank. I compliment myself many times for having chosen him. You know, a man like me, a man of dollars, I didn't get much chance to learn how to appreciate beauty. Kozak has taught me. Now I know what the balance of line means; what the harmony of form is. I'm much richer."

"That's the purpose of the Scheffing process," Santoliquido said sententiously. "To enhance, to enrich. Doubtless he's greatly widened your horizons of perceptions. But tell me, John: how does Kozak find it, seeing the world through the eyes of a billionaire financier?"

"He enjoys it, I believe. He makes no complaints. His world is enriched too. He moved much too much in the company of esthetes; now he sees a different facet of existence. I'm sure that when he makes his next carnate trip he'll try to express some of that new knowledge in art, if he's lucky enough to be acquired by someone with the right skills for practicing sonic sculpture."

"That's far in the future," said Santoliquido nervously. "You look quite healthy, John, and there'll be no new carnate trips for you or your personae for a long time to come, I'm sure."

"I hope so."

"And Walsh? Old Elio? He's thriving too?"

"Oh, yes," Roditis said. "We're kindred spirits. He built a network of power-transmission stations; I've built a network of a different sort of power. He finds his present place quite rewarding. And I regard him as indispensable." Roditis smiled, and held the smile just slightly too long, intentionally. Then he said, "I'm sure you realize that I didn't ask for this appointment so I could discuss my existing personae."

"Of course."

"You realize why I'm here?"

"Naturally."

"Shall I name it or will you?"

"Paul Kaufmann," Santoliquido said. "Yes?"

"Yes. The old man's been dead since the turn of the year. It's nearly May now. There's no reason for keeping him in storage any longer, is there?"

"We're nearing a decision, John."

"I've been hearing that phrase for weeks. I'd like to know how long you plan to go on nearing that decision."

"I'm approaching it rapidly," said Santoliquido.

"And asymptotically?"

"John, you don't appreciate the complexity of what's involved. Here's the persona of one of the world's most powerful men, perhaps *the* most powerful of his age, a uniquely vigorous personality, a man of colossal wealth, of the highest family connections. It takes time to evaluate the applicants for his persona. The decision can have far-reaching consequences."

"How many other applicants are there?" Roditis asked.

141

"Hundreds."

"And how many of them do you seriously think are qualified to handle a persona of such force?"

"Several," Santoliquido said.

Instantly Roditis knew that he was lying. But he did not dare force the situation beyond this point. Obviously Elena's ministrations had clinched nothing yet. Santoliquido was still reluctant to surrender the Paul Kaufmann file.

Roditis said, "It's not my intention to put pressure on you. I feel you owe it to the world to restore Paul Kaufmann to carnate existence, and I'm offering myself as the vehicle for that. As time passes, you know, his persona gets out of touch with the flow of events. We'll forfeit his abilities to evaluate situations if we let the world become incomprehensible to him."

"But do you think you're an adequate vehicle, John?"

Surprised, Roditis answered, "Has anyone ever doubted that I am?"

"The Kaufmann persona is a powerful one."

"I realize that. I'm prepared and capable. You've tested my capacity."

"Yes. Even so, I remain uneasy. A man like Paul Kaufmann could so easily break through to dybbuk—"

"No one," said Roditis stiffly, "is going to reach dybbuk at my expense. Not even Paul Kaufmann."

"There are times," Santoliquido murmured, "when I feel it would be best to leave that old man in storage forever."

"That would be a crime against his persona! You have no right!"

"I didn't say I would. But it's a temptation. Otherwise we run the risk of loosing him on the world again. A buccaneer. A cannibal. A marauder."

"He was merely a shrewd and aggressive businessman," Roditis said. "Give him to me and he'll be under control every minute of the day. I'll harness him."

"You're very confident of yourself, John. Come with me."

"Where?"

"To the main storage vault. I'll give you a closer view of Kaufmann."

Roditis had been in the storage vault before. But yet it never failed to strike pangs of awe in him as he moved through the low-roofed vestibule with its assortment of wary scanners and into the huge gloomy cavern of canned souls. They reached a sampling booth. Santoliquido requisitioned one of the storage caskets and cradled it firmly under one arm.

Looking about the colossal room, with its tier upon tier of racks and urns, Roditis said softly, "Do you know the eleventh book of the *Odyssey*? Odysseus goes to the Halls of Hades to seek advice of the soul of Teiresias." His hand swept along the dully gleaming balcony. "Here we are. The Halls of Hades, the City of Perpetual Mist. We beach our boat and make our way along the banks of the River of Ocean. Odysseus draws his sword, digs a trench, pours libations to the dead. Honey and milk, wine, water. He sprinkles white barley. He cuts the throats of sheep. The dark blood pours into the trench, and now the souls of the dead come swarming up from below. He sees his unburied friend Elpenor. He is approached by his mother, but waves her away to speak with Teiresias. Then he meets others. The mother of Oedipus. The wife of Amphitryon. Ariadne. Poseidon. These are the Halls of Hades, Santoliquido. We can summon up departed souls."

"You know your Homer well," Santoliquido said.

"I am a Greek," said Roditis calmly. "Are you surprised?"

"You don't usually seem so—literary, John."

"But this is Hades, isn't it? Not a place of punishment, not Dante's Inferno, simply a storage vault. As Homer tells it. Standing here looking into that darkness, Frank, don't you feel it?"

"I've felt it many times. Though not in. Homer's terms, exactly. We Romans have a poet of Hades too. Remember? 'The descent into Hell is easy. Night and day he open the gates of death's dark kingdom.'"

"Virgil?"

"Yes. Aeneas also sees the dead. He plucks a golden bough and inquires after his comrades. A deep, dark cave, with fumes coming up from its throat; he follows a path, he takes the ferry across the river, he encounters the shade of his steersman Palinurus. He finds Dido, weeping. And his father, Anchises. I've often thought of it, John."

"Open Hades for me, then. Show me Paul Kaufmann."

"Come inside the booth."

They entered. Roditis was in a dark mood now; he stared at the coppery casket containing the persona of Paul Kaufmann, and a terrible desire came over him to seize it from plump Santoliquido and run off. But that was foolishness. He waited while Santoliquido set up the equipment.

"What are you going to do?" Roditis asked finally.

"Allow you to have a thirty-second peek at Paul Kaufmann. It's a standard scanning. Once it begins, I'll let it continue no matter how you react, and afterward we'll know how eager you really are to have him with you forever."

"You don't frighten me."

"I don't mean to. But I want you to realize that there are risks."

"Go ahead," said Roditis.

He accepted the electrodes. Through slitted eyes he observed the final preparations.

"Now," Santoliquido said.

Roditis jerked and quivered in the first impact of union with the persona of Paul Kaufmann. It was as if he had plunged into a boiling, sulfurous lake, dropping straight to the bottom, engulfed in it, fighting for breath. But he did not drown. Within moments he was rising, finding his level, learning the art of swimming in this medium.

Incredible!

Such strength, such vitality, such intensity that old man had had! Roditis examined strands of memory; not tangled knotted ones, but firm hawsers of recollection, stretching across the void of years. He acknowledged a formidable mind when he met one. Had old Kaufmann ever forgotten anything? Had he ever blun-dered? Roditis stared in delight at serried rows of archives, at a comprehensive and flawlessly arranged memory bank. Kaufmann must not have been human, but some sort of computer. But no, he was human enough: here were lust, rage, avarice, triumph, all the passions, throbbing chords of emotion slashing in bright primary hues across the purpled backdrop of that powerful mind. To and fro Roditis moved, examining everything, passing freely down the frozen canyons of that awesome persona, admiring stalactites and stalagmites of desire, glittering crystals of achievement, the ropy fabric of maturity. Kaufmann at seventy had been a phe-nomenon, but not a sudden one; roving backward, Roditis saw the unity of the man, saw the same unbending purpose at forty, at twenty, even at ten. How could there be a man like this, all fire and ice at once? Having entered that realm of wonders, Roditis could not leave. He heard the sound of distant music, resonant, somber, a chromatic symphony of great power. He saw towering Gothic arches receding to infinity. In his nostrils was the scent of grandeur. Roditis planted his feet firmly on a broad plain beneath a black sky. He threw his head back and roared joyous laughter at the heavens.

The images dissolved. He sat in a small room, electrodes on his forehead, Santoliquido studying him with interest.

"Give him to me," Roditis said at once.

"The risks—"

"There are no risks. I can handle him. He belongs to me! He must be mine!"

"You're shaking all over," Santoliquido pointed out.

Roditis discovered that it was so. He stared at his trembling fingers, his quaking knees. The harder he tried to regain muscular control, the more violent the tremors became. He said, "It's nothing but a reaction to tension. I don't pretend it was like nothing, scanning that mind. But I am well. I am strong. I have the right to receive that persona."

"How do your own personae feel about it?"

Roditis realized that he had lost contact with Kozak and Walsh. He had to grope uncertainly in the recesses of his own mind a moment before he located them. Walsh seemed dazed; Kozak, sullen, withdrawn, wounded. As he probed them they stirred gradually, as if thawing after a freezing bath. They had not enjoyed their brief exposure to Paul Kaufmann, it appeared. Roditis tried to cheer them. They would get used to their new neighbor in his mind.

He said to Santoliquido, "Well, they're a little shaken up, I suppose. He was a rough dose for them. But it'll wear off."

"I'm worried, John."

"About them?"

"About you. If you took on Kaufmann, what the long-term effects might be. You're an important man nowadays, with plenty of responsibility. If you should cave in under the weight of this new persona you want—"

"I won't."

"*If,*" said Santoliquido. "There could be serious economic consequences."

"How many different ways do I have to put it? I'm capable of bearing up. Do you know, Frank, I feel such exultation now, having seen that man's mind—such a sense of *widening,* after only half a minute. You've *got* to give him to me!"

Santoliquido's tongue appeared and made a slow circuit of his lips. After a moment's silence he rose and beckoned to Roditis. "Let's take a walk," he suggested. "If you've recovered from those tremors by now."

Roditis stood up with exaggerated agility. Santoliquido put the Kaufmann persona back in its casket and stuffed it in a hopper slot; it vanished from sight, to Roditis' sharp regret. They left the sampling booth. Santoliquido led him out on the catwalk that rimmed the circumference of the storage vault.

"We're going to take a tour of Hades," he said. "I want to show you some possible alternate personae."

"I don't—"

"At least consider them," said Santoliquido. He tapped out digits on a data terminal. One of the sealed storage banks opened and he pulled out an urn, examined it, frowned, replaced it, removed the adjoining one. He held it up. "Elliot Sakyamuni," he said. "You know him? An outstanding guru, one of the architects of the new religion, a truly powerful man. He died in March. We've had him here, waiting for the right recipient. John, if you were to take him on, you'd have the added spiritual depth, the extra dimension of wisdom, that

147

only a fully trained guru of the highest degree could offer. You're the first person I've suggested giving him to. Consider it."

"In addition to Kaufmann?"

"In place of Kaufmann," said Santoliquido. "I think the guru would be better for you."

"No," said Roditis. "I can get along without extra spiritual depth. I've got Noyes to recite mantras for me. Put Sakyamuni back."

Santoliquido sighed and put the urn away. They climbed to another catwalk. Indicating a frosted glass panel, Santoliquido said, "The world-famous mathematician Horst Schaffhausen. He has waited nearly two years now to return to carnate form. A mind like yours would be well-suited—"

"Stop it, Frank."

"You oughtn't turn away from Schaffhausen that lightly. His unique powers would be of great value to you in—"

"I'll take him three years from now," said Roditis. "Give me a chance to digest Kaufmann first."

Beads of sweat burst out on Santoliquido's forehead. Hoarsely he said, "Won't you get off that obsession, John? Kaufmann's a burden for anyone. He'll weigh you down."

"I want him."

"You and he are too much alike. In the Scheffing process we should seek for complements, not supplements. There'll be war between you and Kaufmann over every business decision. He'll want to do it his way, you'll want to do it yours—"

"And I'll win," said Roditis. "I'm alive, he'll just be carnate. I'll use his judgment, but I won't let him call the tunes for me."

"If he goes dybbuk—"

"Impossible."

Santoliquido said, "I offer you your free choice of any persona we have here, but that one."

"Are you trying to torture me?"

In a low voice Santoliquido said, "It might even be possible to arrange something slightly irregular. Would a transsexual transplant interest you? What if I made available to you the persona of Katerina Andrabovna, say. An extraordinary combination of sensuality and intellect, a truly blazing woman—"

"Is it that bad?" Roditis asked. "Are you in such a mess, Frank, that you have to consider breaking the law? What hold do they have on you, anyway?"

"Who?"

"The Kaufmanns!"

"No one has any hold on me whatever," said Santoliquido with obvious strain. Roditis was amazed at the anguish visible on the plump face. "I make my own decisions."

"Mark Kaufmann doesn't want me to get his uncle's persona. He's fixed things so I won't. You're willing to offer me the whole vault, if I please, so long as I keep away from old Paul. You've even offered me an abomination. So you must be really trapped. You'd like to make me happy, but you're afraid to offend Mark, and that leaves you ripping in half." Roditis put his hand on Santoliquido's shoulder. "I know what it must be like for you," he said more gently. "But all I ask is that you do your duty. I'm the logical recipient of Paul Kaufmann. Mark would get reconciled to the idea after a while, once he finds out I'm not a monster."

"We can't talk about such things out here."

"In your office, then."

But even amid the Babylonian splendor of his office Santoliquido was ill at ease. He took several drinks in quick succession, paced the floor, stood for a long moment before the Kozak sonic sculpture. Finally he said, "I need more time, John."

"You're just stalling."

"Maybe so. But I'm not ready to move. You know, I'll have to live with my decision forever. Give me a few more weeks. By May 15 I'll announce the disposal of the Kaufmann persona, all right?"

"I have no way of holding you to that," Roditis noted.

"I pledge my word."

Roditis let his eyes linger on Santoliquido's. He knew that such a pledge meant a great deal to a man like Santoliquido, who had centuries of ancestors peering down at him all the time. A Roditis, a *condottiere,* might break a solemnly given word when it suited his needs; but not a Santoliquido. Or so Roditis tried to persuade himself.

"Very well," he said. "Weigh your decision carefully, Frank. Don't let Mark pressure you into doing something shortsighted."

Outside the building, Roditis gave way to an access of rage. He sat in his hopter a long while, burning with fury, while angry spasms of heat ripped through him. So much for Elena's help! So much for all Noyes' scheming! The situation was right where it had been since Paul Kaufmann's death . . . a stalemate. Santoliquido still equivocated. The administrator was all façade; beneath, he quivered with fright at the possibility of offending someone mighty, and so took no action.

When ten minutes had passed, and Roditis felt somewhat calmer, he ordered the hopter to lift and head out over the ocean, due east. The machine throbbed into the air.

"Is there any specific destination?" the robopilot asked.

"Just keep going east till I tell you to go somewhere else."

Roditis closed his eyes. Instantly there came flooding into his mind the renewed presence of Paul Kaufmann. Just that tiny tantalizing taste of Kaufmann's persona had been enough to leave Roditis unalterably convinced that the old man must be his. It was more than mere desire now. It was destiny.

What if Santoliquido should rule against him?

That was hard to imagine. Roditis knew of no one else who could handle the high-voltage mind of Paul Kaufmann. Of course, Santoliquido could take the coward's way out, and simply leave Kaufmann in the storage vault, as he had hinted he might do, as he seemed to be doing with that mathematician, Schaffhausen. But Santoliquido was a man of honor. He could not expose himself that way to shame. He would have to allot Paul Kaufmann to someone.

What if, at Mark's prodding, Santoliquido found some innocuity and impressed the persona on him?

Roditis smiled. Instantly a dybbuk would be created. His investigators would demand the penalty of the law. Erasure would be imposed. Kaufmann would go back into the soul bank, and Roditis could reapply.

On the other hand, Roditis reflected, suppose Santoliquido discovered a person who was strong enough to cope with the Kaufmann persona?

That would be awkward, but it could be handled. Roditis saw that in that event it would be necessary to arrange a discorporation. There would be an accidental death; Paul Kaufmann and his late host would both revert to the soul bank; Roditis could begin the quest anew. One way or another, he would obtain that persona. Having tasted it, he could not now relinquish his need.

He opened his eyes. The small hopter was far out over the Atlantic now. Though spring had formally arrived, the water far below was gray and ominous. High waves surged like mobile mountains, rising and crashing. Through the audio Roditis picked up the sound of that baleful sea. He ordered the hopter to dip low, skimming no more than three hundred feet above the water. The vehicle was meant for short-haul transport, and it was unsafe to have come out here, alone, in such a fragile craft, but Roditis felt soothed by the dangers. The fusion pack below his seat could power the hopter all the way to Europe, if he chose.

On the face of the water the dull tubular bulk of a whale appeared suddenly. Roditis studied the fleshy mass, observing the gray-white spout of water that flumed abruptly from the broad forehead. There was strength! There was power! The tail came up; the flukes lashed the waves. The whale sounded and was gone. A Paul Kaufmann of the seas, Roditis thought. A watery titan.

"Return to New York," he ordered the hopter.

Stormy winds sped the craft landward. As he neared shore, Roditis put through a call to Noyes and found him, tense and knotted, in his apartment.

"It was no good," Roditis said. "Santoliquido still hesitates."

"But Elena said—"

"Elena is a worthless slut. Santoliquido is terrified of Mark Kaufmann, and Mark still refuses to let me have the old man. We're stuck. Santoliquido was willing to give me any persona in the place, except that one. Even a woman."

"You're joking, John!"

"I could have had Katerina Andrabovna. That's how panicky he is."

Noyes bowed his head. He muttered, "I was sure it was all fixed up. Elena was positive too."

"Santoliquido promised to make a decision by May 15," said Roditis. "He didn't promise that the decision would be favorable to me. If it goes some other way—"

"It won't, John."

"If it does, there'll be work for you to do. We can't let that persona slip away. Do you know, Charles, he let me sample the old man! I saw into that mind. I would do anything to have it now. *Anything.*"

"Perhaps I should talk to Elena again," Noyes ventured.

"It can do no harm. But probably little good, either."

"I'll try. I'm in this as deep as you are, John. I've got a lot staked on success. I'll speak to her and get her to put the screws on Santo all over again."

Roditis nodded. He made a dismissing gesture. The screen went blank.

Behind him an ocean storm was rising. He felt the winds buffet his hopter, and ordered the craft upward to safer altitudes. It was late in the afternoon when he landed. He went at once to his nearest office, mind churning with half-conceived ideas. The storm broke in full impact, and, as he looked from his tower window, it seemed to him that he saw the gigantic and powerful figure of Paul Kaufmann raging in the dark sky.

# 10

Where is Risa today?" Elena asked.

"Chasing about Europe," said Mark Kaufmann. "Doing some detective work on behalf of her persona. Last I heard of her, she was in Stockholm, but that was a few days ago."

"You don't worry about her?"

"She can look after herself. Besides, I have her under surveillance."

Elena laughed. "How typical of you! In one breath you tell me that she's self-reliant, and that you're having her watched anyway. You never leave anything to chance."

"I have only one daughter," Kaufmann said quietly. "My dynastic urge won't allow me to leave Risa's welfare to chance."

"Would you have wanted a son?"

He shrugged. "The name won't die. Only my line of it. And I'll be right there, watching the future unfold." Kaufmann got easily to his feet. They were lying on the resilient tile beside his private swimming pool, a hundred feet beneath the Manhattan streets. Warm pinkish light filtered down. "Shall we swim?"

"I'll watch you from here," said Elena languidly.

Leaping into the pool, he swam three lengths in some sudden furious haste, then, more calmly, let himself drift back and forth across the width. The pool had been designed for Elena's tastes. The water contained a fluorescing compound, so that his body left vivid streaks of gold and green as he sliced through it. Below, sparkling globes of captive living light glowed on the pool's floor. The sides of the pool were studded along the waterline with silicaceous thermotectonic gems. The entire installation had run him into many thousands of dollars fissionable. Elena rarely used the pool her whims had created; she was content to be naked beside it, soaking up warmth from the battery of overhead lamps. Kaufmann disliked the decorative effects, but he humored her.

He surfaced. His hand came up over the margin of the pool and seized her thigh, inches from her groin. He began to draw her to the water. Elena shrieked. Her buttocks bounced and skidded over the tile, and her free leg poked futilely at him.

"*Mark!*"

He tugged her in. She landed with a radiant fluorescing splash and came up sputtering and blinking, her ebony hair in disarray, her tanned skin shining. "*Birbone,*" she muttered. "*Scelerato!*"

"Sticks and stones will break my bones." He pulled her to him and kissed her, standing upright in the shallows of the pool. Her body resisted him stiffly for a moment, but only for a moment, and then she flowed against him, and her rigid nipples drew a tickling line across his chest. When he released her, she was pouting with what he knew to be mock rage. He watched the sparkling water stream from her skin as Elena hauled herself out of the pool and flounced to a vibrator to dry. She stood with her back to him, combing out her hair. His eyes followed the supple line of her spinal column downward from her long neck through the widening hips, the delightful dimples, the fleshy blossoming of her rump.

"I'll get even with you for that," she told him. "I'll make Santo give your uncle's persona to an Arab."

"Better that than to Roditis," Kaufmann said.

Elena stared at him over her shoulder. "I almost believe you mean that. You'd have Paul saying prayers to Mecca before you'd let him into Roditis."

"Yes. Yes, I'm sure of that."

She finished at the vibrator and sprawled on the tile again, well out of reach of his grasping hand. He remained at the edge of the pool.

She said, "Shall I do a three-dollar frood job on you, Mark? I'll tell you why you hate Roditis so much."

"Why?"

"Because he's so much like you."

"What do you know about Roditis? Have you ever met the man?"

"Not yet."

"I have," Kaufmann said. "He's a little thick coarse fellow with big muscles and no grace of soul. He's a walking bank account. He dreams money day and night, and if he's got any other interests they don't show."

"He gave more than a million dollars to a lamasery in San Francisco a few weeks ago," Elena pointed out. "The same one your uncle used to give so much to."

"And for the same reasons, too. You think Paul was a Buddhist? You think Roditis gives a damn about karma? He's looking for publicity, and maybe he'd like the guru to lobby for him with Santoliquido. I'm surprised you're taken in."

"And I'm surprised that you underestimate him so much," said Elena. "He's not quite the ugly dollar-chaser you say he is. One of his personae is the sonic sculptor Kozak. Roditis is a connoisseur of the arts. He collects rare books. Do you know, he's got an entire building full of editions of Homer?"

"How do you know all this?"

"I've been reading about him. I mean, he'll be practically a member of the family soon, and so I thought I'd better—"

Kaufmann was out of the water instantly. He rushed toward her, knowing that he must look absurd in his angry dripping nakedness. He dropped down beside Elena and shouted, "What's that? A member of the family?"

"After he gets your uncle's persona."

"There's no chance of that!"

Elena smiled sweetly. She appeared to be enjoying his discomfiture. She placed one hand flat on the tile at either side of her, leaned back, inflated her lungs to give her breasts maximum display. Coolly she said, "I talked to Santo about it. Santo expects to award the persona to Roditis any day now."

"No," Kaufmann said. "Impossible! I've talked to Santo also about this. He promised—"

"What did he promise?"

Kaufmann hesitated. "Well, perhaps not exactly a promise. But he indicated he didn't want to see Paul go to Roditis, any more than I did."

"That was some time ago. Santo is discovering that there's no other qualified recipient. Roditis is clamoring for the persona, and without a valid reason for denying it, Santo is going to have to give it to him. He's holding back only because he's searching for some way to break the news to you."

"No, no, no, no!"

"Yes, Mark!" Elena's face was strangely animated. "You're jealous, aren't you? Roditis is going to get him, and you want him yourself! You can't bear to see anyone else have Paul Kaufmann persona."

"Stop it," he said.

"I offered you the three-dollar frooding. Take the ten-dollar job instead. It's as I said: you and Roditis are practically alike. The same drives, the same hungers. You have ancestry and he doesn't; that's the only difference. He came out of the dirt and you were born to the Kaufmann billions. Now he's going to grab himself a Kaufmann, and everything will be even. You can't bear that thought."

Kaufmann slapped her across the face. She jumped back, the meaty mounds of her bare breasts leaping toward her chin. Trembling but not in tears, she glowered at him.

"I'm sorry," he said after an endless moment. "You pushed me too far."

"Was I wrong in what I said?"

"I don't know. I don't know." He crouched on the tile and pressed his forehead against his knees. Looking up, he said, "How does it happen that you've been discussing all this with Santoliquido? And why are you suddenly so fascinated by Roditis?"

"Strong men have always interested me, Mark. I shouldn't need to tell you that. And I've neglected Roditis up till now. I should have paid more attention to him while he was on the way up. Now it's clear to me that he's the coming man."

"And so you're preparing to make the hop from my bed to his," Kaufmann said. "Eh?"

"That's an overstatement. But I mean to know him better. And I hope you'll bring yourself to get over your hatred of him. The two of you, working together, could control the world. Particularly with your Uncle Paul guiding him."

"*I* should have Uncle Paul."

"But you can't, Mark. So let him go to Roditis, and then make terms with them. Are you afraid you'll be outnumbered? Aren't you a match for Roditis and Paul together?"

"No," said Kaufmann. "No man ever born could be a match for those two in one mind."

"All the more reason for you to make peace," Elena told him. "He's going to get that persona, and if you haven't come to terms with him, he'll try to break you. Don't be stubbornly proud, Mark. Don't let anger get in the way of common sense. As of now you're richer and stronger than Roditis, but not by much, and the balance is going to tip."

"You sound so sure of that, Elena. Exactly what did Santo tell you, anyway?"

"You've heard it already. It's inevitable that Roditis will get your uncle's persona."

"I'll block it."

"You can't," Elena said in exasperation.

"I'll speak to Santoliquido! I'll—"

"Santo's been having a terrible enough time over this thing as it is, Mark. And you're the cause of all his trouble. Let him alone! It's not proper for you to interfere this way. He's trying to look at things objectively, and here you are in the background, throwing your weight around as a Kaufmann, threatening, cajoling—"

"I can't let Roditis do this," said Kaufmann stubbornly, feeling more and more like a blind, obstinate fool, but unable to let himself turn back from his chosen course.

Elena yawned prettily. "I'm tired of this discussion. We're at a dead end. You're giving me a headache. Come swim with me."

"You don't like to swim!"

"What of it?" She sprinted past him, reached the rim of the pool, catapulted herself out into space. For an instant she seemed to hang there, for at her request Kaufmann had lowered the gravity of the room they were in, and he watched the heavy mounds of her breasts extend themselves into downward-pointing cones. Then she slipped sleekly into the water, leaving a bright streak that outlined her nudity in an appealingly sensuous way.

He went diving after her. She eluded him for several moments as they crisscrossed the pool. At last he caught her, and she struggled playfully in his arms. He pulled her toward the shallow end of the pool. His lips descended into the hollow between her cheek and her shoulder.

Panting, she slipped away and sprang from the pool. She went only a few paces, turning, going to her knees, then reclining to await him. Tense and uneasy, Kaufmann came after her. She drew him down against the soft cushion of her flesh, and he entered her quickly, fiercely, and together they shuddered out their ecstasies.

He was calmer afterward. He lay beside her, caressing her, apologizing for his loss of temper, for his shouted words, for the slap.

His busy mind prepared new plans.

He had no reason to doubt Elena's statements. He knew that she had been spending time with Santoliquido lately, both at the beach party at Dominica and in New York. It was no secret to him that she had seen the Scheffing administrator on several occasions. He had not objected, partly because he was not possessive toward Elena, and—he admitted to himself now—partly in the unconscious hope that Elena would influence Santoliquido in his favor. It appeared that Santoliquido inclined in the opposite direction. Kaufmann had sensed that, too, from the recent nervousness of Santoliquido in his presence. And he did have to concede that a rational, impartial verdict would award the disputed persona to Roditis.

It was time to stop fighting the inevitable.

There were other ways to keep abreast of Roditis' ambitions. He had tried subtle agitation, and it had failed. Now he would have to go beyond the law, or else he was lost.

Risa spent three days in Monaco before she learned anything of the fate of Claude Villefranche's persona. There were worse places to be hung up, she realized; but yet it was bothersome. Ancient traditions of secrecy interfered with her quest. She could not simply pick up a data line and demand the information she needed. She had to go through channels, and the channels were not always clear.

In late April the weather here was mild, almost balmy, bringing an advance taste of summer. Purple bowers of bougainvillea blossomed on the ramparts of Monte Carlo. The sun was dazzling against the white towers of the tiny principality. She stood in the princely cactus gardens and looked out across the blue Mediterranean, and it seemed to her that she could see Africa slumbering in the hazy horizon. Risa had never been here before. Of course, Tandy had, many times, and she was Risa's guide.

Little had changed in Monaco since the grand days of the nineteenth century. The Hotel de Paris still dominated the waterfront, with the baroque magnificence of the Casino alongside. Pavilions of feathery palm trees swayed in every breeze. Here were dandies and belles cast forward into time, as though this were some pocket of the preserved past. Some of these buildings had been continuously inhabited for more than five hundred years.

At the Hall of Records Risa learned quickly enough of Claude's death, confirming the story Stig had told. On December 18 last, he had been caught in a tidal surge on the Great Barrier Reef and swept out into the open sea. His body had not been recovered. Meat for the sharks, no doubt.

Who had received his persona?

Nothing in the records about that. So far as the principality was concerned, the story of Claude Villefranche had ended on December 18 through accidental discorporation. If his persona had moved on by now to a new carnate existence, it mattered not at all, officially; carnates paid no taxes, did not vote, held no passports. In the United States it was possible to obtain details of a persona's migration from body to body, but not here.

"What will we do?" Risa asked Tandy.

—Can't your family help you?

"Of course. Of course, that's the answer!" She hurried to the offices of Kaufmann et Cie, in a gilded building on the esplanade just below the Hotel de Paris. The bank was operated by the European branch of the family, and actually there were no Kaufmanns currently involved in its management; the directors now were entirely Loebs and Schiffs. Yet Mark Kaufmann's only daughter was certain to get a hospitable welcome. Risa, dressed chastely and sweetly, presented herself to M. Pierre Schiff, her cousin by some intricate prank of genealogy, and explained her problem.

The banker was fifty, portly, staid. He paid Risa the courtesy of addressing her in English; she felt obliged to speak to him in French, which made for an odd conversation.

"I remember the incident," he said. "Last winter, yes. I believe he was a client of ours."

"I've asked the soul bank in Paris for information on him. They wouldn't tell me a thing."

"You gave your name?"

"Yes. It didn't matter."

"Let me try," said Pierre Schiff. He asked his telephone for a number, and did not bother with the vision element. Quickly he made contact. He spoke in rapid, slurred French, pitching his voice so low that Risa could not follow the words. The soft flesh of his face creased into deepening frowns; after a few moments he dropped the phone into his cradle.

He said, "The persona of Claude Villefranche was taken from storage in February and implanted."

"In whom?"

"The name was not available. Even to me. Even to me." He studied his pudgy palm as though it held the answer. "They are quite secretive, those people. But of course there are ways of dealing with them. They are in need of constant credit for the expansion of their services, and we—" He smiled eloquently. "My son will help you. Let me summon him."

An hour later, Risa found herself on a balcony overlooking the sea, lunching with Jacques Schiff, who was also her cousin, apparently, and far less portly than his father. She had changed from her chaste girlish clothes into something more likely to please Cousin Jacques: a scalloped shell of sprayon that lanced across her slender body to reveal a flawless shoulder, a small firm breast, and a rounded hip. Cousin Jacques was twenty-five, unmarried, tall, attractive. His eyes had a Gallic sparkle, brighter even than the sunlight dancing through the golden-yellow wine they drank with their oysters.

"I knew this Villefranche, yes," he said. "Was he a friend of yours?"

"Of my persona," Risa said.

"Ah! Yes, so. Do you think I knew her?"

"You didn't know her personally. If you did, she's got no recollection of you, and I doubt that she'd have forgotten you, Jacques. Tandy Cushing."

"Yes. So. I knew her by name. Claude described her to me. A beautiful, beautiful girl, he said. With—ah—" He laughed awkwardly. "Very adequate body. She is dead?"

"She was discorporated at St. Moritz last summer. A skiing accident. Claude was with her at the time. She'd like to know more about what happened."

"But Claude himself has since been discorporated too," Jacques mused. "It is a sad world, even now. Dangers lie everywhere for the young, the strong, the rich. Only the poor live long lives."

"But they live only once," Risa pointed out.

"True. True." Jacques steepled his fingers. "After lunch," he said, "I will trace Claude's persona for you."

They ate well. For her main course Risa had a mousse of sole, and vegetables of some unfamiliar sort braised in a sauce that was clearly Venusian in origin. Yet the wine that flowed so copiously throughout the luncheon was quite Terrestrial, a lively Chablis four years old. Elderly men passing beneath the veranda paused and looked up at them and made mental calculations, wondering who it was who might be lunching with Pierre Schiff's son, that pale girl in the revealing costume. Did any of them realize that it was not Pierre Schiff's son but Mark Kaufmann's daughter who should concern them on that veranda? Risa enjoyed her anonymity here.

After they had eaten, Jacques suggested that they go to his office while he made the necessary calls. Risa nodded toward the nearby hotel.

"My room is closer," she said.

He looked startled for a moment, but only for a moment. At his insistence, though, they entered the hotel through different doorways. She left the door to her room unsealed, and he slipped through it a moment after she arrived. The large, cavernous room was dark. Jacques produced a portable cesium-powered MHD torch and set it on the ornate dresser. Then he settled in a chair before the old-fashioned telephone and punched out a number.

"This will take a while," he said.

She went into the bathroom, removed her clothing, and stepped under the vibrator. When she felt thoroughly clean, she wrapped herself in a cloud of grayish mist and emerged. Jacques still sat at the telephone, taking notes. At length he grunted in satisfaction and hung up.

"Any luck?" she asked.

He turned to look at her. He frowned, and his eyes pierced the quasi-concealing mist to survey the essential points of her body. "Yes," he said absent-mindedly. "I have the details. His persona was awarded to Martin St. John, a resident of London, several months ago."

"Who's he?"

"The third son of Lord Godwin. Here is his address. I have requisitioned his photograph, and it will be coming by slow transmission in a few moments."

"I'm very grateful to you, Jacques. You've done me a great service."

"Say nothing of it," he replied.

But he seemed willing enough to be rewarded for his activities on her behalf. His body was supple, lean, and skilled. It was the first time Risa had made love since taking on Tandy Cushing's persona, and when she slipped into Jacques' arms she felt a sudden wild surge of embarrassment, for there was something enormously public about this lovemaking, with Tandy watching everything through her eyes. Risa was not accustomed to feeling inhibited. After a moment she realized that it was not the lack of privacy that troubled her, but rather that she sensed the much more experienced Tandy sitting as a judge of her erotic performance. Tension gripped her.

—Loosen up, Tandy said. Are you always like this?

Risa felt a flood of encouragement coming from within. She ceased to think of Tandy as a critical observer; Tandy was a participant, a cooperative entity. That made it much more interesting for her. Risa wriggled prettily; she put her lips to Jacques'; she surrendered to him with that mixture of kittenish girlishness and precocious womanhood that she knew was the best weapon in her armory. Tandy guided her. Without her help, Risa might not have been so successful in meeting Jacques' sophisticated approach.

When it was over, and Jacques had donned his banker's solemn garb and was gone, Risa lay sprawled pleasantly on the rumpled bed, recapitulating with Tandy what had taken place, enjoying an amiable post mortem on her responses. It was wonderful to be able to speak so frankly and to know that every thought was perfectly understood.

"I feel so good having you with me," Risa said. "To know that I'll never be alone again. I wish I could reach out and hug you, Tandy."

—Why not?

Risa laughed. She thrust her arms about herself and squeezed tight, twisting on the bed as though she were in another's embrace. Then she relaxed. She waved her legs playfully about.

—We ought to get going, Risa.

"Where to?"

—London. To find Martin St. John.

"What's the hurry?" Risa asked.

But Tandy insisted. And so Risa phoned for reservations on the next flight to London, due to leave at five that afternoon. She just barely made it to the airport in time. En route, she studied the photo of Martin St. John that had come from the data file. Though only a flat, it gave a fair likeness: a man in his early thirties, light-haired, pale-eyed, with a soft face of no particular character. Flabby chin, loose sensual lips, pasty cheeks. Tandy was shocked. She sent up an image of the late Claude Villefranche for comparison: the hard face, the cruel eyes, the tight skin, the thin, curved line of the lips, all were the direct contradiction of the physiognomy of Martin St. John. Could Claude be happy in such a slack, soft-bodied individual?

Moments after she landed at London, Risa put through a call to Martin St. John. It was gratifying to find him at home. Peering at the three-square-inch screen of the airport telephone, though, Risa was struck by his lack of resemblance to the man in the photo. This Martin St. John looked tougher, harder, leaner. He's been sick lately, Risa guessed. He's lost a lot of weight. That must be it.

"Yes?" he said.

"I'm Risa Kaufmann. You don't know me, but we've got a great deal in common."

"How so?"

"You carry the persona of Claude Villefranche," she said. "I'm carrying the persona of Tandy Cushing."

Martin St. John's lips flickered, but he said nothing.

Risa went on, "I know it isn't proper to talk persona-to-persona. But Tandy's very eager to get some information from Claude. If we could meet, and transmit through ourselves the contact between them, it would make Tandy and me very happy."

"I don't know if we should do that."

"Please," Risa said meltingly. "I've chased all over Europe to find you. Don't refuse me now. Give me just half an hour of your time—"

"Very well."

"This evening?"

"If you insist."

"It's very kind of you."

He gave her the address of a coffee shop in the Finchley Road. Risa caught a hopter and was there within the hour. The place was a dark, oblong room, decorated in an arty fake twentieth-century style, with lots of plastic flowers and other foolishness. He sat alone at a table just within the door.

His appearance was unexpected. There was no trace of the flabbiness of feature and expression that characterized the photograph. This man was brusque, taut, and dynamic. His eyes, though a washed-out light blue in tone, were fixed and gleaming, and burned with a feverish intensity. His lips were tense, with the muscles poised in a way that minimized their natural fullness. There was little excess flesh on his face, and apparently none on his body, but about his chin and eyelids there were indications that he had recently lost perhaps forty pounds, for the skin had not yet completely adopted its new outline. When he rose to greet her, his motions were swift and aggressive.

He took her hand in the continental manner. His smile was the briefest of flickers, on and off.

He said in a harsh voice, "Claude Villefranche sends greetings to Tandy Cushing."

Risa was taken aback by the unconventionality of that welcome. "It's good to have located you finally, Mr. St. John. I won't trouble you for long."

"What will you drink?"

"Would you care to recommend something?"

"There's a filtered rum punch here. It's excellent. I'll order two."

Risa said, "I'd love it."

He turned to place the order. But there were no servitors in sight. Then one appeared, moving behind their table without appearing to notice him. St. John called out, and still was ignored. He rose from his seat, turning, and his motion was clumsy for a moment, but then he seemed to change gears inwardly; he uncoiled and nearly sprang at the servitor, his hand pouncing down at the robot's nearest limb to spin it about.

"*Will* you give me some service?" he demanded.

It was an amazing performance, a show of temper, agility, and impatience that was as impressive as it was unexpected. Tandy had remained silent thus far in Risa's meeting with Martin St. John, but now she reacted. Waves of sheer terror rose from the persona and washed through Risa's mind.

"What's wrong?" Risa whispered.

—Can't you see? There's nothing left of Martin St. John! Claude's ejected him! Claude's gone dybbuk!

It was only a guess, a quick flash of intuition. Yet Risa was convinced. Tandy seemed clearly to recognize the characteristic inflections and responses of Claude Villefranche, not veiled and distorted as they would be if Claude were only a persona reaching them indirectly through the mind of Martin St. John, but overt and definite, immediate, direct.

Still, caution was advised. Risa could hardly sound an alarm and call in the quaestors this early to arrest and mindpick the alleged Martin St. John.

Over filtered rum punches she said, "Tandy's memory line ends in June of last year. She died in August. What she wishes to know is how she came about her discorporation."

"Her skis failed as she was crossing a ravine. It happened rapidly and without warning."

"Claude was with her?"

"They started down the slope together. They were in the air together over the ravine. Then—suddenly—she was no longer with him. It was a terrible experience."

"It must have been," said Risa. "I can see that you're moved by it, and you weren't even there."

"My persona was there, though," St. John pointed out.

Risa nodded. It seemed odd to her that the memories of Tandy's death should he so near the surface of St. John's mind. He did not give the appearance of reaching into a persona's crowded memory bank for the details, but rather of reading them right off his own backlog of experience.

She said, "What happened after the accident?"

"Claude saw that she had fallen. He turned upslope to find her. But she was gone from sight. It took a great deal of work to uncover her body. Claude was demoralized. He went off to Australia to forget what had happened. And there, as you perhaps know, he met discorporation last December."

"Can you tell me anything about Tandy's last few weeks with Claude?"

St. John shrugged. His eyes never wavered from Risa's, making her feel acutely uncomfortable. "They met in Zurich at the end of July. After a week there they went on to St. Moritz, for the summer skiing. They were both in high spirits. Occasionally they quarreled a bit, nothing serious, lovers' tiffs."

"They were in love?"

"Oh, yes. The second week in August Claude asked her to marry him."

—That's a lie, came Tandy's furious denial. Claude would never have married anyone!

"Did she accept him?" Risa asked.

"She hesitated. She told him she would have to wait until later in the year to make up her mind. But of course there never was any later in the year for her."

"I wonder if they would have been happy together."

"I'm sure of it," said St. John. His nostrils widened with some inner tension. "Investigate her earlier memories of him. You'll see how powerfully she was drawn to him."

That was true in its way, Risa knew. Certainly Tandy's feelings toward Claude had been far more powerful than what she felt for the detached, cool Stig Hollenbeck. But she had feared Claude as well as loving him.

"What about you?" Risa said. "Did you know Claude at all when he was alive?"

"We never met. It simply seemed to me his persona would be of interest to me. I needed someone more vigorous than myself, someone with athletic interests. It is always best to choose one's complement, of course."

"He seems to have had quite an effect on you."

"What do you mean?"

Risa hesitated. "Well—that is, when I began to trace you, I received a photo of you. With—I don't mean offense—a very different appearance. You looked softer, more plump."

"Do you have this photo? May I see it?"

She produced it. He studied it intently, his forehead furrowing, his lips curling in a feral scowl. At length he said, "It was taken about a year ago. I've lost a good deal of weight. I've been tak-

171

ing more exercise. Claude's helped me shed all that jelly." St. John glanced up and smiled for the first time. "I feel I'm the better man for having him aboard. Another rum punch?"

"I'd rather not."

"Must you be going?"

"I have—family to visit," Risa said lamely.

"They can wait. Let me show you London. We'll do the town tonight. After all, as you said, we have a great deal in common. Even though we're strangers, a bond of love unites us vicariously. We owe it to Claude and Tandy to come together."

Wavering, Risa felt herself captured. For all his ominous coldness and enigmatic intensity, this man had an undeniable appeal. She was always willing to have an adventure. And with Tandy's lover lurking behind those pale blue eyes—

St. John excused himself to pay the bill.

—Now's your chance. Get out of here, said Tandy.

"Why?"

—He's dangerous. You don't want to fool with a dybbuk. Find a quaestor and have him mindpicked!

"We've got no proof."

—Don't you think I know Claude? His way of speaking, his movements, his facial expressions? He can fool the whole world, but he can't fool me. He's done a countererasure on his host and taken over. First he murdered me, then he murdered Martin St. John. And if you give him a chance tonight, you'll be taking a new carnate trip too. Get out of here!

St. John was returning from the billing plate now. Abruptly, Risa scrambled to her feet.

She rushed from the coffee shop. St. John came after her, calling her name. But he did not pursue her beyond the front of the building.

A thin, acrid smell was in her nostrils: fear. Risa rushed to the corner, shouldering past pedestrians uncaringly. Time seemed to accelerate oddly for her, so that she was unaware of individual moments. In a blur of panic she came to a message box on the corner and opened the speaker hood.

"Quaestor!" she blurted. "I want to report a dybbuk!"

It took only an instant for the robots of the quaestorate to get a fix on the street. Two personnel hopters appeared, and gleaming figures dropped from them. Risa pointed back toward the coffee shop. "Martin St. John," she said. "There he goes!"

The robots surrounded him. Risa saw the man struggling in vain.

—They've got him, Tandy cried. Come on! We'll have to testify.

"I'd better call my father first. I'm in this too deep."

—All right. Get him to ship a lawyer over. We'll post the challenge and demand a mindpick with me as the injured party. And I want an autopsy report on my body, too. I'm beginning to figure this business out, Risa.

"What if we're wrong? What if it's all a mistake?"

—Then he'll sue you for false arrest and it'll cost your father some money. It's worth the risk. Do you want dybbuks walking around free?

"Of course not," Risa said softly. She began to walk like a figure in a dream toward the middle of the block. "Of course not. I'll call my father. He'll know what to do."

# 11

"Send in Donahy," Mark Kaufmann said.

The door of his inner office flickered open, and the Scheffing-process technician stumbled in. He looked awed to the point of collapse. His huge bushy eyebrows were thrust up to the top of his wide pale forehead, and his hands plucked tensely at the fringes of his tunic. Within the confines of the Scheffing Institute building, men like Donahy taped the personae of the rich and mighty with little deference, blandly relying on their array of intricate equipment to give them the upper hand. But here, on the home ground of so potent a person as Mark Kaufmann, Donahy was devoid of confidence, a cipher, a twitching pleb smitten with terror, wholly unable to imagine why he had been singled out and summoned here.

Kaufmann said, "We're all alone in here, Donahy. There's no one with us, no one watching us, no miniviewers, no monitor of any kind. Whatever's said in here remains absolutely private, between the two of us. Sit down."

Donahy remained standing. He shifted his weight from leg to leg.

"You don't trust me?" Kaufmann asked. He opened a panel on his desk and unclipped a microspool monad. "Do you see this? It's a spy detector. It's programed to set off an alarm if any outside entity taps into this room. So long as it quietly glows green like this, we can say what we please, we can plot to blow up the universe, and no one will know. So relax. Sit down and have a drink. I don't bite."

"I can't understand why you've asked me to come here."

"Because I want you to do something for me, obviously," Kaufmann said. He extended the tray of drinks as Donahy nervously lowered himself into the chair at last. Silently they went through the ritual of the drink. By every motion Donahy showed his fear and uncertainty. He'll be tugging at his forelock next, Kaufmann thought.

On Kaufmann's desk sat a small portrait of Uncle Paul, one of the many in his possession. He thrust it forward and let Donahy contemplate the patrician features, the sly, veiled eyes, the magnificent chin.

"Do you know this man, Donahy?"

A nod. "It's Paul Kaufmann, isn't it?"

"Yes. My late uncle. He'll soon be back in carnate form, I believe."

"I don't know anything about that, sir."

"The information I have is that Administrator Santoliquido intends shortly to approve the transplant of my uncle's persona to John Roditis."

Donahy looked blank. Kaufmann realized that he was speaking

beyond the technician's comprehension; Roditis and Santoliquido and old Paul were simply not part of Donahy's world except as friezes on some titanic façade far overhead. They were demigods, and Donahy did not concern himself with their wishes, conflicts, or plans.

Kaufmann said, "How would you like to be earning twenty thousand bucks fish a year, Donahy?"

"*Sir?*"

"I need a favor. You're in a position to grant it. I could have picked any one of a hundred technicians to handle the job for me, but I've dealt with you before and I know you're capable and trustworthy. And I assume you could always use more money. What do you get paid, anyway?"

"Seven thousand, sir. With an annual increment of two hundred fifty."

"Which means that if you stick to your job and don't make any conspicuous mistakes, you're likely to be making as much as ten thousand by the time you're middle-aged, right? And there you stick until you retire and die. Well, I'm offering you an extra twenty thousand, on a lifetime annuity. Out of that you should be able to put aside enough money to make the down payment on a Scheffing persona recording. Would you like to live again, Donahy?"

The man looked utterly sick now. Rivulets of perspiration streamed down his face. He reached impulsively toward the tray of drinks, and then, as if deciding that it was impolite to serve himself without being asked, drew back, his fingers quivering.

Kaufmann smiled. "Go on. Have another. Have two. If you're tense, why not?"

Donahy jabbed the snout of a drink tube against his arm. When he spoke, he had difficulty framing his words.

"Could—could you be more specific, Mr. Kaufmann?"

"Certainly. I'm sure you know that the Scheffing Institute retains all persona recordings it makes, storing them in various depots around the world. For example, John Roditis is shortly going to receive a transplant of my uncle's persona recorded last December, but there's also a Paul Kaufmann persona that was recorded last spring, and one made the year before that, and so on over quite a span of time. And these previous recordings remain in dead storage. Are you aware of that?"

"Yes."

"Now, then, suppose you were to locate the whereabouts of my uncle's last-but-one recording, which shouldn't be too difficult for you to find, and remove it from storage. Then, suppose you were to bring this recording with you to a certain lamasery in San Francisco which is in the process of setting up its own soul bank. They've already installed enough equipment to do transplants and make recordings. What if you were to supervise the transplant of this borrowed persona at the lamasery? And then you'd undergo a blanking that would wipe all this incriminating evidence from your mind, so that no one could possibly prove that you had done any of these things. When you came to, you wouldn't know what you had been up to, but you'd discover you had suddenly become the recipient of an annuity which automatically transferred twenty thousand bucks fish into your credit balance each year. That's the equivalent of half a million dollars invested at four percent, which is considerable capital. With that kind of stake, you'd be able to buy yourself onto the wheel of rebirth. The risk is very small and the reward is infinite. What do you say, Donahy?"

"I've always been a law-abiding man, Mr. Kaufmann."

"I know that. But would you give up your chance of eternal life for the sake of respecting the regulations? Look, Donahy, the rules about transplants aren't graven on tablets of stone. They don't represent basic, moral commandments. If you kill a man, that's evil, I agree. If you molest a child and warp its life, that's evil. If you mutilate another human being for arbitrary amusement, that's evil. But the regulations governing the Scheffing Institute don't grow out of fundamental ethical constructs. They're just working rules set up to avoid confusion and possible conflicts. I don't say that they ought to be disregarded lightly, but they mustn't be looked upon as immutable. When there's a chance to have rebirth by winking at the rules for a moment, it's suicidal to be a stickler for the letter of the law."

Donahy appeared to be impressed by that argument. But he was not altogether tempted.

"How can I be sure that this isn't some kind of trap?" he asked.

"Trap?" Kaufmann exploded. "*Trap?* You mean that I've had you hauled over here for purposes of entrapment? That I've given you this much of my time simply for the sake of finding out whether your loyalty to the rules is unshakable? Don't be absurd."

"I've got to look at this thing from my own viewpoint. You don't know me at all, Mr. Kaufmann, except that I've worked on your recordings at the Institute. All of a sudden you send for me and offer me a fantastic reward if I'll do something wrong. I can't begin to understand any of this."

"Let me spell it out for you, then. I'll give you some insight into my motives. The recipient of the transplant will be myself."

"*You?*"

"Me. I'm determined not to let John Roditis gain advantage on me by taking on my uncle's persona. I'll have a slightly earlier persona, slightly less complete, but good enough to match him anyway. That'll nullify what he gains by getting Uncle Paul."

Donahy was drawn back in his chair as though gripped by

total panic. His eyes bulged; a muscle in his cheek danced about. Clearly he had no wish to be privy to these secrets of the great.

Kaufmann said, "Now you understand what's at stake. Will you help me?"

"What would happen to me if I refused?"

"I'd have you mindpicked and blanked to get all the details of this conversation out of your head. Then I'd send you back to your apartment and have another Scheffing technician brought here, and I'd make the same offer."

"I see."

"What's your answer, Donahy?"

"Can I have a little time to think things over, sir?"

"Of course." Kaufmann looked at his watch. "Take sixty seconds, if you like."

"I meant several days, Mr. Kaufmann."

"You can't have several days. You've heard the terms of the offer. I'll shield you from all consequences and give you an annuity that will make you a rich man. What do you say?"

Donahy let nearly a full minute spill away before he replied.

"Yes," he whispered. "Yes. I'll do it! But you've got to protect me!"

"You have my assurance," said Kaufmann. He stood up. "One of my associates will accompany you to your home. He'll remain with you overnight. In the morning you'll arrange to get access to the archive of old persona recordings. At the close of your working day you'll be picked up and taken to San Francisco with the recording. I'll meet you there tomorrow evening and you'll perform the transplant. When you report for work in New York the day after tomorrow, your part will be complete and you'll be blanked to protect you against possible interrogation. Your annuity payments will begin to accrue to your account that day. Is it a deal?"

Donahy nodded numbly.

"Your hand," Kaufmann said. He grasped the limp, cool fingers in his own. Then he buzzed for an aide to take the technician away. Donahy would not be alone again until the work was finished.

Moodily, Kaufmann let the tension ebb from his system. The interview had gone about as well as he could have expected. He disliked the shady nature of what he was doing; but at this stage he was compelled to take these protective steps. Above all else, a Kaufmann was bound by honor, yes. But if honor dictated that he preserve the family's position no matter by what means, he could hardly afford to boggle at shady doings. Normal concepts of honor were not framed to include the existence of a Roditis.

He flipped the retrofile, triggering it to see what calls might have come in while he spoke with Donahy. Risa's image appeared. The file told him that she was waiting in London to speak with him.

"Put her on," he said, transferring the call to the large screen.

A moment passed; then Risa appeared, life-size, on the screen. She looked frayed and weary. It was after midnight in London. No doubt this legal business involving her persona was taking a heavy toll of her energy.

"Well?" he said. "How does it go?"

"It's moving very fast, Mark. The autopsy report on Tandy came in this morning."

"And?"

"She was almost four weeks pregnant at the time of her death. That checks with the mindpick information they got out of Claude Villefranche's dybbuk."

"I see," Mark said. "She went to Claude and told him she was pregnant and wanted him to marry her, and he refused, and they had a fight over it and he killed her."

Risa laughed. "Oh, no! The way you tell it, it's straight out of one of the old melodramas. Tandy wouldn't have tried to use a pregnancy to blackmail a man into marrying her. Especially not a man like Claude."

"What's the story, then?"

"The gene tests show that she was pregnant by Stig. The Swede, her other lover. Sometime between the time Tandy made her last persona recording in June and the time she died in August, she decided that it would be interesting to have a baby, I guess. So she stopped the pill and Stig filled her up. She knew that Stig would be willing to marry her. He's a decent sort. Claude excited her more, but she didn't trust him. Then she went off to Switzerland to have her last fling with Claude. At St. Moritz she broke the news to him that this was where he got off. He was furious and told her to have the fetus aborted, to forget about getting married to Stig."

"But you said that Claude wasn't interested in marrying her," Mark said, puzzled.

"He wasn't. But he wasn't about to let Stig have her either. Or put a child in her. He saw that as an attack on his reputation for virility. He was wild with jealousy. So they had a fight, and finally they went out on the ski slope and he took the feeder pin out of her gravity repulsor, and down she went. If he couldn't run her life, she had to die. It's all there in the persona he last recorded. He made the recording two months after the killing."

"Didn't anyone think of examining her skis after the accident?"

"They were badly damaged, Mark. It was impossible to determine anything."

"And there was no autopsy?"

Risa shrugged. "When a girl is smashed up in a hundred-meter fall, there's no real point in an autopsy, is there? No one suspected she might be pregnant."

"What happens to this dybbuk now?"

"Claude? Well, they've got him on a double murder charge. The mindpick evidence shows that he killed Tandy, and there's also the little matter of what he did to his host. So the quaestorate has requested a complete erasure. They're going to blot him out entirely. He's being shipped to New York tomorrow and the job will be done at the Scheffing Institute. They'll clean him out of his host's mind and also destroy all his existing persona records."

"You must feel very proud of yourself, Risa, exposing this criminal."

"Well, actually, I could never have done it without Tandy. She was the one who guessed she'd been murdered, and she put the finger on Claude as a dybbuk. After that it was just a matter of seeing what was in his mind."

"And in Tandy's uterus," Kaufmann observed.

"Yes, that too. Well, now it's over, anyway."

"I'm glad. Risa, are you all through playing detective?"

"I think so. Why?"

"It would be nice if you'd stay closer to home for a while, with this business settled."

"I'll be home in about a week," she said. "Is that all right?"

"Fine," said Kaufmann. "Do you have enough money?"

"I'm drawing on the general family balance. All right?"

"Have mercy," he told her.

"I will. I'll see you soon."

Out of her tired eyes there twinkled a look of warmth, love, kinship. He smiled at her. She was a fine girl, he decided. A credit to their line. She had the promise of true greatness. He blew her a kiss, and the screen darkened.

A pity she was a girl, he thought.

Of course, they had had an option to fix that. But Kaufmann's wife was delicate, and he hadn't cared to dabble in uterine adjustments. He had taken his chances, and had had a girl, and there had been no more children after that. Risa was masculine enough in her thinking, at any rate. A time would come when she'd enter the family enterprises as a full partner, and Kaufmann knew she'd do well. His only objection to her sex was an esthetic one: a woman in business was in some way an unattractive sight, no matter how beautiful she might be. That was archaic foolishness, he knew, but he could not escape the thought that it was somehow ugly to watch a woman at work in front of a data console, making executive decisions involving millions of dollars. Women should be gentler creatures. But there was nothing gentle about Risa, female or not. It would be interesting to follow her progress down the generations as they leapfrogged from one carnate trip to the next.

He turned back to his ticker. Three quick trades produced a handsome profit for him. A cheerful omen.

By the end of this week he'd have all the shrewdness of Paul Kaufmann to add to his own. At last. At last. Naturally, he'd have to go warily, lest anyone find out that he carried an illegal persona. But Roditis would be perplexed when he discovered that each of his new strategic thrusts, inspired by Paul's persona, was being countered by strategies just as shrewd. Would he suspect that a second Paul Kaufmann was at work to thwart him? Would it occur to Roditis that such a thing was possible—a duplicated transplant? Few people were even aware that old recordings were preserved. Mark himself had not known it, despite his wide range of information, until Santoliquido had told him. So Roditis, though he was naturally suspicious, would have no inkling of the truth. He would just wonder how it was that his rival stayed abreast of him. Of course, after Mark's death the next possessor of Mark's persona would discover the secret, when he unexpectedly found Paul in his skull as well. But he was not likely to make the news public. Revelation of the irregularity would most likely bring about the erasure of both Kaufmann personae; the lucky man who had received two Kaufmanns for the price of one would make every effort to hide the fact.

Kaufmann laughed softly. His phone lit up. He keyed in, and the monitor said, "Francesco Santoliquido is calling."

Surprised, Kaufmann accepted the call at once. "Yes, Frank?"

Santoliquido looked younger, more carefree than he had appeared for many weeks. The living jewelry at his throat, the cage of tiny crustaceans, seemed to be leaping about jauntily in reflection of his changed mood. "I've reached a decision about your uncle's persona," said Santoliquido briskly.

Kaufmann remained calm. Donahy's assurance of cooperation was his bulwark against any possibility. "Yes?" he said easily. "Who's the lucky man? Roditis, as expected, eh?"

"No."

"*No?*"

"I've weighed this a million times, Mark. I've come around to your way of thinking: that Roditis has such power already that it would be a grave mistake to let him have Paul. That would set up an extraordinary concentration of ability in one individual, with unpredictable results."

"Of course."

"I've also taken into account the objections of the Kaufmann family, as voiced through you."

"Kind of you, Frank. But what will you do with old Paul, then? There can't be many others around you could safely award him to. I suppose it's best simply to leave him in storage a few years, until he's so far out of touch with events that he can be let loose again as someone's persona. I—"

"Oh, he'll be transplanted soon, though."

"To whom?" Kaufmann asked, taken aback.

"We have a rare event scheduled to take place here shortly," said Santoliquido. "The erasure of a dybbuk who's guilty not only of ejecting his host but of deliberately causing the discorporation of a young woman."

"The Tandy Cushing case. Yes, of course. Risa's given me all the details. But what does this have to do with—"

"Once Claude Villefranche has been obliterated, Mark, we'll be left with the empty but living body of Martin St. John, a young man of good family and decent health. Have you considered the status of a blanked-out body of that sort?"

"Why," Kaufmann said, "just take out one of St. John's own recorded personae and imprint it on his own brain. Isn't that the logical solution?"

"It's logical, but it won't work. That's called an autoimprint, and autoimprints can't be made. The brain rejects its own abstracted persona. There are complex reasons for this, partly having to do with the technique of the process, partly with the physiology of the autonomic nervous system, partly with the psychology of the persona. I won't trouble you with the details. But we can't put Martin St. John's persona back into Martin St. John's body. However, there's nothing stopping us from installing some *other* persona in that vacant, healthy body—"

Mark Kaufmann saw where Santoliquido was leading. The impact of comprehension was swift and violent.

"You'll put *Paul* in there?"

"Yes," said Santoliquido smugly.

"But that'll create an instant dybbuk! It'll be Paul Kaufmann operating Martin St. John's body!" Kaufmann cried hoarsely.

"True. However, there's no specific regulation prohibiting such a transplant. We have blank bodies so infrequently that there are no precedents. Paul himself is something of a precedent-setter, too, since his mind is uniquely dynamic and overbearing, and he's almost certain to turn any host he gets into a dybbuk. With a few possible exceptions, such as Roditis. And yourself. But we have a moral obligation to return Paul's persona to carnate form. If we give him an orthodox transplant, and a dybbuk results, the quaestors will insist on mandatory erasure again. If we put him into a wholly empty body, though, so that there's no charge of an unethical takeover of another intelligence, he won't be breaking any laws. In effect, your uncle will return to the world as an independent entity, truly reborn."

Kaufmann was staggered by the idea.

He saw the complacence in Santoliquido's face, and knew that the Scheffing administrator had engineered this most cunningly, as a way of immobilizing both Roditis and himself. Handing the disputed persona to a third party, a zero, a blank, neatly cut the ground from under both of them. Roditis could storm and rant, but unless he found some legal flaw in the transfer, he could not oppose it. And Mark, having put up a successful battle to keep Paul out of Roditis' mind, could not now very well presume to interfere with Santoliquido's further freedom of action.

It was ironic that Risa had provided Santoliquido with the solution to his dilemma. Very conveniently, she had helped to make a blank body available to him at the critical moment. Zip, zip, and Paul Kaufmann would walk the earth again, not merely as a silent persona, nor even as an unlawful dybbuk that had wrested control from a victimized host, but as a true rebirth, given a body of his own with the blessings of the Scheffing Institute!

"What do you say, Mark?" Santoliquido asked coyly.

Shaken, Kaufmann replied, "This is very sudden. It brings up all kinds of complications. What, for example, would be the legal status of this carnate form? Paul's dead. His estate is going through probate."

"Legally, the new entity would assume the property and status of Martin St. John," said Santoliquido. "I've already had a ruling on that. He'd be St. John, carrying the Paul Kaufmann persona. Of course, in effect he'd simply be Paul in St. John's body, but that doesn't give him any title to Kaufmann status. I assume that you'd accept him into your family circle as Paul and find room for him in your business enterprises, but that's strictly up to you. You could just as easily let him try to make his way as St. John. Knowing Paul, I think he'd do all right."

"Yes," said Kaufmann hollowly. "I think he would."

"So what do you say? I've saved you from the monstrous threat of a Roditis in your bosom! That's a relief, eh, Mark? Isn't it? You look a bit uncertain."

The initial shock was wearing off. Kaufmann had begun to see past his amazement at Santoliquido's coup to the deeper implications. Paul would return to life, yes, as shrewd and as energetic as ever, and with the extra benefit of residing in the body of a young man. That posed something of a threat to Mark's own status as head of the Kaufmann clan.

But no Kaufmann could really accept the reborn Paul as a true Kaufmann. The family would draw upon his reserve of experience and wisdom, but could never accord him full status. At best he'd be a secondary focus of power.

I can handle him, Mark thought. After all, what Santoliquido doesn't know is that I'll have Paul's persona myself. That'll enable me to cope, in case it comes to a showdown between Paul and me. And I should be able to count on Paul's support in the struggle against Roditis.

Kaufmann envisioned the possibility of a three-cornered rivalry: himself, the new Paul, and Roditis. But in such a conflict he would invariably emerge on top, since he'd be Mark-plus-Paul, and thus at least one notch ahead of Paul alone, and two notches ahead of Roditis.

He said, "Yes. Very clever of you, Frank. I approve. Have you broken the news to Roditis yet?"

"No. I thought I'd wait another day or two, until the transplant has actually been carried out. I'd prefer to present it to him as a *fait accompli.*"

"That's probably best," said Kaufmann. He chuckled. "I imagine Roditis is going to be surprised."

# 12

Charles Noyes said, "you won't like this, John. Elena says that they've decided not to give Paul Kaufmann to you. They've got some dummy body that a dybbuk was removed from, and they're putting the persona in that."

He waited fearfully for Roditis to react.

They were in the midwestern office of Roditis Securities at Evansville, Indiana, on the top floor of a tower overlooking the river. From the broad windows it was possible to see deep into Kentucky. Noyes had flown to Evansville that afternoon, after lunch with Elena. This was too important to convey to Roditis by phone.

Roditis seemed strangely calm. He walked past Noyes to the window and peered out into the blaze of light that was the city across the river. Then, turning slowly, he went to the Anton Kozak sonic sculpture that dominated one wall of his office and carefully recalibrated its pitch so that it produced a gentle hum at about fifty cycles. A horizontal component in the sculpture began to oscillate at such a frequency that it blurred and became barely visible.

Quietly Roditis said, "Did she learn this from Santoliquido?"

"Yes. She spent much of last night with him, and he told her. According to Elena, Santoliquido is quite proud of what he's arranged, because it thwarts both you and Mark in one stroke."

"What did Mark want done with the persona?"

"Either to be given to him or simply kept in cold storage. Since it obviously couldn't be given to him, Mark preferred that it go to nobody at all. Santoliquido's manipulated things so that neither one of you gets what he wanted, and yet neither one of you has any recourse from the decision."

Roditis, still icily calm, fondled the shining rim of the sonic sculpture. Noyes could not understand his employer's coolness. The man should be raving and shouting. Was Roditis drugged in some way? Up to the eyebrows in pills? System flooded with a chemosterilant to damp down any response?

"Does Kaufmann know of the decision?" Roditis asked.

"Yes," Noyes said. "Santoliquido phoned and told him about it two days ago."

"How did he take it?"

"Angrily. Very angrily. But then he gave his agreement. He had no real choice."

"And when is this transplant supposed to take place?"

Noyes shifted his weight uncertainly from leg to leg. "It was done this afternoon."

"Paul Kaufmann's walking around in a body without a controlling mind?"

Noyes nodded.

"Kaufmann's a dybbuk, then. Without even having to struggle for it."

"Yes."

"Dybbuks are illegal."

"Not this one," said Noyes. "Santoliquido apparently found some sort of legal loophole. Don't you see, this was approved on the highest level, meaning Santoliquido. Therefore, by definition, it can't be illegal. Paul Kaufmann's back in the world, and he's got full command of a body."

"Whose body was it?"

"An Englishman named Martin St. John. One of the younger sons of some lord. He was pushed out of the body by a Frenchman who had earlier murdered a girl at a ski resort, then was killed himself and picked up by St. John as a persona. They tracked him down, erased him after getting a confession under mindpick, and Santoliquido had the bright idea of putting old Kaufmann into the empty body."

"Very clever of him."

"You aren't upset by all this, John?"

"Not at all. I was expecting it, in a way. You can choose not to believe this, but I foresaw some such arrangement down to the actual details. I was braced for it. And I also have a plan of action ready to meet the situation."

"I knew you would, John. What do you have in mind?"

Roditis smiled. "Where is this St. John body now, do you know?"

"Probably still in New York. That's where the transplant was performed. I doubt that he'll do any traveling until he's achieved physical coordination in the new body."

"Good. Go to New York. Find St. John, Charles. Find him and kill him."

"You want me to discorporate—"

"That's right. Kill him. Destroy the St. John body."

Noyes sat down abruptly. His head whirled. Within, James Kravchenko gave a mighty leap, battering against Noyes' defenses. Noyes shivered as the persona assailed him. It was a moment before he could reassert his control over Kravchenko, and another moment before he was able to meet Roditis' level gaze.

"I can't do that, John!" Noyes gasped.

"Yes, you can, and you will. Damn it, do you think I'm going to let a dummy walk off with that persona? Look: Santoliquido doesn't have an infinite supply of empty bodies sitting around ready for Paul Kaufmann to go dybbuk in. Discorporate St. John and you're actually tossing Paul back into the soul bank, right? The master recording is still there, ready to be used again if something happens to the old man's current carnate embodiment. Okay. Remove St. John. I reapply for the Kaufmann persona, which is again available. Only this time I put more pressure on Santo than before. I don't waltz around so diplomatically. I threaten a little. I pound the table. I make it clear to him that I won't tolerate a second trick of that sort. He'll have to give in. I'll get my way at last."

"But I have to commit a discorporation," Noyes said in a weak voice. "What if I'm caught? What if I bungle it?"

"You won't be caught, and you won't bungle it. Don't worry, Charles. I'll arrange everything. As soon as you've done it, we'll whisk you back out here and have you blanked for the hours of the discorporation. We'll fill in false memories, an alibi that nobody can challenge. You'll be beyond the reach of mindpicking. Do you really think I'd allow my oldest and closest friend to run any real risks?"

"Still, can't you hire some thug—program a robot—"

"I need someone I can trust. There's only one person in the world I can rely on for this, Charles. You've been with me on every stage of the operation."

"But—"

"You'll do it, Charles." Roditis came over, standing above Noyes' chair, and put his hands on Noyes' shoulders just alongside the clavicles. His thick, powerful fingers dug sharply into the flesh. His eyes, compelling, almost hypnotic, sought for Noyes' and locked on them. Noyes knew he was being coerced, but he had never been able to resist Roditis' pressures before, and he doubted that he would succeed this time.

Earnestly Roditis said, "Do you have moral objections?"

"Well, in a way."

"Look at it this way. You aren't actually taking life. The real Martin St. John was discorporated long ago. The only intelligent thing in that body is the persona of Paul Kaufmann, which has no right to be there. Kaufmann's had one life already, one body. That's all he's entitled to on an autonomous basis. Now he's supposed to be riding as a passenger, as a persona. You dispose of the St. John body and Kaufmann reverts to his proper status, minus the illegal nonsense Santoliquido has invented out of cowardice. You'll actually be performing a pro-social act, Charles. You'll be canceling out an anomaly. Do you follow that?"

"I think so. I—"

"You can't kill something that's already dead. Both Martin St. John and Paul Kaufmann are already dead: one because his persona ejected him, one because his natural span was over. What you'll be doing is disposing of some superfluous protoplasm. Nothing else. You'll do it for me, Charles. I know you will."

"How will I do it?"

Roditis straightened up, went to his desk, ran his fingers over the protruding green studs of a safety cache. The cache door sprang open and he thrust his hand inside, pulling out a lemon-colored box less than an inch in diameter. Roditis popped the box onto his palm and stuck his hand under Noyes' nose. A touch of his finger and the box fissioned along its vertical axis to reveal a minute capsule containing a few drops of some turquoise fluid.

"This," said Roditis, "is cyclophosphamide-8. It's an alkylating agent that has the effect of breaking down the body's fail-safe system for tolerating its own chemical components. Let a little of this get inside a man and he rejects his own organs, the way he'd reject an organ graft from another person without proper chemical preparation."

"Some kind of carniphage?" Noyes asked uncertainly.

"Not exactly, but close enough. Your true carniphage causes the cells of the body to destroy themselves through autolysis, through enzyme release. This stuff has the effect of turning the body into a conglomeration of alien components that can't function homeostatically any more. Gland secretions become poisons; organ coordination ceases; antigens are poured forth to attack the very tissues they ought to be defending. The loveliness of it all is that nothing the medics can do can possibly save the patient. The more they meddle, the more quickly the rate of destruction accelerates. Death comes in less than an hour usually."

"Carniphage is quicker," Noyes pointed out.

"But carniphage is too obvious. When a man turns to a puddle of slime inside of fifteen minutes, it's a clear case of carniphage dosing. But with cyclophosphamide-8, the cause of death remains in doubt. It's an ambiguous finish."

"How is the drug administered?"

"In the fine old Borgia fashion. Conceal the box in your palm, like so. Offer your victim a glass of water. Pass your hand over it, squeeze the muscles together. The box opens, the capsule drops in. It dissolves in a microsecond. The turquoise color is lost upon contact with any other fluid. No taste. No odor. It's that simple." Roditis closed the lemon-colored box. He presented it gravely to Noyes. "Get aboard the next flight to New York and find Martin St. John. I've never needed your help more, Charlie-lad."

Dazed, Noyes shortly found himself high above Indiana, eastward bound. One of Roditis' secretaries had booked the flight for him; he himself seemed incapable of taking any positive action at the moment. He carried the capsule of poison in his lefthand breast pocket. In his righthand breast pocket there nestled, as always, the flask of carniphage with which he proposed to end his own miserable life just as soon as he found the courage to do it.

This would be an excellent moment, Noyes told himself morosely.

He did not want to be a catspaw for John Roditis any longer. He was tired of rushing around compromising himself for the sake of fulfilling the little entrepreneur's ambitions. Committing murder now. True, true, Roditis had produced a pack of sophistries to persuade him that supping cyclophosphamide-8 into Martin St. John's drinking water was not murder in any valid sense, and so persuasive was Roditis' glibness that Noyes had been nearly taken in. Nearly. Yet he knew that the quaestors would take a harder line with him if he were caught before Roditis could blank the crime from his mind. They'd accuse him of deliberate discorporation, and there was no more serious crime. He'd be erased. A small loss, maybe, to the universe and even to himself; but nevertheless humiliating. A man should destroy himself, not allow others to destroy him.

Gulp the carniphage now, he thought. You'll make a mess in the plane, and the stewardess will throw up, but at least you'll die an honest death.

His hand stole toward his righthand breast pocket.

—Go on, Kravchenko urged. Why don't you do it and get it over with? I'm so sick of being stuck in your lousy head, Noyes, you can't possibly imagine!

The hand halted short of its goal.

Some lingering Puritan sense of obligation assailed him. To kill himself now would be cowardly; he'd be running out on Roditis' assignment. He had no right to do that. Roditis trusted him; Roditis relied on him. And Roditis had given him employment and a purpose in the world for many years past. Sure, Roditis was overbearing, tyrannical, self-centered, and all the rest. Sure, Roditis had bullied him into compromise after compromise, until at the end he was even crashing parties on the man's behalf and sleeping with strange women to win a nugget of useful information. Nevertheless, those were the conditions of his employment. He had accepted them. He could not spurn them now. He owed it to Roditis to carry out this final assignment, this meaningless discorporation, this destruction of a body already dead and tenanted by a dead man's ghost. After that, if he wished, he could swallow his carniphage at last, with even more justification than now. Running out on unfinished business was surely not in the Noyes tradition.

Noyes realized that he had just made use of his New England heritage to justify an act of murder.

So be it, he told himself. So be it.

The decelerating rockets whined. They were landing in New York. Kravchenko, mocking as always, set up a clamor of derision as Noyes moved his hand away from the carniphage. But

Kravchenko, Noyes knew, could not have followed the complex inner processes of decision-making. The persona was simply trying to keep him off balance and unsettled. It was not really in Kravchenko's interest to goad him into actually drinking the carniphage; merely to get him so rattled that he'd be vulnerable to the sudden swift strike of a counter-erasure, the violent ejection by a triumphant dybbuk.

He wondered how he was going to find Martin St. John.

He could not simply look him up in the master directory. St. John was an Englishman, and wouldn't be listed here. Of course, Santoliquido would know where St. John was staying. But Noyes wanted to avoid tipping his hand to Santoliquido. It was too obvious that Roditis had an interest in getting Paul Kaufmann out of his present carnate form, and if Roditis' known confederate Noyes were suddenly to begin making inquiries about St. John, any chance Noyes might have of gaining access to St. John would disappear.

Noyes decided to ask Elena.

Elena seemed to know everything about everyone. She was at the center of the nexus, tentacles reaching toward Mark Kaufmann on the one hand, toward Santoliquido on the other, toward Noyes on the third. And she still had a tentacle or two left to extend in Roditis' direction. She'd be a likely source of information.

She had a small apartment registered in her own name in New Jersey. Noyes scarcely expected to find her there, but it was the logical place to begin. He called from the airport and was surprised to find her answering.

Her privacy code appeared on the screen. Noyes identified himself. The screen cleared, and Elena came into view. She was nude, but the scanner cut her off at the breasts, and in any case the tiny screen in the booth did not give him much of a view.

"I've just come back from a visit to Roditis," he said. "In Indiana."

"You told him about—"

"St. John? Yes."

"He must have been furious!"

"Actually, he was quite cool about it," Noyes said. "He seemed to be expecting some sort of fast shuffle of that kind, and he was braced. Listen, Elena, how soon can I get to see you?"

"Why not right now?"

"You're free this evening?"

"Very much so. Would you like to take me to Jubilisle again?"

"No," he said. "I'd just like a quiet visit. There are—some questions I'd like to ask."

"Questions, questions, questions! Very well. Come to my apartment. When should I expect you?"

"How about an hour from now?"

"That will do." She tapped out the hopter program for reaching her house, fingers moving swiftly over the data keys. An instant later the program card came chuttering out of the data slot in Noyes' telephone booth. He seized it and blew her a kiss. Grabbing his one suitcase, he rushed up the ramp and stepped into a traveler's-aid station, where he underwent a vibrator bath while his clothes were being pressed and refurbished. Freed of the grime of his journey from Indiana, Noyes proceeded toward the hopter zone, pausing on the way for a short snack. He chartered a hopter and slipped Elena's house program into the receptor slot. The vehicle took off, found itself hung up momentarily in a delay pattern over the crowded airport, then discovered an exit vector and made its way toward New Jersey.

He arrived at Elena's place a little after nine that evening.

Noyes had never been there before. His previous meetings with Elena had taken place at his apartment. He did not know what to expect: a place of palatial luxury, perhaps, or some steamy, overdecorated temple of amour. But in reality the apartment was nothing more than a *pied-à-terre,* as simple and austere as his own little suite. Despite Elena's known predilections for opulence, she did not seem to require it here, perhaps because it served only as a way station for her on those rare nights when she was not sleeping out. Greeting him in diaphanous, swirling pink robes that did very little to hide the exaggerated voluptuousness of her body, Elena seemed like some overblown tropical blossom blooming in a humble northern meadow.

They embraced tentatively and distantly. Elena evidently was ready for any kind of overtures he cared to make, but Noyes was too tense, too bound up in his own situation, to do more than go through a kind of ritualistic contact.

They broke away. She offered drinks. He settled into a chair; she chose a divan. Her robes parted to reveal tawny thighs. Noyes wondered if, as a matter of strategy, he should respond to her wanton unvoiced invitation. Or was she only teasing him? He was well aware that in all their relationships she regarded him only as a surrogate for other men. Sexually, she reached through him to make love to Jim Kravchenko. And when she passed secret information to him about the doings of Mark Kaufmann or Santoliquido, it was in the hope of winning favor with Roditis.

He said, "I need your help, Elena. I'm trying to find Martin St. John."

Her eyebrows rose. Her full lips drew apart. "Roditis is after him so soon?"

Noyes made an effort to conceal his reaction. "I'd simply like to talk to the man."

"About what?"

"Does it matter?"

"It might," she said.

Fidgeting, Noyes improvised. "All right. Roditis is interested in working out a deal with Paul Kaufmann. As long as old Kaufmann's back in circulation and Roditis can't have the persona himself, he'd like to come to an understanding with him. You see, Roditis is worried that Paul and Mark will form a family alliance to crush him. So he'd like to drive a wedge between them as rapidly as possible. Does that make sense to you?"

"A great deal of sense."

"So I've been sent here to make contact with Kaufmann/St. John. Only I don't know where to find him."

"And you think I do?"

"If anyone does, you do. Certainly Santoliquido's aware of St. John's location, and probably Mark as well. You're close to both of them. So—"

"You're right," said Elena. "I do know."

"Will you tell me?"

She stirred idly. Her robes opened, probably not by accident, and for a brief dazzling moment her entire body was bare to him. Noyes let his eyes rest on the huge globes of her breasts. She had mounted a fusion node in the great valley between them, and its tireless sparkle lulled him. Just as casually, Elena covered herself.

Softly she said, "Perhaps I might tell you. But there would be a price, Charles."

"Name it. Any amount."

She laughed. "Not money. A favor."

"What?" he asked uneasily.

"You carry the persona of a man who once meant a great deal to me," Elena said. "You stand between me and that man, Charles.

TO LIVE AGAIN

If I lead you to Martin St. John, you will step aside and make that man available to me. Yes? I can take you to St. John tonight."

"You mean I should have Kravchenko erased and let his persona be given to someone else?"

"Not exactly," she replied. "I mean that you should allow him to take you over. So that I may enjoy him directly in your body."

Noyes was thrown into such turmoil that Kravchenko nearly was able to eject him then and there. He struggled for control. Never had he experienced so direct a blow to his ego. Calmly, casually, Elena had invited him to commit suicide for her convenience! His ups worked incoherently. At length he said, "You have no right to ask that of me. It's insane to think that I'd do any such thing!"

"Is it? Why do you carry that flask of carniphage, then?"

"Well—"

"Your suicidal tendencies are well-known. Very well, Charles: here's your moment. Be of some use. Restore Jim Kravchenko to the world he loves, and remove yourself from the world you hate. While at the same time fulfilling your obligations to Roditis by speaking with St. John. Yes? It is perfect, you see."

In a stunned silence Noyes contemplated the symmetry of Elena's proposal. True enough, he had already contracted with himself to swallow the carniphage once he had done this last deed for Roditis. Elena seemed to recognize, somehow, that he had declared himself superfluous. In the long run, what difference did it make which exit he chose? To drink the carniphage would be a petty way of revenging himself on Kravchenko for many slights, but in short order Kravchenko's persona would be in a new body, and what then of his revenge? This way, at least, he could graciously step aside and deliver up his body to Kravchenko, not for Kravchenko's sake but for Elena's.

But yet it was so damned humiliating—to have a woman suggest that he voluntarily let his own persona go dybbuk. Did she really think he was as worthless as that? Yes. Yes, she did. He scowled. Perhaps, he thought, it was time for him to junk his old-line ideals and try a little craftiness. He could always promise to do as Elena wished, and change his mind afterward. The important thing now was to get at St. John.

He said heavily, "You ask a stiff price."

"I know. But there's logic to it. Isn't there?"

"Yes. Yes." He paced about, clenching his fists. "All right," he said. "Damn you, yes! Have your Kravchenko!"

"A deal, then?"

"A deal. Where is Martin St. John?"

"He was taken to Mark Kaufmann's Manhattan apartment."

Noyes gasped. "I should have known it. But I can't see him *there*, Elena! I can't walk right into Mark's own house and—"

"Mark went to California yesterday on business," said Elena. "He won't be back until tomorrow. His daughter's still in Europe. There's no one in his apartment but St. John and the servants looking after him. I'll take you there now."

"Let's go," he said.

She shed her robes with no trace of modesty while he watched, and selected light sprayon garments. They went out. The hopter journey to Manhattan was swift. Noyes felt as though trapped in a dream, with every event converging on a predestined climax with incredible rapidity and ease.

At the door of Kaufmann's apartment, Elena presented her thumb. The door did not open. She explained, "I don't have instant-access privileges. The scanner reports that I'm here, and checks to see if there's any order to bar me. In the absence of a specific order, I can come in."

"Why all the precaution?"

"Mark sometimes has other women with him," she said simply, as the door opened.

Noyes had never been in Mark Kaufmann's home before. It was elegant and spacious, with wings of rooms stretching to the sides and straight ahead. A blank-faced, snub-headed robot appeared. Elena said, "We're here to visit Mr. St. John."

The robot ushered them into a bedroom of huge size, dark, decked with brocaded draperies rising from projectors at the baseboards along the floor. Tones of green, cerise, and violet played across the ceiling. Sitting propped up in bed was a weary-looking, blue-eyed young man with light yellow hair, sallow skin, a rounded nose, a weak chin. Noyes paused at the doorway.

He realized, numbed, that he was in the presence of Paul Kaufmann.

There was an electric moment of confrontation. The unprepossessing figure in the bed seemed to take on strength and intensity as though it were flowing to him from some inner reserve. The eyes brightened; the head rose; the chin jutted. Above the bed was mounted a solido portrait of Paul Kaufmann in late middle age, an imperious eagle of a man. Despite the total difference in physical appearance, the man in the bed suddenly had that same imperious look.

"Yes?" he said. "Who are you?" The voice was cracked and unfocused; Paul Kaufmann, only hours into his borrowed body, had not yet mastered it.

"My name is Charles Noyes. I believe you already know Elena Volterra."

"Noyes? Noyes of Roditis Securities?"

"That's right," Noyes said. "You know me?"

"It was my business to know the Roditis organization, yes. Well, what are you doing here? How did you get in? Roditis men don't belong here."

"I brought him," said Elena. "He asked to see you, and I owed him a favor."

"Take him away," Kaufmann/St. John snapped. He waved his hand in what was meant as a gesture of dismissal; but his coordination was still poor, and his arm flapped in an awkward overswing that brought it slapping against the headboard.

Elena looked stymied. She did not move.

"Away," came the petulant command. "Out of here. *Out of here!* I must rest. I've been through a great deal. If you knew what it was like to die, to awaken, to enter a strange body . . ." His words trickled away into incoherence. The Kaufmann dybbuk seemed exhausted by the effort of speaking. The brilliance and intensity vanished from the eyes as though a switch had been thrown; he was resting, regaining his powers.

Elena said doubtfully, "If he doesn't want to see you—"

"He'll give me five minutes," Noyes told her. "Look, wait outside for me, yes? I won't be with him long."

She nodded and left the room.

Noyes did not pretend to himself that Elena would fail to comprehend what he was about to do. But he doubted that she would expose him. He closed the door carefully behind her.

Kaufmann/St. John looked harsh and arrogant again. "I order you to leave!"

Approaching the bed, Noyes said quietly, "Just a few minutes. I want to talk. Do you find it very confusing, coming back to the world? You expected to have to fight through to dybbuk, didn't you? Not to have a body handed to you like this. You know, there was quite a dispute over who was going to be your carnate. Roditis was very anxious to get you. But Santoliquido flimflammed him by finding this empty body. Don't you agree it might have been more interesting to wake up in Roditis' skull?"

As he spoke, Noyes steadily drew nearer the bed.

Paul Kaufmann glowered at him. The flaccid muscles of his new face strained with the effort to rise and hurl the intruder from his room. But he could not do it.

"If you don't leave here at once—"

"Can't we discuss things peacefully?" Noyes asked. His long fingers enfolded the container of the cyclophosphamide-8 capsule. "Here. Have a drink of water. Let me tell you about a deal Roditis has in mind. A great profit opportunity."

He picked up a drinking glass in his left hand, filled it halfway with water, and began to bring the concealed capsule toward it. But it was no use. Those strange washed-out blue eyes moved twitchingly, taking in everything. Noyes realized he could not bring off the sleight-of-hand successfully. Kaufmann/St. John would guess what he was trying to do and would put up a fight, clumsily, perhaps, but effectively enough to spill the irreplaceable poison or to get the robot servitors into the room.

Noyes could not afford to be subtle.

He leaned toward the man in the bed. In a low voice he said, "You'll be better off in a different carnate form."

"What do you—"

As the lips parted, Noyes shot his hand forward, applied pressure to the lemon-colored box to open it, and sent the deadly capsule into his victim's mouth. At the same time he pressed two forked fingers of his other hand against Kaufmann/St. John's Adam's apple. The man gulped. The capsule went down.

There was scathing fury in the blue eyes.

Kaufmann/St. John flailed impotently at Noyes with weak,

badly coordinated arms. His hands wobbled as if about to fly from their wrists. But the face was a study in malevolence; all the full vitality of Paul Kaufmann was harnessed and hurled forth in a crescendo of frustrated rage and vindictive hostility. Clusters of muscles churned and spasmed beneath the surface of his cheeks. Exposed to that blast of hatred, Noyes recoiled, singed by the fire of this incredible old man.

But then, within the minute, the discorporation began.

Noyes watched only the beginning of it. Backing away from the bed, he saw the fire go out, saw the look of puzzlement and anguish appear. Strange internal events were commencing. The floodgates of the ductless glands had opened all at once, pouring forth an impossible mixture of secretions that mingled and reacted violently. The synchrony of heart and lungs was destroyed. The brain itself scorned the messages of its sensory perceptors. Instant by instant, the body of Martin St. John proceeded toward self-destruction.

Noyes fled.

Elena caught hold of him in the corridor outside. "Where are you going? What happened?"

"Get a doctor," Noyes burst out. "He's sick—some kind of stroke, I don't know—"

"*What did you do to him?*"

"We were just talking. He got angry. And then—"

A wild, screeching groan came from the bedroom, a sound ripped from tortured and disintegrating vocal cords. Elena went in. She emerged only moments later, looking appalled.

"You gave him a poison!" she cried.

"No. I don't know what happened. While I was with him, suddenly—"

"Don't lie. Roditis sent you here to kill him. And you told me you just wanted to talk to him!"

"Elena—"

With savage fury she pulled at him, tugging him out of the apartment. She seemed almost berserk with fear and shock. But in the fresh air she calmed; she had had a moment to digest the event, and her control had returned.

"Now we go to my place," she said. "You tricked me once tonight, Charles, but not again. Now you keep your bargain."

Noyes was close to collapse. Drenched in sweat, trembling, terrified, he let her shepherd him across to her little apartment in New Jersey. He tumbled wearily onto a couch. Elena stood over him, eyes bright, features rigid with malevolence.

"Now, Mr. Discorporator," she said, "you've done Roditis' filthy work and made me an accomplice. You owe me something for that. Out of that body now!"

"No," Noyes said feebly.

"No? *No!* We have a deal! Come, now. Shall I give you a drink? To make it easier? No trickery, Charles!"

Noyes felt Kravchenko hammering vehemently at the fabric of his mind, making a savage attempt to go dybbuk. Desperately Noyes resisted. I won't do it, he told himself. This is one bargain I won't keep. They can't make me destroy myself this way. I've got to get out of here, back to Roditis to get blanked, fast.

—You miserable cheater, Charles. You filthy pig!

It was Kravchenko. Noyes was stunned to realize that he had spoken nothing aloud. Kravchenko had tapped right into his flow of interior monolog! That meant the persona had taken a deeper hold than ever before on him, and was now in direct contact with his mind.

"Let's go, Charles," Elena said. "Out!"

"No. No, please—"

She seized him by the shoulders and shook him in a wild

fury. He tried to push her away, but she was too strong for him; and now he could feel Kravchenko ripping at his brain, uprooting neural connections like saplings, drilling his way through the centers of control. Already it seemed to Noyes that whole sectors of his brain were cut off, that he was being thrust aside, pushed into a single lobe, isolated, undermined—

*Ejected.*

"No!" he cried. "The deal's off! I never meant to—"

"—but now I've changed his mind for him," Kravchenko finished. Elena rose in triumph. "Jim? Jim, that's you, yes?"

"Yes. Me. God, it's good to be free!" Kravchenko stretched lavishly. He took a few steps, stumbled, recovered. "The coordination takes a little while to come back, I guess. But to have a body again! To feel! To breathe!"

"He's really gone?" she asked.

"I've rammed him down far out of sight. Nothing left of him but a few shreds, and I'll hunt those down and pull them out. Free, Elena! After all those years penned up in that sniveling hulk of a man!" He reached for her. His fingers clutched at the taut cones of her breasts, missed aim, got her shoulders instead; with an effort he drew his arms downward.

Softly he said, "I've got some other reflexes to test, Elena!"

He found that coordination returned more swiftly than he expected, although not altogether at a satisfactory level. It would take some time, he decided. Time and practice.

As dawn came Elena said, "Now we head for Indiana."

"What for?"

"So that Roditis can blank you, stupid! As far as the world knows, you're Charles Noyes, right? And Charles Noyes has discorporated Martin St. John. The memory of that must be wiped from your mind. Come. Come."

Kravchenko nodded. "You're right. I'll have to go to Roditis—bluff it through, let him blank me on the killing. Then I'll quit him and we'll go off together, eh?"

"Yes!"

"But why are *you* going to Indiana?" he asked.

Elena gave him a slow, simmering smile. "Do you think I'm going to be apart from you even for an hour, now that I have you again?"

# 13

D ead?" Mark Kaufmann asked. "How could he possibly be dead? The St. John body was in good health. I saw it myself before I went to San Francisco."

The medic shook his head. "There was a total breakdown of autoimmunity. A civil war inside him, so to speak. No hope whatever of saving him."

—Murder, Paul's persona said.

But it did not take any great shrewdness, to see that. Mark said, "Can such a thing happen naturally?"

"Most unlikely. You realize, Mr. Kaufmann, that it's statistically possible for such a thing to occur, but—"

"Not very probable?"

"No. Not at all."

"What was it, then? Carniphage?"

"These are not the effects of a carniphage," said the medic. "How-

TO LIVE AGAIN

ever, the poisoner today has an extremely wide choice of drugs. I've been running a data check, comparing effects with possible causes, and this is what I've come up with."

He handed Kaufmann a data sheet. It was headed:

CYCLOPHOSPHAMIDES-8

Mark scanned it hastily. "Is this drug easily available?"

"I'd say it costs roughly a million dollars fissionable an ounce," the medic replied. "The lethal dose is perhaps a hundredth of an ounce, though."

"Expensive, but not prohibitive. Rare?"

"It can be had. The sources are difficult to reach, but they exist. With enough money—"

"Yes, with enough money," Mark said. "Have you found any traces of this—this cyclophosphamide in the body?"

"It leaves no traces. It metabolizes completely in use, and the only indication it leaves is in its effect."

"In other words, proof of use has to be empirical, deduced from the ruin it makes out of the victim?"

"Essentially, yes," said the medic smoothly. "The quaestorate is now conducting a second autopsy, and naturally will be making every effort to determine the actual cause of death. But I venture to predict that the ultimate verdict will be the same as mine: poisoning by cyclophosphamide-8."

"All right. Thank you. Go."

—You need to tighten your security net, Paul told him. A murder committed in your own apartment is shameful.

"There are finite limits to security," Mark said. He moved about the apartment, scuffing at the carpet. This incident left him tense and baffled and angry. He did not mind at all that someone had discorporated Martin St. John, the dybbuk Paul Kaufmann, so speedily after the transplant. But it offended him that St. John could be discorporated right here, of all places. And he was troubled by the possibility that suspicion of the discorporation might come to rest on him.

It was poor business. If the quaestorate hatched the idea that he was in any way connected with the murder, he'd be hauled down on a mindpick warrant, and not all the money in the universe could buy him out of that. Naturally, the mind-pick would show that he had no complicity in the discorporation of Martin St. John, since in fact he had not been involved at all.

But at the same time the mindpick would reveal the illegal presence in his mind of the persona of Paul Kaufmann.

This had to be the work of Roditis, Mark thought. To take advantage of his absence by sneaking an agent in here to kill St. John, thereby opening him to mindpick and disgrace—no, no, Roditis could have no inkling of what he had been up to in San Francisco, and it was a mistake to attribute to the man more deviousness than he actually possessed—unless, that is, Roditis had his hooks into the lamasery too, and had instantly received word that Mark had come there to undergo a *sub rosa* persona transplant. . . .

Exhausted by the intricacy of his own hypotheses, Mark sank down on a couch to collect himself.

—Fool, you're panicking over this.

"Let me think, Paul. Please."

—Think all you like. But think fast! An hour from now you may be under arrest.

"No, there's more time than that. The quaestorate hasn't finished the autopsy. And then they'll have to move through channels, deciding if they dare to arrest me, swearing out the warrant, arranging the mindpick. I've got at least twenty-four hours."

Paul did not reply. His head aching, Mark attempted to reconstruct the sequence of events.

He had seen Donahy Tuesday afternoon. That same day Santoliquido had called to announce his intention of transplanting Paul's persona into the vacated St. John body. On Wednesday, Mark had inspected the St. John body, then had flown to San Francisco. Also on Wednesday, Donahy had abstracted last year's persona recording of Paul Kaufmann from the archives. Wednesday night, in San Francisco, Donahy had transplanted the persona into Mark. Mark had remained out there on Thursday, resting and adapting to the powerful new persona. Meanwhile, in New York on Thursday, the most recent Paul Kaufmann persona had been transplanted into the St. John body, and St. John had been taken to Mark's apartment for recuperation. Sometime late Thursday night St. John had been murdered.

Now it was Friday afternoon, and Mark, back from San Francisco, found himself in deep trouble.

Just when everything had been going so well, too. He and Paul had adjusted to one another remarkably smoothly. There had been none of the tests of strength, none of the jockeying and probing that might have been anticipated when strong-willed old uncle entered strong-willed nephew's mind. Paul had been delighted at getting a new carnate trip, fascinated by the shady way Mark had obtained his persona, and absolutely overjoyed to learn that a second and later version of himself was also going to be at large in dybbuk form. He showed no resentment of the fact that the provision in his will barring transplant to a member of his family had been circumvented, possibly because that codicil had been added after this particular persona had been

213

recorded. Recognizing Roditis as the real family enemy, Paul was willing to aid his nephew in every way, while at the same time helping to isolate and immobilize the dybbuk-Paul whom Santoliquido had spawned. Of course, Mark was prepared for conflict with his uncle sooner or later, possibly even a sneaky attempt to go dybbuk at his expense. But for now, at least, their mutual adaptation was splendid, and Mark reveled at having the crusty, indomitable old brigand finally safe in his mind.

Then, to fly home and walk into this—

Well, there were certain obvious first steps to take. The most obvious of all was to check last night's scanner records and see who had been in his apartment. He had a pretty good idea. There weren't many people who had even conditional access, and the only one with full access, Risa, was still in Europe, so far as he knew.

The scanner file gave him the quick answer.

Elena had been here. She had applied for admission just before eleven last night, and the robots had let her in. Mark saw her on the tape, and there was nothing unusual about her expression, as there might have been if she had come to commit a discorporation.

But who was this who had come in with her? This tall, blond fellow with the taut, edgy look in his eyes?

Noyes? Charles Noyes?

Noyes of Roditis Securities?

Elena had brought him *here?*

—There's your killer, Paul said. He *must* be.

"Not so fast," Mark muttered. "Noyes is Roditis' man, sure, but Roditis doesn't do foolish things. If he wanted to kill St. John, he wouldn't send someone like Noyes here to do the job. It's too transparent."

—What do you know about Noyes? I recall that he's not too stable.

"No, not very."

—Then perhaps Roditis picked a bungler. Run the tape a little further.

Mark moved it along. The figures of Elena and Noyes appeared at the door again some ten minutes later. Noyes looked more tense than ever, almost close to collapse. And Elena, now, gave every impression of hysteria. Obviously something significant had happened in those ten minutes—such as the murder of Martin St. John. The two figures were exchanging hurried conversation at the door. Mark could not read their lips, nor was there any audio on the scanner tape, but he knew that a simple computer analysis of lip patterns would tell him what they were saying. He watched Noyes hurry from the apartment. Then Elena disappeared from the door. About twenty minutes later she left, looking calmer. That concluded the Thursday night record. The file of outgoing calls showed none until one in the morning, when a robot had noticed St. John dead and had summoned the quaestors.

"That's it, then," Mark said. "She let him in, and he killed St. John."

—There's no proof. It's all circumstantial, Mark. Where's the weapon? Where are the witnesses? St. John might have been killed by someone else before Noyes ever got here, for all your records show. A blowdart through a window, maybe.

"It's enough to authorize a mindpick, Paul. And a mindpick will show Noyes' guilt. I've got to get him picked before anyone thinks of mindpicking me, or they'll find you."

—You might try talking to Elena, Paul suggested.

But Elena did not answer when he called her apartment. Curiously, she had not even left a forwarding number. Mark buzzed

215

her inner number, thinking that perhaps she had posted a forwarding number for limited distribution to close friends, but that drew a blank too. Where was she? She never went anywhere without notifying him first. And she surely knew that he was due back in New York sometime today.

He phoned Santoliquido next.

As usual, it was a slow, bothersome job to get through to him. When Santoliquido appeared, his quizzical expression showed that he had heard the news.

"Where have you been, Mark?"

"Away on business since late Wednesday. And when I got back—St. John—"

"I know. The quaestors notified me."

"What is this all about, Frank?"

"I haven't any idea. But of course I have my suspicions."

"Such as?"

"Never mind," said Santoliquido. "They're unfounded at present. The important thing is that your uncle is discorporate again, and we have to start the whole process from the beginning."

Mark felt a secret pleasure at the knowledge that his uncle was far from discorporate. He heard the old man's silent, complacent chuckle within him.

To Santoliquido he said, "Do you expect Roditis to reapply?"

"Why shouldn't he? The persona's available again."

"And you've run out of ways to avoid giving it to him."

Santoliquido nodded. "For the moment, at least."

"Listen to me, Frank, I want one last favor. Stall him off. If only for a few days. I can't explain now, but I've got reason to think you'll be wasting everyone's time if you give Paul to Roditis now. Will you wait at least until the report of the quaestors is issued?"

"I'll do that, yes," Santoliquido agreed.

"Good." Mark paused a moment. Then, in a carefully more relaxed tone, he said, "You haven't seen Elena lately, have you?"

With the same deliberate casualness Santoliquido replied, "Lately? Well, let's see . . . I had lunch with her yesterday. Is that lately enough?"

"I meant today."

"No. The last I saw of her was one in the afternoon yesterday. You've phoned her apartment?"

"Of course," Mark said. "I suppose she's taken a little trip. I imagine I'll be hearing from her soon."

Roditis said, "So it's all done, and you're back here, and no one's the wiser, Charles. Was that so bad?"

Kravchenko attempted to keep his facial muscles fixed in the bland, idiotic expression of benignity that he imagined Charles Noyes customarily to have worn. He was on edge, here in Roditis' Indiana headquarters, for this was the first test of his dybbukhood. If he failed to fool Roditis, he'd be on the scrapheap by nightfall.

He said carefully, "Well, John, I don't deny I was uneasy about it. But it went off more smoothly than I dared hope."

"And now we'll get you blanked, and splice in a set of phony memories for last night, and you'll be safe. Eh?"

"Yes, John."

"Want to take a little workout first? Get yourself back into shape?"

"I think we'd better tend to the blanking first," said Kravchenko. "I've got a few things on my mind that I'm better off without."

Roditis nodded. "Right. Come with me."

Kravchenko followed the stocky little financier through the maze of the building. He did not much like the idea of submitting to a blanking; he hated to surrender consciousness, hated to go under the machine. But so long as he still carried around memories of the discorporation of Martin St. John, he ran serious risks. Noyes, whom he pretended to be, might well be under suspicion of that discorporation. If they picked him up, ran a routine mindpick on him, and found the evidence, all would be up not only for Noyes—whose personae would be destroyed because of his crime—but for Kravchenko as well, since the routine mindpick would be followed by a deep pick that would reveal who was actually running the Noyes body. Kravchenko thought he could conceal his dybbuk status if the pick merely went scraping around looking for a specific event, the discorporation episode. But he was finished for good if they sank the pick beyond the surface. His only hope of avoiding that was to blank out everything having to do with last night. Which Roditis now proposed to do.

Technicians were readying the blanking apparatus.

Kravchenko studied it warily. A blanking was something like getting a persona transplant—in reverse. Instead of having taped information poured into your receptive brain, you yielded information. Instead of being doped with mnemonic drugs to damp out memory decay, they washed your mind with a selective memory suppressant, carefully measured to obliterate a certain chronological segment of the memory bank. Kravchenko distrusted all this fiddling with the brain. Yet he admitted the necessity of it.

"Will you lie down here?" a technician said.

Kravchenko waited. They gave him injections. They strapped electrodes to his skull. They took EEG readings of Noyes' brain waves. Silently they bustled about, while Roditis hovered somberly in the background.

"Ready, now," someone said.

A helmet was lowered over his head.

"Don't worry about a thing, Charles," came Roditis' confident voice. "We'll clean you up in no time."

"Wow," said a technician.

Kravchenko went tense, imagining that switches were being thrown and contacts made. He could see nothing. His drugged mind grew foggy. Abruptly he heard what sounded like a colossal explosion, and in the same instant a burst of intolerably bright lightning shot through his brain. He felt as though his skull had split apart.

Chaos enfolded him.

He was swept away by a terrible tide—down, down, down—out of control—helpless—and with his last conscious thought he asked himself how this could be happening, when a blanking was supposed to be such a trivial thing. Then he was swallowed up in darkness.

This was her moment, Elena thought. Jim was downstairs undergoing his blanking; afterwards, he'd be resting for a few hours. Now was her chance to add Roditis to her collection.

She hadn't felt like telling Jim that one of her motives in accompanying him to Evansville was to seduce John Roditis. Newly returned to corporate status by her scheming, Kravchenko would not understand that he was not going to be the only man in her life. She loved him passionately; but she wanted Roditis. Two hours ago, when she and Kravchenko had arrived here, Elena had met Roditis for the first time. They had exchanged perhaps ten words; Roditis had hardly seemed to take notice of her. He was too preoccupied with the maneuvers surrounding the St. John discorporation, as was only natural. But she had taken notice of him. That muscular, powerful body held promise of physical delight; and the strength of the man was unmistakable. To Elena, a connoisseur of strong men, Roditis seemed an ideal mixture of raw power and intuitive intelligence. Santoliquido and Mark Kaufmann and the others had palled on her; Kravchenko, now that he was back, offered many pleasures, but he was shallow, a floater, a playboy; new adventures beckoned to her. With Roditis.

She said, "I've always been curious about you. It's strange we never had occasion to meet before."

"I don't move in your high-society circles." Roditis seemed distant, even bored.

"You really should, you know. We aren't such ogres. A man of your vigor, your enterprise—you'd inject some new vitality into our group." Surreptitiously she moved closer to him. Elena regretted that she was not dressed for her purpose; she had flown to Evansville in workaday travel clothes, and there had been no chance to change into something more clinging, something more revealing. In this drab garb she felt, as though locked into armor. Yet it was a handicap she felt she could overcome.

Roditis said, "I object to snobbery, Miss Volterra. I am a wealthy man, yes, but no playboy. My values are not those of your set. I have work to do every day."

"You ought to let yourself enjoy the benefits of your work," she purred. She stood beside him now, at his desk, examining the sonic sculpture. "How beautiful!" she said. As she reached forward to caress the piece the soft hill of her breast pressed into Roditis' elbow. It was hardly a subtle gesture, but she did not regard Roditis as a subtle man.

He moved smoothly away, breaking the contact.

Elena nibbled her lip. She threw him a coquettish glance; she asked him about the sculpture, found that it had been made by one of his personae, praised it extravagantly; she adopted a posture so sensual it might almost have been self-parody. Roditis seemed unmoved. What's the matter with the man, she wondered?

Her approach became even more direct. She flattered him; she told him how thrilled she was to have met him at last; she cornered him behind his own desk and filled his ears with praise. She could not have made it more obvious if she had stripped and sprawled out spreadlegged on the carpet. And Roditis grew more brusque, more withdrawn, as she fought to reach him.

It was a dismal moment. Elena sensed that she was being refused, which had never happened to her before, and she could not imagine why. From what she knew of Roditis he was unmarried, heterosexual, promiscuous. Why, then—?

To hell with it, Elena told herself.

She thrust herself into his arms.

Her breasts crushed up against him. Panting, eager, she hunted for his lips, while her hands clawed the muscular ridges of his back. By now she was so angry that she felt only the counterfeit of desire; but she came on in seemingly uncontrollable passion, determined to sweep Roditis off his feet. He would have her on the floor, she resolved. A wild bestial coupling. She'd show him her abilities, and afterwards he'd need less coaxing.

His hands went to her breasts. Not to caress, though, but to shove. He pushed her back, disengaged himself, adjusted his clothing. He looked ruffled; his eyes were steely. In a frosty voice he said, "This is no pleasure palace, Miss Volterra. This is a workingman's office. I'm not in the mood for a wrestling match now."

She cursed him eloquently in Italian. Then, inspired, she went on to roast him in Greek; but not even that got a rise out of him. Incredulously she stared as he summoned a robosecretary and instructed it to show Miss Volterra to her lodgings.

"Dog!" she cried. "Eunuch!"

Roditis glowered, slammed fist into palm, and switched up the vents to get the reek of her perfume out of the room. Damn her! He could hardly believe what had happened—the coarseness of her, the grossness of her assault. He had known from the very first, naturally, why she was here, hitchhiking along with Noyes to get an introduction to him. All that ogling and rump-wiggling when she had first showed up had not failed to get through to him. And now, in his office, the winks, the ever broader hints, the breast nuzzling against his arm, finally the desperate lunge and clutch—he had not expected the famed Elena Volterra to be quite so blunt.

Unless, he thought, she regarded him as the sort of man who was lured with such tactics.

The episode had jangled his nerves. She was a handsome woman, yes, well up to advance word; no doubt it would have been an interesting hour or two in bed for him. But Roditis had enough handsome women to keep him busy for centuries. This was one he would not touch, though she had the beauty of Helen of Troy. He was unwilling to push Mark Kaufmann too far. He was about to get his uncle's persona; he would not try to take his woman too. Once the elder Kaufmann was safe in Roditis' brain, he planned to strike a truce with Mark; and it would be much harder to arrange that if Elena Volterra were in the picture too.

Of course, Roditis conceded, he had just made an undying enemy out of Elena. Hell hath no fury, etc. That could have its strategic uses too, though. What was Elena, anyway? A bed-hopper, a gossip, a seeker of vicarious power, an animated bundle of desires and greedy ambitions, a fleshy construct of breasts and buttocks and thighs and loins. Mark Kaufmann, who controlled real power, had not been able to harm him; what damage could Elena do?

She might succeed only in forging a Roditis-Kaufmann alliance. If she screamed loudly enough to Mark about the "insult" visited upon her, it might just give Mark the idea that John Roditis didn't mean to grab everything within his reach. And that could be the beginning of the Kaufmann-Roditis *détente* that Roditis saw as the key to major power expansion.

So let her do her worst, Roditis thought.

There's no way the slut can hurt me. None!

Noyes, crouching in darkness, was amazed to find light lancing through. Sudden brightness from above told him that the lid which had been crushing down on him was cracking. He stirred; he tested his strength and found that he could lift the lid.

What was happening? Why was Kravchenko losing control?

For an uncertain and perhaps infinite span of time Noyes had lain huddled in a corner of his own mind, Kravchenko's prisoner. No sensory inputs had reached him here. He was wholly cut off; and he had assumed that eventually Kravchenko would bear down and finish the job of destroying him. First came ejection from motor control, and then loss of the voluntary brain centers, and finally the ripping away of all contacts, so that the dybbuk would be alone in the body they had formerly shared. Bleakly Noyes had awaited his fate. He could not comprehend the turn of events; but quite plainly Kravchenko's grasp had slipped.

Noyes burst from confinement and flooded back into every lobe of his brain.

He encountered Kravchenko. The persona seemed dazed and helpless, lost in a fog. It was an easy matter for Noyes to recapture motor and sensory power from him.

He let his eyelids flutter open and took stock. He found himself lying on a laboratory table, with apparatus strapped to his skull and chest, and technicians bustling about him. "He's coming out of it," one of them said. Noyes thought at first that he was in a soul bank, but then he recognized his surroundings: this was Roditis' place in Indiana. What had they been doing to his body at the moment of his unexpected return to control, though?

A technician said, "You look a little shaken up, Mr. Noyes. Everything all right?"

"I—well, more or less," he said. He sat up. It was not difficult for him to operate his body, and that was encouraging; it told him that relatively little time had passed since Kravchenko had thrust him out. Tentatively he formed a theory that this was only the day after St. John's discorporation. According to the plan, he was supposed to have returned to Evansville to have all knowledge of the crime blanked. Presumably that was what had been taking place in this laboratory.

But if I've been blanked, Noyes wondered, how is it that I still remember the discorporation?

He realized that he would have to move warily until he could draw some clues from those about him. Something very strange had taken place, and he had to be careful not to tip his hand.

Roditis entered the room, scowling, tense. He brightened as he saw Noyes, though, and said, "Well, Charles, how did it go?"

"F-fine," Noyes said. "My ears are ringing just a little, maybe."

"They say you sometimes have a hangover after something like that." Roditis dismissed the technicians with an impatient wave of one hand. His face grew serious once more. In a low voice he said, "Have you heard the news, Charles? Martin St. John was discorporated last night in New York!"

So this was a test of how well he had been blanked.

Noyes said, "St. John? St. John? I'm not sure I place the name."

224

"An Englishman. The persona of Paul Kaufmann had been transplanted to him. You remember, don't you?"

"I'm afraid I'm a little hazy about all that. Discorporated, you say? Do the quaestors have any clues?"

"I doubt it," Roditis replied. "The poor quaestors are always three jumps behind the criminals. It's so hard to enforce the law properly when a murderer can have all sense of guilt blotted from his mind. By the way, Charles, where'd you spend the night?"

He was caught off guard. Desperately improvising, he said, "If you have to know, John, I was with a woman. I'll give you the details if you wish, but a gentleman really doesn't—"

Roditis chuckled. "No, a gentleman doesn't. But she's a hot one, isn't she? Elena, I mean." He slapped Noyes heartily on the back. "She's waiting here in town. I'd like you to escort her back to New York right away, yes, Charles?"

"Whatever you say."

"And now, if you'll excuse me, it's exercise time."

Roditis went out. Noyes, relieved, paced around the room as he drew together the strands of the mystery. He had discorporated St. John, and then Elena and Kravchenko had teamed up to push him out of his mind. Noyes shuddered at the recollection. Afterwards, the dybbuk-Kravchenko and Elena had flown out here, with Kravchenko obviously masquerading as Noyes. That was how it must have been, Noyes decided. And, naturally, Roditis had wanted to blank the crime from Noyes' mind.

But the blanking had gone awry.

Noyes thought he understood why. A blanking was a simple thing, in its way, but only if no unknown factors fouled up the settings of the machine. Doubtless they had calibrated their dials for the brainwaves of Charles Noyes—and then had tried to blank the Noyes brain, unaware that they were really working on the mind of Jim Kravchenko. The clashing of Noyes' brain waves with Kravchenko's consciousness had driven the dybbuk into shock, permitting Noyes to resume control. But Noyes had not been blanked after all, since he had been cut off, beyond the reach of the instruments.

So I am a murderer and still unblanked, Noyes thought, and I have won out over my own dybbuk, and Roditis is sending me back to New York with Elena. What do I do now? May all the Buddhas help me, what do I do now?


Mark Kaufmann spent much of Friday afternoon patiently tracking down leads in the hope of solving the double mystery of St. John's discorporation and Elena's disappearance. Through various channels he was able to gain access to a great deal of information normally available only to the investigators of the quaestorate. The world was full of scanners, monitors, and other data-recording devices that took down impartial, impersonal accounts of the comings and goings of individuals, and with luck and influence one could tap this ocean of data for one's own needs. Not all the information received was immediately relevant, but Kaufmann sifted it, searching out the patterns. He had a better-than-normal faculty for finding patterns in seemingly random data. And now he had the advantage of his uncle's judicious, practiced eye to aid him in his examination.

He knew by now that Noyes had come in from Evansville and had made contact with Elena some hours before the discorporation of Martin St. John. Now both of them had vanished, but this was not a world in which anyone could stay vanished for long. Keying in to the data banks of the transport terminals, Kaufmann succeeded in learning that Noyes had flown to Evansville at one that afternoon. Closer examination of the passenger list of that flight showed that Elena had been with him.

—Has she been keeping company with Roditis in the past?

"No, never," Mark told his uncle's persona. "They haven't even met."

—Sure?

"Positive. Noyes must have set this up for her."

He puzzled over the *quid pro quo.* He knew that Elena had developed a fascination for Roditis and was yearning to meet him. Very well. She had taken Noyes to the apartment where Martin St. John was being kept. St. John had met a mysterious death. Now Noyes had taken her to Evansville, and, presumably, to an assignation with Roditis.

It looked very much like a sellout.

—Put tracers on Elena right away, Paul advised. Get men busy in Evansville. Pick her up and bring her back here for questioning before she does any more damage.

"I'm already doing so," said Mark.

It took him a few minutes to arrange for the surveillance, not only of Elena, but of Noyes as well. Whenever they left Roditis, they'd be watched and followed, and at the proper moment they'd be taken into custody. Elena had never done anything overtly treacherous before, but Mark knew her capabilities. He visualized a conspiracy involving Noyes, Roditis, Elena, and perhaps even Santoliquido, by which Paul's persona was speedily liberated from the hapless St. John body, and just as speedily reincorporated into John Roditis on second application.

The phone chimed.

He switched it on and found that Risa was calling—not from Europe, surprisingly, but from the New York airport.

"You said you were coming back next week," he told her.

"It's a woman's privilege to change her mind. I got bored over there. And I missed you. There's a hopter waiting, and I'll be home in a hurry."

"Wonderful, Risa."

She looked at him strangely. "Mark? Is there anything wrong?"

"Why?"

"You're very drawn. You've got a peculiar expression on your face."

"It's been a hectic day, love. Too hectic for me even to begin explaining now. I'll fill everything in when you're here."

They broke contact. Mark felt pleased at Risa's arrival. In this time of crisis, with unexpected things happening much too swiftly, it would be good to have her around. A man had to depend on family at a time like this. Paul within him . . . Risa beside him . . .

He smiled. It was a tacit admission that Risa had crossed the borderline from childhood to womanhood these past few weeks. You didn't think of a child as a potential ally. But she had shown him her true strength, first in the matter of obtaining a persona for herself, then by her sleuthing to find Tandy's killer. He would cease to delude himself into thinking she was a child, now. She was a woman, a Kaufmann woman, and he wanted her with him.

She reached the apartment more quickly than he expected. Her European adventures seemed to have sobered and matured her; or was it the presence of an extra mind within her own? She was the same slim, boyish-bodied girl who had left so suddenly for Stockholm not long before, but the cast of her features was different now, the set of her lips, the glow of her eyes.

Paul was astonished.

—This is Risa? he asked, as she entered. Your little girl? Mark, how long was I in storage?

"You haven't seen her for over a year, your time," Mark told his uncle quietly. "It's been a big year for her."

—She's impressive. She has the right bearing. There's no doubt she's a Kaufmann, is there?

Moving gracefully, almost sinuously, in a style she must certainly have learned from Tandy Cushing, Risa crossed the room to her father, embraced him, brushed his lips with hers. Then she stepped back and eyed him searchingly.

"You've changed," she said.

"I was just about to say that to you."

"I know *I've* changed, Mark. I have Tandy with me now. But you—you're different too!"

"In what way?"

"I'm not sure," she said. "Your eyes—your whole way of standing—"

"I told you, Risa, it's been a frightful day. I'm tired."

She shook her head. "It's not fatigue I see. Fatigue subtracts. You've got something extra. You're standing taller. You could almost be Uncle Paul, you know, except that the face and hair are wrong. But you hold yourself the way he did."

Mark smiled feebly. "The Kaufmann genes win out."

"I'm serious. Mark, have you had some sort of persona transplant since I went overseas?"

"Sure," he said. "I bribed Santoliquido and he gave me Uncle Paul." Better to make a joke about it, he thought, and destroy the possibility that she'll sniff out the truth.

"Really, Mark. You *did* get a transplant, didn't you? Maybe not Uncle Paul, but it's someone new. I'm sure of it."

"Sorry, sweet. I don't mean to shake your faith in your own womanly intuition, but it just isn't so. What you think you see in me is the nervous reaction of a bone-tired man." The phone chimed. "Excuse me, will you?"

As he turned away from her, Mark passed a mirror and peered

into its oval depths. Yes, he thought. She's right. There is a change. I didn't notice it, but she, who was away—

The effect was an odd one: as though an overlay of Paul's features had been placed on his own. There was a tension about his facial muscles, perhaps resulting from some new disposition of his features. Mark felt a twinge of distress. If Paul had infiltrated him to this extent so fast, was an attempt at going dybbuk lying just ahead? Paul was, above all else, sly. This present mood of benign cooperation might simply be Paul's way of setting him up for the kill.

And, also, he wasn't happy about the accuracy of Risa's guess. She was a smart girl, of course, but was it so obvious that he had taken possession of Paul's persona? If she saw it, would others? He was ruined unless he maintained the secret.

He picked up the telephone on the fifth chime.

"Yes?"

"Miss Volterra is on her way back to New York," a flat, mechanical voice reported. "She left Evansville twenty minutes ago."

"Is she being tracked?"

"Yes, sir."

"And Noyes?"

"He's with her. They seem to have had a quarrel. He looks upset. And she's the angriest-looking woman I've ever seen."

# 14

Risa went to her apartment a floor above her father's, unpacked, changed, and returned to the lower apartment. She had never seen Mark in such a state before. Usually, no matter how severe the crisis might be, he remained at the center of the storm, calm, self-possessed. Something must be very seriously wrong now.

His appearance puzzled her too. A man of forty didn't alter his whole facial makeup between one week and the next, not unless something of impact had occurred, like taking on a new persona. He denied that he had. Why, then, did he have this new gleam in his eyes, that feral radiance that she associated with Uncle Paul? Jokingly he had told her of bribing Santoliquido and getting Paul's persona. Well, Santoliquido was beyond reach of bribery, no doubt, but such things could be arranged in other ways. Risa was aware of her father's tactics, more so, possibly, than he realized; she had seen him many times bluntly admit some outrageous act simply to make it look inconceivable that he had committed it.

The more she mulled it, the more convinced she was that he had somehow obtained the illegal transplant. Only that could account for the alteration in his bearing. Risa knew quite well that a transplant could bring about such changes; she had seen it in herself since Tandy had come to her. Her look was softer, now, more feminine; she had shed the chip-on-the-shoulder tomboy-ishness in favor of a more seductive approach, and she credited that to Tandy.

In her father's apartment Risa listened in astonishment to the story of the discorporation of Martin St. John.

"You helped to solve Santoliquido's problem for him, you know," Mark told her. His hand tapped his knee in a gesture uncomfortably reminiscent of the old man's. "By hunting down that dybbuk, you handed Santo an empty body at just the right time, and he dumped Paul into it."

"Couldn't you have stopped him?"

"I didn't really want to, Risa. Short of keeping Paul in cold stor-age forever, I had to let him go to someone. I figured it was better that he go to St. John than to Roditis."

"Agreed. But the discorporation—"

"It happened last night. As I reconstruct it, Roditis sent his flunky Noyes to Elena. Elena not only told him where St. John was being kept, but brought him here. Noyes gave St. John a tricky poison. This morning, he and Elena flew out to one of Roditis' headquarters. Now they're on their way back."

"I never trusted that bitch, Mark."

He laughed. "I know. I wrote it off to your monstrous Electra complex."

"Which is genuine. But not so monstrous that it distorts every judgment I make. Elena's worthless, and I've been trying to get you to see it all along. But at least she hasn't done you any real harm. You don't lose anything by St. John's discorporation."

"I do," he said, "if Roditis reapplies for Uncle Paul and gets him."

"But if he's part of this discorporation conspiracy, he'll be sent to erasure himself!"

"If anything can be proven."

"You seem to have reconstructed everything," Risa said.

He nodded. "To my own satisfaction. Not necessarily to that of the quaestorate. I've got to get Elena to admit she cooperated in the murder. That'll allow the quaestors to demand a mindpick of Noyes. If Noyes is picked, he'll incriminate Roditis, and we'll have won—maybe. But it's a tricky road."

"If I were Roditis," Risa said carefully, "I'd get hold of both Elena and Noyes and give their minds a good blanking. That'll cut the line of incrimination before it reaches him."

"I suspect he's done just that. They spent the morning with him in Indiana, and now they're on their way back—most likely with their minds swept clean of last night's fun." He clenched his fists and struck an attitude of anger and determination, incredibly Paul-like. "No matter what happens, Roditis won't get Paul! Maybe he's won this round, maybe he's lost everything—but the persona won't go to him. Somehow. Somehow."

Risa was startled by the depths of her father's agitation. She couldn't see why he was so troubled over this discorporation, annoying and infuriating though it was. His reaction seemed all out of keeping with the event. Yes, Elena had betrayed him. Yes, Roditis had managed to make Uncle Paul available again, just when it seemed the troublesome persona was locked away in St. John for keeps. But that simply meant that the status was back to

233

what it had been a few days ago. Why this frenzy of tension? He was so worked up that he had taken her fully into his confidence, something he had never done before. Risa was flattered by that. It wasn't so long ago—only at the beach party—that he had coolly told her to run along and play, that these things did not concern her. The change in him was so dramatic that it was suspicious.

Why was he worried?

Was he afraid that the investigation of the St. John murder would turn on him? That he might be mindpicked by the quaestors? That they might discover something he wished very much to hide—like the presence in his mind of an illegal Paul Kaufmann persona?

Everything seemed to be coming back to that, Risa observed.

Her father excused himself to take another call. Risa wandered about the apartment, assessing the intricacies of the situation. It seemed imperative to discard the notion that her father was in possession of Uncle Paul's persona. The persona had gone to the empty Martin St. John, hadn't it? Then it couldn't simultaneously have been imprinted on Mark. They took strict precautions against a double transplant of that sort, Risa thought. Sealed the master recording away in a special vault, or something, until it was needed again, if ever it was. In this case, since St. John had been so quickly discorporated, the master would be needed again. But ordinarily, the Paul Kaufmann persona would be passed along as a secondary within its next carnate possessor's persona, and so there'd be no call for reverting to the old master.

Yet that recording of Paul Kaufmann would still exist in the files, yes? And what about all the earlier recordings of him? Surely they weren't thrown away.

Risa began to see vast scope for chicanery within the supposedly foolproof regulations of the Scheffing Institute. She began

234

to see how plausible it was that her father might have obtained a bootlegged transplant of Uncle Paul.

—Go easy, Tandy warned her. You're getting all tied up in this thing.

Risa tried to slip her leash of sudden tensions. She noticed a green-bound volume lying on a table and picked it up idly. It was the *Bardo Thödol,* she discovered with some surprise. The Tibetan Book of the Dead, the cult book of the new religion that was sweeping eastward from California. She hadn't known her father owned one. This copy looked brand-new. Risa touched the activator stud and flipped through the book, wondering how people could get so enmeshed in the silly stuff merely because rebirth had become a practicality. To dig up an obscure branch of decadent Buddhism, with absolutely no relevance to the Scheffing process, and to devote time and energy and money to its study—

"From the Eastern Realm of Preeminent Happiness," she read, "the Buddha Vajra-Sattva, the Divine Father-Mother, with the attendant deities, will come to shine upon thee. From the Southern Realm endowed with Glory, the Buddha Ratna-Sambhava, the Divine Father-Mother, with the attendant deities, will come to shine upon thee. From the Happy Western Realm of Heaped-up Lotuses, the Buddha Amitabha, the Divine Father-Mother, along with the attendant deities, will come to shine upon thee. From the Northern Realm of Perfected Good Deeds, the Buddha Amogha-Siddhi, the Divine Father-Mother, along with the attendants will come, amidst a halo of rainbow light, to shine upon thee at this very moment."

Her father returned to the room. Risa held out the book and said, "Mark, what's this?"

"I visited the big lamasery in San Francisco when I was on

the Coast. They gave it to me as a souvenir." He shrugged the book aside. "They've picked up Elena and Noyes at the airport. Elena claims she was on her way to see me anyway. She'll be here any minute."

"And Noyes?"

"He's being brought along separately, and not so willingly. I want to keep him apart from Elena until I've heard her story. I've arranged for him to be held upstairs in your apartment for a little while. All right?"

"I suppose. But where am I going to stay?"

"Right here with me," Mark said. "I'll need your assistance." He tossed her a recording cube. "Get every word of the conversation onto this, and make sure Elena doesn't see you doing it. Also, get ready to jump her if she tries to attack. I'll have her scanned for concealed weapons before she's brought in, but she'll still have her fingernails."

Risa felt a tremor of delight at receiving these responsibilities from her father. She said, "Do you really think you'll learn anything from Elena or Noyes, now that they've been out where Roditis could blank them?"

"I can't say. I doubt that he'd be foolish enough to let them get away with their memories intact. But big men sometimes slip up in the details." A signal flashed at the door. "Elena's here."

He had her sent in—without any of the guards who had picked her up and accompanied her here. Risa was taken aback by the fury in her eyes; Elena seemed to be bubbling with wrath. She was dressed in what was for her a plain, even dowdy costume, and she strode into the room with a vigor far removed from her usual languid saunter.

"Mark! Oh, Mark, I've got so much to tell you!" she burst out.

"I imagine you have," Mark said. He shot a glance at Risa, who had quietly switched on the recording cube. Risa nodded.

Elena looked at her too. "In private," she said.

"You can speak in front of Risa. She's already aware of what's happened. At least, she knows as much about it as I do. But you must know a lot more."

Color came to Elena's cheeks. She looked clearly uncomfortable about Risa's presence. There was an exchange of glares.

Mark said, "I want to know what took place in this apartment on Thursday, Elena."

Elena paced the room in barely suppressed rage. "For most of the day, I have no idea. Martin St. John was here, in the guest bedroom, watched over by a squad of robots."

"Yes. Then?"

"Charles Noyes came to me. He said he had important business to discuss with St. John. He begged me and begged me until I agreed to bring him here."

"That was a grave mistake, Elena."

"I know, Mark. But I brought him. We went into St. John's bedroom together."

"You saw St. John? What condition was he in?"

"Alive," said Elena. "Fatigued, but doing well. Your uncle was working hard to get control over the body. Noyes asked me to leave him alone with St. John for a few minutes. I did. Very shortly Noyes came out of the room. St. John was screaming. He was having peculiar convulsions. Noyes left the apartment, and soon St. John was dead."

"Would you say he was murdered by Noyes?"

"That's reasonable to assume," Elena admitted.

"How did Noyes explain what had happened?"

"He said St. John had had a kind of stroke."

"Did you notify the quaestorate?" Mark asked.

Elena shook her head. "I stayed here for a while after Noyes had left. Then I went home. I notified no one."

"Not even me."

"Not even you, Mark."

"You helped Noyes discorporate St. John, then," Mark said.

"No." Elena's nostrils flared in anger. "I had no idea he would do such a thing! I swear it, Mark! I was wrong to let him in here, to allow him to be alone with St. John, but I never suspected he meant to murder him!"

"Perhaps," said Mark. "But in any case your actions are strange. First you let a known agent of Roditis into my house and give him carte blanche to murder my guest. Then you rush off without calling the authorities. And the following morning you fly away to see Roditis himself. You spent a couple of hours in Evansville today, didn't you? Didn't you, Elena?"

"Yes," she said hoarsely. "But I was never working for Roditis. I had no part in this murder, except through stupidity in giving Noyes access. I'll take a mindpick to prove it. Let the quaestors pick all they want."

"I will," he assured her.

"If Roditis had obtained my help in discorporating St. John, don't you think he would have blanked me while I was in Evansville?"

Kaufmann conceded the point. Clearly Elena hadn't been blanked, which meant that Roditis had no knowledge of her status as an accessory. "But what were you doing there, then?"

"You won't like the answer, Mark."

"Tell me anyway."

"Not in front of your daughter."

"Risa can hear it."

"What I have to say is—not complimentary to you," Elena said. "You would prefer not to have anyone but yourself hear it."

"I'll take my chances."

"Well, then," Elena said, "I went to Evansville to make love with Roditis. I've desired him for months. This was my opportunity. You were away. Noyes was with me, and he was flying to Evansville, and I asked him to take me along. While Noyes was being blanked by Roditis' men, I went to Roditis and—"

"Noyes was blanked?" Kaufmann said leadenly.

"Of course. Roditis knew that he'd probably be traced to St. John. Noyes had to be blanked so that the trail wouldn't lead back to Roditis. So I went to Roditis. He would not have anything to do with me. He refused me!" She was flushed, agitated, her breasts heaving wildly. "I went close to him, and he pushed me, like *this*—away. So it was all for nothing. I humiliated myself to him and he pushed me."

There was a lengthy silence in the room. Risa feared that Elena might hear the throbbing of the recording cube, so silent did everything become. But Elena stood transfixed, hearing nothing but the thunder of her own indignation.

—She was turned down, Tandy said. No wonder she's so mad now! She's willing to tell your father anything, just to get even with Roditis.

Risa agreed. She could not help feel a pang of pity for Elena in this moment of her defeat. To be spurned by Roditis, to have to come back here and reveal not only her promiscuity but her rejection—how that must sting!

Mark said finally, "Noyes was definitely blanked, eh? You're sure of that."

"Positive. He will be of no use to you as a witness. I am the only one who can testify," Elena said.

Mark shook his head. "You didn't see the crime. We've already got evidence that you and Noyes were at the apartment at the time of the discorporation, but the best we could hope for from that would be to get a mindpick on Noyes. Which will come up blank. We couldn't possibly get any court to grant a mindpick of Roditis on your suspicions alone. We're stopped, Elena."

"No! No! Fight, Mark! We all know Roditis was behind this murder! Put your best lawyers to work!"

Mark smiled coolly. "You'd love to see Roditis ruined, wouldn't you, Elena? But only because he turned you down. If he had slept with you, you'd be selling me out right and left, wouldn't you?"

"Don't deal in ifs, Mark. I've told you the truth. You're free to hate me, free to throw me aside, but don't preach to me. All right?"

"All right, Elena. Will you go into that bedroom and wait there? I want to talk to Noyes now."

"He's here?"

"They're holding him upstairs. Please stay out of sight while I'm questioning him."

"You will get nothing from him. Nothing!"

"Please," Mark said.

Elena entered the bedroom and closed the door.

Risa's eyes met her father's. Mark looked wearier than ever, but that strange Paul-like effect was even more pronounced. He appeared to be drawing on an inner reservoir of will.

He picked up the phone and asked to have Charles Noyes brought in.

Noyes edged into the room like a beast brought to bay by hounds. The strain was getting fearful. All the way back from Evansville he had pretended to Elena that he was Kravchenko, to keep her from turning on him again. And meanwhile Kravchenko had recovered from his shock and was awake again, fighting more strongly than ever to gain control, now that he had had a night's taste of freedom.

Kravchenko hammered at Noyes' forehead. Noyes' clothing was pasted to his skin by the sweat of fear. His knees were watery. His eyes moved in quick birdlike flickers, nervously, warily. He knew he was caught, knew that all was over. Elena, in her fury with Roditis, was determined to spill everything. And he, unblanked, was caught in the middle, his mind full of unwanted knowledge that was sure to come out.

Guilty of willful discorporation. Sentenced to erasure.

Not so bad, perhaps. Peace at last. No more turns of the wheel of karma. Oblivion, nirvana. At-one-ment.

Mark Kaufmann confronted him. The financier showed evidences of strain. His face was different, Noyes noticed immediately. Well, no doubt mine is, too. We've all been living on this anvil so long, taking blow after blow.

And there on the couch the daughter sat, Risa, the sexy little minx. She also looked different, older, shrewder, more predatory. They'll devour me alive. Elena's told them everything. I've been betrayed by all of them. Why is she doing this? Did Roditis turn her down? Why couldn't he have bedded her? Why would he choose to antagonize her this way? Didn't he see that by scorning her, he was inviting her to tell the story? I should have let him know that it was through Elena that I had gained access to St. John. But he hustled me off to be blanked while Kravchenko was still running me, and obviously Kravchenko didn't tell him. And afterward there was no way I could, because I wasn't supposed to know anything about the discorporation any more.

Kaufmann said, "I believe you've been in this apartment before, Mr. Noyes."

"Well—"

"Recently. Last night, in fact. Isn't that so?"

"Who gave you that idea?" Noyes said with his last shred of bravado.

"You came here late last evening in the company of Miss Elena Volterra," Kaufmann said. "At your insistence she admitted you to the bedroom of Martin St. John. There, alone with him, you introduced a small but lethal quantity of a drug known as cyclophosphamide-8 into his metabolism, causing a speedy but horrible discorpor—"

*"No!"* Noyes screamed. "I didn't do it! It isn't so!"

"We have mindpick evidence against you."

"You don't! You're bluffing!"

Kaufmann said, "We have conclusive mindpick evidence of your guilt, Noyes. Enough to persuade the quaestorate to conduct a mindpick examination of your own memory bank, after which they'll certainly recommend erasure. Of course, if you agree to testify voluntarily, and explain on whose behalf it was that you committed this foul crime, you may receive better treatment from the law."

Noyes shook. Elena had told him everything, then. As he had expected her to do. He was trapped.

—Might as well make a clean breast of it, Kravchenko advised.

"We're prepared to recommend every leniency," said Kaufmann in a soothing voice. "We understand that you were not acting as a free agent when you committed the discorporation of Martin St. John. If you'll aid us in convicting the motivating force behind this crime—"

Of course, thought Noyes. That's what you're after, to nail Roditis! It figures. You don't care about me any more than anyone else does.

He swayed. Waves of disorientation swept his brain. The world was spinning, the center did not hold, everything was shattering. Six Mark Kaufmanns faced him. Six Risas. His eyes would not focus. It seemed to him he heard Kravchenko's vicious laughter, rising in volume, becoming a howl of triumph.

The flask of carniphage in Noyes' breast pocket seemed to blaze against his skin.

Take it, he told himself. You've threatened to do it for so long— just self-dramatization, isn't it? But now, this is the right moment. Pull it out, gulp it down. They've got you anyway. He talks of leniency, but he's lying. You'll be erased after you've been mindpicked. But at least you can save Roditis. There's no solid evidence against him. Roditis is a bastard, but you owe him your loyalty, you always have, and if you drink the carniphage before Kaufmann gets anything out of you it'll take Roditis off the hook.

—You're a bigger fool than I think you are if you can worry about Roditis at a time like this, Kravchenko burst in.

Once again the persona had tapped his thoughts. The last time that had happened, it had signaled imminent ejection.

—Cook Roditis' goose for him, Kravchenko urged. Tell Kaufmann everything you know. Why not? You don't owe anything to Roditis except credit for wrecking you.

"No," said Noyes. "I won't."

"You won't what?" asked Mark Kaufmann.

"I think he's talking to his persona," Risa said. "Look at his face! He's cracking up!"

Noyes made a heavy gargling sound. It was beginning again: Kravchenko rising from captivity, uncoiling, filling his mind, grasping the levers of control.

"Stop it!" Noyes shrieked. "Let me alone! I won't let you—get out of there—"

He was silent.

Kravchenko said coolly, "If you don't mind, Kaufmann, we'll call this inquisition to a halt right now. I'd like to consult my lawyer. And I'll answer the questions put to me by the quaestors, not by you. Is it understood?"

"It's a different voice," said Kaufmann. "A different persona. Calmer—the eyes—"

"Will you excuse me, please?" Kravchenko asked. "You've brought me here by abduction, and I intend to make you pay for it, but this kangaroo court is hereby adjourned. Don't try to prevent me from leaving."

He walked gracefully toward the door.

Risa burst from her seat. *"Dybbuk!"* she yelled. "Don't you see, the persona's gone dybbuk right in front of us!"

The bedroom door opened. Elena appeared, pale, extending a quivering hand. She looked altogether confused. "Jim?" she said. "Noyes? Which are you? What's happening?"

"Quiet, Elena!" Kravchenko said.

In that moment Charles Noyes launched a desperate and instantly successful counterattack. Erupting from the corner of his own mind in which Kravchenko had penned him, Noyes sped through the neural wreckage within his skull, taking Kravchenko off guard. They grappled. Kravchenko, not as thoroughly in control as he had believed, was thrown from command, hurled down only moments after his brief triumph.

Noyes sagged to the floor and crouched there.

"Listen to me," he said, shaping the words with terrible effort. "This is Noyes again. Noyes. See, the right voice? He didn't quite reach dybbuk. A good try, that's all. Listen. Are you recording this, Kaufmann?"

"Every word."

"Good. I've been an idiot. I've let everyone use me. But no more. My mind's my own. Last night—Roditis sent me here. John Roditis of Roditis Securities. With orders to kill St. John.

So that he could reapply for the Paul Kaufmann persona. I gave St. John a drug—cyclo—cyclophosphamide-8. I confess this of my own—free—will."

He could not sustain even the crouching position any longer. Now he lay on his left side, half his body limp.

"I repeat: I killed St. John at Roditis' orders. Mindpick Roditis and you'll see it's so. Two favors, please. Don't let Kravchenko have another carnate trip. You saw—he almost went dybbuk. *Did* go dybbuk, for a minute. And also—for me—no more trips either. Just sleep. I want to get off the wheel."

I ought to utter a mantra now, Noyes thought. Go out with a flourish. *Om mani padme hum.* But why bother?

His hand went into his breast pocket.

He felt Kravchenko fighting him, furiously trying to seize their shared body again. But Noyes held him off. His coordination was almost destroyed, yet he was able to get his hands on the beloved flask of carniphage, fondled so often, so sensually, his constant companion, his dearest friend.

He brought it to his mouth. He bit down.

The flask shattered and its contents spurted down his throat.


Mark Kaufmann stared in shock at the writhing, deliquescing thing on the carpet.

"Carniphage," he said thickly. "Risa—Elena—don't look!"

Elena had fled. But Risa was watching the process of decay with somber fascination. Kaufmann did not try to cover her eyes.

Surely Noyes must be dead. The inward rot was nearing the

surface; his body was chaos. Yet still it moved, jerking and twitching as it traveled its one-way road to destruction.

Risa said, "Why did he confess? He was trying to be defiant at first."

"He was showing everyone. Roditis. Kravchenko. Right at the end, he finally found a little strength."

The limbs were flowing into shapelessness. The motions of the body were ceasing.

"Will that confession be any good?" Risa asked.

Mark nodded slowly. "The voiceprints will show that it was really Noyes speaking. The recording will show that he was nearly ejected by a dybbuk, fought back, blurted his story, and killed himself. It'll be good enough to convince the quaestors that Roditis should be mindpicked."

"And then?"

"They'll erase him," Kaufmann said. He felt little triumph, somehow. He took one more look at the ghastliness on the floor, and then went to put in a call to the quaestors.

# 15

It was July now. A season of stifling weather had set in, beyond the capacity of the weather controllers to handle, and many people had fled to cooler climes. Risa remained in New York. The trial of John Roditis had just ended, and now there was a great deal for her to do.

Roditis had been found guilty, of course. Noyes' recorded testimony had induced the quaestorate to seek a mindpick against him, and the motion had been granted. Roditis' lawyers had undertaken a delaying action based on the ancient constitutional principal of freedom from self-incrimination; but the legality of the mindpick was firmly established, and Roditis was put to the test. His complicity in the deliberate discorporation of Martin St. John was undeniable after that.

The defense tactics shifted. Now the lawyers asserted that, while Roditis and Noyes had undoubtedly conspired to destroy the St. John body, there was no injured party, since St. John was not his own body's tenant. The only occupant of the body, the persona of Paul Kaufmann, was legally dead and therefore not capable of suffering discorporation.

It was a fine point, and gave the jurists of the quaestorate considerable exercise. It caused a good deal of embarrassment for Francesco Santoliquido, too, since he was responsible for creating the anomaly of the deliberate dybbuk. In the end, the decision went against Roditis, but the charge was reduced from murder to antisocial actions of the first degree. Which, when Roditis was found guilty, resulted in these sentences:

- Forfeiture of citizenship and civic privileges.
- Mandatory destruction of any recorded Roditis personae on file with the Scheffing Institute.
- Erasure of all present personae carried by Roditis, and their return to the soul bank for redistribution to others.
- Five years of corrective therapy, including, if needed, a total reorientation of personality to remove aggressive impulses.

"He's finished now," Mark Kaufmann said to his daughter as the verdicts were announced. He'll come out of the therapy a broken man—polite, amiable, lacking in purpose and direction. A pleasant nobody. A nothing. A shell."

"It seems like such a waste," said Risa. "All that drive—all that energy thrown away—"

"He was too dangerous to remain as he was, Risa. He had a greatness, I'll admit, but his ambitions weren't tempered by the moral sense. He was without a governor."

"And you? And Uncle Paul?"

Kaufmann looked at her sharply. "We have our family traditions. We have our sense of what is honorable. Roditis was a wild beast. Now he'll be tamed. There's no comparison between a Roditis and one of us, Risa. None."

Risa had private reservations about that. She had no wish to anger her father; but it seemed to her that the real difference between the shattered, defeated Roditis and the triumphant Mark Kaufmann was more a matter of luck and diplomacy than of breeding and honor. Roditis had overreached himself, and Mark had destroyed him. But Mark's methods, though they stopped short at murder, had hardly been gentle.

Roditis disappeared behind the fortress walls of Belle Isle Sanatorium for corrective therapy. No one would ever again see the old John Roditis in public, that man seething with vitality and shrewdness. When Roditis emerged, several years hence, he would still be a wealthy man, but he would be an aimless, smiling ruin, cheerfully acquiescing in the decisions of the court-appointed trustees who managed his financial empire.

A great waste of dynamism, Risa decided.

Perhaps, she thought, such a squandering might be in some way avoided.

On the hottest day of that July heat wave, soon after the sentencing of John Roditis, Risa brought her hopter down in the employee lot of the Scheffing Institute building. She parked it deftly and crossed the sweltering strip of ferroconcrete in a hurry. It was three in the afternoon; the first shift of technicians was about to leave.

Within the building Risa picked up the first telephone she came to and requested to speak to a certain employee. Moments later, his face appeared on the screen.

He looked baffled.

"Hello, Leonards. Remember me?"

He was young, pale, good-looking, pinch lines forming between his eyebrows. He moistened his lips. "M-Miss Kaufmann?"

"That's right, Leonards. Go to the head of the class."

He forced an uneasy smile. "Is there something wrong? Can I be of service?"

"No, there's nothing wrong, and yes, you can be of service. You're finished working for the day, aren't you?"

"Yes."

"Good. My hopter's parked in Employee Lot D. Meet me there right away and we'll take a little trip."

"But—"

"I'll be waiting, Leonards!"

He did not disappoint her. He did not dare.

Looking mystified, he entered the hopter, taking his seat beside her as she indicated. The little craft lifted and headed north. Risa said, "You did an excellent job with my transplant, Leonards. Tandy and I are very happy together."

"That's good, Miss Kaufmann. Perhaps you could tell me—"

"Where we're heading? Of course. We're going uptown. To my apartment."

He scarcely seemed to believe any of this was happening to him. His posture was rigid; he looked straight ahead, never venturing a glance in her direction. He was terrified of her.

She brought the hopter in for a smooth landing at her home lot. Minutes later, they entered her apartment.

"Take a good look around," she told him. "It's nice, isn't it? Ever been in a place like this before?"

"N-no, Miss Kaufmann."

"Call me Risa. Why are you so frightened, Leonards? You're a big, handsome young fellow, aren't you? A skilled technician, a man with a bright future? Are you married?"

"Yes, Miss Kaufmann."

"Children?"

"One child. We're going to have another after my next incre-ment comes through."

"Fine, Leonards. I'm sure you're a wonderful family man. And I'm glad to know you're so virile." She put her hand to her shoulder, touched a stud. Her light summer clothing fell away in a rustling swirl. She stood before him incandescently nude, and he gaped at the sudden sight.

He backed away from her, shielding his eyes.

"Come here, Leonards," she said in a husky voice Tandy Cush-ing had taught her how to use. "You're not really afraid. You want me, don't you? Admit it. I'm yours for the taking. The experience of a lifetime. A Kaufmann in your arms. Why run away?"

"Please—I don't understand—"

She swept up against him. She took his hand and put it to her small breasts. Her own hand traveled expertly over his body. Leonards gasped. Leonards moaned. Leonards shook his head and tried to push her away, but the attempt was not a success.

"I want you, Leonards! What's your first name?"

"Harry."

"Harry! Harry! Harry! Love me, Harry!"

She tugged at him and they toppled to the floor. Her lithe body entwined itself with his. Urgently she awakened his desire and banished his timidity.

"Harry," she whispered. *"Harry!"*

He made a sound that was half a protest, half an acceptance. And then, with sudden desperate willingness, he pulled her against him.

He was not very good, Risa concluded. But he was appeal-ingly earnest.

When it was over, she slipped away from him and got nimbly to her feet. He lay still, rumpled and glassy-eyed.

"You've just committed an act of rape," Risa told him. "Your helpless victim was a girl of the highest social position, less than seventeen years old. You'll get your mind blotted out for a crime like that."

Leonards came to a sitting position, and the color drained from his face a moment, then returned in a crimson rush. "What are you saying?"

"I'm explaining to you the nature of the trouble you're in. Forcibly entering my hopter while I was visiting the Scheffing Institute, compelling me to bring you here, disrobing me, inducing me through superior strength to submit to sexual violation—oh, it's bad, Leonards, it's very bad!"

"I feel like I'm in a dream," he whispered.

"It's real enough. I'll have the quaestors here any minute."

"Why are you doing this?"

She crouched before him, her face close to his. "Would you like to avoid going to trial? Would you like me to forgive you for your audacity in perpetrating this hideous rape?"

"What do you want from me?"

"A favor," she said harshly. "A small favor, and I'll forget all about what happened here today, and leave you with your memories of pleasure."

"What kind of favor?"

"You'll have to break the rules of the Scheffing Institute," she said. "But that's a much smaller crime than raping a girl my age, and if you're smart and lucky you'll get away with it. There's a certain persona I want, Leonards. Get it for me from the files, just borrow it for a little while tomorrow. And transplant it to me. That's all I ask. I'll come to the tower, and you'll handle the transplant, and we'll call it quits. But we'll have to move swiftly, because this particular persona recording is due to be destroyed very soon. All right, Leonards? Do we have a deal?"

"Everything's settled, then," Mark Kaufmann said. "My uncle's persona remains in storage indefinitely."

"Yes," said Santoliquido. "Which is to say, at least another year or two."

"Long enough for some of the voltage to bleed out of the dynamo, at any rate. He'll be less formidable coming back then. If he comes back at all."

Santoliquido shrugged. "I'll hold him in storage until a qualified recipient appears, Mark. And with Roditis permanently disqualified, it might be a long, long time. You don't need to worry about that."

"Fine. See you at my party on Saturday?"

"Of course," said Santoliquido. "I'll reach Dominica about noon, I suppose. It'll be a novelty, going south to the tropics to find cooler weather. My best to Elena, yes?"

"Of course."

Kaufmann broke the contact. He smiled, leaned back, touched the tips of his fingers together. All was well at last. Roditis was neutralized, entirely out of the scene. Santoliquido, who had come out of this affair very poorly indeed, was helpless before his wishes. There would be no extra Uncle Paul at liberty to interfere now. Elena, a chastened woman, had settled into something very much like fidelity. Risa, taking on new depth and maturity day by day, had ripened into a fitting Kaufmann heiress, ready to assume new responsibilities in the family empire. And he himself was home free with his uncle's potent persona well integrated into his awareness, unknown to the rest of the world.

"How do you like that, you old fox? I've handled things pretty well, haven't I, eh?"

—You've done well for yourself, Paul replied. But don't get overconfident. Smugness was Roditis' undoing.

"Don't worry about me," Mark replied. "I try to calculate all the angles. And with you in there helping me, we shouldn't miss very many of them."

—There's always the unpredictable. Be on guard for it.

"Mark?" It was Risa's voice, outside. "I'm here, Mark."

"Come in," he said.

She entered his office. In her sketchy summer wrap she looked crisp and cool, and she carried herself with a no-nonsense self-possession that he admired greatly. Here was the one person in the world who mattered most to him; and also the one person to whom he might be vulnerable. He had an idea that Risa suspected what he had done with Paul's persona. She knew Paul's mannerisms, and of course she knew his own, and she seemed conscious that a fusion had taken place. But after the first day she had ceased to betray any suspicions. Mark had no way of telling what was going on behind the smooth mask of his daughter's face. Somehow, though, he felt certain that she knew the truth.

"I'm here for a business discussion," Risa announced.

"What kind of business?"

"Preliminary business, really. I'd like to get some idea of the family assets. What we have where, in whose name, what slice of equity in each."

Kaufmann nodded. "It's time we went over all that anyway, I suppose. I mean to bring you much more closely into our activities. To groom you for the time when you're running the show. The world of business genuinely interests you, eh, Risa?"

"You know it does. And now that Roditis is through, we can begin to make a new move, Mark. I'd like to close in on that Latin American electrical empire of his. I've been thinking, we could undercut the Roditis trustees by a takeover of the company that makes the transmission pylons, and then—"

"Do you have a cold, Risa?"

"Why?"

"Your voice sounds odd. Deeper. Hoarser."

She shook her head. "That's just Tandy's influence, I guess. She must have had a very lush contralto, and she's trying to pitch my voice down there too. You know how it is, the way a persona influences the host in little ways, certain mannerisms—"

"Yes," Kaufmann said. "I know."

"Very well, then. If we can get a grasp on the pylon company, we'll have Roditis Securities caught between Scylla and Charybdis, and—"

"Between who and whom?"

"Scylla and Charybdis," she repeated impatiently. "The monster and the whirlpool. Book Twelve of *The Odyssey*. By Homer."

"Yes. I know. I didn't realize you were a student of Homer, Risa."

"Every civilized person should have a deep knowledge of Homer," she said. "Has there ever been a greater poet? A man with a more vivid imagination? There are lessons we can learn from him even today." Risa laughed self-consciously. "Back to the transmission pylons, though. Here's what I have in mind—"

Mark Kaufmann watched his daughter construct an elaborate holding-company scheme with quick scrawled strokes of stylus against pad. But he paid little attention to her financial theories just now. A sudden implausible notion sent a chill of disbelief through him.

Homer? Holding companies? Transmission pylons?

A deeper voice?

No, he thought. No, it isn't possible. She wouldn't—she couldn't—

From somewhere far away, Paul Kaufmann's persona delivered a silent booming laugh.

—There's always the unpredictable, Mark.

Quietly Mark agreed. He peered closely at Risa, seeking for signs, for proof, for confirmation of this strange and frightening fantasy of his. If it were true, a new, invincible force had entered their family, and all plans must be reconsidered. But it could not be true. It could not be true. It *could not* be true.

"There we are," Risa finished. She shoved the pad toward her father. "What do you say, Mark? How does the plan look to you?"

"I'll have to think about it," he said warily. "But it's worth considering. If we can use Roditis' own way of thinking to cut chunks out of his holdings, why not?"

Risa grinned. She pointed to the somber, brooding portrait of Uncle Paul hanging behind her father's desk. "I think *he'd* go for the idea. I think the old buccaneer would be very amused by it. Perhaps a little proud of me. Perhaps even a little jealous."

"He is," Mark Kaufmann said, and looked beyond his window to see the sky suddenly grow dark with the fury of a summer storm.

# THE SECOND TRIP

# 1

Even the street felt wrong beneath his feet. Something oddly rubbery about the pavement, too much give in it. As though they had changed the mix of the concrete during the four years of his troubles. A new futuristic stuff, the 2011-model sidewalk, bouncy and weird. But no. The sidewalk looked the same. *He* was the new stuff. As though, when they had altered him, they had altered his stride too, changing the swing of his knees, changing the pivot of his hips. Now he wasn't sure of his movements. He didn't know whether he was supposed to hit the pavement with his heel or his toe. Every step was an adventure in discovery. He felt clumsy and uncertain within his own body.

Or *was* it his own? How far did the Rehab people go, anyway, in reconstructing your existence? Maybe a total brain transplant. Scoop out the old gray mass, run a jolt of juice through it, stick it into a waiting new body. And put somebody else's rehabilitated brain in your vacated skull? The old wine in a new decanter. No. No. That isn't how they work at all. This is the body I was born with. I'm having a little difficulty in coordination, true, but that's only to be expected. The first day out on the street again. Tuesday the something of May, 2011. Clear blue sky over the towers of Manhattan North. So I'm a little clumsy at first. So? So? Didn't they say something like this would happen?

Easy, now. Get a grip. Can't you remember how you used to walk? Just be natural.

Step. Step. Step. Into the rhythm of it. Heel and toe, heel and toe. Step. *Step.* That's the way! One-and-two-and-*one*-and-two-and-*one*-and-two. This is how Paul Macy walks. Proudly down the goddam street. Shoulders square. Belly sucked in. Thirty-nine years old. Prime of life. Strong as an—what did they say, strong as an ox? Yes. Ox. Ox. Opportunity beckons you. A second trip, a second start. The bad dream is over; now you're awake. Step. Step. What about your arms? Let them swing? Hands in pockets? Don't worry about that, just go on walking. Let the arms look after themselves. You'll get the hang of it. You're out on the street, you're free, you've been rehabilitated. On your way to pick up your job assignment. Your new career. Your new life. Step. Step.

One-and-two-and-*one*-and-two.

He couldn't avoid the feeling that everybody was looking at him. That was probably normal too, the little touch of paranoia. After all, he had the Rehab badge in his lapel, the glittering bit of yellow metal advertising his status as a reconstruct job. The image of the new shoots rising from the old stump, warning everybody who had known him in the old days to be tactful. No one was supposed to greet him by his former name. No one was supposed to acknowledge the existence of his past. The Rehab badge was intended as a mercy, as a protection against the prodding of absent memories. But of course it attracted attention too. People looked at him—absolute strangers, so far as he knew, though he couldn't be sure—people looked and wondered, Who is this guy, what did he do that got him sentenced to Rehab? The triple ax murderer. Raped a nine-year-old with pinking shears. Embezzled ten million. Poisoned six old ladies for their heirlooms. Dynamited the Chartres Cathedral. All those eyes on him, speculating. Imagining his sins. The badge warned them he was something special.

There was no place to hide from those eyes. Macy moved all the way over to the curb and walked just along the edge. Right inside the strip of gleaming red metal ribbon that was embedded in the pavement, the stuff that flashed the magnetic pulses that kept autos from going out of control and jumping up on the sidewalk. It was no good here either. He imagined that the drivers zipping by were leaning out to stare at him. Crossing the pavement on an inward diagonal, he found another route for himself, hugging the sides of buildings. That's right, Macy, skulk along. Keep one shoulder higher than the other and try to fool yourself into thinking that it shields your face. Hunch your head. Jack the Ripper out for a stroll. Nobody's looking at you. This is New York, remember? You could walk down the street with your dong out of your pants and who'd notice? Not here. This city is full of Rehabs. Why should anybody care about you and your sordid eradicated past? Cut the paranoia, Paul.

*Paul.*

That was a hard part too. The new name. *I am Paul Macy.* A sweet compact name. Who dreamed that one up? Is there a computer down in the guts of the earth that fits syllables together and makes up new names for the Rehab boys? *Paul Macy.* Not bad. They could have told me I was Dragomir Slivovitz. Izzy Levine. Leroy Rastus Williams. But instead they came up with Paul Macy.

I suppose for the holovision job. You need a name like that for the networks. *"Good evening, this is Dragomir Slivovitz, bringing you the eleven-o'clock news. Speaking from his weekend retreat at the Lunar White House, the President declared—"* No. They had coined the right kind of name for his new career. Very fucking Anglo-Saxon.

Suddenly he felt a great need to see the face he was wearing. He couldn't remember what he looked like. Coming to an abrupt stop, he turned to his left and picked his reflection off the mirror-bright pilaster beside an office building's entrance. He caught the image of a wide-cheeked, thin-lipped, standard sort of Anglo-Saxon face, with a big chin and a lot of soft windblown yellow-brown hair and deep-set pale-blue eyes. No beard, no mustache. The face seemed strong, a little bland, decently proportioned, and wholly unfamiliar. He was surprised to see how relaxed he looked: no tension lines in the forehead, no scowl, no harshness of the eyes. Macy absorbed all this in a fraction of a second; then whoever had been walking behind him, caught short by his sudden halt, crashed into his side and shoulder. He whirled. A girl. His hand went quickly to her elbow, steadying her. More her fault than his: she ought to look where she's going. Yet he felt guilty. "I'm terribly sor—"

"Nat," she said. "Nat Hamlin, for God's sake!"


Someone was slipping a long cold needle into his eye. Under the lid, very very delicately done, up and up and around the top of the eyeball, past the tangled ropes of the nerves, and on into his brain. The needle had some sort of extension; it seemed to expand telescopically, sliding through the wrinkled furrowed folded mass of soft tissue, skewering him from forehead to skullcap. A tiny blaze of sparkling light wherever the tip of the needle touched. Ah, so, ve cut out dis, und den ve isolate dis, and ve chop here a little, ja, ja, ist gut! And the pain. Oh, Christ, the pain, the pain, the pain, the fire running down every neuron and jumping every synapse, the pain! Like having a thousand teeth pulled all at once. They said it absolutely wouldn't hurt at all. Those lying fuckers.

They had taught him how to handle a situation like this. He had to be polite but firm. Politely but firmly he said, "I'm sorry, but you're mistaken. My name's Paul Macy."

The girl had recovered from the shock of their collision. She took a couple of steps back and studied him carefully. He and she now constituted an encapsulated pocket of stasis on the busy sidewalk; people were flowing smoothly around them. She was tall and slender, with long straight red hair, troubled green eyes, fine features. A light dusting of freckles on the bridge of her nose. Full lips. No makeup. She wore a scruffy blue-checked spring coat. She looked as if she hadn't been sleeping well lately. He guessed she was in her late twenties. Very pale. Attractive in a tired, frayed way. She said, "Don't play around with me. I know you're Nat Hamlin. You're looking good, Nat."

Each time she said the name he felt the needles wiggle behind his eyeballs.

"Macy. Paul Macy."

"I don't like this game. It's a cruel one, Nat. Where have you been? What is it, five years?"

"Won't you please try to understand?" he asked. He glanced meaningfully at his Rehab badge. Her eyes didn't follow his.

"I understand that you're trying to hurt me, Nat. It wouldn't be the first time."

"I don't know you at all, miss."

"You don't know me at all. You don't know me at all."

"I don't know you at all. Right."

"Lissa Moore."

"I'm sorry."

"What kind of trip are you on, Nat?"

"My second one," Macy said.

"Your—second—one?"

He touched the badge. This time she saw it.

"Rehab?" she said. Blinking a couple of times: obviously adjusting her frame of reference. Color in her cheeks now. Biting her lip, abashed.

He nodded. "I've just come out. Now do you understand? I don't know you. I never did."

"Christ," she said. "We had such good times, Nat."

"Paul."

"How can I call you that?"

"It's my name now."

"We had such good times," she said. "Before you went away. Before I came apart. I'm not working much now, you know. It's been pretty bad."

"I'm sorry," he told her, shifting his weight uneasily. "It really isn't good for me to spend much time with people from my first trip. Or any time at all with them, actually."

"You don't want to go somewhere and talk?"

"I can't. I mustn't."

"Maybe some other time?" she asked. "When you're a little more accustomed to things?"

"I'm afraid not," he said. Firmly but politely. "The whole point is that I've made a total break with the past, and I mustn't try to repair that break, or let anyone repair it for me. I'm on an entirely new trip now, can you see that?"

"I can see it," she murmured, "but I don't want it. I'm having a lot of trouble these days, and you can help me, Nat. If only—"

"*Paul.* And I'm not in any shape for helping anybody. I can barely help myself. Look at how my hand is shaking."

"And you've started to sweat. Your forehead's all wet."

"There's a tremendous strain. I'm conditioned to keep away from people out of the past."

"It kills me when you say that. *People out of the past.* Like a guillotine coming down. You loved me. And I loved you. Love. Still. Love. So when you say—"

"Please."

"You, please." She was trembling, hanging onto his sleeve. Her eyes, going glassy, flitted and flickered a thousand times a second. "Let's go somewhere for a drink, for a smoke, for a talk. I realize about the Rehab thing, but I need you too much. Please. Please."

"I can't."

"*Please.*" And she leaned toward him, her fingertips clutching hard into the bones of his right wrist, and he felt a baffling sensation in the top of his skull. A sort of intrusion. A tickling. A mild glow of heat Along with it came a disturbing blurring of identity, a doubling of self, so that for a moment he was knocked free of his moorings. Paul Hamlin. Nat Macy. In the core of his mind erupted a vivid scene in garish colors: himself crouched over some sort of keyboard, and this girl standing naked on the far side of a cluttered room with her hands pressed to her cheeks. *Scream,* he was saying. *Go on, Lissa, scream. Give us a good one.* The image faded. He was back on a street in Manhattan North, but he was having trouble seeing, everything out of focus and getting more bleary each second. His legs were wobbly. A spike of pain under his breastbone. Maybe a heart attack, even. "Please," the girl was saying. "Don't turn me away, Nat Nat, what's happening? Your face is so red!"

"The conditioning—" he said, gasping.

The pressure eased. The girl backed away from him, touching the tips of her knuckles to her lips. As the distance between them increased he felt better. He clung to the side of the building with one hand and made a little shooing gesture at her with the other. Go on. Away. Out of my life. Whoever you were, there's no room now. She nodded. She continued to back away. He had a last brief glimpse of her tense, puffy-eyed face, and then she was cut off from him by a stream of people. Is this what it's going to be like every time I meet somebody from the old days? But maybe the others won't be like that. They'll respect my badge and pass silently on. Give me a chance to rebuild. It's only fair. She wasn't being fair. Neurotic bitch, putting her troubles above mine. Help me, she kept saying. Please. Please, Nat. As if I could help anybody.

Twenty minutes later he arrived at the network office. Ten minutes overdue, but that was unavoidable. He had needed some time to recover after the encounter with the girl on the street. Let the adrenalin drain out of the system, let the sweat dry. It was important for him to present an unruffled exterior; more important, in fact, than showing up on time the first day. The network people were probably prepared to be tolerant of a little unpunctuality at first, considering all that he had been through. But he had to demonstrate that he had the professional qualities the job demanded. They were hiring him as an act of grace, yes, but it wasn't pure charity: he wouldn't have been accepted if he hadn't been suitable for the job. So he needed to show that he had the surface slickness, the smoothness, that a holovision commentator had to have. Pause to catch the breath. Get the hair tidy. Adjust the collar. Give yourself that seamless, sprayed-on look. You had a nasty shock or two in the street, but now you're feeling much better. All right. Now go in. A confident stride. One-and-two-and-*one*-and-two.

The lobby was dark and cavernous. Screens everywhere, a hundred sensors mounted in the onyx walls, anti-vandal robots poised with bland impersonality to come rolling forth if anybody tried anything troublesome. Standing beneath the security panel, Macy activated one of the screens and a cheery female face appeared. Just a hint of plump bare breasts at the bottom of the screen, cut off by the prudish camera angle. "I have an appointment," he said. "Paul Macy. To see Mr. Bercovici."

"Certainly, Mr. Macy. The liftshaft to your right. Thirty-eighth floor."

He stepped into the shaft. It was already programmed; serenely he floated skyward. At the top, another screen. Face of an elegant haggard black girl, shaven eyebrows, gleaming cheekbones, no flesh to spare. The expectable gorgeous halo of shimmering hair. "Please step through Access Green," she said. A throaty, throbbing contralto. "Mr. Fredericks is expecting you in Gallery Nine of the Rotunda."

"My appointment is with Mr. Bercovici—"

Too late. Screen dead. Access Green, an immense oval doorway the color of a rhododendron leaf, was opening from a central sphincter, like the irising shutter of an antique camera. Abandon all hope, ye who enter here. Macy stepped hastily through, worrying about having the sphincter reverse itself when he had one leg on each side. Beyond the doorway the air was soft and clammy, heavy with a rain-forest warmth and humidity, and mysterious fragrances were adrift. He saw low, dim passages radiating in a dozen directions. The walls were pink and rounded, no corners anywhere, and seemed to be made of some spongy resilient substance. The whole place was like one vast womb. Trapped in the fallopian tubes. Macy tried to persuade himself not to start sweating again. There was a popping sound, of the sort one could make by pushing a fingertip against the inside of one's cheek and sliding it swiftly out of one's mouth, and the black girl emerged from a gash in the wall that promptly resealed itself. She was sealed too, encased in purple plastic from throat to toes, like a chrysalis, everything covered but nothing concealed: her tight wrap startlingly displayed the outlines of her bony body. Superb skeletal structure. She said, "I'm Loftus. I'll show you to Mr. Fredericks' office."

"Mr. Bercovici—"

She didn't wait Hurrying down the hall, legs going like pistons, bare feet hitting the spongy floor, thwunk thwunk thwunk. Trim flat rump: no buttocks at all, so far as he could tell, merely a termination, like a cat's hindquarters. He was upset. Bercovici was the one who had interviewed him at the Rehab Center, all smiles and sincerity, thinning blond hair, pudgy cheeks. Don't worry, Mr. Macy, I'll be looking after you personally during your difficult transition back to daily life. Bercovici was his lifeline. Without looking back, the black girl called out, "Mr. Bercovici's been transferred to the Addis Ababa office."

"But I spoke to him only ten days ago, Miss Loftus!"

She halted. Momentary blaze of the eyes. "*Loftus* is quite sufficient," she said. Then the expression softened. Perhaps remembering she was dealing with a convalescent. "Sometimes transfers happen rapidly here. But Mr. Fredericks has your full dossier. He's aware of the problems."

Mr. Fredericks had a long cavernous office, rounded and womby, from the sloping ceiling of which dangled hundreds of soft pink globes, breast-shaped; a tiny light was mounted in each nipple. He was a small dapper man with a moist handshake. Macy received from him a sweet sad embarrassed smile, the kind one gives a man who has had a couple of limbs or perhaps his genitals amputated to check the metastasis of some new lightning cancer. "So glad you've come, Mr. Macy. Paul, may I make it? And call me Stilton. We're all informal here. A wonderful opportunity for you in this organization." Eyes going to Macy's Rehab badge, then away, then back, as though he couldn't refrain from staring at it. The stigmata of healing.

"Show you around," Fredericks was saying. "Get to know everybody. The options here are tremendous: the whole world of modern data-intake at your service. We'll start you slowly, feed you into the news in ninety-second slices, first, then, as you pick up real ease at it, we'll nudge you into the front line."

*Good evening, ladies and chentlemen, this is Pavel Nathaniel-ovitch Macy coming to you from the Kremlin on the eve of the long-awaited summit.*

The rear wall of Frederick's office vanished as though it had been annihilated by some wandering mass of antimatter, and Macy found himself staring into an immense stupefying abyss, a dark well hundreds of feet across and perhaps infinitely deep. A great many golden specks floated freely in that bowl of nothingness. He was so awestruck by the unexpected sight that he lost a chunk of Fredericks' commentary, but picked up on it in time to hear, "You see, we have thousands, literally thousands of free-ranging hovereye cameras posted in every spot throughout the world where news is likely to break. Their normal altitude is eighty to a hundred feet, but of course we can raise or lower them on command. You can think of them simply as passive observers hanging everywhere overhead, little self-contained self-propelled passive observers, sitting up there soaking in a full range of audio and visual information and holding it all on twenty-four-hour tape-scanning drums. Those of us here at Manhattan North Headquarters can tap in on any of these inputs as needed. For instance, if I want to get some idea of what's doing at the Sterility Day parade in Trafalgar Square—" he touched a small blue button in a broad console on his desk, and up out of the darkness one of the golden specks came zooming, halting in midair just beyond the place where the wall of Fredericks' office had been. "What we have here," Fredericks explained, "is the slave-servo counterpart of the hovereye camera that's hanging above that parade right now. I simply induce an output—here, we get a visual"—Macy saw gesticulating women waving banners and setting off flares— "and here we get the audio." Raucous screams, the chanting of slogans.

Macy hadn't heard of Sterility Day before. The world becomes terribly strange when you spend four years out of circulation.

"If we want any of this for the next newscast, you see, we just pump the signal into a recorder and set it up for editing—and meanwhile the hovereye is still up there, soaking it all in, relaying on demand. Gathering the news is no frigging chore at all when you have ten thousand of these lovely little motherfuckers working for you all over the place." A nervous giggle. "Sometimes our language gets a little rough around here. You stop noticing it after a while." One doesn't speak crude Anglo-Saxon to a man who wears the badge of his trauma on his lapel, is that it?

Fredericks had him by the arm. "Time to meet your new colleagues," he was saying. "I want to fill you in completely. You're going to love it working here."

Out of the office. The rear wall mysteriously restoring itself as they leave, the dark well of the hovereyes vanishing once more. Down the humid fallopian passageways. Doors opening. Neat, well-groomed executives everywhere, all of them getting up to greet him. Some of them speaking exceptionally loudly and clearly, as if they thought a man who had had his troubles might find it difficult to understand what they said. Long-legged girls flashing the promise of ecstasy. Some of them looking a trifle scared; maybe they were hip to the evil deeds of his former self. Macy was aware of what crimes the previous user of his body had committed, and sometimes they scared him a little, too.

"In here," Fredericks said. Into a bright, gaudy room, twice the size of Fredericks' office. "I'd like you to meet the chief of daytime news, Paul. One hell of a guy. Harold Griswold, and he's some beautiful son of a bitch. Harold, here's our new man, Paul Macy. Number six on the late news. Bercovici told you the story, right? Right He's going to fit in here perfectly."

Griswold stood up, a slow and complex process, and smiled. Macy smiled. His facial muscles were beginning to ache from all the smiling he had done in the last hour and a half. One doesn't smile much at a Rehab Center. He shook the hand of the chief of daytime news. Griswold was implausibly tall, slabjawed, perhaps fifty years old, obviously a man of great prestige; he reminded Macy somehow of George Washington. He wore a bright-blue tank suit, an earwatch, and an elaborate breastplate of several kinds of exotic polished Woods. His office was like a museum annex, with works of art everywhere: shaped paintings, crystallines, talk-spikes, programmed resonances. A million-dollar collection. In the corner, to the right of Griswold's kidney-shaped desk, stood a striking psycho-sculpture, a figure of an old woman. Macy, who had been glancing from piece to piece by way of an implied compliment to Griswold, lurched forward at the sight of the last work, coughed, grabbed the edge of the desk to steady himself. He felt as though he had been clubbed at the back of the neck. Instantly friendly hands clutched at him. "Are you all right? What's the trouble, fella?" Macy fought off dizziness. He straightened and shook himself free of the propping hands.

"I don't know what hit me," he muttered. "Just as I looked at that sculpture in the corner—"

"The Hamlin over there?" Griswold asked. "One of my favorites. A gift from my first wife, ten years back, when Hamlin was still an unknown—"

"If you don't mind—some cold water—"

Two gulps. Another cup. Three gulps. Carefully averting his eyes from the figure of the old woman. The Hamlin over there. The sleek smooth network men frowning at him, then erasing the frowns the instant he noticed. Everyone so solicitous. "Forgive me," he said. "You know, it's only my first day on the outside. The strain, the tension."

"Of course. The tension." Griswold.

"The strain. We understand." Fredericks.

He forced himself to look at the psychosculpture. The Hamlin over there. An excellent piece of work. Poignance; pathos; a sense of the tragedy of aging, a sense of the heroism of defying time. A soft hum coming from its resonators, subtly coloring the mood it was designed to stimulate. The Hamlin over there. Macy said, "That's *Nathaniel* Hamlin who did it?"

"Right," Griswold said. "God only knows what it's worth now. On account of Hamlin's tragic fate. Not that I have the slightest interest in selling, but of course when an artist dies young his work skyrockets amazingly in value."

He didn't know, then. He couldn't just be pretending. And he couldn't be that dumb. Either Bercovici hadn't told him, or he'd been told and hadn't cared enough to remember. That was interesting. Macy was shaken, though, by the intensity of his reaction to the unexpected sight of the sculpture. They hadn't warned him at the Rehab Center that such things might happen. He made a mental note to ask about it when he went back next week for his first session of outpatient post-therapy therapy. And a mental note, also, to stay out of Griswold's office as much as possible.

The sculpture was still exerting an effect on him. He felt an undertow, the sucking of a subcerebral ocean in his mind. Hollow echoing sounds of surf from far below. A hammering against the threshold of consciousness. The Hamlin over there. That's *Nathaniel* Hamlin who did it? On account of his tragic fate. Jesus. Jesus. A bad attack of wobbly knees. Sweaty forehead. Paroxysms of confusion. Going to collapse, going to fall down in a screaming fit, going to vomit all over Harold Griswold's nappy green electronic carpet. Unless you regain control fast. He turned apologetically to Stilton Fredericks and said in a thick furry voice, "It's more upsetting than I thought. You'd better get me out of here fast."

Fredericks took his arm. A firm grasp. To Griswold: "I'll explain afterward." Propelling Macy urgently toward the door. Stumbling feet. Head swaying on neck. Jesus. Outside the office, finally.

The moment of intolerable *angst* ebbing.

"I feel much better now," Macy murmured.

"Can I get you a pill?"

"No. No. Nothing."

"Are you sure you're all right?"

"Sure."

"You don't look all right."

"It'll pass. It shook me up more than I expected. Listen, Fredericks—Stilton—I don't want you to think that I'm fragile, or anything, but you know I've just been released from the Rehab Center, and for the first few days—"

"It's perfectly natural," said Fredericks. A comradely pat on the shoulder. "We understand the problem. We can make allowances. This was my fault, anyway. I should have checked things out before I brought you in there. He's got so many works of art in his office, though—"

"Sure. How could you have known?"

"I should have checked anyway. Now that I see the difficulty, I'll check the whole building. I simply didn't realize that it would upset you so much to come face to face with one of your own sculptures."

"Not mine," Macy said, shaking his head emphatically. "Not mine."

# 2

Daytime it wasn't so bad. He built a cozy routine for himself and lived within it, just as they had advised him at the Center to do. The Rehab people had found him a little apartment near the upper tip of Old Manhattan, five minutes from the network office by short-hop tube, forty minutes if he walked; he hadn't wanted to risk exposing himself to the chaotic rush-hour environment of the tubes too soon, and so at first he went to work on foot. The exercise was good for him, and he had nothing better to do with his time anyway. But from the fourth day on he took the tube. The jostling and the screeching of wheels turned out not to bother him as much as he feared it might, and packed belly to rump in the cars, he didn't have to worry about people staring at him or his Rehab badge.

At work he slipped easily and comfortably into the network's news-broadcast operation. He had had six months of vocational training at the Center, and so he came to his new career already skilled in voice projection, sincerity dynamics, makeup technique, and other such things; he needed only to learn the details of the network's daily practice, the authority levels and flow patterns and such. Everybody was kind to him, although after the first few days most of them dropped the maddening exaggerated courtesy that made him feel like such a cripple. They showed him what to do, they covered his blunders, they responded patiently and good-humoredly to his questions.

In the beginning Fredericks didn't let him do any actual broadcasting, just dummy off-the-air runs under simulated studio circumstances. Instead he was put to work reading scripts aloud for the timing, and monitoring air checks of the other broadcasters. But he did so well at the dummy runs that by the fifth day they were putting him on the late news to do ninety-second capsule reports in what they called the mosaic-texture section, in which a bunch of broadcasters offered quick bouncy segments of the news in swift succession. Fredericks told him that in another few weeks he'd be allowed to handle full-scale stories, even to select his own accompanying hovereye coverage. So all went well professionally.

The nights were something else.

Lonely, for one thing. *You'd be wisest to avoid sexual liaisons, at least at the outset,* the Center therapists had suggested. *They could be disturbing during the initial two or three weeks of adjustment.* He paid heed. He refrained from bringing any of the network girls home with him, though plenty of them made it clear that they were available. Just ask, honey. At night he sat alone in the modest apartment. Watching a lot of holovision. Pretending that it was important to his career to study how the various networks handled the news. In truth he simply wanted the companionship of the bright screen and the loud audio; he left it on even when he wasn't watching anything.

He didn't go out in the evenings. A matter of economy, he told himself. Supposedly he had been a wealthy man in his former life, or at least pretty damned prosperous. A successful artist, work in constant demand, prices going up at the gallery every year, that kind of thing. But his assets had been forfeit to the state. Most of his money had been used up by the costs of his therapy and the termination settlement awarded his wife. What little was left had gone into renting and furnishing his apartment. He was essentially a pauper until the network salary checks began coming in. But he knew that the real reason for staying home was fear. He wasn't ready yet to explore the night world of this formidable city. He couldn't go out there while his new self was still moist and malleable around the edges.

Then there were the dreams.

He hadn't had nightmares at the Rehab Center. He had them now. Traumatic identity crises punctuated his sleep. He ran breathlessly down long gleaming ropy corridors, pursued by a man who wore his face. He stood by the shore of a viscous gray-green pool that bubbled and steamed and heaved, and a gnarled hairy claw reached up from its depths and groped for him. He tiptoed across a sea of quicksand, sinking deeper and deeper, and something underneath plucked at his toes. Pulling him under with a loud plop. A coven of monsters waiting down below. Teeth and green horns and yellow eyes. Often he woke up shrieking. And then lay awake, listening to something knocking on the inside of his skull. Let me out, let me out, let me out, let me out! Great gusts of wind blew through his brain. Vast snorting snores setting the medulla atremble. A slumbering giant, restless, cranky, trapped behind his forehead. Belching and farting within his head. Knock. Knock. Knock.

277

Also the peculiar doubleness of self assailed him, the sensation of being enshrouded and entangled in the scraps and threads of his old identity, so that he momentarily was sucked back into it. I am Nat Hamlin. Married, successful. Psychosculptor. This is my face. These are my hands. Why am I in this unfamiliar little apartment? No. No. I am Paul Macy. I used to be. Formerly was. In another country, so to speak. And besides the stench is dead. Why does he haunt me? I am not Nat Hamlin.

Sometimes at night it was hard to be sure of that, though. By the third night Macy dreaded going to bed. There was that man with his face, always haunting him when he crossed into dreamland. Waking in distress, he wanted to call a friend and ask for reassurance. But he had no friends. The old ones had been washed away by the therapy, and he hadn't made any new ones yet, except a few people he had come to know at the Rehab Center, fellow reconstructs, and he didn't want to bother them in the middle of the night. Maybe they had demons of their own to wrestle with. And the people from the network. Mustn't call them. You'd blow the whole pretense of your stability in one gush of panicky talk. Nor could he call any of his therapists. Dr. Brewster, Dr. Ianuzzi, Dr. Gomez. You're on your own, they said. We're cutting the umbilicus. So. So. All alone. Sweat it out. Eventually, no matter how bad a night it was, he would sleep. Eventually.


"Is there any chance," Macy asked, "that the Rehab job didn't completely take? I mean, sometimes I think I can feel Hamlin trying to break through."

A Tuesday late in May, 2011. One week after his discharge from the Rehab Center. His first session of post-therapy therapy. Dr. Gomez, round-faced, swarthy, drooping black mustache, not much chin, scowling and chewing on a computer stylus. Soft buzzing voice. "No chance of that at all, Macy."

"But these dreams—"

"A little psychic static, is all. What gives you the idea Hamlin still exists?"

"During these nightmares I feel him pushing inside my head. Like somebody trying to get out."

"Don't mess things up with your pretty imagery, Macy. You've been having some bad dreams. Everybody has bad dreams. You think I'm immune? I've got my share of lousy karma. Without any fancy hypotheses, tell me why you think it's Hamlin."

"The man with my face chasing me."

"A metaphor for our own unfocused past, maybe."

"A sense of confusion. Not knowing who I really am."

"Who are you, really?"

"Paul Macy. But—"

"That's who you really are. Nat Hamlin doesn't exist any more. He's been stripped out of your body, cell by cell, and extinguished. You really surprise me, Macy. I thought you were going to make one of the best adjustments I ever saw."

"I felt that way too," Macy said. "But since I've been outside there have been these—these bursts of psychic static. I'm scared. What if Hamlin's still there?"

"Hamlin exists only as an abstract concept. He's a famous psychosculptor who ran into trouble with the law and was eradicated. Now he exists only through his works. Like Mozart. Like Michelangelo. He isn't in your head."

Macy said, "My first day at the network, I walked into the office of one of the high executives and there was a big Hamlin sculpture in the corner. I looked at it and I recognized it for what it was and I just took it in, you know, the way I'd take in a Michelangelo, and after a fraction of a second I had this sensation like somebody had banged me on the head with a mallet. I almost fell over. The impact was tremendous. How do you account for that, Dr. Gomez?"

"How do *you* account for it?"

"Like it was Hamlin still inside me, standing up and yelling, 'That's mine, I made that!' Such a surge of pride and identity that I felt it on the conscious level as physical pain."

"Balls," the doctor said. "Hamlin's gone."

"How can you be sure of that?"

Gomez sighed. "Look," he said, and jabbed an output node. On the walls of his office blossomed screened images of Macy's psychological profiles. Gomez pointed. "Over on the left, that's the EEG of Nat Hamlin. You see those greasy waves of psychopathic tendency, those ugly nasty jiggles? You see those electrical storms going on in that man's head? That's a sick EEG. That's sick as hell. Right?

"Now look over here. We've begun the mindpick operation. We're wiping out Nat Hamlin. The waves get smoother. Sweet as a baby. Chart after chart. Look. Look. Look. As Hamlin goes, we bring in Macy. You can see the overlay here. *This* is what a double mind looks like. Vestigial Hamlin, incipient Macy. Yes? Two distinct electrical patterns, no problems at all distinguishing one from the other. And now, this side of the room, you can see Hamlin wiped out entirely. Can you find any of the typical Hamlin waveforms? By shit, can you?

"You aren't saying anything, Macy. There's your brain on the wall. Alpha, beta, the whole mess. Compare your waves and Hamlin's. Altogether different. Two separate patterns. He's him, you're you. The machine says so. It isn't a matter of opinion, it's a matter of voltage thresholds. A voltage doesn't lie. Amperes don't have opinions. Resistances don't fuck around with you for sly tactical reasons. We're dealing in objective facts, and the objective facts tell me that Nat Hamlin has been wiped out. They ought to tell you that too."

"The dreams—the sight of that psychosculpture—"

"So you're a little unstable. A couple of surprise adjustment traumas. But Hamlin? No."

"Another thing. My first day out, that came day, I met a girl in the street, somebody from Hamlin's life. She kept calling me Nat. Telling me she loved me."

"Weren't you wearing your Rehab badge?"

"Of course I was."

"And the dumb bitch still dumped all that garbage on you?"

"I suppose she's disturbed mentally herself. I don't know. Anyway," Macy said, "she was doing all this to me, Nat this and Nat that, paying no attention when I told her I was Paul Macy, and out of nowhere I felt, well, like hot on top of my head, and for half a second I didn't know who I was. Which one of me I was. It was like something had reached into my head and mixed everything up. I could even remember myself making a psychosculpture of the girl. You see, she was one of Hamlin's models, apparently, and I had this flickering memory of her posing, me at a sculptor's keyboard—"

"Crap," Gomez said.

"What?"

"Crap. It wasn't a memory. You couldn't possibly remember anything out of Nat Hamlin's life."

"What was it, then?"

"It was an episode of free-floating masochism, Macy. A normal self-injury wish. You invented this phantom image of yourself sculpting the girl because you wanted to fool yourself into thinking that Hamlin was breaking through."

"But I don't see why—"

"Shut up and I'll explain the mechanism; You lived at this Center for four years, right, and you got constant attention. It was like being in the womb. Every need instantly attended to. Okay, it's time for Paul Macy to be born, and we toss you out into the world on your ass. Not exactly as rough as that, we find you a job first, we find you a place to live, but it's still a ballbreaker to get evicted. Out you go. Suddenly no umbilicus to feed you. Suddenly no placenta to cuddle in.

"Well, you want attention, and one way to get it is to come here yelling that your personality reconstruct didn't take, that Hamlin is knocking around inside your head. I don't mean that this is a conscious thing. It's a mechanism. Your rational self just wants to make a decent adjustment to outside life and live happily ever after as Paul Macy, but there's this irrational side of us too. Which often operates directly counter to the needs and desires of the rational side.

"Suppose I tell somebody that his sanity depends on never calling his mother-in-law by her first name, okay? And he nods, he says, 'Yes, I understand, if I do that it'll really wreck me.' So of course every time he sees the old witch he finds that her first name is on the tip of his tongue. He'll have dreams in which he calls her by her first name. He'll fantasy it while he's sitting at his desk. Because it's the most destructive fucking thing he could possibly do, so of course the temptation to do it keeps rising out of his head, and he's constantly imagining he *has* done it.

"Now back to you. The last thing you want to have happen is for Hamlin to come back to life, so naturally you fantasy yourself making a sculpture of this girl. Which upsets you and sends you in a sweat back to me, screaming for help. The immediate result of this mechanism is to give you bad dreams and general trauma, and an incidental side-effect is to supply you with that claim on my attention that you unconsciously crave. You see how the dark side of our mind always craps us up? But don't worry about it, Macy. None of this is real, in the sense that Hamlin *is* there. Oh, sure, it's real in a psychological sense, but so what?" Gomez grinned triumphantly. "You're a smart boy. You've been following all this, right?"

Macy said, "Isn't it possible to run some new EEGs all the same? What if I did come up with a double wave pattern?"

"You really want me to coddle you, don't you?"

"Would it be so hard to make an empirical test?"

"I could do it in five minutes."

"Why not, then?"

"Because I don't believe in giving in to an outpatient's weepy fantasies. You think you're my first reconstruct job? I've had a hundred of you. I know what's possible and what isn't. If I tell you Hamlin is eradicated, it's because I *know* Hamlin is eradicated. I'm not just being a bull-headed bastard."

"All right, so I'm irrational," Macy said. "But if I had the evidence of the EEG in front of me—"

"I won't play that game with you. The fantasy came from inside you; let the cure for it come from in there too. Sweat it out. Convince yourself that your belief in Hamlin's continued existence is nothing but a move to get sympathy from us."

"And if the hallucinations don't go away?"

"They have to."

"If they don't, though?"

"You'll be here again next Tuesday," Gomez said. "I won't be seeing you then. Dr. Ianuzzi will, and as you know she's an entirely different kind of doctor. Sweet and refined and sympathetic, whereas I'm a vulgar and hostile son of a bitch. If this stuff is still bothering you then, maybe she'll run an EEG for you, though I hope she doesn't I won't, Macy. I can't. The top sergeant never kisses you and tucks you in, no matter how piteously you ask him, and I'm top sergeant on this team. So come back next week."

Gomez stood up. "I saw you on the late news last night. You weren't bad at all."

The next morning he found a message cube addressed to him in his box at the office. Puzzled, he plugged the glossy little cassette into his desk's output slot. The face of the girl who had talked to him on the street the week before appeared on the screen. Red-rimmed eyes, hollow cheeks. Her hair straggly, unkempt. She offered the camera an uncertain lopsided grin and said, "I saw you on holovision and so I knew where to send this. Please, Nat, don't just ignore me. I can't tell you—"

His hand shot out and killed the playback. *Please, Nat.* He couldn't take that. The use of his old name: it was like slivers of wood under his fingernails, needles probing behind his eyes. Last night the dreams had been worse than ever. Seeing himself as Siamese twins, one body ripping and clawing at its identical brother. And then the trapdoor opening in the attic floor and the shambling disemboweled thing lurching up out of it. The girl had initiated all his traumas; there hadn't been bad dreams before that miserable accidental meeting. He wasn't going to give her a second chance to screw him up. If that bastard Gomez wouldn't offer supportive therapy, he was simply going to have to defend himself against potential inner turmoil. And therefore it was necessary to avoid new sources of anguish.

Macy switched the output control to *Erase* and reached for

the button. Then he saw the girl's sad, eroded face in his mind. A fellow human being. She also suffers. I could at least listen once.

He turned to *Playback* again and she reappeared, saying, "I saw you on holovision and so I knew where to send this. Please, Nat, don't just ignore me. I can't tell you how much you still mean to me, even after everything. I know you've been through Rehab and things must be very strange to you, and you don't want to hear from people out of your old life. But finding you like that was such a miracle that I can't simply pretend you don't exist. Because I can't keep going like this much longer, Nat I'm in bad shape. I need help. I'm sinking and somebody's got to throw me a rope."

There was more in that vein. She said she'd wait for him Wednesday night at six o'clock on the northeast corner of 227th and Broadway, opposite the network building, and that she'd be waiting for him the same time the next two nights also, in case he wasn't free Wednesday. Or if he wanted to make other arrangements he could call her at her home, any day after eleven in the morning, such-and-such a number. With all my love. Yours truly, Lissa Moore.

I can't, he thought. I don't dare. He erased the cube. That night he left ten minutes early, going out the building's east entrance to avoid her. He did the same on Thursday and Friday.

On Monday there was a new cube from her. He carried it around for three hours, unwilling to erase it, afraid to play it, and finally slipped it into the slot. On the screen, her pale face against a black velvet backdrop. The mouth drawn into a quirky grimace. A hypothyroid bulge to the eyes that he hadn't noticed before. The lighting in the booth where she'd recorded the message was too bright, and it struck her cheeks so fiercely that it seemed to strip them to the bone. Her voice, blurting, unmodulated: "You didn't come. I waited, but you didn't come. All right Nat Paul. Maybe you don't give a damn about me. Maybe you've got your own neck to look out for and can't fool around with me. I won't bother you after today. I'll wait tonight, six o'clock, same corner, Broadway and 227th, northeast side. You aren't there by half past eight I'll be dead by nine. I mean it. Now it's up to you."

# 3

A few minutes past six, he was still in the central newsroom, finishing his last piece of the day. A cold sullen anger still gripped
him. Let the bitch kill herself. I won't be blackmailed like that. She
doesn't mean anything to me except trouble.

With a sharp stabbing gesture he summoned control of the
hovereye that patrolled the street outside the network office
building, forever keeping watch for demonstrators, bombers,
self-immolators. With newly skillful motions Macy brought the
airborne camera down the block until it was scanning the street-
corner where Lissa had said she'd wait. Now the fine control, the
vernier.

Yes, there she is. Pacing in a taut little circle. A self-contained
zone of tension on the busy street. Damn her. She can do whatever she likes to herself. Whatever she likes.

Macy signed himself out of the newsroom and, gliding on the

glacial flow of his rage, drifted toward the liftshaft. Down forty stories. Sweeping quickly through the lobby. Outside. A soft spring evening. Long lines of patient homegoers wearily filing into the tubemouth. So easy to avoid her, in this crowd. Just slide on past.

He found himself walking toward her, though. One-and-two-and-*one*-and-two; he couldn't stop. She seemed to be talking to herself; eyes turned inward, she didn't notice him approaching. From twenty yards away he glowered at her. Who the hell does she think she is, trying to use me this way? Playing on my sympathies. Oh, I need you, I need you so much! With throbbing violins. And working on my sense of guilt. Meet me on the corner or I'll jump off the Palisades Bridge! Sure. What business is it of mine if you want to jump off a bridge, baby? I've got nothing to feel guilty about. Guilt? I haven't done a thing. I'm brand new in the world. Christ, I'm even a virgin. That's right: Paul Macy is a virgin. A goddamn virgin.

He was only a few feet from her, now, but she hadn't seen him yet. He started to touch her arm, but halted as a curious discomfort flitted across his skull. That sense of doubleness, again, that scrambling of identities. Disorientation. A bonging sensation like the muffled tolling of a distant bell. With it came a fast spasm of nausea, a light tightening around his Adam's apple.

Then all the disturbing symptoms vanished. He nudged her elbow. "All right," he said gruffly. "Wake up! Here I am. You're pulling a lousy stinking trick, but I fell for it. And here I am."

"Nat!" Looking at him in mingled amazement and delight. Color stippling her cheeks. Eyes fluttering: she's scared of me, he realized suddenly. He experienced a second spasm of strange uneasiness, here and gone before it had any real effect. "Oh, Nat, thank God you came!"

"No," he said. "Let's get this established once and for all. My name's Paul Macy. You want to have anything to do with me, you call me by that name, and no options about it. Paul Macy. Say it now."

"P-Paul."

"Say it all."

"Paul Macy. Paul Macy."

"Good." He was starting to get a headache: two spikes of pain converging on the center of his head. This girl was no good for him. "Nat Hamlin doesn't exist any more, and don't you forget it," he said. "Now: you wanted me to meet you, and I met you. What's on your mind?"

"You sound so cruel, Paul." She stumbled on the *Paul*.

"Just annoyed. Your suicide threat—what a miserable tactic that is. I goddam well should have called your bluff."

"I wasn't bluffing."

"Whatever you say. I fell for it I'm here. What do you want?"

"We can't talk here," she said. "Not in the middle of a crowd. Not out on the street."

"Where, then?"

"Your place?"

He shook his head. "Absolutely not."

"Mine, then. We can be there in fifteen minutes. Everything's filthy, but—"

"What about a restaurant?" he suggested.

She brightened. "That would be okay. Any place you like. One of your favorites, where you'd feel comfortable."

He tried to think of one of his favorite restaurants.

"I don't know any restaurants," he said. "You pick one."

"You don't know any? But you always ate out, practically every night. It was like a compulsion with you. You—"

"That was Nat Hamlin," he said. "Hamlin might have been the one who ate out a lot. If you say so. But not me. Not yet."

He reached into his stock of memories, looking for the names of some Manhattan restaurants. Zero. They really should have given him some restaurant memories when they were constructing the Paul Macy persona at the Rehab Center. It wouldn't have been any big effort for them. They had given him all kinds of other things. Star of the high school lacrosse team. Chicken pox. A mother and a father. Breaking his leg on the slopes at Gstaad. Reading Proust and Hemingway. Putting his hand under Jeanie Grossman's polo shirt. Thirty-five years of ersatz memories. But no information about restaurants. Maybe Gomez, Ianuzzi, and Brewster didn't eat out much. Or perhaps the restaurant stuff was hidden in some cranny of his mind that he hadn't found yet. He said, "I mean it. I've got no suggestions. You pick."

"There's a people's restaurant two blocks from here. I've been having lunch at it a lot. You know it?"

"No."

"We could go there," she said.

It was a deep, narrow room with tarnishing brass walls and a bunch of sputtering defective light-loops threaded through the thatchwork ceiling. Service was cafeteria-style; you took what you wanted from servo-actuated cubbyholes along the power-counter. Then you found seats at dreary long community tables. Macy, following Lissa to the counter, whispered, "How do you know how much anything costs?"

"It's a people's restaurant."

"So?"

"You don't know what that is?"

"I'm new to a lot of this."

"You pay whatever you can afford," she said. "If you don't have any money, you just eat, and make it up next time. Or you go around back and help wash dishes."

"Does the system work?" he asked.

"Not very well." She smiled bleakly and began piling food on her tray. In a few moments she had it completely crammed with dishes. Five different kinds of synthetic meats, a mound of salads and vegetables, three rolls, and other things. He was more sparing: vegetable juice, proteoid steak, fried kelp, a cup of no-caffy. At the end of the counter stood a central-credit console. Lissa walked by it without giving it a glance. Macy hesitated a moment, confused, peering into the glossy dark-green screen. In a flustered way he authorized the console to charge his credit account ten dollars. A fat flat-faced girl waiting behind him in line snorted contemptuously. He wondered if he had paid too much or too little. Lissa was already far down the aisle, heading for an empty table at the back of the restaurant. He seized his tray and hurried after her.

They sat facing each other over the bare grim plank of the tabletop. "I've got some golds," she said. "Want one?"

"I'm not sure."

"Try." She pulled out a pack. Its brim snapped up and a cigarette popped out. He took it. She took one also, and he carefully watched her nip the ignition pod with her nail. He did the same. A deep pull. Almost at once he felt the dizziness and the acceleration of his heartbeat. She winked at him and blew smoke in his face.

Then she started to eat, stuffing the food down as if she hadn't had anything in weeks. The way she wolfed it, so unselfconscious in her gluttony, fascinated him: it was like watching a fire sweep through a dry meadow. Head forward, jaws working frantically. Sounds of chewing. White teeth flashing. He sat still, dragging on the cigarette, ineffectually trying to spear a strand of kelp with his fork. She looked up. "Aren't you hungry?" she asked, mouth full.

"Not as hungry as you are, I guess."

"Don't mind me."

Her wrists were dirty and there was a film of grime visible on her neck. She was wearing the same blue coat as the other day. Again, no makeup. Her fingernails were ragged. But she wasn't merely outwardly unkempt; she conveyed a sense of inner disintegration that terrified him. Obviously she had once been a beautiful girl, perhaps extraordinarily beautiful. Traces of that beauty remained. She had a parched, ravaged look, though, as if fevers of the soul had been consuming her substance. Her eyes, large and bloodshot, never were still. Always a birdlike flickering from place to place. Cheeks hollower than they ought to be. She could use about ten pounds more, he figured. And a bath. He stubbed out his roach and cut himself a slice of steak. Filet of papier-mâché. He gagged.

Lissa said, "God, that's better! Some food in the gut again."

"Why were you so hungry?"

"I always am. I'm burning up."

"Are you sick?"

She shrugged. "Who knows?" Her eyes momentarily rested on his. "I'm trying to think of you as Paul Macy. It isn't easy, sitting here with Nat Hamlin opposite me."

"Nat Hamlin doesn't exist."

"You really don't remember me?"

"Zero," he said.

"Shit almighty! What did they *do* to you at the Rehab Center?"

He said, "They pumped Nat Hamlin full of memory-dissolving drugs until every bit of him was flushed away. Which left a kind of zombie, you see? A healthy empty body. Society doesn't like to waste a good healthy body. So then they built me inside the zombie's head."

"Built you? What do you mean, built?"

"Created an identity for me." He shut his eyes a moment. There was a tightness at his collar. Choking sensation. He wasn't supposed to have to explain any of this. The world was supposed to take it all for granted. "They built up a past, a cluster of events that I could move around in as if it had really happened. Like I grew up in Idaho Falls, Idaho, and moved to Seattle when I was twelve. My father was a propulsion engineer and my mother taught school. They're both dead now. No brothers. No sisters. I collected African stamps and I did a lot of hunting and fishing. I went to college, UCLA, class of '93, got a degree in philosophy of communication. Two years of national service, stationed in Bolivia and Ecuador, doing voice-overs for the People's Democratic Channel. Then various TV and HV jobs in Europe and the States, and now here in New York. Et cetera, et cetera."

"God," she said. "And it's all phony?"

"Pretty near. It follows Nat Hamlin's biography only as closely as it has to. Like in age. Or Hamlin broke a leg when he was twenty-six and you can see that in the bone, so they've given me a skiing accident for that year."

"What would happen if I checked the UCLA alumni records, looking for Paul Macy in the class of '93?"

"You'd find him. With a Rehab asterisk saying that this is a pro forma entry covering a retroactively established identity. Same thing if you looked up the Idaho Falls birth register. They do a very thorough job."

"Christ," Lissa said. And shivered. "How creepy this is! You actually are a whole new person."

"I don't know how whole I am. But I'm new, all right."

"You don't have any idea who I am, then."

"You used to pose for Nat Hamlin, didn't you?"

She looked startled. "How come you know that? I haven't said anything about—"

"The day you stopped me in the street," he said, "while we were talking, I got a flash picture of you naked in a kind of studio, and I was leaning over a complicated keyboard thing and telling you to scream. Like a psycho-sculptor trying to get an emotional effect. I saw it maybe half a second, then it was gone." He moistened his lips. "It was like a piece of Nat Hamlin's blotted-out mind surfacing into mine."

"Or a piece of my mind reaching into yours," she said.

"Eh?"

"It happens. I can't keep it under control." A shrill giggle. "Wherever you got it from, it was right. I was one of Nat Hamlin's models. From January to August, '06, when he was working on his *Antigone 21*. The one the Metropolitan bought. His last big work, before his breakdown. You know about his breakdown?"

"Some. Don't talk about it." He felt a band of fire across his forehead. Simply being close to someone out of the old existence this long was painful. "Can I have another gold?"

She offered the cigarette and said, "I was also his mistress, all through '05 and most of '06. He said he'd get a divorce and marry me. Like Rembrandt. Like Renoir. Falling in love with the model. Only he went out of his head instead. Doing all those crazy things."

Macy, suddenly vulnerable, tried to stop her with an upraised hand, but there was no halting the flow of her words. "The last time I saw him was Thanksgiving Day, 2006. At his studio. We had a fight and he threw me down the stairs." She winced. Into his mind a searing image: an endless flight, the girl falling, falling, skirt up around her thighs, legs kicking, arms clutching, the dwindling scream, the sudden twist and impact. A sound of something cracking. "In the hospital six weeks with a broken pelvis. When I got out they were hunting him from Connecticut to Kansas. And then—"

"*No more!*" he yelled. People turned to look.

She shrank away from him. "I'm sorry," she said, folding into herself, huddling, shaking. His cheeks were hot, were shame and turmoil. After a moment she said softly, "Does it hurt a lot when I talk about him?"

A nod. Silence.

"You asked me to see you because you were in trouble," he said at length.

"Yes."

"Would you honestly have killed yourself if I hadn't shown up?"

"Yes."

"Why?"

"I'm all alone. I have nobody at all. And I'm going out of my mind."

"How do you know?"

"I hear voices. Other people's minds come into mine. And mine goes into theirs. Extrasensory perception."

"ESP?" he said. "Like—what is it, mental telepathy?"

"Telepathy. That's what it is. ESP. Telepathy."

"I didn't think that that really existed."

A bitter laugh. "You bet your ass. Sitting right here in front of you. The genuine article."

"You can read minds?" he said, feeling dreamfogged and unreal.

"Not exactly read. Just touch, mind to mind. It isn't under my conscious control. Things drift in, drift out. Voices humming in my brain, a word, a phrase, an image.

It's been happening since I was ten, twelve years old. Only much worse now. Much, much worse." Trembling. "The past, two years. Hell. Absolute hell."

"How so?"

"I don't know who I am any more a lot of the time," she said. "I get to be five, six people at once. This mushy noise in my head. The buzzing. The voices. Like static, only sometimes words drift in on the static. I pick up all these weird emotions, and they scare me. Not knowing if I'm imagining or not. There's somebody two tables away who wants to rape me. Wishes he dared. In his head I'm naked and bloody, spreadeagled, arms and legs tied to the furniture. And over to my left, someone else, a woman, she's transmitting the odor of shit. She sees me like some kind of giant turd sitting here. I don't know why. And then you—"

"No," he said. "Don't tell me."

"It isn't really ugly. You think I'm dirty and you want to take me home and give me a bath. And fuck me afterward. That's okay. I know I'm dirty. And I'd like to go to bed with you, too. But I can't stand all this crosstalk in my head. I'm wide open, Nat, wide open to every stray thought, and—"

"Paul."

"What?"

"I said, call me Paul. It's important to me."

"But you're—"

"Paul Macy."

"Just now, though, you were coming through as Nat Hamlin to me. From deep underneath."

"No. Hamlin's gone," he said. "I'm Paul Macy." A feeling of sea-sickness. The light-loops swaying and hissing overhead. He found himself covering her hand with his. Ragged cuticles against his fingertips. He said, "If you're suffering so much, why don't you get some help? Maybe there's a cure for ESP. Is that what you want, a cure? I could take you to see Dr. Ianuzzi, she's a very sensitive woman, she could get you into the right kind of psychiatric hospital and—"

"And they'd give me shock treatment," Lissa said. "Memory dislocation with drugs, like I was a criminal. They'd wash half my brain out trying to heal me. There wouldn't be anything of *me* left I'm afraid of therapy. I haven't ever gone. I don't want to go."

"What do you want to do?"

"I don't know."

"Then what am I supposed to do for you?" he asked.

"I don't know that either, Paul. I'm absolutely fucked up in the head, so there's no use asking me rational questions." Her eyes glittering eerily. Sick, sick, sick. "What you really ought to do," she said, "is get the hell away from me, right now, like you've wanted to do since the first minute you saw me. Only don't. God, please, don't. Help me. Help me."

"How?"

"Just be with me a little. I'm all alone. I've cut myself off from the whole world. Look, you know how it is with me? I don't have a job. I don't have friends any more. I look in the mirror and I see my own skeleton. I sit home and wait for the voices to go away, and they scream and scream at me until my head is coming off. I live off the welfare checks. Then I go out for a walk one day, on and on and on, way the hell uptown, and I crash into some guy on the street and he turns around and he's Nat Hamlin, he's the only man I ever really loved, only he isn't Hamlin any more, he's Paul Macy, that's what he says, and—" She caught her breath. "All right. You don't know me at all and I guess I can't say I know you. But I know your body. Every inch. That's a familiar thing to me, a land-mark, something I can anchor myself to. Let me anchor. Let me hold on. I'm going under, Paul. I'm drowning, and maybe you can hold me up, for the sake of what I used to mean to the person you used to be. Maybe. Maybe for a little while. You don't owe it to me, you don't owe me anything, you could get right up and walk out of here and you'd have every right. But don't. Because I need you."

Sweat-soaked, numb, fists pressed together under the table, he felt a wild surge of pity for her. He felt like saying, Yes, of course, whatever I can do to help you. Come home with me, take a bath, let's blow a few golds and talk about things, this telepathy of yours, this delusion. Not because I ever knew you. Not because the things that happened between you and Nat Hamlin give you any claim on me. But only because you're a suffering human being and you've turned to me for help, and how can I refuse? An act of grace. Yes, yes, I will be your anchor.

Instead he said, "You're asking a hell of a lot from me. I'm not the most stable individual in the world either. And I'm under doc-tor's orders to keep away from people out of Nat Hamlin's life. You could be big trouble for me. And me for you. I think the risks for both of us are bigger than the rewards."

"Does that mean you don't want to get involved?"

"I'm afraid so."

"Sorry I wasted so much of your time," she said. In a dead voice. No change of expression. Not really believing he means it, maybe.

"It wasn't wasted. I only wish I was in shape to do you any good. But a Rehab lives right on the edge of collapse himself, in the beginning. He's got to build a whole new life. So when you ask somebody like that to take on the additional burden—" All right, Macy. Stop explaining things, get up, walk out of here, before she starts crying and you start listening to her again. Up. You don't owe her a thing. You have your own troubles and they aren't small ones. Getting to his feet, now. The girl watching him, stricken, incredulous. Giving her a sickly smile, knowing that a smile of any kind is out of context when you're condemning somebody to death. Turning. Walking away from her, up the aisle of the people's restaurant, past the counter, the sauerkraut and the algaecakes. Another ten stride's and you're out the door.

A scream from the back of the room.

"No! Come back! Paul! Paul! *Nat!*"

Her words leaped across the gulf between them like a flight of arrows. Six direct hits. Thwack thwack thwack thwack thwack *thwack!* The last one a killer, straight through from back to chest. He staggered. St. Sebastian stumbling in the restaurant aisle. His brain on fire, something very strange happening in there, like the two hemispheres splitting apart and taking up independent existence. And then a voice, speaking quite distinctly from a point just above his left ear, saying:

—How could you walk out on her like that, you snotty creep?

He hit the floor hard, landing elbow-first. A stunning burst of pain. Within that cone of red agony a curious clarity of perception.

*Who said that?* he asked, losing consciousness. And, going under, he heard:

—I did. Nat Hamlin. Your twin brother Nat.

# 4

He was at work in his studio again, after too long a layoff. All the sculpting equipment covered with a fine coating of dust. Maybe the delicate inner mechanisms are ruined, or at least imprecise. Try to build an armature for a man, end up with a chimp, something like that. He checked all the calibration carefully: everything in order, surprisingly. Just dusty. Ought to be, after all these years. A wonder it wasn't busted up by vandals. Fucking vandals all over the place. Goths, too. He touched the main keyboard lightly. This was going to be his chef d'oeuvre, a group composition, a contemporary equivalent of *The Burghers of Calais*. But fragmented, intense, multivalued. Call it something unpretentious, like *The Human Condition*.

A fucking headache getting all the models together at the same time. But the group interactions are important: shit, they're the whole point of the thing! There they all stand, now. The fat lady from the circus, eight hundred pounds of quivering suet. Half a ton of laughs. The kid from the student co-op, the one with the shaven head. Gomez, the skull doctor, for that little touch of hostility. The pregnant chick from the supersupermarket. Get the clothes off, baby, show that bulge. Bellybutton sticking way out like a handle. And the vice-president from the bank, very very proper, turn him on a little when we're ready to start. Also the old plaster model from art school days, Apollo Belvedere, missing his prick. A real technical stunt, trying to make psychosculpture out of a hunk of plaster. Faking in the appropriate responses: the test of a master. A cat, too, the one-eyed one from downstairs, gray and white with maybe a dozen claws on each paw, the way it looks.

Lastly, Lissa. My beloved. Stand next to the banker, honey. Turn a little to the left. The banker lifts his hand. He wants to grab your tit, but he doesn't dare, and he hangs there caught in the tension between wanting and holding back. Your nipples ought to be erect for this: you ought to be in heat, some. Wait, I'll do it. A tickle or two down here, yes, look at them standing up.

Okay! Okay! Places, everybody! Group interaction, take one! I want each of you to project the emotion we talked about before, project just that emotion, as purely as you can. And really *live* it. Don't say to yourself, I'm posing for an artist, but say, I'm so-and-so and this is my life, this is my soul, and I'm radiating it in big chunks so he can grab it with his machine and turn it into a masterpiece. Ready? Ready? Hey, you sucks, why aren't you holding the pose? Who gave you permission to dissolve? Let's have some fucking *stability* in here! Hold it! Hold it! Hold it!


He was running as fast as he could, and the effort was killing him. A band of hot metal around his chest. His eyes ready to pop out of his head. He had turned left outside the restaurant, onto Broadway, down the dark street in long loping strides, thinking at first that he was going to get away, but then he heard the footsteps precisely matching his, a clop for his clop, on and on, and knew he wouldn't escape. Don't look back. Something may be gaining on you.

Nat Hamlin running smoothly behind him, wearing the same body as his only four years younger. Shouting obscenities as he ran. What a foul mouth he has! You'd think artists were aesthetic types, more refined, and yet here comes this anthology of smut running after me. Shouting, Hey, you, Macy, you dumb cocksucker, slow down! We got a lot to talk about, you asshole!

Sure we do. The first thing we talk about is which of us dies and which of us lives, and I know right away what your position is on *that,* Nat. So I'm just going to keep on running until I drop. Maybe you'll drop first, even though you're younger. With your acid and your golds and your broads tearing you down, and I've lived a clean life in the Center all these years.

On. On. Almost at the bridge, now. The shining towers of Old Manhattan ahead of me. Hamlin still screaming garbage. Isn't that one of the network hovereyes up there? Sure it is! Following right along, taping the whole thing, just in case a nice sweet murder happens. Call the police, you dumb machine! Look, there's a lunatic on my ass, a convicted criminal making an illegal breakthrough to life after having been eradicated! See, see, he's got my face! Why don't you do something? I'm a network man, can't you tell? Paul Macy. Number six on the late news. I know, you're just a machine, an objective reporter, a self-contained self-propelled passive observer, but screw all that now. My life's at stake. If he catches up with me. And I can't hold out much longer. Fire in my guts. All that spaghetti in there going up and down with every stride. Liver and lights ajiggle. Oh, Christ, a hand on my shoulder. Tag, I'm it!

Down on the ground. His knees on the crooks of my arms. Pinned. His lips drooling. A lunatic with my face. Get off! Get off! Get off! And he laughs. And over his right shoulder I see the hovereye recording everything. Wonderful. *Now we bring you the final moments of Paul Macy, thirty-nine, tragically slain by his berserk alter ego. After this brief message from the makers of Acapulco Golds.* Going. Going. Go—

He was moving warily through a sleepy suburb, Queens or Staten Island, he wasn't sure which. They all looked the same. A biting January day. High-pressure system sitting on the city: not even a cloud in the sky, just a bright blank blue shield pressing down, no hint of oncoming snow, though some blackened heaps of the Christmas snowfall still lined the curb. In this sort of dryness it was difficult to believe it would ever snow again. The leafless trees like gaunt bundles of sticks, silently shouting, I am an oak, I am a maple, I am a tulip tree, and nobody listening because they all look the same. Squat two-story brick houses, reasonably far apart, on both sides of the street. The kiddies at school. The hubbies at work. A hot little wifey behind each picture window.

He wasn't sure how he had found his way here. Starting out from Connecticut about half past nine in the morning, the work going all wrong, a fucking nightmare in the studio finishing in a horrid botch of a week's good labors, and then driving into the city, crossing two or maybe three bridges, ending up here. And the familiar yellow haze now swathing the temples and forehead, the steamy mist of madness. He welcomed it. There comes a time when you have to surrender to the dark forces. Yes, yes, go on, take possession of me. Nat Hamlin at your service. Call me Raskolnikov Junior. Ha, that crazy Rooshian understood something about intensity! How we boil inside. And sometimes boil over.

Look at this house, now. A completely stereotyped suburban villa, maybe fifty years old, product of the buggy seventies, the creepy sixties. I shall bring some illumination into its dreary existence. By an act of will I shall intensify the life-experience of its inhabitant. See how easy it is to force the side door? Just this flimsy little latch: you insert the slicer, you waggle it, you push . . . yes.

Now we go inside. Good morning, ma'am, this is the mad rapist, the Darien cocksmith, I'm peddling ecstatic terror this happy day. No, don't scream, I'm friendly. I never do unnecessary injury. I assure you that I wouldn't be here at all except for this irresistible compulsion I have. Is it my fault I'm off my hinges? A man is entitled to have a breakdown. Especially if he's a serious important artist. You ought to be thrilled to know who's going to fuck you. You're part of one of the most significant personal disintegrations in the history of western art. Like, suppose I was Van Gogh and I cut off my fucking ear right here on your kitchen linoleum? Wouldn't that give you at least a peripheral place in his biography? Well, all right, then. He had his collapse, I'm having mine. Come here, now. Let's get this tunic off you. See what kind of merchandise you're offering. Sorry, I wouldn't have ripped it if you had been cooperating. Why fight it? This can be much more meaningful for you if you just spread and give in. There. There. See, you're creaming for me! How can you deny the activity of your own Bartholin glands? This lubrication brands you whore, milady! Ah, In. In. In. That's the ticket. In and out, in and out. *Con amore. Allegro, allegrissimo!* Wham, bam, thank you, ma'am. Zip it up. Out the door. Mad rapist strikes again. Thus we enact the latest fascinating episode in our case of personality disruption. I look so cleancut for being a psychopath. Oops! Hey, no, officer! Put that stunner down!

Don't—hey, watch it—I surrender, damn you, I surrender! I'll go peacefully! I'll—go—peacefully—

Blinking furiously, soggy-headed, disoriented, he woke up. He found himself in bed, his own bed, the covers up around his chin, the lights on in the bedroom. Darkness beyond the window. The sheets cool against his skin: somebody has undressed him. From his elbow there flowed rivulets of agony. For a moment he was totally unable to recollect his last previous period of consciousness; then the incident in the people's restaurant came back to him. Walking out on Lissa. The girl calling after him. Nat Hamlin's voice whispering snakelike in his ear. Calamity. Collapse. Chaos. "Hello?" he said, voice breaking, ragged. "Is anybody here? Hello? Hello?"

Out of the other room came the girl. Framed in the doorway, naked. Even more slender than he had imagined, ribcage visible, the double ridge of muscle on the flat belly, thighs lean with a gap of an inch or two between them all the way up. The breasts still full, though. Not big boobs but nicely shaped. Triangular red bush. Her skin pink, scrubbed-looking, still moist. She's had a bath. Looks about five years younger now.

"How long have you been up?" she asked him.

"Maybe half a minute. What day is this?"

"It's still the same Monday night. No, it's Tuesday morning by now. Half past one in the morning."

"You brought me home?"

"With some help. There was this cabdriver in the people's restaurant. He carried you out. Christ, I was scared, Paul. I thought you were dead!"

"Did you try to get a doctor?"

She laughed. "At this time of night? I just sat here and watched you and hoped you'd snap out of it. You seemed to be having nightmares. Your eyeballs rolling around under the lids. I touched your mind just once, more or less an accident, and it was pretty scary, something about being chased through a dark alley." Coming over to the bed, she said, "Do you feel all right? Headache?"

"Headache, yes. Jesus."

"After a while it looked like you were just sleeping. So I took a bath, like you said I needed. You should have seen the mud come off me. But you get to feeling so shitty sometimes that you don't even bother to wash yourself, and that's where I was at. Well, that's over, now. I couldn't figure out how to work your cassette player, so I've been inside reading a book, and—"

"What happened to me in the restaurant?" he asked.

She sat on the edge of the bed. He looked at her thighs and wanted to let his hand rest on them, but it took two tries before the quivering arm would lift itself and make the ten-inch journey. Her skin was cool and smooth. He stroked her thigh, up and down, midway between knee and crotch.

She said, "You got up to leave, remember? I didn't think you were going to do it, but you did, and there you were, walking away from me. The one hope I had, walking away from me. And I knew I had hit bottom right there."

"So you called out to me."

"No," she said. "I *reached* out. With my mind."

"You didn't shout my name? Yell at me to come back?"

"I didn't open my mouth. I reached. And I made contact. With both of you."

"Both?"

"I went right into your head, and there was someone called Paul Macy there, yes, but I hit you on another level, too, and I found Nat Hamlin. Coiled up like a spring. Hiding in the dark. I'll never forget it in a million years. My mind arcing across the gap from me to you, and finding two of you. The hidden one. Or the sleeping one, I guess."

—Sleeping is more accurate.

Hamlin's voice. Macy jumped, yanking his hand back from Lissa as though she were a stove.

"Did you hear that?" he asked.

"I didn't hear anything. But I felt a kind of twinge. A little jolt of ESP action."

"It was Hamlin, talking inside me. He said, 'Sleeping is more accurate.' What the hell's going on, Lissa?"

"He's still inside you," she said.

"No. No. That's impossible. They all said he was gone forever."

"I guess he wasn't," Lissa said. "A little bit of him left, down in the bottom of your head. Maybe you can't ever fully wipe out a personality. Like you can breed a whole new frog if you've got a single cell of the old one's body, and the new one will be identical to the old. Is that right? And so you had a couple of cells of Nat Hamlin still in your head, and I brought them back to life by touching them. I'm sorry, Paul. It's all my fault."

"It isn't possible," he said. "It's just some hallucination I'm having."

—You wish, brother.

"He's really there," Lissa said. "I *felt* him. A presence inside you. The two of you in one head."

"No."

—No?

307

"I didn't mean to bring him back, Paul. I mean, I loved him, yes, but he was no good, he hurt people, he was a criminal. When they sentenced him to be wiped out, they did the right thing. I don't want him back. How can we get rid of him?"

"Don't worry about that," said Macy. "He was got rid of before. He can be got rid of again."

—Up yours, friend.

Lissa managed a brave smile. She took his hand between hers and clamped it. She looked transformed by soap and hot water, no longer the moody, embittered, disturbed waif of the restaurant. He realized that his collapse now tied her to him. She had brought him home. She had cared for him. He couldn't throw her out. She said, "Can I get you anything? A drink? A gold?"

"Not right now. I'd like to see—if I can stand up—"

"You ought to rest A nasty shock you had."

"Nevertheless." He swung his legs over the side of the bed and tested his feet a couple of times before putting his weight on them. Precariously rising. Wobbly. Standing there showing his nakedness to her. Then a gesture that astounded him: modestly moving his hand to cover his crotch. Immediately pulling it back; he could think of six different reasons why it was crazy to want to hide himself from her, starting with the fact that she had been this body's other owner's mistress for all those months years ago.

He took a step and another, and found himself in the middle of the room, lurching a little. His left elbow was stiff and sore, which was expectable enough, considering that all his weight had landed on it. Lucky thing it wasn't broken. But there was also a curious numbness around the right side of his face. No sensation in the cheek, and his lips felt funny in the corner of his mouth. As though he'd had an anesthetic shot at the dentist. As though he'd had a stroke, maybe.

He looked at his face in the bedroom mirror. Yes, a little lop-sided, the way his father had looked after *his* stroke. The mouth pulled back, the lower eyelid drooping. Macy prodded the numb part of his cheek and tried to push the lips into their proper con-figuration. Everything hard, like plastic flesh.

—Hi ho.

"Are *you* doing that?"

"What's the matter, Paul?"

"My face. He's holding the muscles. I can't get him to ease off."

"Oh, Christ, Paul!" Terrified.

A battle of wills. Her terror infected him. This was grisly, hav-ing the side of your face held captive by something in your brain. Like going swimming and coming up with a lobster pinching your cock. He fought back. Tugging at the muscles, trying to soften the flesh. Re-lax—re-lax—re-*lax*. Yes. Getting the upper hand, or whatever. Some sensation returning, now. The mouth no longer distorted. Hamlin scuttling lobsterlike into deeper recesses of his brain, letting go. Tomorrow I scoot over to the Rehab Center and have this taken care of. A complete and exhaustive burnout of whatever vestiges of the previous self still remain. Macy glanced at the mirror again. Opening and closing his mouth, practicing big grins. The first round goes to me. He stumbled back to the bed and toppled onto it, quivering.

"You're soaked with sweat!" Lissa cried.

"It was a real struggle. The muscles."

"I watched it. Your face was writhing and grimacing. It looked like you were going crazy. Here, get back under the cover. You ought to rest. Would you like to smoke?"

"Maybe that's not such a bad idea."

She brought two golds over. Solemnly they lit up and went through the ritual of puffing, the deep drag, suck in lots of air. As the hallucinogenic smoke wandered through his lungs he imagined it traveling swiftly to his brain and befuddling the demon that Lissa's ESP had conjured into life there. Lull him back to sleep. And then, when Hamlin's groggy, drive a silver spike through his heart. Macy couldn't feel any trace of the other's presence now. For all he knew, the pot really knocked him out.

"Turn out the light," Macy said. "Get into bed with me. We'll lie here and smoke."

Her thighs cool against his. He felt feverish. The strain of the last few hours, no doubt. The tips of the golds glowing in the dark. They don't burn as fast now as they did when you had to roll your own. Time to meditate, time to contemplate. But eventually they were gone. Stubbing out the roaches. He was still unable to detect the presence of the passionate, warped soul of Nat Hamlin within him. Pot the panacea, maybe.

He reached toward Lissa.

Moving about in the bed was difficult, because of his sore elbow. Yet he managed. His right arm curling around her back and the hand coming out front on the far side to cup her distant breast. Soft firm bouncy globe, overflowing his clutching fingers. Trapping the nipple gently between index and middle, twitching his digits tenderly to excite her. Then, not easily, he pivoted upward, wriggled, touched his bad arm briefly and dismayingly against the headboard, and succeeded in wedging his right knee between her thighs without losing his grip on her breast. Her legs parted and he got the top of his knee up against the warmth of her. She made little purring sounds. The trouble was that he couldn't kiss her in this position, his neck simply wouldn't reach, but okay, this would do for now. Tentatively he flexed the stiff arm, planning to slide it across to her groin if it wasn't too painful for him.

310

This was the first time since he had become Paul Macy that he'd been in bed with a woman.

Oh, they'd given him a set of memories. Probably Gomez had taken care of the programming job, the little horny bastard. Dreaming up phantom lays for him. A proper heterosexual background, not even neglecting a spot of innocent pubescent homophily. Here he was with Jeanie Grossman in the cabin at Mount Rainier. Sweet sixteen, both of them, tiny boobies cold and hard in his hands, Jeanie's long black hair all disheveled, her thighs clamped tight on his probing hand. Oh, no, no, Paul, don't, please don't, she was saying, and then she was breathing hoarsely and murmuring, Be gentle, darling, just the way they said it in the dumb romantic novels Gomez most likely had stolen all this from, Oh, be gentle with me, Paul, it's my first time. On her and in her, wham and bam. Frantic hasty poking. My first time too, but he doesn't tell her that. Jeanie Grossman gasping out her inaugural orgasm with the white bulk of Mount Rainier peering over her shoulder. But of course it hadn't happened. Not to him. To Gomez, maybe, long ago; maybe Gomez programmed his own sex life into all his reconstructs, for lack of imagination. Poor Jeanie, whoever you are, a hundred different men think they've had your cherry.

And there was much more to Macy's curriculum vita. The married woman, really old, easily past thirty, who had fallen upon him with sudden ferocity when he was seventeen years old and selling encyclopedias in the summer. Sitting next to her on the couch with all his charts outspread, saying, This is an outstanding feature, our three-dimensional visual aids presentation, and we have a choice of six bindings in beautiful decorator colors, and would you like to hear about our brand-new home videotape supplement, and while he prattles she pushes the brochures off his lap and dives for his zipper and then the amazing shattering sensation of her lips engulfing his cock.

Good old Gomez. And the nurse at Gstaad, seducing him in his huge plaster cast. And the plump German girl who liked him to use the butler's entrance. And the one with the rubber underwear and the whip. The endurance contest in Kyoto, too. The orgy on the beach at Herzlia. The dear doctor had stocked him amply with vivid and varied erotica. But what was the use? None of it was real, at least not so far as Paul Macy was concerned, and so he could no more claim it as earned experience than if he had got it all from Henry Miller and the divine marquis. He was minus any authentic lovemaking memories. So in effect he was about to lose his innocence at the age of thirty-nine. But as he fondled Lissa's slim sleek body he realized the value of having had all those imaginary episodes of the flesh implanted in him. A real virgin would be up against anatomical confusions, the mechanics of the thing, the correct angle of entry, all those problems. He at least knew where the way in was to be found. Secondhand knowledge, maybe, but useful. The Rehab Center hadn't turned him loose unable to cope.

One small problem, though. He didn't seem to be able to get it up.

Lissa was primed and ready, nicely lubricated, and his item still hung slack. Through slitwide eyes she watched him and frowned. The juices souring and curdling in her as she waited to have her vacancy filled. At last understanding the reason for the delay. Cuddling against him; her hand to the scrotum, a light tickling, very skillful. Ah. Yes. Some wind in the sails, finally. The old familiar rigidifying that he had never before experienced. Up. Up. Up. At full mast, now. Swing smoothly around, slide yourself into her. They made adjustments of their positions. She prepared herself to receive him. He was athrob, inflamed, aloft.

Then came a laugh from within and a cold devilish voice:

—Take a look at this, pal.

Blossoming on the screen of his mind the image of Lissa spread wide on another bed in another room, and himself—no, not himself but Nat Hamlin—poised above her, seizing the calves of her legs, draping them over his shoulders, now lowering himself to her with ithyphallic vitality. Nailing her. And as that inward consummation took place Macy felt his own rod lose its vehemence. Limp again; shriveled, infantile, a wee-wee instead of a cock. Wearily he sagged against the girl. Doing it was impossible for him now. Not with *him* watching. I carry my own audience in my head. Hamlin, still roaring with turbulent inner laughter, was sending up scene after scene out of his no doubt actual experience, coupling with Lissa in this position, in that one, Lissa on top, Lissa down on her knees being had dogwise, the whole copulatory biography of their long-ago liaison, and Macy, helpless, his phantom images of Jeanie Grossman and the encyclopedia woman swept away by this gushing incursion of reality, lay stunned and sobbing and impotent waiting for Hamlin to stop tormenting him.

Lissa didn't seem to understand what was happening, only that Macy had lost his hard at a critical moment and was plainly upset about it. Her long thin arms cradled him affectionately. "It's all right," she whispered. "You've been under a terrible strain, and anyway that kind of thing can happen to anybody. It'll be better later. Just lie here and rest. It doesn't matter. It's all right. It's all right." Pressing his cheek against her breast. "Try to get some sleep," she said. He nodded. Closing his eyes, trying to relax. Out of the darkness Hamlin's voice:

—That was just to let you know I'm still here.

# 5

Sometime during the night there must have been a flow of strength from her to him, for he had fallen asleep being comforted by her, and he was awakened by the sounds of her sobs. The room very dark: morning some hours away, yet he felt as though he'd had enough sleep. Lissa had her back to him, her bony spine pressing into his chest; she was curled up knees to breasts, making snuffling sounds, and every thirty seconds or so a great racking open-mouthed bed-shaking sob came out of her. Before he could tend to her he had to survey the condition of his own head. All seemed well. He was rested and loose. There was a delicious sense of aloneness between his ears. When he was in contact with Hamlin he felt inwardly cluttered, as though bales of barbed wire were coming unraveled in his skull. None of that now. The alter ego was sleeping, maybe, or at any rate busy in some other realm. Macy put his hand lightly on Lissa's bare shoulder and called her name. She went on sobbing. He shook her gently.

"What?" she said, sounding foggy and far away.

"Tell me what the trouble is."

A long silence. No reply. Had she gone back to sleep? Had she ever been awake?

"Lissa? Lissa, what's the trouble?"

"Trouble?"

"You've been crying."

"It's all a bad dream," she said, and he realized that she was still asleep. She pulled away from him, getting even more tightly into the fetal position. Heaving a terrible sigh. Sounds of weeping. He wrapped himself around her, thighs to her buttocks, his lips just above her ear. Her skin was cold. She was shivering. "Chasing me," she murmured. "Ten arms, like some kind of octopus."

"Wake up," he said. "It'll all go away if you wake up."

"Why are you so sure?"

And she sent him her dream, nicely wrapped. Popping from her mind to his, clicking smartly into place like a cassette. Jesus. A lunar landscape of crumbling concrete, thousands of miles wide, a million cracks and furrows and fissures. Not a building, not a tree, not a shrub in sight, only this gray-white plateau of flat ruinous stony pavement covering the universe. From above a fierce white light plays on the concrete, so that the upthrust rims of the fissure-lines cast long harsh shadows. A frosty wind blowing. Footsteps. Lissa appears from the right, naked, breathless, running hard, her hair streaming behind her, streaming *into* the wind. Her pale white skin is marked by dozens of circular red cicatrices, suction marks. And now her pursuer thunders after her. Nat Hamlin, yes, wearing his bland even-featured Anglo-Saxon face, but he has eight, ten, a dozen curling tentacles coming out of his shoulders, tentacles equipped with big rigid sucker-cups. Not hard to tell where Lissa got the red marks on her body. And a dick a yard long sticking out in front of him, like a club. His feet are frog-flipped the size of snowshoes. Thromp! Thromp! Thromp! He comes flapping toward her at an incredible speed. And then there are the voices. People are saying things about her in Sanskrit, in Hungarian, in Basque, in Hopi, in Turkish. Unfavorable comments about her breasts. Snide remarks about her unshaven armpits. A cutting reference to a mole on her left hind cheek. They are laughing at her in Bengali. They are offering her perversions in Polish. She hears everything. She understands everything. Hamlin now has split in two, a double pursuer, one of him somehow coming from the other side of her, and she is trapped between them. Closer . . . closer . . . impaling her fore and aft . . . she screams . . .

I reject this dream, Macy thought. It isn't a necessary nightmare. To hell with it.

"Wake up," he said again, loudly.

Waking her wasn't so easy. She was hovering in a peculiar borderline state, almost a hypnotic trance, in which she was able to hear him and even give him rational answers, without, however, being plugged into the waking world in any meaningful way. Lost in her hallucinatory horrors. He switched on the light. Half past four in the morning. He'd been sleeping only about two hours, then. Seemed like a full night. Pulling her to a sitting position, he opened her eyes with his thumbs.

She stared blearily at him. Eyes like mirrors, seeing nothing. "Lissa? Jesus, Lissa, *snap out of it!*" Waves of terror rippling across her face. Her sharp little elbows digging hard into her sides, fists balled and held tight to her clavicles. Still sobbing, a quick panicky inhaling and exhaling. Macy hauled her from the bed and frog-marched her into the bathroom. His palm touching the shower control. A computerized cascade of chilly water. Get under, girl. A shriek. As though he were flaying her. But she was awake now.

"My God," she said. "I was on some other planet."

"I know. I know."

"My head's all full of it. A million square miles of cracked pavement. I still see it. And that light shining overhead, such a fucking bright light. And those tentacles."

"They're gone now," he said.

"No. They came out of my head, didn't they? They're still in there, the way Nat Hamlin's in you. I'm going crazy, Paul, isn't that obvious? Christ, hold tight to me. Maybe the octopus is real and this is the dream."

Her teeth were chattering. He wrapped a towel around her and guided her back to the bedroom. Her cheeks felt hot. A high fever raging in her. "I just want to hide somewhere," she said. "To disappear into my own brain, you understand what I mean? To get away into some inner world where nobody can find me. Where I can't hear the voices."

She slithered under the covers, pulling the blankets over her head. A thick mound in the bed, a lump, like a rabbit in a snake's belly. From underneath came muffled words. "What's going to happen to us, Paul? We're both crazy."

Macy got in beside her, and abruptly she turned to him with such fantastic ferocious passion that the breath was knocked from him. Grappling with him, knotting her arms and legs about his. Her belly pushing at his. Her pubic bone jabbing him painfully. Lissa clutching him as if she wanted to devour him. As a boy living in Seattle in the life he hadn't lived, he had watched a starfish in a tidepool going to work on a clam, pulling its shell open with its suction cups, then turning itself inside out so that its stomach might go forth and ingest. He thought of that now as Lissa

317

writhed against him. Waiting for something long and slimy to extrude from her slit and begin digesting him. Thank you, Dr. Gomez, for that lovely image. Do you hate women too, you mind-fucking bastard?

"Paul," she murmured. "Paul. Paul. Paul." Rhythmic exclamations. To his surprise he found his member stiffening despite everything, and in a single swift gesture he slipped it into her. She was hot and wet. As he speared her he expected Hamlin to surface and interfere with things again, but this time he was allowed the privacy of his genitals. Lissa cried out and came almost immediately. Her spasms were still going on when his began, a million and a quarter years later.

At half past seven he woke again. Lissa seemed to be sleeping soundly. Hamlin quiescent. He showered and went into the little kitchen-cum-dinette. Picked up the phone, tapped out the delayed-message code, and instructed it to call the network at nine to say that he was sick and wouldn't be coming in. Then he called the Rehab Center and arranged for today's post-therapy session to be moved up from four in the afternoon to nine in the morning. He didn't want to lose any time getting the Hamlin problem dealt with. "Will you hold?" the Center's computer asked him, and he held, and two or three minutes later the machine came back to him and said, "I've checked Dr. Ianuzzi's schedule, Mr. Macy, and it will be possible for her to see you at nine today." The computer's face, on the telephone screen, was that of an efficient, good-looking brunette. "Fine," Macy said, winking at her.

He peered into the bedroom. Lissa lay face down, one arm dangling to the floor. Snoring faintly. Well, she'd had a hard night He programmed breakfast for himself.

Macy wondered if Dr. Gomez would be at the Center today. He wanted to see the look on the little Mex's face when he showed up with a supposedly obliterated identity surfacing in his brain. Macy could still hear the doctor's cocky spiel. "If I tell you Hamlin is eradicated, it's because I *know* Hamlin is eradicated." Sure. "I'm not just being a bullheaded bastard." No, of course not. "Nat Hamlin doesn't exist any more." You tell it, baby. "Hamlin exists only as an abstract concept." Right on, sweetheart. How was Gomez going to explain any of last night's events? I hope Hamlin spits right in his goddam face. With my mouth.

He thought he had a good idea what had brought Hamlin back to life. Who. Lissa was who. This telepathy business of hers had somehow managed to nudge the expelled ego out of limbo and give him at least a partial grip on his former body. Looking back over his relationship with Lissa, Macy saw the pattern clearly. That first day, two weeks ago exactly, when she'd collided with him on the street, that first moment of recognition, Lissa refusing to honor his Rehab badge and calling him by Nat Hamlin's name: right then, at the beginning, he'd felt a stabbing pain, as if he were Hamlin and back at the Center having his past uprooted. And then, a few minutes later, same incident, when Lissa had leaned close and grabbed his wrist: that feeling of heat in his brain, that sense of an intrusion. Clearly it was her ESP stirring things up in him. Producing an instant of confusion, of double identity, when he wasn't sure whether he was Hamlin or Macy. Probably that was the moment at which Hamlin's return to conscious existence was stimulated. When I got that vision of myself in Hamlin's studio, Lissa posing for me. And thought I was having a heart attack on the street.

And then? Later the same day, when he almost passed out in front of Harold Griswold's Hamlin sculpture, that must have been Hamlin giving a wild whoop and a leap inside him at the sight of something familiar. That night he had the first of his pursuit dreams. Hamlin loose in his head, and chasing him. Next? When Lissa sent the letter threatening suicide, and he met her on the street. Good Christ, was that only last night? And he walked up to her and there was that doubleness again, the nausea, the confusion. No doubt she had given Hamlin another little nudge. Lastly, when he tried to leave her in the restaurant, and she cried out for him to come back. The sheer mental voltage of that must have been the clincher, awakening Hamlin fully, giving him a chance to jump to the conscious level. He was so stunned by Lissa's telepathic scream that Hamlin was able to grab some of the cerebral centers and start talking to him. Even to seize the facial muscles on the right side, for a little while. He doesn't have solid control of anything, not for long, he holds on a while and slips away, but he's there. Lissa's fault. Of course she didn't intend to. A weird telepathic accident, is all. Or maybe not so accidental. It was Hamlin she loved, he thought; I'm just a stranger in his body. Suppose this is her way of getting rid of me and helping him come back.

No.

He didn't want to believe that. She hadn't meant to yank Hamlin into consciousness. All the same, she was responsible. Now he had to get Hamlin removed again. Anguish and turmoil, most likely. After which he'd better not fool around with Lissa. Self-preservation has to come before concern for others, right? Out she goes.


The Rehab Center was just across the Connecticut line in Greenwich. Ten minutes by long-hop gravity tube, from Manhattan North. Macy took the uptown shuttle to the nearest loading point for the tube. A gray, misty morning, more like late autumn than late spring. Taut-faced commuters running this way and that. Most of them going the other way, thank God. They kept bumping into him. Giving him funny stares and going on. For over a week now he had been free of his obsession that people were staring at him, but this morning it returned. The Rehab badge seemed like a beacon drawing all eyes. Announcing: Here walks a former sinner. Doer of dreadful deeds! Behind this bland mask lurks the purified brain of a famous criminal. Do you recognize him? Do you remember the news stories? Go up close, take a good look, enlarge your life-experience through a moment of proximity with somebody who has been a household word. Guaranteed not to harm you. Guaranteed to be regenerated and redeemed from sin. He walks, he talks, he suffers like an ordinary human being! See the former monster! See! See! See!

"Greenwich," Macy said huskily to the ticket-scanner, and tapped out his account number. From the slot came a plastic ticket with thin golden filaments embedded in it Clutching it tightly, Macy made his way to the loading gate. The doors of the train were open. Plenty of seats inside. He found one next to the wall. No windows in here. People drifting aboard. He sat passively, thinking as little as possible. Floating in here. Just as the train itself, within its tube, floated in a larger tube on a two-foot-deep cushion of water.

"All aboard," the computer voice calls. The pressure-tight door sliding shut. We are sealed within. Gliding forward, through the airlock. The valve swinging open. Near-vacuum in front of the train, full pressure behind: the train goes squirting into the tube. Very clever. Little sensation of motion, because of the dynamic notation system and the sleek roller-bearing wheels. Onward, zooming silently eastward, driven by cunning pneumatic forces, the air to the train's rear gradually becoming more tenuous, the air in front undergoing steady compression. Ultimately the air in front will be our cushion for deceleration. Meanwhile gravity also drives us as we swoop through a gently sloping tunnel. To the midpoint, where we will begin to rise and slow. How shrewd these engineers are. If he could only ride the tube all day, coasting from here to there and back again at a lovely three hundred miles per hour. The ecstasies of free fall. Or almost free.

Macy sat with eyes closed. Not a twitch out of Hamlin. Stay hidden, you murderous bastard. Stay hidden.

He didn't understand how it was possible for Hamlin to have come back. At the Center he had picked up a good working knowledge of the Rehab process, and from what he knew of it he couldn't see any chance for the spontaneous or evoked resurrection of an obliterated identity. What's identity, after all, if not just the sum of all the programming we've received since the initial obstetrical slap on the rear? They pump into us a name, a set of kinship relations, a structural outlook toward society, and a succession of life experiences. And after a while feedback mechanisms come into play, so that what we've already become directs our choice of further shaping experiences, thereby reinforcing the contours of the existing self, creating the attitudes and responses that we and others consider "typical" of that self. Fine. And this accumulation of events and attitudes is engraved on the brain, first in the form of electrical impulses and patterns, then, as short-term memories are accepted for long-term storage, in the form of chains of complex molecules, registering in the chemical structure of the brain's cells.

And so, to undo the identity-creating process, one merely undoes the electrochemical patterns by which the identity is recorded. A little electronic scrambling, first, to inhibit synapse transmission and rearrange the way the electrons jump in the brain. Then, when defenses are down, start the chemical attack. A shot of acetylcholine terminase to interfere with short-term memory fixation. One of the puromycin derivatives to wash out the involuted chains of ribonucleic acid, brain-RNA, that keep memories permanently inscribed in the brain. Flush the system with amnesifacient drugs, and presto! The web of experiences and attitudes is wiped away, leaving the body a tabula rasa, a blank sheet, without identity, without soul, without memory. So, then: feed in a new identity, any identity you like. Building takes longer than destroying, naturally. You start with a vacant hulk that has certain basic motor reactions left and nothing else: it knows how to tie its shoelaces, how to blow its nose, how to make articulate sounds. Unless the wipeout job has been done with excessive zeal, it can even speak, read, and write, though probably on a six-year-old level. Now give it a name. Using nifty hypnagogic techniques, feed it its new biography: here is where you went to school, this is your mother, this is your father, these were your childhood friends, these were your hobbies. It doesn't have to be crystalline in its consistency; most of our memories are mush anyway, out of which a bright strand projects here and there. Stuff the reconstruct with enough of a past so he won't feel disembodied. Then train him for adult life: give him some job skills, social graces, remind him what sex is all about, et cetera, et cetera. The peripheral stuff, reading and writing and language, comes back faster than you'd imagine. But the old identity *never* comes back, because it's been hit by fifty megatons of fragmentation bombs, it's been totally smashed. Right down on the cellular level, everything making up that identity has been sluiced away by the clever drugs. It's gone.

Unless. Somehow. Skulking in the cellular recesses, traces of the old self manage to remain, like scum on a pond, a mere film of demolished identity, and from this film, given the right circumstances, the old self can rebuild itself and take command of its body. What are the right circumstances? None, if you listen to Gomez & Co. No recorded case of an identity reestablishing itself after a court-ordered eradication has been carried out. But how many reconstructs have ever been exposed to ESP? The full blast of a telepath reaching out toward old and new identities simultaneously? It's a statistical problem. There are $x$ number of reconstructs walking around today. And $y$ number of telepaths. $X$ is a very small number and $y$ is even smaller than that. So what are the odds against an $x$ meeting a $y$? So big, apparently, that this is the first time it's ever happened. And now look. That psychopathic fucker Hamlin crawling around loose in my brain. Why mine?

"Greenwich," said the voice of the computer, and the train slid placidly to a halt on its cushion of compressed air.


The Rehab Center was north of the city, in the old estate district, which through inspired and desperate zoning arrangements had managed to resist the grinding glacier of population pressures which had devastated most of suburbia. Several acts of reconstruction and rehabilitation had been performed on the Center itself. The main building, a gray pseudo-Tudor stone pile three stories high, with groined stockbroker-Gothic ceilings and leaded-glass windows, had been a private residence in the middle twentieth century, the mansion of some old robber baron, a speculator in energy options. In the end the speculator had outsmarted himself and gone into bankruptcy; the big house then had been transformed into the headquarters of a therapy cult that relied a good deal on year-round nudity, and it was in this era that the five plastic geodesic domes had been erected, forming a giant pentagram around the main building, to serve as wintertime solaria. Recriminations and lawsuits did the cult in within five years, and the place became an avant-garde secondary school, where the scions of the Connecticut gentry took courses in copulatory gymnastics, polarity traumas, and social relativity. The various minor outbuildings, with many ingenious electronic facilities, were added at this time. The school collapsed before it had produced its first graduating class, and the county, taking possession of the premises for nonpayment of realty taxes, speedily turned it into the first Rehab Center in the western half of the state in order to qualify for the federal matching-funds grant then being offered; the national government, eager to get the Rehab program off to a fast start, was throwing its meager resources around quite grandly then.

As one rode up the thousand-yard-long driveway leading to the main building, one could behold all the discrete strata of construction marking the epochs of the Center's past, and, if one were imaginatively inclined, one might envision the old speculator placing phone calls from pool-side, the health fanatics toasting in the solaria, the youthful scholars elaborately fornicating on the lawn, all at once, while through the leafy glades wandered today's candidates for personality rehabilitation, smiling blankly as voices out of earphones purred their past to them.

Macy saw none of these things today, not even the driveway. For, as he emerged from the tube station in downtown Greenwich and looked about for an autotaxi to take him up to the Center, he felt a sensation much like that of a hatchet landing between his shoulder blades, and toppled forward, dazed and retching, sprawling to the pavement. For some moments he lay half-conscious on the elegant blue and white terrazzo tiling of the station entrance. Then, recovering somewhat, he managed to scramble up until he crouched on hands and knees, like a tipsy sprinter awaiting the starter's gun. More than that he could not do. Rising to a standing position was beyond him now. Flushed, sweating, stricken, he waited for his strength to return and hoped someone would help him up.

No one did. The commuters obligingly parted their ranks and flowed by him to either side. A boulder in a stream. No one offers to assist a boulder. Perhaps they have a lot of epileptics in Greenwich. Can't let yourself get worked up over one of *those*. Damned troublemakers always flopping on their faces, chewing on their tongues: how's a man going to get to work on time if he stops for them every morning?

Macy listened to time tolling in his head. One minute, two, three. What had happened? This was the second time in the last eighteen hours that he'd been clubbed down from within. *Hamlin?*

—You bet your ass.

*What did you do to me?*

—Gave you a leetle twitch in the autonomic nervous system. I'm sitting right here looking at it. A bunch of ropes and cords, the most complicated frigging mess you could imagine. I just reached out and went *plink*.

Another shaft of pain between the shoulder blades.

*Stop it*, Macy said. *Jesus, why are you doing that?*

—Self-preservation. Like you said a little while ago, self-preservation has to come before concern for others, right?

*Can you hear all my thoughts?*

—Enough of them. Enough to know when I'm being threatened.

*Threatened?*

—Sure. Where were you heading when I knocked you off your feet?

*The Rehab Center,* Macy admitted.

—That's right. And what were you going to do there?

*I was going for my weekly post-therapy therapy session.*

—Like shit you were. You were going to tell the doctors that I had come back to life.

*And if I was?*

—Don't try to play innocent. You were going to have them blot me out again, right? Right Macy?

*Well—*

—Admit it!

Macy, crouching on the shining tiles, attempted to call for help. A soft mewing sound came from him. The commuters continued to stream past A flotilla of attaché cases and portable terminals. Please. Please. Help me.

From Hamlin, a second time:

—Admit it!

*Let me alone.*

Macy felt a sudden explosion of agony behind his breastbone. As if a hand had clasped itself about his heart for a quick powerful squeeze. Setting the valves aflap, emptying the ventricles, pinching the aorta.

—I'm learning my way around in here, pal. I can do all kinds of things today that I couldn't swing yesterday. Like tickling your heart. Isn't that a lovely sensation? Now, suppose you tell me why you were in such a hurry to get to the Rehab Center, and it better be the right answer.

*To have you obliterated again,* Macy confessed miserably.

—Yes. Yes. The dirty truth will out! You were conspiring in my murder, weren't you? I never murdered anybody in my life, you understand, I merely took a few liberties with my prick, and nevertheless the state was pleased to order my death—

327

*Your rehabilitation,* said Macy.

—My death, Hamlin shot back at him, giving him a tug on the right triceps by way of emphasis: They killed me and put somebody else in my body, only I came back to life, and you were going to have them kill me again. We don't need to debate the semantics of the point. Stand up, Macy.

Macy cautiously tested his strength and found that his legs now would support him. He rose, very slowly, feeling immensely fragile. A few tottering steps. Knees shaking. Skin clammy. Dryness in the throat.

—Now, friend, we have to get something understood. You aren't going to go to the Rehab Center today. You aren't going to go there at all, ever again, because the Center is a dangerous place for me, and so in order to keep you away I'll have to make it a dangerous place for you too. Let me give you just a taste of what will happen to you if you come within five miles of a Rehab Center. Just a taste.

Again, the hand tightening around his heart. But no mere squeeze this time. A fierce, gripping full-strength clench. It knocked Macy down once more. Gradually the inner grasp was relaxed, but it left him nauseated and feeble, and a terrible thunder reverberated in his chest. Cheek to the tile, he kicked his legs in a frenzy of pain. This time his anguish was too visible to be ignored, and he was seized by passersby and hoisted to his feet.

"You okay? Some kind of fit?"

"Please—if I could just sit down somewhere—"

"You need a doctor?"

"It's only a little chest spasm—I've had them before—"

They took him inside. A bench in the waiting room. Advert globes floating in the air. Blinking their messages into his face. He was numb. Impossible even to think. A constant stream of people flowing by. Trains arriving, departing. Voices. Colors. After a while, his strength returned.

—If you try to go back for reconditioning, Macy, that's what I'll do to you, and not just a little squeeze. If necessary I'll shut off your heart altogether. I can do it. I see where the nerve connections are now.

*But then you'll die too,* Macy said.

—That's true. If it's necessary for me to interrupt the life processes of this body that we're sharing, we'll both die. So what? I don't expect you to commit suicide for the sake of getting rid of me. But I'm perfectly prepared to commit suicide for the sake of *keeping* you from getting rid of me, because I've got no choice. I'm a dead man anyway if you get inside a Rehab Center. So I offer you the ultimate threat. Keep away, or else. It wouldn't be smart of you to call my bluff. For both our sakes, don't.

*I'm supposed to show up for weekly post-therapy sessions, though.*

—Skip them.

*It's part of the court decree. If I don't show up, they're likely to issue a warrant for me.*

—We'll worry about that when the time comes. Meanwhile forget about therapy sessions.

*But we can't share a body,* Macy protested. *It's insanity. There's no room for two of us.*

—Don't worry about that now, either. We'll work something out. For the time being we're sharing, and you fucking well better accept the idea. Now get yourself aboard a city-bound train. Put some distance between me and that Center.

# 6

Home again, mid-morning. His head throbbing. Not a peep out of Hamlin all the way back. The apartment seemed to have undergone a strange transformation in the two hours of his absence: previously a neutral place, wholly lacking emotional connotations, and now an alien and sinister cell, cramped and repellent.

The flat's dark new tone astonished him. Its mysterious autumnal resonances. Its shadows where no shadows had been. Nothing had changed in it, really. Lissa hadn't moved any furniture around or sprayed the walls a different color. And yet. And yet, how frightening it all looked now. How out of place he felt in it. That L-shaped bedroom, low ceiling, narrow bed jammed up against flimsy wall, old-fashioned light fixture dangling, bilious green paint, cheap smeary Picasso prints, slit of a window revealing splotchy May sunshine and two scraggly trees across the street—how ugly it looked, how coarse, how constricted, how squashed! Did people really live in places like this? Tiny bathroom, slick pink tiles. Not even an ultrasonic cleanser, just archaic sink and tub and crapper. A microscopic kitchen-dinette affair, everything jammed together, table, freezer, telephone screen, disposal unit, stove. At least a tiny buzz-cleanser for the dirty dishes. A sitting room, cheap red plastic couch, some books, cassettes, a video unit.

A prison for the soul. Our impoverished century: this is the best we can afford for human beings, after our long orgies of waste and destruction. For the last couple of weeks, this apartment had been his refuge, his harbor, his hermitage; if he thought about it at all, which he doubted, it had been in a friendly way. Why did it turn him off now? After a moment, he believed he knew. Hamlin's sensibility now underlay his own. The sculptor's sophisticated perceptions bleeding through to the Macy levels of their shared mind. Hamlin's loathing for the apartment tinged Macy's view of it. To Hamlin the proportions were wrong, the ambiance vile, the psychological texture of the place slimy and grimy, the inner environmental color a nasty one. Macy shivered. He visualized Hamlin as a kind of abscess in his brain, a pocket of pus, inaccessible, destructive.

Lissa was still in bed. That bothered him. The Protestant ethic: sleeping late equals rejection of life.

But she wasn't asleep. Stirring lazily, sitting up, knuckles to eyes. A purring yawn. "Everything taken care of?" she asked.

"No."

"What happened?"

He told her about the episode at the Greenwich terminal. Writhing on the blue and white terrazzo with fire in his chest. Hamlin playfully strumming the harp of his autonomic nervous system. Lissa listened, big-eyed, somber-faced, and said finally, "What are you going to do?"

"I haven't any idea."

"But that's hideous. Having him inside you like a parasite. A crab hiding in your head. Like a case of brain cancer. Look, maybe if I call the Rehab Center—"

A warning twinge from Hamlin, deep down.

"No," Macy said.

"I could tell them what's happened. Maybe this has happened before. Maybe they know some way to deal with him."

"The moment they tried anything," he said, "Hamlin would stop my heartbeat. I know that."

"But if there's some drug that might knock him out—I could slip it to you somehow—"

"He's listening right now, Lissa. Don't you think he'll be on guard constantly? He may not even need to sleep. We can't take chances."

"But how can you go on with somebody else inside your head, trying to take you over?"

Macy pondered that one. "What makes you think he's trying to take me over?"

"Isn't it obvious? He wants his body back. He'll try to cut you down, one block of nerves at a time, until there's nothing left of you at all. He'll push you out. And then he'll be Nat Hamlin again."

"He just said he wanted to share the body with me," Macy muttered.

"Will he stop there? Why should he?"

"But Nat Hamlin's a proscribed criminal. Legally he doesn't even exist any more. If he tried to return to life—"

"Oh, he'd go on using the Macy identity," Lissa said. "Only he'd take up sculpting again, in another country, maybe. He'd look up his old friends. He'd be the old Hamlin, except his passport would say Macy, and—" She halted. "He'd look up his old friends," she repeated. She seemed to be examining the idea from various angles. "Old friends such as me."

"Yes. You." In a tone that he recognized as unpleasant, but which he found impossible to alter, Macy said, "He could even marry you. As he was originally planning to do."

"His wife is still alive, I'm sure."

"That marriage was legally dissolved at the time he was sentenced," Macy said. "It's automatic. They cut all ties. Officially, he wouldn't be Hamlin even if he took over. He'd be Macy, and Macy is single. There you are, Lissa." The edge of cruelty coming into his voice again. "You'd finally get to be his wife. What you've always wanted."

She shook her head. "I don't want it any more."

"You said you loved him."

"I once did love him. But I told you, that's all dead now. The things he did. The crimes. The rapes."

"The first time we met," said Macy heavily, "when you were still insisting on calling me Nat, you made a point of saying you were still in love with me. The old me. *Him.* You said it two or three times. Talking about how much you missed him. Refusing to believe that there was somebody new living behind his face."

"You misunderstand," she said. "I felt so lonely. So fucking *lost.* And all of a sudden I was standing next to somebody I knew; somebody out of the past—I just wanted help, I had to talk to him—I mean, I crashed right into you in the street, was I supposed to walk away and not even say hello?"

"You saw my Rehab badge and you ignored it."

"I didn't see it at all."

"You must have blanked it out deliberately. You knew Nat Hamlin had been put away for Rehab."

"You're shouting at me."

"I'm sorry. I can't help it. I'm tense as hell, Lissa. Look, so you saw somebody in the street and you thought he was Nat Hamlin, so you said hello, but did you have to tell him you were still in love with him, too?"

"I didn't mean it."

"You said it."

"What else could I do?" she asked. Her voice was shrill now. "Stand there and say, Hello, you look like Nat Hamlin who I used to love, and of course I don't love him any more and in any case he's been wiped out but since you look just like him I'll fall in love with you instead, so let's go home and ball a little? How could I say that? But I couldn't let you just vanish without saying something to you. I was making a stab at the past, trying to catch it, trying to bring it back. The beautiful past, before the hellish part started. And you were my only link to that, Paul, and I was excited, and I said Nat, Nat, I talked about being in love—"

"Exactly. You called me Nat, and said you were still in love with—"

"Why are you doing this to me, Paul?"

"Doing what?"

"Chewing on me. Shouting. All these questions."

"I'm trying to find out which one of us you're really loyal to. Hamlin or me. Which side you're going to take when the struggle for this body gets rough."

"You aren't trying to find out any such thing. You just want to hurt me."

"Why should I want to—"

"How would I know? Because you blame me for bringing him

334

back to life, maybe. Because you hate me for having loved him once. Because he's sitting inside you right now forcing you to hurt me. I don't know. Christ, I don't know at all. Only why do you need to find out where my loyalty is? Didn't I tell you last night that I didn't want him coming back? Didn't I offer to call the Rehab Center just now?"

"Yes. Yes."

"So how could I possibly be on his side? I want him to be wiped out. I want him gone forever. I want—oh, Christ—"

She halted suddenly. Leaping from the bed as though stung, arms and legs flying stiffly out from her torso. Turning toward him. Her face contorted, the eyes bulging, the mouth a rigid hole, the muscles of her throat bunched and jutting. From her lips a bizarre clotted baritone, hoarse and unfocused, like the blunt blurtings of a deaf mute, no words intelligible: *"Mfss. Shlrrm. Skk-kk. Vshh. Vshh. Vshh."* A terrible gargling cry, all the more horrible because of the deep masculine tongue in which it was delivered.

She lurched around the room, stumbling into things, clawing at the air. A plain case of demonic possession. What rides her?

*"Grkk. Lll. Llll. Pkd-dd."* Eyes wild, pleading. Bare breasts heaving wildly. A sheen of sweat on her skin.

Macy rushed toward her, trying to embrace her, calm her, ease her back to the bed. She pivoted like a robot and her arm crashed across his chest, doubling him up in gasps. When he looked at her again her face was scarlet with strain and her mouth was open to the full reach of her jaws, beyond it perhaps. The wild gargling sounds still erupted from her, and her eyes registered total horror and despair.

Once again Macy tried to seize her. This time successfully. Muscles leaping and churning and twitching all over her spare naked form. He forced her down on the bed and covered her with his body, hands gripping her wrists, knees imprisoning her thighs. A sour smell of sweat rising from her, bad sweat, fear-sweat.

Some kind of epileptic fit? Epilepsy was much on his mind this morning. In a low urgent voice he talked to her, tried to soothe her, to reach her somehow. More baritone drivel coming out of her in halting husky bleeps of thick noise. The static of the soul.

"Lissa?" he said. "Lissa, can you hear me? Try to go limp. Let all your muscles hang loose."

Easier said than done. She still twitched. While in the midst of this he felt a hot sensation at the base of his skull, as of an auger drilling into him. Or drilling toward the outside from the soft center of his brain. Something jumped frantically within his mouth, and it was a moment before he realized that it was his tongue, jerking itself crazily backward toward his gullet *"Vshh. Vshh. Pkd-dd. Slrr. Msss."* The sounds not from Lissa this time. From him.

Lying there congealed and coagulated on top of Lissa, he understood perfectly what was happening. Nat Hamlin, having conserved his strength for a couple of hours, was trying to achieve a takeover of a new level of their shared brain. Specifically, Hamlin was attempting to grab Macy's speech centers.

Macy knew that that would mark the start of his own obliteration; once Hamlin had control of the voice, it would be *his* thoughts, not Macy's that their body would express. Hamlin would have access to the external world and Macy would be shut inside. But at the moment Hamlin wasn't doing too well. He had grabbed the neural sectors governing speech, only his grasp was incomplete, and the best he could manage were these bursts of nonsense. Somehow, Macy realized, Lissa had become entangled in the battle before he himself had known it was going on. Her brain hooked into his; Hamlin speaking, or trying to, through her mouth. A microphoning effect of some kind. Now they were both doing it, the two of them bellowing like demented seals. Feeding hour at the zoo. Is this where it ends? Does Hamlin take over from me now? No. No. Fight back. Stop him here and drive him into a corner.

How, though?

The way you did last night, when he had hold of the side of your mouth. Pry him loose. Through sheer strength of concentration, break his grip.

Macy tried to visualize the interior of his brain. Telling himself, This is where Hamlin lives, this pocket of gunk, and these are the pathways he's been building to other parts of my brain, and this is the place he's attacking now. It was a purely imaginary construct, but it would serve for the moment. Try to visualize the speech centers themselves. Say, row upon row of tight-strung pink cords, a kind of piano deal, with a switchboard attached. Hamlin at the switchboard, plugging things in, looking for the right connection; and the pink cords, all ajangle, giving off weird groaning noises. Come up behind him. Grab his arms. He isn't any stronger than you are. Pull him away, knock him on his ass. Jump on him. Careful, don't smash any of the machinery. You'll need it when this is over. Just hang on to him. Stay on top. Pin him, pin him, pin him! Good! Smash his head against the floor a couple of times! Okay, the floor's spongy, it gives a little, smash him anyway. Stun him. Right. Now start hauling him the hell out of there. Heavy fucker, isn't he? One hundred ninety pounds, same as you. Heave. Heave. Heave. Into this musty corridor. A hot humid smell coming out of it. Things must be rotting in there. In with him! Down the chute! Slam the door. There. Easier than you expected, eh? All it takes is some mental energy. Perseverance. You can relax now. Catch your breath.

ROBERT SILVERBERG

Hey, Jesus, what's this? He must have come to, in there. Hammering on the other side of the door. Starting to push it open. Wow, you can't let him do that. Hold it closed! Push . . . push . . . push . . . a stalemate. He can't get it open any farther, you can't close it that last crack. *Push.* He's pushing back. *Push. Push.* Bear down. Oh, Jesus. There! It's closed again. All right, keep your shoulder to the door, hold it tight. The bear's locked in his cave; you don't want him coming out again.

Now fasten the door. With what? Slip a bolt in place, dodo. But there isn't a bolt. Sure there is. This is your mind, your own fucking mind, can't you use a little imagination? Invent a bolt! Like that. Fine. Now ram it home. In the slot. In. In. There. Okay, step back. See if he can break out. Be ready to clobber him if he does. He's banging on the door. Throwing himself against it. But the bolt holds. It holds. Good deal. Let's check out the machinery now. Make sure he didn't screw it up. Loud and clear, let's hear it:

"My name is Paul Macy."

Good. Nice to hear some sense out of your mouth again. Keep going.

"I was born in Idaho Falls, Idaho, on the twelfth of March, 1972. My father was a propulsion engineer and my mother was a schoolteacher."

Voice production generally okay. A little rusty around the edges, a little froggy in the lower frequencies, but that's only to be expected, the way he was abusing your pipes. It'll clear up fast most likely.

You win this round, Macy.

Slowly, shakily, he rose from the bed. Lissa still lay there, looking crumpled and flattened. She didn't move.

Her face had resumed its normal appearance. Her eyes were open. No glow in them. A sullen, absent expression.

338

"Are you all right?" he asked.

No response. Off in another galaxy somewhere.

"Lissa? Are you okay?"

Staring blankly at him, she said, "Do you give a shit if I am?" Her voice was as hoarse as his.

"What kind of question is that?"

"You were really letting me have it before all the fireworks started," she said. "Telling me you suspected I was on his side, and a lot of other crap. If I had any sense I'd get the hell away from you, fast. I don't need to be pushed around like that." She stood up, huddling her arms against her sides, looking more vulnerable than ever. The blue streaks of veins visible in her breasts. Stretch marks in the skin of her hips, showing where she had lost weight lately. Quick angry motions. Snatching at her clothes, throwing things on. A blouse, a tunic. She said, "That was him, wasn't it? Hamlin? Trying to talk through my voice?"

"And then through mine, yes."

"Where did he go?"

"I beat him down. I made him let go."

"Hurray for you." Tonelessly. "My hero. You see my sandals anywhere?"

"Where are you going?" he asked.

"This is a crazyhouse. I'm worse off here than I was alone. I'm going home."

"No," he said. He remembered that he had decided, only this dawn, to sever her from his life once the Rehab Center had plucked the resurgent Nat Hamlin from his brain. Telling himself then that it was too dangerous to have her around him, because of her gift, her curse, whatever it was that had awakened Hamlin. Out she goes, he had decided. Self-preservation first and always. Out she goes. How hollow that sounded to him

339

now. He still had Hamlin inside him, and he was frightened by the thought of having to grapple with him in solitude. Lissa wasn't as dispensable now as she had seemed earlier. "Don't go," he said. "Please."

"I'll get nothing but trouble here."

"I didn't mean to yell at you. My nerves were raw, is all. You can understand that. I didn't intend to accuse you of anything, Lissa."

"Even so. You got me all stirred up. And then *him,* jumping into my head. The sounds I was making. I never did that before. Like I was some kind of ventriloquist's dummy, and I could feel Nat trying to move my lips, trying to push my vocal cords, trying to get his words out through me—" She seemed to gag on something. "It was coming out of you, Paul. I thought my head would blow. I don't want to go through that again."

"I beat him back," Macy said. "I shut him off."

"And if he gets out again? Or if you start suspecting me again? Asking me if I'm really on his side? Maybe next time you'll bang me around some. You could break my arms. You could knock all my teeth out. And then you'd apologize later."

"There's no possibility of that."

"But you've got reason to be hostile. I'm responsible for waking him up inside you, right? Even if I wanted to stay here, you know, it wouldn't be smart for you if I did. Maybe he'll use me now to finish the takeover of your body. Play his mental energy through my ESP output, or something. He almost did that just now, didn't he? Do you want to chance it?"

"Who knows?" Macy said. He caught her by the arm as she moved slowly toward the door. "Do I have to beg you, Lissa? Don't leave me now."

"First you didn't want anything to do with me. Then you screamed at me that you didn't trust me. Now you don't want me to go. I can't figure you, Paul. When somebody comes out of a Rehab Center, he's supposed to be sane, isn't he? You scare me too much. I want to get out of here."

"Please. Stay."

"What for?"

"To help me fight against him. I need you. And you need me. We can support each other. Separately we're both going to go under. Together—"

"Together we'll both go under too," she said. Moving no closer to the door, though. "Look, I thought you could help me, Paul. That's why I wrote you at the network, that's why I begged you to see me. But now I realize that your troubles are as bad as mine. Worse, maybe. I just hear voices from outside. You've got somebody else in your head. On account of me. We can only harm each other."

"No."

"You ought to believe it. Look what I've already done to you, bringing *him* back. And then you, bouncing him into my head for a couple of minutes. And on and on and on like that, things getting worse and worse and worse for both of us."

He shook his head. "I'm going to fight. I've beaten him twice in two days. Next time I'll finish him altogether. But I don't want to be alone while I'm doing it."

Shrugging, she said, "Don't blame me if—"

"I won't." He looked at the time. A sudden bold idea hooking him. By their works ye shall know them. Yes. Go to the museum, see his version of Lissa. Look at her through his eyes.

An unexpectedly powerful hunger rose in him to know the real past, to find out what manner of man he had been, what he had been capable of creating. In a sense what *I* was capable of, in my other self. And the sculpture of Lissa a bridge to that hidden past. Leading him out of this shadowy unlife into the realm of authentic experience. *He* did this, *he* made it, *his* unique and irreplaceable vision was at work. And I must understand him in order to defeat him.

Macy said, "Listen, there's no sense in my going to the office this late in the day. But we've still got the whole afternoon. You know where I want to go? The Metropolitan Museum. To see the sculpture he did of you, the *Antigone 21*."

"Why?"

"Old maxim: Know your enemy. I want to see his interpretation of you. Find out what his mind is like. Size him up, look for the places where I can attack."

"I don't think we should go. It could trigger anything, Paul. You said yourself, how at your office you saw one of his pieces and it almost knocked you out. Suppose at the museum—"

"I was caught by surprise that first time. This is different I've got to take the offensive, Lissa. Carry the battle to him, do you see? And the museum's as good a place to start as any. Showing him that I can hold my own under any conditions. All right? Let's go, shall we? The museum."

"All right," she said distantly. "The museum."

# 7

Entering the huge building, he felt apprehensive and ill at ease. An overwhelming sense of not belonging in this vast and labyrinthine palace of culture oppressed him.

Searching his stock of synthetic memories, he couldn't find any recollection of having been here before. Or any other art museum. The Rehab people hadn't built a strong interest in the visual arts into him, it seemed. Music, yes. The theater. Even ballet. But not sculpture, not painting, not anything that was likely to impinge on the world Nat Hamlin had inhabited. A deliberate divergence from the abolished past.

Still, why was he so edgy about going in? Afraid of being recognized, maybe? People turning, whispering, pointing? Look, that's Nathaniel Hamlin, the famous psychosculptor. He did that naked woman we saw before. Hamlin. Hamlin. That man looks just like Hamlin. Requiring you to say something by way of correction. Pardon me, ma'am, you are in error. My name is Paul Macy. Never done a sculpture in my life. Ostentatiously rubbing your Rehab badge. Thrusting it in her eyes. I must tell you, ma'am, that Nathaniel Hamlin has become an unperson. And the woman fading, away in embarrassment, heels clicking on the stone floor, looking back at him over her shoulder, sniffing a little in disdain. Maybe even reporting him to a guard for molesting her.

Macy smiled sourly and swept the whole scenario away. Not much chance of any of that happening. Rembrandt could walk through this place and nobody'd recognize him. Michelangelo. Picasso. Mommy, who's that funny little bald-headed man? Shh, dear, I think that's some senator. Yes. Macy shook off his apprehensions. They went inside.

Just within the main entrance they were held for a moment in a cone of tingling blue light, some kind of scanning device ascertaining that they carried no explosives, knives, cans of paint, or other instruments of vandalism. Evidently there was a lot of free-floating masterpiece-directed hostility in this city. They passed the test and advanced into the colossal central hall. Pink granite pharaohs to the left; bleached marble Apollos to the right. Straight ahead, an immense dizzying vista of receding hallway. The dry smell of the past in here: the nineteenth century, the fourteenth, the third.

"Where is it?" he asked. "Your statue."

"Second floor, all the way in the back, the modern-art wing," Lissa said. Once again she seemed remote and abstracted. She slipped easily into that kind of withdrawal, that closed-and-sealed surliness. "You go, Paul. I'll wait here and do the Egyptian stuff or something. I don't want to see it."

"I'd like you to come with me."

"No."

"Jesus, why not?"

"Because it shows how beautiful I was. I don't want to be in the room with you when you see it. And when you turn and look at me afterward and see what I've become. Go on, Paul. You wont have any trouble finding it."

He was stubborn. Refusing to leave her. Unwilling to face the Hamlin piece without her. Suppose the sight of it struck him down again; who would help him up? But she was equally firm. Not going with him, simply not going. The museum expedition was his crazy idea, not hers. She couldn't bear to see that piece. Won't you? I won't. I wont. A tense little scene in the grand hallway. Their harsh whispers echoing from alabaster arcades. People staring at them as they bickered. He half expected someone to say, any minute, Say, isn't that the sculptor Nathaniel Hamlin? Over there, the big one arguing with the redhead. Terrified by that irrational prospect. His discomfort grew so strong that he was on the verge of letting her have her way when suddenly she nipped her upper lip with her lower teeth, pressed her knuckles to her jawbone, hunched her shoulders as if trying to touch her earlobes with them, sucked in her cheeks. Began quirking her mouth from side to side. Possibly she was being skewered by invisible darts. Eyes wild. Glossy with panic. Saying to him, after some moments, in a veiled, barely audible voice: "Okay, come on, then. I'll go with you. But hurry!"

"What's happening to you, Lissa?"

"I'm picking up voices again." A fusillade of twitches distorting her face. "They're bouncing off the walls, a dozen different strands of thought. Getting louder and louder. All garbled up. Christ, get me out of this room. *Get me out of this room.*"

Everybody in the museum must have heard that. She seemed about to come apart.

He took her elbow and steered her hastily into the long hallway facing them. Hardly anyone here. Without any real idea of where he was going, he hustled her along, infected by the urgency of her distress; she slipped and slid on the smooth polished floor, but he kept her upright. Mounted figures in chain mail streaming toward them and vanishing to the rear. Shimmering tapestries looming in the dusk. Swords. Lances. Engraved silver bowls. All the loot of the past, and no one around, just a couple of blank-faced robot guards.

When they had gone about a hundred yards he halted, aware that Lissa had grown more calm, and they stood for a moment in front of a case of small iridescent Roman glass flasks and vases with elaborate spiral handles. She turned to him, haggard, sweat-streaked, and clung to him, cheek to his chest. Her anxiety definitely subsiding, but she was still upset.

Finally she said, "How awful that was. One of the worst ones yet. A dozen of them all talking at once, each one with a pipeline right into my skull. A torrent of nonsense. Swelling and swelling and swelling my head till it wants to explode."

"Is it better now?"

"I don't hear them, anyway. But the echoes inside me . . . the noise bouncing around upstairs . . . .You know, I wish I could go far away from the whole human race. To some icy planet. To one of the moons of Jupiter. And just live there in a plastic dome, all by myself. Although even there I'd probably pick up the static. Minds radiating at me right across space. Can you imagine what it's like, Paul, never to have real privacy? Never to know when your head is going to turn into a goddam two-way radio?" Then a chilly laugh from her. "Hey, that's funny. Me asking you about privacy. And you with your own ghost sitting in your head. Worse off than I am. Paul and Lissa, Lissa and Paul. What a pair of fucking cripples we are, you and me!"

"Somehow we'll manage."

"I bet."

"We can get help, Lissa."

"Sure we can. He'll kill you as soon as you go within a mile of your doctors. And nobody can fix me without chopping my brain into hamburger. But we can get help, yeah. I like your optimism, kid." She pointed. "We can take that staircase. Nightmare Number Sixteen is waiting for us."

Up the stairs, through another hall full of Chinese porcelains and Assyrian palace reliefs, past a room of Persian miniatures, one of Iranian pottery, gallery after gallery of archaic treasures, and emerging ultimately in an opulent cube of clear plastic cantilevered out of the rear of the building to overhang the wilted greenery of Central Park. The modern-art wing.

Crowded, too; Macy looked nervously at Lissa, fearing she would tumble into another telepathic abyss, but she appeared to be in control of herself. Guiding him coolly down yards of gaudy paintings and sculpture and tick-tock artifacts and dancing posters and metabolic mirrors and liquespheres and all the rest.

Left turn. Deep breath. A small room, no door, just a circular entrance. Over the entrance, in raised gilded letters: ANTIGONE 21 BY NATHANIEL HAMLIN. Jesus. A private exhibition hall for it. What he had taken to be the absence of a door was in fact the presence of an invisible airseal, providing secret shelter for the masterwork within, ensuring it its own environment and psychological habitat. They stepped through. No sensation while breaching the seal; cooler on the other side, the air tingling, full of wandering ions. A faint chemical odor. A low hum.

"That's it," Lissa said.

Ten, twelve people clustered in front of it; he couldn't see. She hung tensely against him, arm jammed through his, ribs raking his side. Her tautness leaked through to him, a mental emanation of something just short of fear. He felt the same way. The knot of onlookers parted and as though through a rift in the clouds he beheld Nathaniel Hamlin's *Antigone 21.*

Nude female figure, larger than life. Unmistakably Lissa, yet no danger that anyone in the room would turn from that radiant statue to the drab drained girl and connect the two of them. Firm, full body. The breasts higher and heavier: had the sculptor idealized them or had Lissa lost weight there too? The pose an aggressive, dynamic one, head flung back, one arm outstretched, legs apart. O Pioneers, that sort of thing. Emphasizing the strength of the woman, the resilience of her. Eyes bright and fierce. Mouth not quite smiling but almost. The entire solid figure crying out, I can take it, I can handle anything, stress and turmoil and flood and famine and revolution and assassination, I have endured, I will endure, I am the essence of endurance. The eternal feminine. And so forth.

But of course the sculpture was not merely just a sexy academic nude in a high-powered nineteenth-century mode, nor was it only a sentimentally conceived monument to stereotyped concepts of womanhood. It was those things, yes, but it was also a psychosculpture, meaning that it approached the condition of being alive, it was a whole cosmos in itself. It did tricks. The room was rigged to heighten the effects. Imperceptible changes of lighting. That odd humming sound, coming from a battery of hidden sonic generators, controlled the mood through its pattern of modulations, hitting the onlookers at some subterranean level of their psyches.

The degree of ionization in the room was constantly changing, too. And the statue itself. Going through a cycle of transformations. Look, the nipples are erect now, the breasts are heaving (but are they, or does it just seem that they move?), the eyes are those of a woman in heat. What has become of the defiant, all-enduring woman of three minutes ago? Now we behold the essence of cuntliness. One could rush forward gladly and prong her.

And yet she changes again. Her juices going sour, her nipples softening: a woman thwarted, a woman denied. How bitter that fractional smile! She holds grudges. In the darkness of the night she would gladly castrate the unsuspecting male. But the strength of hatred ebbs from her. She is afraid; she knows that there are questions for which she has no answers; she feels the phantoms of the night fluttering against the windows, wings beating harder and harder. Terror closes its hand on her. She is alone, naked and vulnerable, not half so strong as she would have the world believe.

If they came to attack her now—but what comes is dawn. A brightening. Finding her place in the universe under a friendly sky. She seems taller. Older, though no less beautiful; voluptuous, though cooler than before; in command of herself, beyond doubt Venus ascendant. A totally different self each few minutes.

What machinery is at work beneath that figure's supple skin? How is this cycle of transformations propelled? Watching it, the constantly shifting play of emotions and impressions, the subtle mutations of posture and attitude, Macy feels awed and overpowered but also vaguely cheated. He had not known what to expect of the art of his former self, other than that it would be dramatic and impressive. But is this really art, this clever robot? Will all this mechanical trickery be able to stand alongside the true artistic achievements of the ages? He is no critic, in truth he knows nothing at all, yet the intense realism of the sculpture that is its outstanding characteristic makes it seem aesthetically primitive to him, a toy, a stunt, a triumph of craft, not art.

But even so. But even so. Impossible not to respond to the power of the thing. How thoroughly Lissa has been captured in those gears and cogs; not his Lissa, not the broken dazed girl he knows, but Nat Hamlin's glorious Lissa, whose caved-in shell has fallen to Hamlin's successor. What Hamlin has created here may be simpleminded next to Leonardo and Cellini and Henry Moore, but behind the superficial superficiality may lie a carefully masked profundity, Macy suspects. He could stand here studying the figure for hours. Days. As others seem to be doing. Those students muttering notes into hand recorders, and that one, holographing the work from every conceivable angle—they are trapped by it too, plainly. A masterpiece. Undoubtedly a masterpiece.

With an effort he turned away from it, feeling an almost audible snap as the sightlines of his contact with the sculpture broke, and glanced at Lissa. She was drawn back, hunched against the wall, lips parted, eyes fixed and glassy, caught by the mesmerism of her overpowering simulacrum up there. A gasp frozen on her face. What currents of identity, he wondered, were flowing from her to the sculpture, from the sculpture to her? What draining of self was going on, and what recharging? What must it be like to behold yourself made into such a work of art?

And where was Hamlin? Why wasn't he jumping and cavorting in pride before his wondrous achievement, as he had that first day in Harold Griswold's office? Hamlin was quiescent. Not absent, though. Macy became gradually aware of him glowing far below the surface, embedded deep in his brain. A thorn in his paw. A pebble in his hoof. Macy hadn't expected Hamlin to remain bolted inside his dungeon for long.

Nor did he. Rising slowly now, bubbling toward the top. Evoked into consciousness by the *Antigone 21*. That's all right, Macy thought. Let him come up. I can handle him. Bracing himself, battening down, Macy waited for his other self to finish drifting toward the surface. Not hostile, this time. Not even aggressive. A prevailing air of calmness about him. No resentment apparent over his defeat in their last battle. Perhaps a strategy of deception, though. Get me off guard, then make another quick leap for the speech centers. I'm ready, whatever he tries. But when Hamlin opened their inner conversation, his tone was easy, civil:

—What do you think of it?

*Impressive. I didn't know you had it in you.*

—Why? Do I seem second-rate to you, Macy?

*The only aspect of you that I know is the violence, the criminality. It turns me off. I don't associate great art with that kind of personality.*

—What a load of bourgeois crap that is, friend.

*Is it?*

—Item one, a man can be a thief, a killer, a baby-buggerer, anything, and still be a great artist. The quality of his morals has nothing to do with the quality of his perceptions, hip? You'd be surprised how much of the stuff in this museum was produced by absolute bastards. Item two, I happened to have been a pretty fair artist fifteen years before I became what they call an enemy of society. This piece you see here was entirely finished before I had my breakdown. Item three, since you never knew me, you don't have any goddam right to judge what kind of person I was.

*I concede item two and maybe item one. But why should I yield on number three? I know you plenty well, Hamlin. You've knocked me down, you've played games with my heart, you've attempted to seize sections of my brain, you've threatened outright to kill me. Should I love you for that? This is the first time since you surfaced that you've seemed even halfway civilized. You come on like a thug; do you blame me for being surprised you could produce a sculpture like this?*

—You really think I'm a villain?

*You're a convicted criminal.*

—Forget that shit I mean my relationship to you. You think I'm acting out of evil impulses?

*What else can I think?*

—But I'm not, Macy. I don't dislike you, I don't want to harm you, I have no negative feelings toward you at all. It just happens that you're in the way of a man who's fighting for his life.

*Meaning you.*

—Exactly. I want to be myself again. I don't want to stay submerged inside you.

*The court decreed—*

—Fuck the court. The whole Rehab system is hysterical nonsense. Why wipe me out? Why not rehabilitate me in the real sense of the word? I wasn't hopelessly insane, Macy. Shit, yes, I did a lot of awful things, I admit that freely, I was off my head. But in the year 2007 they could have some better way of coping with insanity than the death sentence.

*But—*

—Let me finish. It *was* a death sentence, wasn't it? To rip me out of my own body and throw me away, and pour someone else into my head? What happened to my whole accumulation of experiences? What happened to my skills and talents? What happened to me, damn it, what happened to *me?* Killed. Killed. Nothing but a zombie body left. It's only by the merest fluke that I'm still here, even in this condition, hanging on inside you. What kind of humanitarianism is that? What are they saving, when they keep the body and throw away the soul?

*I didn't make the laws.*

—Agreed, Macy. But you're no fool. You can see how flagrantly unjust Rehab is. They want to separate me from society because I'm dangerous, okay, I agree, I agree, put me away, try to fix me, drain all the poison out of me. Right. But instead this. The super resources of modern science are employed to murder a great but somewhat deranged sculptor and invent a dumb holovision commentator to replace him.

*Thank you.*

—What else can I say? Look up there, at my *Antigone.* Could you do that? Could anybody else do that? I did it. My unique gift to mankind. And fifty others almost as good. I'm not bragging, Macy, I'm being as objective as hell. I was somebody valuable, I had a special gift, I had intensity, I had humanity. Maybe my gift drove me crazy after a while, but at least I had something to offer. And you? What are you? *Who* are you? You're nothing. You have no depth You have no texture. You have no past. You have no reality. I've been sitting here inside you, taking an inventory. I know what you're made of, Macy, and it's all ersatz. You have no purpose in existing. You can't do anything that a robot couldn't do better. A holovision commentator? They can program a machine with pear-shaped tones, and it'll broadcast you off the map.

*I admit all this,* Macy replied. He stood stiffly, pretending to study the sculpture. He wondered how much time had elapsed during his colloquy with Hamlin. Five seconds? Five minutes? He had lost track of external things. *Granted that you were a genius and I'm a nobody, what am I supposed to do about it?*

—Vacate the premises.

*Just like that.*

—Yes. It wouldn't be hard. I could show you how. You relax, you lower your defenses, you let me administer the *coup de grace*. Then you disappear back into the limbo they whistled you out of, and I can function as Nat Hamlin wearing the mask of Paul Macy. I can begin to sculpt again. Quietly. As long as I don't harm anybody, I'd get away with it

*You'd harm me.*

—But you have no right to exist! You're fiction, Macy. You're not real.

*I exist now. I'm here. I have feelings and ambitions and fears. When I eat a steak I taste it. When I fuck a girl I enjoy it. You know how it goes. Cut me and I bleed. I'm real, as real as anybody who ever lived.*

—How can I persuade you that you aren't?

*You can't. I'm as real to me as anybody else is to himself. Look, Hamlin, look, this isn't a thing for logic. I can't just say to you, Okay, you're a genius, I bow to the demands of culture, lop off my head and take my place. A far, far better thing, et cetera, et cetera. No. I'm here. I want to go on being here.*

—Where does that leave me?

*Up shit creek, I guess. Right now you're the one who's unreal, you know that? Officially you're dead. You're just a spook wandering around my skull. Why don't you do the noble thing? Stop fucking up a decent and inoffensive human being's life, and clear out. Vacate the premises, as you say. Lower the defenses and let me clobber you.*

—Some chance.

*You've given the world enough masterpieces.*

—I'm still young. I'm better than you. I deserve to live.

*The court said otherwise. The court sent you out of the world for God knows what kind of crimes, and—*

—For rape. That's all it was, rape.

*I don't care if it was for reusing old postage stamps. A verdict's a verdict. I'm not giving up my life to remedy what you consider to have been a miscarriage of justice.*

—You don't *have* a life, Macy!

*Sorry. I do.*

A long silence. Macy peered at the sculpture, at the onlookers, at the walls. His head was spinning. Hamlin's presence remained manifest within him as a steady pressure, wordless, heavy. And then, finally:

*All right. We're getting nowhere like this. Go stroll around the museum. We'll continue the discussion some other time.*

Sensation of Hamlin letting go. Dropping once more into the depths. Plop. Splash. The illusion of solitude. Solemn trombone music marking the alter ego's exit. Macy was drenched in sweat. Unsteady on his feet.

Lissa: "Have you seen enough yet?"

"I think so. We can go. Wait, let me hold your hand."

"Is something wrong, Paul?"

"A little wobbly." He wasn't able to look at her. Clutching her cool fingers between his. Step. Step. Through the invisible door. In the gallery outside he found a bench and sank down on it. Lissa fluttering over him, bewildered. He said, "While I was looking at it, I had a sort of conversation with Hamlin. Very quietly. He was almost charming."

"What was he telling you?"

"A lot of insidious bullshit. He invited me to get out of our body so he could have it On the grounds that he's a great artist and deserves to live more than I do."

"That's just the sort of thing he'd say!"

"It's just the sort of thing he did say. I told him no, and he went back to his cave. And now I realize I must have put more energy into that chat than I thought."

"Sit. Rest."

"I'm going to."

"How about the *Antigone?*" she asked.

"Incredible. Demolishing. I almost feel a kind of secondhand paternal pride in it. I mean, these hands here made it. This brain conceived it. Even if I wasn't there at the time. And—"

"No," Lissa said. "These hands made it, yes, but not this brain." She tapped his skull lightly, affectionately, with three fingertips. "A brain's just a globe of gray cheese. Brains don't conceive sculptures. *Minds* do. And this wasn't the mind that conceived the *Antigone.*"

"I realize that," he told her stiffly. Somehow her quibbling upset him. A show of loyalty for Hamlin, perhaps. Arousing jealousy in him. Hard to accept the truth that she had been there while that piece was being fashioned, she posed, she was in on the white-hot hours of creation, she and Hamlin, in the days before Paul Macy was born. To think about that made him feel like an intruder in his own body. What ecstasies had Lissa and Hamlin shared, what joys and griefs, what moments of exaltation? He was shut out of all those events. Cut off by the impenetrable wall of the past. Other times, another self. But *she* could remember. Scowling, he watched the museum-goers filing by threes and fours into the Hamlin room. Hamlin is right, he thought gloomily. I'm nothing. I have no texture. I have no past. I have no reality. Abruptly standing, he said, "Is there anything else you'd like to see, as long as we're in the museum?"

"This trip was your idea."

"As long as we're here."

"No, nothing," she said. "Not really."

"Let's go, then."

"Did you learn whatever you wanted to learn from the *Antigone?*" she asked.

"Yes," he said; "All that I wanted to learn. And more. Maybe too much more." They hurried from the building by a side door in the Egyptian wing.

# 8

Emerging into the sunlight revived his vigor a bit. It was still only about four in the afternoon. At Lissa's suggestion they went uptown, to her place; there were some things she needed to get, she said. Unspoken in that was the assumption that she would be moving in with him. He didn't object. He couldn't say that he loved her, as Hamlin evidently had, or that he was even on the verge of falling in love with her; but their individually precarious circumstances demanded a mutual defense treaty, and living together was the obvious logistical arrangement. For the time being, at least.

In the tube heading north she was cheerful, even a little manic: definitely up, despite the throngs of fellow travelers pressing close. Her ESP didn't seem to operate all the time. It was something like Hamlin was for him, he imagined: coming and going, ebbing and flowing, now virtually in full possession, now weak and indetectable. When the demon was on her, she came close to disruption and collapse. At other times, such as now, she was lively, alert, buoyant. Yet there was a hard fretful edge to her gaiety. As if she were contemplating at all times the possibility that her telepathic sensitivity would switch itself on, here in the tube, and plunge her once more into frenzy.

Her apartment was grim: one shabby room in an antique building on a forgotten limb of the city. Something out of Dickens. The lame, the halt, and the blind infesting the place, dirty children everywhere, fat old women, sinister cutthroaty young men, dogs, cats, screams, shrieks, wild laughter from behind concave doors. A prevailing odor of urine and exotic spices. Not just the twentieth century surviving here; more like the nineteenth. The booming of holovision sets in the halls seemed like a grotesque anachronism.

They walked up, five flights. One didn't expect to find liftshafts in this sort of house, but one hoped it dated at least from the era of elevators. Apparently not. Why did she live here? Why not go to one of the people's cooperatives, stark but at least clean, and surely no more costly than this? She preferred this, she told him. He couldn't follow her mumbled explanation, but he thought it had to do with the construction of the walls; was she saying that in an old building like this she wasn't as bothered by her neighbors' telepathic emanations as she would be in a flimsily built co-op?

Within this dismalness she had carved an equally dismal nest. A squarish high-ceilinged room with clumsy furniture, patched draperies, simple utensils. A tiny stained power-pack to cook on, a cold-sink in lieu of real refrigeration. He didn't see toilet facilities. Everything in disarray. No housekeeper she. The bed unmade, the exposed sheets carrying half a dozen layers of yellowish stains—that bothered him, he could guess at the origin of the stains—and books scattered everywhere. On the windowsill, on the floor, even under the bed.

So she was a diligent reader. Interesting. You could judge a person's character by his reading.

Macy realized he scarcely knew Lissa at all. What could he say about her? That she seemed fairly bright but had shown no signs so far of having intellectual interests, that she was a passably good lay (so far as he was capable of telling, given the synthetic nature of his available past experience), that she once had been closely associated with an important contemporary artist. Period. Had she had an education? A career of her own, goals in life, talents, skills? A model is only a cipher, a shape, a set of curves and planes and textures; Hamlin was too complicated a man to have fallen in love with her purely as model, so there had to be something back of the exterior, she must have had some kind of interior substance, she must have done something in the world other than pose for Nat Hamlin. At least until her increasingly more turbulent inner storms had driven her to take refuge in this squalid place.

But he knew nothing. Had she traveled? Did she have a family? Dreams of becoming an artist herself? Perhaps her books might tell him something. Helplessly, he surveyed and inventoried her library while she bustled around collecting her other possessions.

Immediately he found himself in difficulties: he was no reader himself, had merely skimmed a few popular novels during his stay in the Rehab Center, and whatever Hamlin had read, if he had read anything at all, was of course gone from Macy's mind. Macy had only the *illusion* of a familiarity with literature. Dr. Brewster, the literary one, had programmed him with hazy plot summaries and dislocated images and even with the physical feel of some books, so that he knew quite clearly that the *Iliad* was a tall orange volume with cream-colored paper and elegant rounded print But what was it about? A war, long ago. A quarrel over a woman. Proud barbarian chieftains. Who was Homer? Had he lived before Hemingway? Jesus, he was an illiterate!

And so, looking through Lissa's heaps of books, he could draw no certain conclusions, except that she seemed to read (or at least to own) a lot of novels, thick serious-looking ones, and that perhaps a fifth of the books were works of biography and history, not casual light stuff by any means. So she must be a more complex person than she had revealed herself to him thus far to be. Anybody, no matter how dim, might happen to pick up a book occasionally, but Lissa had surrounded herself with them, which argued for the presence within her of psychic hungers for knowledge.

He tried to touch up his image of her, making her less waiflike and dependent, less the hapless, whining victim of circumstances, more of a self-propelled inner-guided individual with purpose and direction and a sphere of interests. But he still had difficulty seeing her as anything other than part of the furniture in Nat Hamlin's studio, or as a pitiful casualty of modern urban life. She refused to come alive for him as a genuine, fully operative human being.

Maybe it's because I don't understand people very well, being so new in the world, he thought. Or perhaps one of the doctors built his own archaic attitudes toward women in general into me—does Gomez, say, see them only as extensions and pale reflections of the men they live with? Mere bundles of foggy emotion and woolly response? But they don't just drift from event to event, letting things happen to them. They won't forget to get out of bed if nobody tells them to. Women have minds of their own. I'm sure they do. They must. They must. And interesting minds. Some commitment to something besides survival, meals, fucking, babies. Then why does she seem so hollow to me? I have to try to get to know her better.

She was filling a large battered green suitcase with her things. Clothes, knicknacks, a dozen books. Something large and flat, maybe a sketchpad. A folder of old letters and papers. She stuffed five more books in at the very last.

A tepid evening, an indifferent night Dinner at a beanery a few blocks from his place. Afterward, home, a couple of golds, some desultory chatter, bed. No outbursts of telepathy to plague her. No resurgences of Hamlin to bother him. They were free to pursue one another's innerness without distractions, but somehow it didn't happen; they talked all around their troubles without coming to any of the main issues. He was surprised to learn she was not quite twenty-five years old, four or five years below his guess. Born in Pittsburgh, no less. Father some kind of scientist, mother an expert on population dynamics. Good genes. They sounded like acceptable types. Lissa hadn't seen them in years. Came to New York, age seventeen, to study art. (Aha!) Thought also of writing novels. (Ahahaha!)

Turning point in life June 15, 2004, age eighteen, meets famed artist Nathaniel Hamlin. Falls wildly in love with him. He doesn't notice her at all, so she thinks (scene is a meet-the-faculty party at the Art Students' League, everybody wildly stoned, Hamlin— guest lecturer or something that semester—urbanely putting on all the pretty girls.)

But a week later he calls her. Drinks? Stroll in Central Park? Of course. She is terrified. Hopes he'll accept her as a private student. Wants to bring him to her apartment (not this present uptown hovel) and show him her sketches. Doesn't dare. A nice chaste summertime stroll.

Afterward she is sure he found her too trivial, too adolescent, but no, he calls again, exactly seven days later. What a sweet time that was. Care to see my studio? Out in Darien, Connecticut. She has no idea where is Darien. He'll pick her up, never fear. Long sleek car. Driving it himself. She has brought her portfolio, just in case. He takes her to flamboyant country estate, unbelievable place: swimming pool, creek, pond full of mutated goldfish in improbable colors, big stone house, medium-big studio annex.

Turns out he isn't interested in her as an artist at all, wants her as model: has some ambitious project in mind for which she would be perfect. She is awed. Her portfolio lying neglected in the car. I need to see the body, he says. Of course. Of course. Strips: blouse, slacks. Thoughtfully omitted to don underwear that day. He studies her carefully. Oh, God, my backside's too flat, my boobs are too big, or maybe not big enough! But no, he compliments her, good tight fanny, cute shape, will do, will do. And suddenly his pants are open in front. Thick reddened organ sticking out. (Oh, you've seen it, Macy, you know it like your own!) She is thrown into panic. She's been laid before, yes, eight, ten fellows, not coming on as timid innocent at all, but yet this is the authentic erect cock of *Nathaniel Hamlin* that now approaches her, which is something very special. Admired his work all her life, never dreamed that one day he'd be presenting his mast to her. Can't take her eyes off it until it disappears into her box.

In and out. In and out. Nathaniel Hamlin's authentic thing knows its business. Such terrific intensity boiling within him, and he expresses it with his pecker. She comes a thousand times. Afterward they both run naked around the estate, swim, laugh, get stoned. He grabs a camera and holographs her for an hour. You and me, he says, we're going to make a masterpiece the world won't ever forget. Then they dress, he drives her to a restaurant near the Sound, such glamour that it dizzies her, and finally, late at night, deposits her, an exhausted astounded adolescent heap of much-fucked flesh, at her apartment. An unforgettable experience.

Then she doesn't hear from him for three months. Despair. At last an apologetic postcard from Morocco. Another, a month and a half later, from Bagdad. At Christmastime a card with Japanese stamps on it. Then, January '05, a phonecall. Back in town at last. See you at nine tonight, break all other engagements.

And from then on she is more or less his full-time mistress, living at Darien much of the time, naturally dropping out of art school, drifting away from old friends, who now seem naive and immature to her. New friends, exciting ones. Even becoming friendly with Hamlin's wife. (A peculiar marital relation there, Macy concluded.)

Early in '06, after nearly a year of planning, he gets down to serious work on the *Antigone 21*. Months of toil for him and for her; he is a demon when he works. Twelve, fifteen, eighteen hours a day. Finally almost finished. Almost finished with her, too. He has been talking of marrying her since the summer of '05, but their relationship grows increasingly tense. Physical violence: he slaps her, kicks her a couple of times, balls her once by main force when she doesn't want it, ultimately knocks her down the stairs and breaks her pelvis. Hospital. During which time he succumbs completely to the disintegration of personality that has, unknown to her, been going on in him for most of the year, and commits Dreadful Deeds upon the persons of a variety of women. He is arrested and tried; she sees him no more until that eerie day in May of 2011 when she crashed into Paul Macy on the streets of Manhattan North.

And your telepathy problem, Macy wants to ask? When did that start? When did it become severe? But obviously she doesn't want to talk about that. She will speak to him tonight only of old business, her romance with the defunct great artist. And now she has talked herself out Silence. Lights out Two red roaches in the darkness. Pungent smoke rising ceilingward. This would be the sort of moment Macy thought, when Hamlin would appear. To append footnotes to Lissa's story. But Hamlin, missing his cue, did not appear. It began to occur to Macy that each of his encounters with Hamlin might drain the other's strength as much as it did his, possibly more; between colloquies, Hamlin had to lie doggo, recharging. Maybe not so, but a cheering possibility. Tire him out, wear him down, eventually eject him. An endurance contest.

Macy turned dutifully to Lissa, not particularly in need of her but feeling that they ought to commemorate her moving-in with some kind of celebration of passion; his hand slipped over one of her breasts, but she responded not at all, merely lying there in a passive stony haze, and an uncheering possibility struck him: When she makes love with me, is she really only trying to recapture those moments of fire with *him?* I am Nat Hamlin's well-endowed body minus Nat Hamlin's troublesomely violent nature; is that not all she seeks from me?

The thought that he might be, for her, nothing but a dead man's reanimated penis did not amuse him. Of course she said she enjoyed him for his own sake, but of what did his own sake consist? Having loved a genius, could she love a nonentity equally well? Or at all? A young, impressionable art student would of course be drawn automatically to a magnet such as Nat Hamlin, but Paul Macy should have no pull. Who am I, what am I, wherein lies my texture, my density? I am nothing. I am unreal. Hamlin's shadowy successor. His relict Macy attempted to check this cascade of negativisms, telling himself that Hamlin was undoubtedly causing it by releasing a river of poisons from his subcranial den. But he could not coax himself just now to a higher self-esteem. Entering her, he pushed the piston mechanically back and forth for three or four minutes, feeling wholly detached from her except at the point of entry, and, since she gave no hint of being with him in any way, he let himself go off and sank into the usual bothered sleep, infested by incubi and revenants.

Many sympathetic glances at the network office the next day. Everybody tiptoeing around him, speaking in soft tones, grinning a lot, sidestepping every situation of potential stress or conflict. Obviously all of them afraid he might flip at the first jarring stimulus. It was a regression to the way they had treated him weeks ago, when he had first come here, when they thought a Rehab needed to be handled as carefully as a barrel of eggs. He wondered why. Was it because he had called in sick yesterday, and now they assumed he had been suffering from some special affliction of Rehabs, some slippage of the identity, that required extracautious handling? Their excessive kindness, implying as it did that he was more vulnerable than they, irritated him. After two and a half hours of it he cornered

Loftus, Stilton Fredericks' executive assistant, and asked her about it.

He said, "I want you to know that what kept me home yesterday was simply an upset stomach. A case of the runs and a lot of puking, okay?"

She looked at him blankly. "I don't remember asking."

"I know you didn't ask. But everybody else around this place seems to think I had some sort of nervous breakdown. At least, that's how they've been treating me today. So fucking kind it's killing me. So I thought I'd let you spread the word that I'm all right. A mere internal indisposition."

"You don't like people to be nice to you, Macy?"

"I didn't say that I just don't want my fellow workers making inaccurate assumptions about the state of my head."

"Okay, so you didn't have a nervous breakdown. So why do you look so strange?"

"Strange?"

"Strange," Loftus said.

"What way?"

"Look in the mirror." Then, a moment of tenderness breaking through the steel: "If anything's the matter that any of us could fix—"

"No. No. Honestly, it was only an upset stomach."

"Uh-huh. Okay, if anybody asks, I'll tell them. Nobody's going to whisper behind your back."

He thanked her and made a quick escape. Executive washroom: amid all the electronic gimmickry, the sonic shavers and the Klein-bottle urinals, he found a mirror, standard variety, silver-backed glass as in days of yore. A fierce, bloodshot face looking back at him. Furrowed forehead. Nostrils flaring. Lips compressed, mouth drawn off to one side. Jesus, no wonder! He was Mr. Hyde and Dr. Jekyll both at the same time, his features all snarled up, reflecting the most intense kind of interior agonies.

And this without a buzz from Hamlin for the past eighteen hours. This double existence, this squatter occupation of the lower reaches of his mind, was corroding his face, turning him into an ambulatory flag of distress. Of course they were all being sweet to him today; they could see the signals of imminent collapse inscribed on his brow.

Yet he felt relatively relaxed today. What must he look like when Hamlin was near the surface and prodding him? Macy ventured an exploratory sweep. *Hamlin? Hamlin, you there? My private permanent bad dream. Come up where I can see you. Let's have a chat.*

But no, all quiet on the cerebral front Feeling snubbed, Macy set out to repair his face. Stripped to the waist. Sticking his head into the hot-air blower. Loosen the muscles, soften the scowl. A little humidity, maestro. Ah. Ah, how good that is on the tactile net. Thrust noggin now into whirlpool sink. Round and round and round, bubble bubble bubble, hold your breath and let the lovely water work its magic. Ah. Ah. Splendid. Back to the hot air to dry off. Now pop a trank. Blow a gold Survey the map. Better, much better. The tension draining away; a lucky thing, too, they wouldn't have let you step in front of a camera looking all screwed up.

Macy was still refurbishing himself, putting his clothes back on, when Fredericks walked into the John. A hearty phony laugh out of him, ho ho ho. "Interrupting you in a moment of relaxation, Paul?"

"No. All done relaxing now. And feeling much better."

"We were all quite concerned when you phoned in yesterday."

"Just a jumpy stomach, was all. Much better now. See?" Flashing his rehabilitated features at Fredericks. "I appreciate the concern, but I'm really pretty tough. Stilton," he added reluctantly. A hell of a name to carry through life.

Fredericks addressed himself to the task of unloading his bladder. Macy went out, working hard at looking loose. The effort must have been worthwhile; people stopped pampering him.

At half past two he picked up his script for the day, ran through the visuals four or five times, rehearsed the audio. A two-minute squib on the coronation in Ethiopia, surging throngs, lions marching on chains through the streets, a herniated corner of the fifteenth century poking into the twenty-first.

Macy wondered how Mr. Bercovici, he who had selected him at the Rehab Center for this job, was making out in Addis Ababa. Was that him at the edge of the crowd, picked up by the trusty hovereye, that plump white face among the hawk-featured brown ones? Here and gone; probably the South African consul-general, or whoever. Macy carried off his voice-over nobly. *"Amid the pomp and glamor of a medieval empire, the former Prince Takla Haymanot today became the Lion of Judah, King of the Kings of Ethiopia, His Excellency the Negus Lebna Dengel II, newest monarch in a line of royalty descended from King Solomon himself . . ."* Beautiful. And then home to Lissa through thin rain.


She was in bed, reading, wearing a tattered green housecoat that looked old enough to be one of the Queen of Sheba's hand-me-downs, nothing at all underneath it, pinkish-brown nipples peeping through. One quick look and he knew, as if by telepathic transmission, that she had had a bad day. Her face had that sullen, pouty look; her hair was uncombed, a wild auburn tangle; the stale smell of dried sweat was sharp in the air of the bedroom. He felt strangely domesticated. Hubby coming home from hard day at office, slatternly wife about to tell him of the day's petty crises.

She tossed aside her book and sat up. "Christ," she said. Her favorite expletive. "An all-day bummer, this was. Rainy weather indoors and out."

He kicked off his shoes. "Bad?"

"The anvil chorus in my head." Shrugging. "Let's not talk about it I was going to whip up a fancy dinner, but I didn't get up the energy. I could put something together fast."

"We'll go out. Don't bother." He eased out of his over-clothes. Fifteen seconds of dead air. Despite her saying she didn't want to talk about today, she seemed obviously waiting for him to start questioning her. Gambit declined. He was tired and fretful himself: Hamlin beginning to clamber toward the surface again, maybe.

He looked at her. She at him. The silence continued, dragging on until it had attained a tangible presence of its own. Then Lissa appeared to tune the tension out; she disconnected something in herself and slumped back against the pillow, sinking into that brooding withdrawal that she affected about half the time.

Macy got himself a beer. When he returned to the bedroom she was still eighteen thousand light-years away. A curious notion came to him: that unless he made contact with her in some fashion this very minute, she would be wholly lost to him. Her closedness annoyed him, but he hid his pique and, going to her, pulled back the coverlet to caress the outside of her bare thigh. A friendly gesture, loving almost. She didn't seem to notice. He touched his cold beer to her skin. A hiss. "Hey!"

"Just wanted to find out if you were still here," he said.

"Very funny."

"What's the matter, Lissa?" The question out of him at last.

"Nothing. Everything. This shitty rain. The air in here. I don't know." Momentary wildness in her eyes. "I've been picking up noise all day in my head. You and Hamlin, Hamlin and you. Like a kind of radioactive trance in the air. I shouldn't have moved in here."

"Surely you can't pick up telepathic impulses from someone who isn't even in the room!"

"No? How do you know? Do you know anything at all about it? Maybe your ESP waves soak into the paint, into the woodwork. And radiate back at me all day. Don't try to tell me what I've been feeling. The two of you, banging at me off the walls, blam blam blam, hour after hour." These sharp sentences were delivered in an inappropriately flat, absent tone. At the end of which she disconnected again.

"Lissa?"

Silence.

"Lissa?"

"What?"

"Remember, you came looking for *me*. I told you it wasn't good for us to be together. And you said we needed each other, right? So don't take it out on me if it doesn't work well."

"I'm sorry." A ten-year-old's insincere apology.

More silence.

He tried to make allowances for her mood. Cooped up all day. Raining. Hostile ions in the air. Her period coming on, maybe. A woman's entitled to be bitchy sometimes. Still, he didn't need to take it. If there was too much telepathic noise here, she could go back to the pigsty.

"I heard that," she said.

"Oh, Jesus."

"My period isn't due for a week. And if you want me to go to the pigsty, say it out loud and I'll pack right now."

"Do you read my mind all the time?"

"Not like that, no. What I get, it's a general hazy fuzz that I can identify as your signal, and a different fuzz that's *his,* but not usually any sharp words. Except that time it was perfectly clear. Am I really being bitchy?"

"You aren't being much fun," he said.

"I'm not having much fun, either."

"How about a shower? And then a good dinner." Trying to repair things. "A dress-up diner, downtown. All right?" Like humoring a cranky child. Did she hear that too? Apparently not. Getting up, shucking her housecoat. Not bothering to hold herself upright; shoulders slumped, breasts dangling, belly pushed outward. Padding across and into the shower. Well, we all have our bad days. Sound of water running. Then her head sticking into the bedroom.

She said, "By the way, the Rehab Center phoned this morning."

Macy looked up, and in the same instant Hamlin awoke and did something to his heartbeat, something, transient and painful, that made him gasp and clap his hand to his breastbone.

"I said, the Rehab Center phoned—"

"I heard you." Macy coughed. "Wait a second. Hamlin acting up." He shot a furious thought downward. *Let me be. Knock it off.* The pain subsided. Macy said, "Who was it?"

"A woman doctor with an Italian name."

"Ianuzzi."

"That's the one. She wanted to know why you hadn't shown up for your therapy yesterday. After making a special early appointment and everything."

"What did you tell her?" he asked.

Hopes suddenly soaring. His previous identity has surfaced and is trying to take him over, Dr. Ianuzzi. A terrible struggle going on inside him. Oh, is that so, Miss Moore? How unexpected. But we can handle it, of course. We'll have our mobile ego-smashing unit on the spot at seven o'clock sharp. Three quick bursts of rays from the egotron machine, beamed up from the street, and that'll be the end of Mr. Nat Hamlin for once and all, oh, yes, oh, yes. Tell Mr. Macy not to worry about a thing. Thank you for giving me the details, Miss Moore.

Lissa very far away. Dreamy. Macy said again, more sharply, "What did you tell her?"

"I didn't tell her anything."

"What?"

"She called at a bad time for me. I don't even know why I answered. I couldn't make much sense out of what she was asking me until afterward."

"So you just hung up?"

"No, I talked, more or less. I said I didn't know much about why you missed your appointment. Or where you were at the moment." A distant shrug. "I guess I was pretty foggy."

"Jesus, Lissa, you had a chance to help me, and you blew it! You could have told her the whole story!"

She said, "Didn't you tell me that Hamlin threatened to kill you if you brought the Rehab Center into the picture?"

"That's right. But he wouldn't have known it if *you* had given them the story while I was at work. It was a perfect chance. And you blew it. You blew it."

"Sorry." But not very.

"If they phone again, will you do things right?"

"What do you want me to tell them?"

"The straight story. Hamlin coming back. And especially the part about his saying he'll stop my heart if I go near a Rehab Center. Make sure they know he means it. How I set out to go there, how he knocked me down at the Greenwich terminal. You won't forget that part of it?"

"Maybe you better call them yourself."

"I told you, I can't. Hamlin monitors everything I think or say. The moment I pick up the phone, he'll have his clutches on my—" *Jesus!* Another twinge in the chest Clammy invisible fingers tweaking the aorta. A cough. A gasp. A slow shivering recovery. Lissa watching, unconcerned. "There," Macy said finally. "He just did it. To let me know he's tuned in."

"What good is having them know, though, if he'll kin you if they try to help you?"

"At least they'll know. Maybe they have a remote-control way of dealing with situations like this. Maybe they can sneak up on him somehow. They've got their tricks. It can't hurt to have them realize what's happened. Provided they're aware of the risks involved for me. You won't forget that part?"

"If they call," Lissa said vaguely, "I'll try to tell them everything. I'll try." She didn't sound too sure of it.

In the night, fragmentary episodes of not-quite-night-mare, slippery bulletins issued by the psychic underground. Oddly unfrightening moments out of an unremembered past arriving on top deck for the sleeper's inspection and enlightenment. Bucolic scenes: the arrest, the arraignment, the detention center, the courthouse, the trial, the verdict, the sentence. *Keep your fucking hands off me, I told you I'd go peacefully!*

Lights flashing in his eyes. A hovereye camera practically touching his nose. Viewers around the world enjoying the spectacle. See the famed doer of abominations! Watch justice triumph! Death to the enemies of chastity! A jury of twelve honest computers and true.

*Sweartotellthetruththewholetruthnothingbutthetruth. IdoIdoIdoIdo.* See the sobbing witnesses! Observe their haunted, vindictive faces! What memories of obscene violations blaze in their souls? *Yes, that's the man, he's the one! I'd know him anywhere.* The courtroom silent. *Your honor, I ask permission to enter as evidence the taped record of the defendant's intrusion into the home of Maria Alicia Rodriguez on the night of*—Red light flickering on the lawyerboard. *Objection! Objection!* Commotion. *Denied. Prosecution may proceed.*

On the wallscreen the defendant appears, bent on rape. Had he but known he was performing for a camera, he would have been ever so much more stylish about it. Up onto the windowledge, hup! Pry the window open. Hands cold; this miserable winter weather. Yes. Inside. The trembling victim. And the camera descends to get a good view of the action. If they were so concerned about chastity, why did they let him consummate the rape? A good question for the victim to ask. But of course it was all taped automatically; not till later did anyone realize that the hovereye had caught the mad rapist at his trade. White thighs gleaming in the moonlight. Wiry black bush, almost blue. Push. Push. Wham!

*Will the defendant please rise. Nathaniel James Hamlin you have heard the verdict of your peers. This court now declares you guilty on eleven counts of aggravated assault fourteen counts of unsolicited carnal entry five counts of third-degree sodomy seven counts of irremediable psychic injury seventeen counts of violation of marital propriety seven counts of first-degree illicit proximity nine counts of eleven counts of sixteen counts of.*

The sleeper becomes restless. Let us perhaps turn our attention to happier times. The artist at work in his splendid studio, cascades of spring sunlight pouring through the grand window. Cleverly constructing the armature for the latest masterpiece. First comes the all-encompassing vision, you understand, the sense of the work as a wholeness, without which it is impossible to begin. This hits you like a bolt of lightning; if it comes any other way, don't trust it. Afterward it's just plonking drudgery, a lot of soldering. I wouldn't bother except that I have to. It's the first moment, the white light falling out of heaven, that makes it all worthwhile.

But of course any shithead phony can say he has inspirations. Can he realize them? I can. You build the armature, see, which means you have to crap around with relays and solenoids and connectors and power-shunts and gate-nexuses and such. You calculate the atmospherics you want; a computer gives you the ionization tables, but then you have to make the corrections yourself, intuitively. You do the lighting. Then you put the skin on. Throughout the whole business you never lose sight of the initial impulse, which is, item one, a matter of form, of the actual goddam shape of the piece, and, item two, a matter of psychological insight, of the particular movement of the spirit you mean to express. Now you know as much about my working methods as I do. You want to know more, buy one of my pieces and take it apart.

The scene changes. At the gallery now, we are watching the elite of the art world scrambling to buy his 2002 output; that was the year of the phallic miniatures, they walk, they talk, they jerk off, eight grand apiece, every distinguished creator is entitled to have his little black jest. Sold like hotcakes. Better than hotcakes: did you ever buy a hotcake in your life? The hotcake market is extremely depressed these days.

Macy, slumbering, maybe even snoring, makes desperate mental notes. I must remember all this when I wake up. This is my genuine past, accept no substitutes. Is Hamlin sending all this stuff up by way of making friendly overtures to me, or is he trying to torment me? In any event, more. More, he cried, give me more! So more. Look at the world through a madman's eyes. Take the hallucinogenic trip for free. Breathe in, breathe out, turn on, *tilt!* What are those streaks spanning the sky? That cockeyed rainbow, black, green, turquoise, gray, purple, white. And what colors do you see when your eyes are closed? The same. The very same.

Why is there so much pressure in the groin? You can feel the pulsations, the throbbings. It's like being sixteen all over again. You want to plant it fast, you want to pump yourself dry. Insatiable. But only in strange and reluctant cunts. Why is that? Can you offer a rational explanation? Ha. Time to prowl the winter streets. A tightness in the ass, a dryness in the throat. Your own sweet wifey willing to come across for you, any time, any place, and the same is true of a myriad of others, hot available Lissa, so why endanger yourself in this fashion? But danger defines the man. I climb these peaks because they're here.

Do you realize, though, that you're out of your mind? Naturally I do. *Will the defendant please rise. Nathaniel James Hamlin you have heard the verdict of your peers.* There, you see the risks? You know what those bastards can do to you? Sure I know. I accept the risks. Let them do their worst. *It is the decision of this court that the identity known as Nathaniel James Hamlin having been found guilty of repeated and numerous instances of intolerably antisocial activity and having been declared an incurable and incorrigible sociopathic menace by a properly constituted panel of authorities shall be withdrawn permanently from access to society and shall be at once expunged under the provisions of the Federal Social Rehabilitation Act of 2001 and that in accordance with the terms of that act the physical container as legally defined of the proscribed identity be reconstructed and returned to society at the earliest possible time.*

Let me have your left arm, please, Mr. Hamlin. No, this isn't a needle, it's an ultrasonic injector, you won't feel a thing. How long will it be before it takes effect? Oh, you'll sense some effects almost immediately, I'd say, as the short-term memory processes begin to break down. The left arm, now? Thank you. There. See how easy it was? We'll be back in ten hours to begin the next phase. *What is my name? Who am I? Why are they doing this to me?* Now the right arm, please, Mr. Hamlin. *Who?* Mr. Hamlin. That's you, Nathaniel Hamlin. *Oh.* The right arm, please? No, it's not a needle, it's an ultrasonic injector, just like the last one. You don't remember the last one? Well, of course, I should have realized that. Here we go! *They're washing away my mind! No no no no no no no no no no no*

At the office the next afternoon Hamlin, who had not been heard from in any overt way for almost two full days, made another attempt at seizing the speech centers of Macy's brain. He chose his moment carefully. Late in the day; Macy trying for the tenth or twelfth time to tape his commentary for the evening news; inner tensions high.

The words weren't flowing and the tones were thorny. He was covering the presumed assassination of the Croatian prime minister, a particularly nasty incident: a gang of monadist radicals had kidnapped the man a week ago and, spiriting him away to an illegal mindpick laboratory thought to be located somewhere in the Caucasus, had subjected him to an intensive three-day personality deconstruct that had wholly obliterated his identity. His soulless shell had been picked up during the night in Istanbul and was now in Zagreb, where platoons of neurologists now were converging in the hope of summoning back his eradicated self. Scarcely any chance of success, according to a British authority on deconstruct techniques. If an identity is taken apart properly, there's no known way of reassembling it. All the king's horses and all the king's men, and so forth. A bad show.

When the story had started to come off the pipe around lunchtime, Macy had instantly volunteered to handle it. He felt he had to prove to his colleagues that he did not need to be sheltered against references to deconstructs and reconstructs, rehabilitation work, and related matters. But it was proving unexpectedly difficult for him to carry out the assignment. The story was full of lumpy Croatian names that refused to cross his tongue in the right order of syllables. Moreover, he was more sensitive to the theme of the incident than he had realized; he burst into uneasy sweats at odd moments while reading his script, usually around the place where he was doing the lead-in to the statement from the London neurologist.

Take it slow, the platform monitor kept calling out to him. You're pressing, Paul. Just go easy and let the words slide out. Everybody was being kind to him, again. A whole taping crew immobilized here for well over an hour while he blundered and staggered his way through an infinity of faulty takes. Take it slow, take it slow.

This time he thought he had it. The polysyllabic names all safely taped. The intricate explication of Balkan politics handled without calamity. For the first time this afternoon, a single usable take covering ninety percent of the script. Now to clinch things: "This morning in London, we spoke with the celebrated British brain expert Varnum Skillings, who *vdrkh cmpm gzpzp vdrkh—*"

"*Cut!*"

"*Shqkm. Vtpkp. Smss! Grgg!*"

People rushing toward him from all sides of the studio. His skull ablaze. Eyes unfocused. Macy knew precisely what had happened, and after the first instinctive moment of terror he began to take counteroffensive action. Just as he had on Tuesday, he labored to pry Hamlin's mental grip loose. There was a complicating factor here, the public nature of his fit, the disturbed colleagues fluttering around him, asking him things, loosening his collar, otherwise distracting him. And the feeling of calamity that came over him at the realization that he had suffered this upheaval in front of everybody, exposed himself thoroughly as too sick to hold this job. Brushing aside those matters, he worked on Hamlin. The devil had bided his time, collected his strength, made his try when Macy was least prepared for it. All the same, Macy was more powerful. He had the leverage that controlling the body's main neural trunks provided. Back, you fucker! Back! Back! Let go!

Hamlin let go. Foiled again.

Macy's vision returned and he found himself staring into the agitated onyx face of Loftus. Asking him over and over what had happened, was he all right, should they send for a doctor, an ambulance, get him a drink, a gold.

"I'll be fine," he said. Voice like corroded copper.

"You sounded so weird just then—and your face was so twisted up—"

"I said I'd be all right." Normal tone returning.

No one must know. No one.

The platform monitor, Smith, Jones, some name like that, coming up to him. "We got a nearly perfect take, Macy. If you'd like to rest a while, and then you can do the finale for us—no problem to splice it—"

"Well do it now," said Macy.

No one must know.

The camera crew returning to places. Confusion defused. Macy, alone under the lights, swaying a little, searched his mind for Hamlin, could not find him, decided that he really had succeeded once again in thwarting a takeover. Nevertheless, he would keep on guard. If it happened again under the cameras he'd be in trouble. No room in this organization for newsmen who throw fits at unpredictable moments.

"Roll it," said Jones or Smith.

"This morning in London," Macy said smoothly, "we spoke with the celebrated British brain expert Varnum Skillings, who gave us this assessment of the situation."

"Cut," said Smith or Jones.

Macy smiled. Almost home free, now. The platform monitor gave the signal. Macy delivered the final line. Done. Sighs of relief. People trooping out. Low whispers, everyone no doubt talking about his creepy paroxysm.

Let them talk. I beat him down again, didn't I? He loses every time.

For once Macy thought it might be almost tolerable to have Hamlin alive within him. Hamlin was the perpetual challenge that defined him. Every man needs a nemesis. He arises, I smite him. He arises again, I smite again. And so we go on together through the busy, happy days. He gives me texture and density. With him, I am a man with a unique affliction; I carry tragic *angst*. Without him I would be a shadow. And so we are comfortable with one another. Until the time when the pattern of testing, of thrust and parry, is broken. Until he conquers me. Or I him. When it comes, it will come with one quick sudden triumphant thrust, and one of us will succumb. He? I? We'll see. Home, now. A long wearying day.

# 9

issa wasn't there. He looked through the apartment with great care, methodically passing several times from one room to the other and quickly doubling back, as though she might be slipping invisibly through the door just ahead of him; but no, she wasn't anywhere around. He checked the bathroom and the closets. Her things were still hanging helterskelter among his. Not gone permanently, then. A note from her? No, nothing. Might have gone out to take a walk. Or to buy some groceries for dinner. At this hour, though? Knowing he always came home punctually? Briefly alarmed, he searched the place once again, looking now for traces of violence. No. A mystery, then.

She had her own key, and he had reprogrammed the thumb-plate safety latch to accept her fingerprint; she could come and go as she pleased. But she should have been on hand when he arrived. He couldn't understand why she wasn't. What now? Notify the police? There was this girl, officer, she's been living with me since Tuesday night, she wasn't home when I returned from work, I wonder if you—No. Hardly. Ask the neighbors if they had seen her? No. Go out and look for her in the local shops? No. Search for her at her own apartment? Maybe. Do nothing, stay here, wait for her to show up? Maybe. For the time being, yes. Give her an hour, two hours. She has her moods. Maybe she went to a show. Feeling tense, just went off by herself. Odd that there's no note, anyway.

He showered, put on his worn dressing gown, poured himself a little cream sherry to blunt the edge of his appetite. Getting later all the time. Half past six, no Lissa. Worry mounting in him. They had not, in the course of constructing him at the Rehab Center, prepared him to handle this sort of situation. He reviewed the possible options. Police. Local shops. Her apartment. Neighbors. Sit and wait. No tactic seemed adequate.

Out of the silence, the voice of the serpent:

—Don't worry about her.

Right now, in his jangled state, even the presence of Hamlin was a comfort. His other self had spoken in a casual, easy way; no challenge, at the moment, merely conversation. Macy was grateful for the muted approach. He wondered how to be properly hospitable. Offer Hamlin some sherry? A gold? Sit down, Nat, make yourself at home. An impulse of lunatic sociability.

*I can't help worrying,* Macy said.

—She can look after herself.

*Can she, though?*

—I know her better than you.

*You haven't had anything to do with her for almost five years. She's unstable, Hamlin. I don't like the idea of her wandering off by herself this way.*

—She probably felt she needed some fresh air. Bad telepathic vibrations bouncing off the walls in here, isn't that what she told you? Getting her down. So she went out.

*Without leaving a note?*

—Lissa doesn't leave notes much. Lissa's not awfully big on responsibility. Relax, Macy.

*That's easy enough to say.*

—You know, maybe she walked out for good. Sick of us both, maybe. All the tension and brawling.

*Her things are still here, though,* Macy pointed out Grasping at straws. Lissa! Lissa!

—That wouldn't matter to her. Abandoned possessions fall from her like dandruff. Hey, cheer up, will you? The worst that can happen is that you won't ever see her again. Which maybe would be not such a terrible thing.

*You'd like it a lot, wouldn't you?*

—What's it to me?

*You don't want me to have anything to do with her. You're jealous because I'm alive and you're not. Because I have her and you don't.*

Robust interior chuckles bubbling in the brain. Derisive guffaws echoing through the involuted corridors.

—You're such a prick, Macy.

*Can you deny what I said?*

—What you said had more nonsense per square inch than is allowed under present brain-pollution laws.

*For example?*

—Where you say you "have" Lissa. Nobody "has" Lissa, ever. Lissa floats. Lissa drifts in a private orbit. Lissa lives inside a sealed airtight glass cage. She doesn't involve herself with other people. She spends time with them, yes, she talks with them, she fucks them sometimes, but she doesn't surrender anything that's real to her.

*She involved herself with you.*

—That was different. She loved me. The great exception in her life. But she doesn't love you or anybody else, herself included. You're fooling yourself if you think you mean anything to her.

*How can you claim to know so much about her when you haven't seen her in five years?*

—I've had all this week to watch her too, haven't I? That girl is very sick. This ESP thing is pulling her apart. She thinks she has to be alone in order to keep the voices out of her head. She can't give herself to anybody for long; she has to retreat, pull back, sink into herself. Otherwise she hurts too much. So you mustn't be surprised that she's walked out. It was inevitable. Believe me, Macy, I'm telling the truth.

A strange note of sincerity in Hamlin's tone. As if he's trying to protect me from a troublesome entanglement, Macy thought. As if he's got my welfare at heart. Curious.

Seven o'clock, now. No Lissa. Another sherry. Feet up on the hassock. Feeling almost relaxed, despite everything. Hardly even hungry. A slight headache. Where is she? She can look after herself. She can look after herself.

—Have you done any further thinking about the proposal I made?

*What proposal?*

—On Tuesday, in the museum. That you go away and let me have my body back.

*You know the answer to that one.*

—You're being unreasonable, Macy. I mean, look at it objectively. You may think you exist, but you actually don't. You're a construct. You don't have any more genuine reality as a person, as a human being, than that wall over there.

*So you keep telling me. If I don't exist, though, why do I worry about Lissa? Why do I enjoy sipping this sherry? Why do I work so hard at the network?*

—Because you've been programmed to. Crap, Macy, can't you see that you're only a clever machine that's been slipped into a vacant human body? Which turned out to be not quite vacant, which still had some bits of its former owner hiding in it. If you were capable of facing your own situation decently and honestly, you'd recognize that—

*Right,* Macy cut in. *I'd recognize that I'm a nothing and you're a genius, and I'd get the hell out of your head.*

—Yes.

*Sorry, Hamlin. You're wasting our time asking me to. Why should I commit suicide just to give you a second chance to mess up your life?*

—Suicide! Suicide! You've got to be alive before you can commit suicide!

*I'm alive.*

—Only in the most narrow technical sense.

*Fuck you, Hamlin.*

—Let's try to keep the conversation on a friendly basis, okay?

*How can I be friendly when you invite me to kill myself? Where's the advantage for me in accepting your deal? What do you have to offer that makes it worth my while to give you this body back?*

—Nothing. I can only appeal to your sense of equity. I'm more talented than you. I'm more valuable to society. I deserve to live more than you do.

*I'm not so sure of that. Society's verdict was that you had no value at all, in fact that you were dangerous and had to be destroyed. Not even rehabilitated, in the old pre-Rehab sense of the word. Destroyed.*

—A miscarriage of justice. I could have been salvaged. I went insane, I don't deny it, I did a lot of harm to a bunch of innocent women. But that's all over. If I came back now, I'd be beyond all that crap. I'd keep to myself and practice my art.

*Sure you would. Sure. Look, Hamlin, if you want this body back, take it away from me—if you can. But I'm not giving it to you just for the asking. I don't think as little of myself as you do. Forget it.*—I wish I could make you see my point of view.

Half past seven. Still no Lissa. Macy switched from sherry to bourbon. Also lit the first gold of the evening. A deep drag; instant response, lightheadedness, a loss of contact with his feet. Just a touch of pot-paranoia, too: suppose Hamlin made a grab for his brain while he was fuddled with liquor and fumes? Could he fight back properly? His skullmate had been quiet for ten or fifteen minutes now. Gathering strength for an assault, maybe. Keep your guard up.

But no assault came. The intoxicants that lulled Macy seemed to lull Hamlin as well.

Eight o'clock.

*Hamlin? You still there?*

—You rang, milord?

*Talk to me.*

—Four score and seven years ago, our fathers brought forth upon this continent a new nation conceived in liberty and—

*No, be serious. Tell me something. What's it like for you, inside there?*

—Crowded and nasty.

*How do you visualize yourself?*

—As an octopus. A very small octopus, Macy, maybe a millionth of an inch in diameter, sitting smack in the middle of the left side of your head. With long skinny tentacles reaching out to various parts of your brain.

*Can you see the outside world?*

—When I want to. It uses some energy, but it isn't really hard. I hook into your optic input, is all, and then I see whatever you're seeing.

*What about hearing?*

—A different kind of hookup. I keep that one patched in nearly all the time.

*Sense of touch? Smell? Taste?*

—The same. It's no great trick to cut into your sensory receptors and find out what's going on outside.

*What about reading my thoughts?*

—Easy. A tentacle into the cerebral cortex. I monitor you constantly there, Macy. You think it, I pick it up instantly. And I can sort out your consciously directed mental impulses from the mush of mental noise that you put out steadily, too.

*How did you learn these things?*

—Trial and error. I woke up, see, not knowing where I was, what had happened to me. Lissa gave me a telepathic nudge, not even realizing she was doing it, and there I was. Locked in a dark room, a coffin, for all I knew. So I started groping around in your head. Accidentally touched something and made a connection. Hey, I can see! Touched something else. I can hear! What's this? Somebody else is wearing my body! But if I make contact here, I can pick up his thoughts. And so on. It took a few days.

*And you keep learning things all the time, eh, Hamlin?*

—Frankly, I haven't been making much progress lately. I'm

finding it hard to override your conscious control, your motor centers, your speech center. To make you walk where I want you to walk, to make you say what I want you to say. I can do a little of that, but it costs me a terrific load of energy, and sooner or later you pull me loose. Maybe there's a secret to overriding you that I haven't found yet.

*You manage to mess with my heartbeat pretty easily, though.*

—Oh, yes. I've got decent control over most of your autonomic system. I could turn your heart off in five seconds. But what's the use? You die, I'd die too. I could play with your digestive juices and give you an ulcer by morning. Only this is my body as much as yours: I don't gain anything by damaging it.

*Nevertheless you can cause me plenty of pain.*

—Indeed I can. I could harass you most miserably, Macy. How would you like the sensation of a toothache, twenty-five hours a day? Not the toothache itself, nothing a dentist could fix, just the sensation of it. How would you like a premature ejaculation, every time? How would you like a feedback loop in your auditory system so that you heard everything twice with a half-second delay? I could make your life hell. But I'm not really a sadist. I don't have any hard feelings toward you. I simply want my body back I still hope we can work things out in an amiable way, without the need for me to apply real pressure.

*Let's not start that routine again.* Macy reached for the bourbon. *I want to know more about you. What it's like for you in there. Can you actually see the interior of my brain?*

—See it? The neurons, the synapses, the brain cells? Not really. Only in a metaphorical sense. A visionary sense. I can set up one-to-one percept equivalents, such as my perception of myself as a miniature octopus, do you follow? But I don't actually see. It's hard to explain. I'm aware of things, structures, forms, but I simply can't communicate that awareness to someone who hasn't ever been on the inside himself. You have to remember that I don't have an organic existence. I'm not a lump of something solid under your headbone, a kind of tumor. I'm just a web of electrochemical impulses, Macy, and I perceive things differently.

*But aren't we all just webs of electrochemical impulses? What am I if not that?*

—True. Except that you're linked with this brain at so many points that you don't have any sense of yourself as something distinct from the bodily organ through which you perceive things. I do. I'm dissociated, disembodied. I sense my own existence as something quite separate from the existence of this brain, here, through which I get various sensory inputs when I ask for them, and through which I can force an output by working at it. It's weird, Macy, and it's lousy, and I don't like it at all. But I can't achieve a real hookup, because you're in the way in so many places, entrenched too deeply for me to dislodge you.

*What are we going to do, then?*

—Continue annoying each other, I suppose.


Quarter to nine. Really ought to check up on Lissa somehow, go down to her apartment, ask the cops to investigate. Not very ambitious right now, though. Maybe she'll come in soon. A long long walk on a spring night, home after dark.

—You're in love with her, aren't you, Macy?

*I don't think so. A certain physical attraction, I don't deny that. And a kind of solidarity of the crippled—she's got troubles, I've got troubles, we really ought to stick together, that kind of feeling. But not love. I don't know her that well. I don't even know myself that well. I have no illusions about that. I'm inexperienced, I'm emotion-ally immature, I'm brand new in the world.*

—And you're in love with her.

*Define your terms.*

—Don't hand me that sophomoric manure. You know what I mean. Let me tell you a few things about your Lissa, though, that somebody who is as you rightly say emotionally immature might not have noticed.

*Go ahead.*

—She's completely selfish. She exists only for the benefit of Lissa Moore. A bitch, a witch, a cunt that walks, a life-force eater. She'll try to suck the vitality out of you. She tried it with me, hoping she could drain some of my talent out of me and into her. I was fighting her all the way. I held her off pretty well. Although I think that ESP of hers infected me somehow and caused my breakdown. I didn't realize that at the time it was happening, Macy, but it occurred to me later, that she was fas-tening onto me, messing up my mind, robbing me of strength, pushing me over some sort of brink. And after a year or so I fell in. She won't need as long with you. She'll bleed you dry in a month.

*You make her sound like a monster. She strikes me as being an awfully pathetic monster, Hamlin.*

—That's because you've come to know her only when she's in trouble. This ESP of hers, do you think it was an accident? Some-thing that just sprouted in her, like the measles? It's that hunger of hers. To use people, to devour people, to drain people, to engulf people. Which finally got out of hand, which ran away with her. Now she drains automatically, she pulls in impulses from all sides, more than her mind can stand, and it's killing her. It's burning her out. But she asked for it.

*How harsh you are.*

—Just realistic. I never knew a woman who wasn't some kind of vampire, and Lissa's the most dangerous one I knew. A cunt is a cunt. A little bundle of ambitions. I fell for it, for a while. And it ruined me, Macy, it used me up.

*I think your whole outlook on women is distorted.*

—Maybe yes, maybe no. But at least I came by it honestly. Through living. Through experiencing. Through drawing my own conclusions. I didn't pick up my ideas vicariously. I didn't have them pumped into me at a Rehab Center.

*Granted. Which still doesn't make your ideas Tighter than mine.*

—Whatever you say. I just wanted to warn you about her.

*I'm amazed at the difference in our images of her. You see her as a marauder, a vampire, a drinker of souls. My impression is just the opposite: that she's a weak, passive, dependent girl, terrified by the world. How can they be reconciled?*

—They don't need to be. Why shouldn't my image of her be different from yours? I'm different from you. We're two very different persons.

*And if an outsider tried to make an assessment of Lissa based on what we told him?*

—He'd have to make parallax adjustments to compensate for our differences in perspective.

*But which is the real Lissa? Yours or mine?*

—Both. She can be passive and weak and still be a monster and a vampire.

*You really believe, though, that she deliberately sets out to drain vitality from people?*

—Not necessarily deliberately, Macy. She may not even realize what she's doing. I'm sure she didn't realize it until her inputs got too intense to cope with. It was just a thing she had, a telepathic thing, a need, a hunger. Which had the incidental effect of destroying people who came close to her.

*I don't feel that she's been destroying me.*

—You're welcome to her, pal.


Twenty minutes to ten. Another shot of bourbon. Smo-o-oth. Another Acapulco special, long and luscious, in the all-new, improved, negative-ion-filter format. The good haziness happening now. Perhaps Lissa's dismembered body has by this time been scattered throughout the six boroughs of the city. She seems remote and unreal to him. For the past ten minutes he has allowed himself to indulge in a mood of intense nostalgia. A curious species of nostalgia for the life he did not live. Meditating on the fragments of Hamlin's experience that have bled through to him across the boundaries that separate their identities. And yearning for more.

*Hamlin?*

—Yes.

*How hard would it be to merge our memory files entirely?*

—I don't follow you. What do you mean?

*So that I'd have access to everything you can remember. And you'd have access to all that had happened to me.*

—I imagine it wouldn't be hard.

*I'm willing if you are.*

—It would amount to a merging of identities, you realize. We wouldn't be sure where one of us ends and the other begins. We'd blend, after a while. Frankly, I'd wipe you out.

*You think so?*

—A pretty good chance of it.

*What makes you so sure?*

—Because I'd bring to the blending thirty-five years of genuine experience. Your thirty-five years of synthetic memories would overlay that like a film of dirt, and after a time I'd polish it away, leaving my real life blended to your four years in the Rehab Center, with some interplays from your ersatz existence coloring my recollections of the things I actually did. What would emerge would be a Nat Hamlin somewhat polluted by Paul Macy. Is that what you want? I'm willing if you are, Macy.

*I didn't mean such a complete joining. Just an exchange of memory banks.*

—I already have as much access to what the Rehab Center gave you as I need.

*But I don't have any access to your past, except some stuff that came floating through the barrier while I was asleep. And I want more.*

—What for?

*Because I'm starting to recognize it as my own identity. Because I feel cut off from myself. I want to know what this body did, where it traveled, what it ate, who it slept with, what it was like to be a psychosculptor. The need's been growing in me for a couple of hours now. Or maybe longer. It frustrates me to know that I was somebody important, somebody vital, and that I'm completely cut off from his life.*

—But you weren't anybody important, Macy. *I* was. You weren't anybody at all. A Rehab doctor's wet dream.

*Don't rub it in.*

—You admit it?

*I never denied I was only a construct, Hamlin.*

—Then why don't you just step aside and let me have the body, then?

*I keep telling you. My past may be a fake, but my present is real as hell, and I'm not giving it up.*

—So you want to add my past to yours, to give you that extra little dimension of reality. You want to go on being Paul Macy, but you want to be able to think you used to be Nat Hamlin, too?

*Something like that.*

—Up yours, Macy. My memories are my own property. They're all I've got. Why should I let you muck around in them? Why should I sweat to make you feel realer?

Ten-fifteen. How quiet it is at this time of night Somehow went without dinner and never even noticed. Sleepy. Sleepy. Phone the police? Tomorrow, maybe. She must have gone back to her own place. I guess. Mmmm. Mmmmmm.

—I have a new proposition for you.

*Eh? Huh?*

—Wake up, Macy.

*What's the matter?*

—I want to talk to you. You've been dozing.

*Okay. So talk. I'm listening.*

—Let's make a deal. Let's share the body on an alternating basis. First you run it, then me, then you again, then me again, and so on indefinitely. Operating it under the Paul identity, naturally, so we don't get into legal difficulties.

*You mean we switch every day? Monday Wednesday Friday it's me in charge, Tuesday Thursday Saturday it's you, Sunday we hold dialogs?*

—Not exactly like that. You need the body four days a week to do your job, right? Those four days it's yours. Saturdays and Sundays and holidays are mine. Weekday evenings we divide in such a way that you get some, I get some. We can work out ad-hoc arrangements for swapping time back and forth as the occasion demands.

*I don't see why I have to give you any time at all, Hamlin. The court awarded your body to me.*

—But I'm still in it. And I'm prepared to be a mammoth pain in the ass unless I'm allowed to take charge some of the time.

*You want me to yield half my lifespan to you under duress.*

—I want you to be sensible and cooperative, that's all. Can you function freely with me playing games inside your nervous system? Do you enjoy being harassed? I can cripple your life, Macy. And what about me? Must I be condemned to be bottled up without any autonomy, with my gifts? Listen, even if you run the body for half the time, that's three and a half days a week more than fate originally intended. By rights you shouldn't be here at all. So why not accept a reasonable compromise? Half the time you'll be you, and you can do any fucking thing you please. The other half you'll surrender autonomy and ride as a passenger while I go about my business. Sculpting, screwing, eating, whatever I feel like doing. We'll both benefit. I'll get to live again, a little, and you'll be free from the annoyance of having me constantly interfering with you.

*Well—*

—Another incentive. I'll give you the free run of my memory bank. What you were asking for a little while ago. You can find out who you really were, before you became you.

*Get thee behind me, Satan!*

—Will you tell me what's wrong with the goddam deal?

*Nothing wrong with it. It's too damned tempting, that's what.*

—Then why not go along with it?

A taut uneasy moment. Considering, weighing, mulling. Blinking his eyes a lot. Aware that his head is really too foggy now for such perilous negotiations. Why surrender a chunk of his life to a condemned criminal? Wouldn't it be better to fight it out, to try to expel Hamlin altogether, to break his grip once and for all? Maybe I can't. Maybe when the showdown comes he'll expel me. Perhaps it makes more sense to accept the half-and-half. But even so—a flood of suspicions, suddenly—

*How would we work this switch?*

—Easy. I'd penetrate the limbic system. You know what that is? Down underneath, in the depths of the folds. Controls your pituitary, your olfactory system, a lot of other things, blood pressure, digestion, and so forth, Also the seat of the self, so far as I can tell. You have it pretty well guarded, whether you know it or not. A wall of electrical charge sealing it off. But I could come in by way of the thalamus, reverse the charge—if we cooperate, it would be just a matter of a few seconds and we'd have our shift of identity polarity—I've worked out the mechanisms, I know where the levers are—

*All right. Let's say I cooperate and you take over. What assurance do I have that you'd let me back on top again when your time was up?*

—Why, if I didn't, you could pull all the stuff I've been pulling on you! The situations would be entirely reversed. You could mess around with my heart, my sex life—you'd learn the right linkups fast, Macy, you aren't dumb—

*I'm not convinced what you say is true. Maybe you'd have a natural advantage, because it was your body originally. Maybe when you were in charge again you could evict me altogether.*

—What an untrusting bastard you are.

*My life's at stake.*

—All I can say is you've got to have more faith in my good intentions.

*How can I?*

—Look, I'll open wide to you for a minute. I'll give you a complete unshielded entry into my personality. Poke around in there, make your own evaluation of my intentions—you'll see them right up front—decide for yourself whether you can trust me. Okay?

*Go ahead. But no funny stuff.*

—I'm baring my soul to him, and he's still suspicious as hell.

*Go ahead, I said. How do we work this?*

—First, we make some little electrical adjustments in the corpus callosum—

Odd sensations along the back of the neck. Prickling, tingling, a mild stiffening of the skin. Not entirely unpleasant; a certain agreeable feel to it, in fact. Unseen fingers stroking the lobes of his brain, caressing the prominences and corrugations. A tickling on the underside of the skull. Moss beginning to sprout between the white jagged cranial ridges and the soft cerebral folds below. And the oozing of warm fluids. Pulse. Pulse. A wonderful sleepy feeling. Passivity, yes, how splendid a thing is passivity. We are merging. We are opening the gates. How could one have thought that this admirable human being meant to do one harm? When now his soul is thuswise displayed. Its peaks and valleys. Its exaltations and depressions. Its hungers and fears. See, see, I am as human as thou! And I yearn. And I lament. Come let me enfold you. Come. Put aside these unworthy untrustingnesses. Open. Open. Open. Bathed in the warm river. Lulled on the gentle tide. Tick. Tock. Tick. Tock. This is how we come together. The avoidance of all friction. The total lubrication of the universe. And we dissolve into one another. And we dissolve.

What's that sound?

Buzz saw at work in the forest! Dentist's drill raping a

bicuspid! Jackhammers unpeeling the street! Braked wheels squealing! The fury of clawed cats!

Key turning in the lock!

Lissa! Lissa! Lissa!

Standing on the threshold. Fingertips pressed to lips in alarm. Body curved backward, recoiling in shock. Then the scream. And then:

"Leave him alone! Get your filthy hands off him, Nat!"

Followed by a sudden instinctive bombardment of mental force, a single massive jolt out of her that sent Macy crumpling stunned to the floor. Blackout Internal churning. Clicking of defective gears. Slow return to semiconsciousness. Lissa embracing him, cradling his throbbing head. A coppery taste in his throat. Incredible lancing pain between the eyes. Her face, smudged, strained, close to his. Her faint worried smile. And Hamlin nowhere within reach. There was in Macy's head that strange blessed aloneness that he had experienced so few times since the first awakening of his other self. Alone. Alone. How quiet it is in here.

# 10

Paul? Can you hear me?"

"From a million miles away."

"Are you all right?"

"Dazed. Groggy. Jesus, groggy!" Trying to sit up. She tugging him back into his chair. Surprising how strong she is. He looked at his hands. Quivering and twitching. As if a powerful electrical current had passed through his body and was still recycling itself through the peripheral circuits, touching off a muscular spasm here and here and here.

Searching for Hamlin. No, not in evidence. Not at the moment.

"What happened?" he said.

"I was at the door," said Lissa. "And from outside, I could feel the waves coming from his mind and yours. Mostly from his. You were—asleep, drugged, drunk, I don't know. Passive, anyway. And he was taking you over, Paul. His mind was wrapped around yours, and he was turning you off switch by switch—that's the only way I can describe it—and you were about half gone already. Submerged, dismantled, switched off, whatever word is best."

"We made a deal. We were going to share the body, half the time him running the show, and me the rest of the time. He promised me that if I let him take over, he'd turn the body back to me when it was my time to have control."

"He was tricking you," she said. "What were you, drunk? Stoned?"

"Both."

"Both. It figures. He was just getting you to lower your defenses so that he could get full control. I felt the whole thing from outside. I opened the door. It was much stronger in here. You sitting there with an idiot smile on your face. Eyes open, but you couldn't see. Hamlin swarming all over you. So I—I don't know, I didn't stop to think, I just *hit* him. With my mind."

"I think you killed him," Macy said.

"No. I hurt him, but I didn't kill him."

"I can't feel him any more."

"I can," she said. "He's very weak, but I can sense him down at the bottom of your brain. It's like he fell off a twenty-five-foot wall. I don't know how I did it. I just lashed out."

"Like you did that time in the restaurant."

"I suppose," she said. "Why did you let him do that to you?"

Macy shrugged. "We were talking to each other all evening. While I waited for you to come home. Getting chummy with him. We were proposing deals to each other, compromises, arrangements. And then this talk of sharing came up. I was pretty stoned by then, I suppose. Lucky thing you came in." He glanced up at her and said, after a moment, "Where the hell were you, anyway?"

Out, she told him. She just decided to go out around five

o'clock. Back to her apartment to pick up some of her things. He gave her a fishy look. Even in his present shellshocked condition he was able to see that she had come in emptyhanded. He taxed her with the inconsistency, and she made a stagy attempt to seem innocent, with much shrugging and tossing of the head, telling him that when she had reached her place she had decided she didn't need those things after all, and had left them there. And the rest of the evening? From six o'clock till now? Chatting with old friends down at the house, she said. Sure, he thought, remembering the sort of neighbors she had had there, the shimmies, the bandits.

Without in so many words accusing her of lying to him, he accused her of lying to him. She was indignant and then at once contrite. Admitting everything. Left here without intending to come back. The strain, too much strain, too much mental noise, the yammering of the double soul within the single brain getting to be more than she can handle. All night long, lying next to him, picking up the blurred shapeless echoes of the conflict going on within his head. You maybe don't even realize it yourself, she told him. How Hamlin hammers all the time, let me out, let me out, let me out. Deep down below the levels of consciousness. That constant agonized cry. And you fighting back, Paul. Suppressing him, squashing him. Don't you know it's going on?

And he shook his head, no, no, I'm only aware when he surfaces and starts talking to me, or when he grabs parts of my nervous system. Tell me more about this. And Lissa told him more. Conveying to him, in short nervous blurts of half-sentences, how much she was suffering from her mere proximity to him, how much it had cost her in extrasensory anguish since she had moved in. It would be bad enough if there was only one of him, but the double identity, no, too much, too fucking much, all that telepathic pressure, her head was splitting.

And it got worse every day. Cumulative. Rebirth of the old overpowering impulse to hide herself away from the whole human race. Not your fault, Paul, I know, not your fault, I asked you to take pity on me and help me, but yet, but yet, this is what happens. Even when you aren't here I feel you and Hamlin hemming me in. Pushing against my temples.

Like a kind of air pollution, it was: he gathered that she felt the sweaty residue of their grappling selves enfogging and enfouling the place, greasy molecules of disembodied consciousness drifting in the rooms, sucked into her lungs with every breath. A daily poisoning. So at last she simply had to get out and clear her head. Setting out at five, a long twilight walk downtown, hour after hour, mechanically moving along, lift foot put foot down lift other foot. Finally reaching the vicinity of West 116th Street by nightfall. A somber prowl in darkness through the ruins of the old university.

He stared at her in alarm. You really went there? Those charred shells of buildings were, they said, a rapist's heaven, a mugger's paradise. Suicidal to stroll there alone after dark. And she gave him an odd masked look, faintly guilty. What had she done this evening? His imagination supplied a possible answer—or was Hamlin planting the thought, or had it come from her, bleeding across the line of mental contact? A dimly perceived figure, say, pursuing her through the shattered campus. But Lissa crazily unafraid, perhaps half eager to court death or mutilation, defiant, turning to the unknown pursuer, winking, pulling up her tunic, waggling her hips. Here, man, bang away, what do I care? Thrust and thrust and thrust on a bed of rubble. Afterward the man giving her a funny look. You must be real weird, lady. And running away from her, leaving her to proceed on her solitary wandering way. Had it happened? Her clothes weren't rumpled or stained or soiled.

Macy told himself that it was all his own ugly fantasy; she had merely been out for a walk, hadn't spread her legs for a stranger, hadn't purged her head of echoes by inviting rape. Go on, he told her. You walked through the ruins. And then? I did a lot of thinking, she said. Wondering if I ought to head back to my old place and stay there. Or go uptown to you. Maybe even to kill myself. The easiest way. Misery no matter what I do, you see, that's no joke. And finally, beginning to tire, to regret her long nocturnal expedition, beginning to worry about worrying him by her disappearance. Getting on the tube, returning. Standing outside the door and becoming aware of the tricky takeover in progress within. The entry. The last-minute rescue. Tarantara!

"Why did you come back here?" he asked.

A shrug. Vague. "I can't say. Because I was lonely, maybe. Because I had a premonition, maybe, that you were in trouble. I didn't think about it I just came."

"Do you want to move out for good?"

"I don't know. I'd like to be able to stay with you, Paul. If only. The pain. Would. Stop." Drifting away from him again. Her voice dreamy and halting. "A river of mud flowing through my head," she murmured. Flopping down on the bed, face in arms. Macy went to her with comfort. Such as he could offer. Stroking her tenderly despite the ache behind his eyes. Again, it seemed, the curious flow of strength had taken place. From her to him. The odd sudden reversal of roles, the comforter becoming the comforted. Ten minutes ago she had been striving to put him back together, now she was crumpled and flaccid. And Hamlin thinks this girl is destructive. A monster, a villainess. Poor pitiful monster.

She said indistinctly, not looking up, "Your Rehab Center phoned again this morning. A doctor with a Spanish name."

"Gomez."

"Gomez, yes, I think so."

"And?"

Pause. "I told him the whole thing. He was very upset."

"What did he say?"

"He wanted to see you right away. I said no, it was impossible, Hamlin would attack you if you went near the Rehab Center. He didn't appear to believe that. I think I convinced him after a while."

"And then?"

"He said finally he'd have to discuss things with his colleagues, he'd call back in a day or two. Said I should phone him if there were any important new developments."

Macy considered calling him now. Wake the bastard up. Yank him from his bed of pleasure. He could be at the Rehab Center by one, half past one in the morning; maybe they could give him a shot of something while Hamlin was dormant, knock him out for keeps. Lissa vetoed the idea. Hamlin's not as dormant as you think, she said. He's down, but not out. Sitting there trying to collect some of his power. No telling what he'll do if he feels threatened.

Macy searched his cerebral crannies for Hamlin and could not find him, but left Gomez unphoned anyway. The risks were too great. Lissa probably was right: Hamlin still maintaining surveillance down there, capable of taking severe and possibly mutually fatal defensive action if attempt was made to reach the Center. Paul didn't dare try calling his bluff.

They prepared for bed. Flesh against flesh, but no copulatory gestures. He was carrying too heavy a burden of fatigue to

405

think about mounting the doubtfully willing Lissa just now. Still obsessed by the image of the stranger balling her in the university ruins, too. Tomorrow's another day, heigh-ho! As Macy was falling asleep he heard her say, "Gomez doesn't want me to stay with you any more. He thinks I'm dangerous for you."

"Because you awakened Hamlin in me?"

"No, I didn't go into that with him. I didn't say anything to him about my—gift."

"Then why?"

"Because I'm out of your other life, is why. You aren't supposed to be seeing Nat Hamlin's cast of characters, remember? They conditioned you against it."

"He knew who you were?"

"I told him I used to model for Nat. Our accidental meeting on the street. He pretty much ordered me to go away from you."

"Is that why you walked out tonight?"

"How do I know?" she said petulantly. Curling close against him. Tips of her breasts grazing his back. Turn around and do her? No. Not tonight. That lousy meddling fucker Gomez. Like to tell him a thing or two. If only I could. If only. What a bitching mess. But tomorrow's another day. She's snoring already, anyway. Let her rest. Maybe I will too. To sleep. Perchance to dream.


Three days of relative tranquility. Friday, Saturday, Sunday. His first weekend with Lissa. No news out of Hamlin, save only some irregular psychic belchings and rumblings. Obviously the shot that Lissa had given him had left him pretty feeble. No news out of Gomez, either. A quiet weekend together. Where to go, what to do? The first edge of summer heat lapping the city. We stay in bed late. We screw to Mozart. Dee-dum-dee-dum-dee-*dum*-

dum, diddy-dum diddy-dum diddy-*dum*. Her legs up over his shoulders in a nicely wanton way. Her eyes aglow afterward in the shower. Playful, kittenish. Soaping his cock, trying to get him up again and succeeding. For a man of my mature years I'm pretty virile, *hein?* Laughter. Breakfast. The morning news coming out of the slot.

Then out of the house. Her mood already descending; he could sense her turning sullen, starting to withdraw. It just didn't seem possible to keep her happy more than two hours at a stretch. He tried to ignore her darkening outlook, hoping it would go away. Such a beautiful day. The golden sunlight spilling out of the Bronx.

"Where do you want to go, Lissa?" She didn't answer. It seemed almost that she hadn't heard him. He asked again.

"Voices," she muttered. "These fucking voices. I'm a crapped-up Joan of Arc." Lissa? Lissa? Turning toward him, torment in the ocean-colored eyes. "A river of mud," she said. "Thick brown mud piling up in my head. Coming out my ears, soon. A delta on each side."

"It's such a beautiful day, Lissa. The whole city's ours."

"Wherever you want to go," she said.

At his random suggestion they went to the Bronx Zoo. Wandering hand in hand past the cunning habitat groups. Hard to believe that those lions really had no way of jumping the moat. And what kept those birds from flying out of their dome? Wide open on one side, for Christ's sake! But of course they did clever things with air pressure and ion-flows these days. The zoo was crowded. Families, lovers, kids. Most of them funnier-looking than the population behind the moats. The raucousness of the animals. Wet twitching noses, sad eyes.

Every third cage or so was marked with a grim black star,

signifying that the species was extinct except in captivity. White rhinoceros. Pygmy hippo. Reticulated giraffe. European bison. Black rhinoceros. South American tapir. Wombat. Arabian oryx. Caspian tiger. Red kangaroo. Bandicoot. Musk-ox. Grizzly bear. So many species gone. Another hundred years, nothing left but dogs and cats and sheep and cattle. But of course the Africans had needed meat in the famine years, before the Population Correction. The South Americans, the Asians. All those babies, all those hungry mouths, and still it hadn't done any good, by the end of it they were eating each other after the animals were gone. Now the zoos were the last refuge. And for some it was too late.

Macy remembered a trip with his father, when he was a boy, ten, twelve years old, the San Diego Zoo, seeing the giant panda they had there. "That's the last one left in the world, son. Smuggled out of Commie China just before the blowup." A big two-toned fuzzy toy sitting in the cage. No giant pandas left anywhere, now. Some stuffed ones, as reminders. His father? The San Diego Zoo? Really? Who was his father? Where had he grown up? Had he ever been to the San Diego Zoo? Did they truly have a giant panda there, once? The oscillations of memory. Surely it had never happened. Perhaps there had never been any such animal.

Lissa said, "I can feel their minds. The animals."

"Can you?"

"I never realized I could. I never went to the zoo before."

He was poised, wary, ready to rush her toward the tube if the impact overwhelmed her. It wasn't necessary. She was joyful, ecstatic, standing in the plaza by the seal tank and drinking in the oinks and bleats and honks and nyaaas of a hundred alien species. "Maybe I can transmit some of what I'm getting to you," she said, and held both his hands and frowned earnestly at him and peered into his eyes, so that passersby nodded and smiled at the sight of true love being expressed between the seals and the tigers, but he was unable to pick up a shred of what she sent him.

So she described it, in intermittent bursts, whenever she could spare him a moment out of her contemplations. The high piping throaty thoughts of the giraffe. The dull booming ruminations of the rhino. The dense, complex, bleak, and bitter output of the African elephant, he of the big ears, a Kierkegaard of zoology. The sparkling twitter of the chimps. The flippant outbursts of the raccoon. The Galapagos tortoise pondered eternity; the brown bear was surprisingly sensual; the penguins dreamed icy dreams.

"Are you making all this up?" he asked her, and she laughed in his face, like Aquinas accused of inventing the Trinity. Within an hour she was wholly spent. They snacked on algaeburgers and Lenin soda, and took the conveyor to the exit. Lissa giggling, manic, stoned on her beasts. "The orangutan," she said. "I could tell you exactly how he'd vote in the next election. And if I could only let you hear the gnu! Oh, shit, the gnu!"

But she was brooding again before dark. They went into Manhattan in the afternoon, circling around the burned-out places and drifting through the flamboyant new downtown section, and he tried to interest her in the amusement parlors, the sniffer palaces, the swimming tanks, and such, only she was glassy and distant. They had dinner at a Chinese restaurant on one of the Hudson piers, and she picked idly at her food, leaving most of it, getting clucked at by the waiter. A quiet evening at home. We have no friends, Macy realized. They played Bach and smoked a lot.

Just before bedtime Hamlin seemed to stretch and yawn within him, or was it an illusion? Bad sex that night, Lissa very far down, he not much better, both of them clumsy and halfhearted as they groped each other in bed. He tried to go into her and she was dry. Persevered, God knows why. Finally some lubrication. Not much

response from her, though. Like fucking a robot; he was tempted
to quit in the middle, but thought it would be impolite, and he
chased himself on to a solitary, unrewarding coming. Some nasty
dreams later, but nothing he hadn't had before.

Saturday a fizzle. Lissa vacant, absent An endless day. Sunday
much better. Throwing herself on him at sunrise, straddling him,
lowering herself until impaled. Good morning, good morning,
good morning! Up and down, up and down. Breasts jiggling overhead. His startled fingers encircling the smooth cool globes of her
ass. After which she fixed a hearty breakfast. Bouncy, a breathless
adolescent giddiness about her, perhaps fake: trying hard to be a
good companion, he suspected. After that sulking bitchy day she
gave me yesterday. Lose one, win one.

"Where to?" she asked.

"Museum of Modern Art," he suggested. "They've got some
Hamlins there, don't they?"

"Five or six, yes. But do you really think it's wise to go? I mean,
he's been so quiet the last couple of days. The sight of his work
might stir him up again."

"That's exactly what I want to find out," he told her. They went.
The museum, it developed, had *seven* Hamlins, two big pieces
almost though not quite as impressive as the *Antigone,* and five
minor objects. They all were on display in the same room, four
grouped in one corner and three assembled against the opposite
wall, which gave Macy the opportunity for a critical test: would
the presence of so much of Nat Hamlin's handiwork arouse the
submerged artist by some process of psychic leverage?

Boldly Macy planted himself between the two groupings,
where he would be exposed to the maximum output of the
pieces. Well, Hamlin? Where are you? But though Macy detected
some cloudy subliminal squirmings, there was nothing else to

indicate Hamlin's existence within him. He studied the sculptures closely. The connoisseur making his lofty observations. Only a few weeks ago, in Harold Griswold's office, the sight of a Hamlin piece had knocked him slappy, and here he was listening critically to the resonances, noting the subtle recurvings of the contours, doing the whole art-appreciation number with great aplomb.

Some kids in the room, researching a report on Hamlin, maybe. Apparently recognizing him. Looking at his face, then at his Rehab badge, then at his face again, then at the sculptures, then at each other. Whispering. Even that didn't bother him, being found out as the walking zombie relict of the great artist. The kids didn't dare approach him. Macy gave them a benevolent smile. I'd give you my autograph if you asked. With these very hands, you know, those masterpieces were created.

He was impressed by his own newfound resilience. To come here, to confront Hamlin's work, to take it all so calmly. Although not entirely calmly. He found the sight of these pieces gradually stirring in him that dismal depressing nostalgia, that yearning to have access to the past in which this body had brought into being those sculptures. His true past. As he was starting to regard it. Implying that his own past was unsatisfactory, insufficient insubstantial, inadequate. As if he too had come to agree with Hamlin that he was mere fiction, a freakish aberrant unreality that had been appended to Nat Hamlin's authentic life. So he craved knowledge of that other time. Who was I when I was he? How did I bring forth these works? What was it like to be Hamlin? A bad moment. The subtle corrosive influence of Hamlin within me, undermining me even when he's quiescent. So that I have begun to doubt myself. So that I have started to scorn myself. And hunger to be him. This is the road to surrender; let me turn from it.

Lissa seemed troubled by the Hamlin group too. Remembering a jollier past, perhaps. The happy days of first love. The awesome sensation of being chosen by Nathaniel Hamlin for his bed, for his studio. A world of endless sunrises before her. All highways open. And to have come to this. How great the contrast Macy could see the bleakness spreading across her face. A mistake to inflict Hamlin's art on her? Or maybe she merely felt oppressed by the museum's Sunday throng. We will go now, I think.

Midmorning, Monday, Macy hard at work. Griswold had just assigned him to a new story. Preliminary charisma-level statistics for the 2012 election came out last night, late; let's do a feature on all the candidates, run up a chart of pulse-figures, hormone counts, recognition profile, the whole multivalent works, right? Right. And so to the task. Research assistants scurrying madly. Their pretty pink boobies hobbling. Stacks of documents. Fredericks stopping by to offer bland, useless suggestions. Loftus staggering in with a load of simulations and color overlays for his approval. The hours whisking swiftly by; the mind fully engaged in purposeful activity.

And then an unscheduled interruption. Someone down here to see you, Mr. Macy. No appointment. A visitor for me? Who? Image of Lissa, bedraggled, obsessed, freaking out in the reception hall. Please, I must see him, matter of life and death, I'm going to snap, I'm going to blow, let me go upstairs! A messy scene. Only his visitor wasn't Lissa. His visitor turned out to be a Dr. Gomez.

Panic. Gomez, here? Hamlin'll kill me!

After the first quick surge of fright, some rethinking. Hamlin had warned him not to go to the Rehab Center, or to telephone his doctors, yes. But the doctor had come to him. Was that covered by the threat? A debatable point. In any case, Hamlin didn't seem to be raising objections. Macy waited a long troubled moment, expecting a sign from within, a squeeze of his heart, a pinching of his nerves, some sort of don't-fool-around signal. Nothing. He sensed Hamlin's presence like a dull heavy weight in his gut, but he got no specific instructions about seeing Gomez. Perhaps Hamlin wants to find out what Gomez will say. Maybe he's still recovering from the jolt Lissa gave him. Anyway. Tell Dr. Gomez he can come up.

Gomez, out of context, looked unfamiliar. At the Rehab Center, surrounded by his phalanxes of computers and his electronic pharmacopoeia, Gomez was dynamic, formidable, aggressive, indomitable, confidently vulgar. Entering Macy's sleek office he was almost meek. Without his throne and scepter a king's but a bifurcated radish. Gomez came slipping hesitantly through the fancy sliding door. Dressed in excessively contemporary business clothes, greens and reds, much too young for him, instead of the customary monochrome lab outfit. Looking shorter and more plump than in his own domain. His thick drooping mustache seedy and in need of trimming. The weakness of his chin somehow mattering much more here. Ten feet apart; eyes meet eyes. Gomez moistening his lips. How strange to see him on the defensive.

Macy said, "I guess you've decided to believe me after all."

"We've been discussing your case nonstop for three days," said Gomez hoarsely. "But I had to have firsthand data. And since you wouldn't come to us—"

"Couldn't."

"Couldn't." Gomez nodded. Scowled. Not at Macy but at himself. His distress was apparent. Coming here today was a considerable gesture. The cocky doctor eating crow. He said, voice ragged, "I didn't want to chance phoning you. In case it might provide too much time for the former ego to build up negative reactions. Is my presence here causing any repercussions?"

"Not so far."

"If it does, tell me and I'll leave. I don't want to endanger you."

"Don't worry, Gomez, I'll tell you fast if anything begins." Checking to see if Hamlin is stirring. All calm. "Hamlin hasn't been very active since Thursday night."

"But he's still there?"

"He's there, all right. Despite your loud assurance that it wasn't possible for him to come back."

"We all make mistakes, Macy."

"That was a pretty fucking big one. I asked you to run an EEG. You said no, I was merely hallucinating, merely having a fantasy, there was no chance in the world that Hamlin was intact and surfacing. And then you said—"

"All right. Let's not go into that now." Dabbing at his sweaty forehead. "I'm concerned with therapy for this, not with placing blame. When did it start?"

"The day I left the Center. When I met the girl, Hamlin's old model, mistress, the one you spoke to a couple of times on the telephone."

"Miss Moore."

"Yes. Bumped into her, literally, on the street. I told you all this. She kept calling me Nat, ignoring my badge—you remember?"

"I remember."

"I saw her again, last Monday. She said she was in trouble and wanted me to help her. I didn't want to get involved and started to leave. She hit me with a two-pronged blast of telepathy. Which woke him up fully, completing the job of arousing him that had started when—"

"Telepathy?"

"ESP. Communication between minds. You know."

"I know. This girl's a telepath?"

"I'm trying to tell you."

"You knew she was a telepath, and also that she was a figure out of Hamlin's past who you therefore were under instructions not to see, and nevertheless you arranged to meet her and—"

"I *didn't* know she was a telepath. Until it was too late. Not that I'd have had any particular reason to avoid her because of that You never said anything about telepaths, Gomez. I didn't even know there were such things as telepaths, not real ones, not walking around in New York City."

Gomez closed his eyes. "All right. I get the picture. What we have here is an apparent case of induced identity reestablishment under telepathic stimulus. Of all the shit. A minute theoretical possibility, but who ever expected to run into an actual case of—no fucking literature on the whole subject—no tests, no background, no data—"

"You can write a wonderful paper on me some day," Macy said bitterly.

"Spare me the crap. You think I'm happy about this?" Indeed genuine agony was visible in Gomez' fleshy features. "Okay, so she woke Hamlin. Meaning what? Give me the symptomology."

"He talks to me."

"Out loud?"

"In my head. A silent voice, but it doesn't seem silent. Twice now he's tried to grab my speech centers. All he can say is gibberish, though, and I knock him away. He also took hold of the muscles of the right side of my face once. I made him let go. Two or three times he's given me a physical shock, a jolt, knocked me down. Last Tuesday, when I set out to the Rehab Center, he staged a little heart attack for me, telling me that he'd give me a niftier one if I persisted in going to the Center. This is no goddam hallucination, Gomez. I've had conversations with him, long rational conversations. He's got very ambitious ideas.

He's been inviting me to let him finish me off so he can have his body back."

"Obviously we can't allow that."

"Obviously there isn't a fucking thing you can do. If I let you make any hostile moves toward him at all, he'll kill me. It's like I'm carrying a bomb inside me."

"He's bluffing."

"You're very sure of that," Macy said.

"If your body dies, he'll die with it. Whatever he is, he can't survive the decay of your brain cells."

"He can't survive another round in the Rehab Center, either. So he'd be willing to take any step to keep me from going there, right up to and including killing us both. If I go to you, he dies. Why shouldn't he kill me anyway and take me along? Or at least threaten to, knowing it'll stop me from going to the Center?"

Gomez considered that. He didn't seem to arrive at any immediate conclusions.

Macy said, "I'll tell you what's going to happen. One of two things. He'll knock me out and take over the body, or I'll find some way of chopping him up so he can't hurt me.

"You're playing dangerous games, Macy. Come to the Center. I know Hamlin better than you do: he won't carry out his threat, he won't do anything ultimately to harm you. Killing you would mean the decay and ruin of his own physical self, the last legitimate vestige of Nat Hamlin in the world. He wouldn't do it. He's always been body-proud."

"Balls. I'm no gambler. He said keep away from you and I'm going to keep away."

"We can't let you remain at large with the ego of a condemned criminal in partial control of your brain," Gomez said.

"What will you do, then? Order my arrest? He'll kill me. I

believe him when he says that. Do you want to take the chance? It isn't your life on the line, Gomez. You've been wrong in this case once already."

Twitchings of the mustache tips. The tongue moving restlessly between teeth and lips. Gomez in a pickle. Macy staring across the desk at him. He felt his heart hammering. Was it Hamlin, waking up? Or just the excitement, the adrenalin flow?

Gomez said finally, "We'll have to put you under surveillance. The legal problems, the presence of a potentially dangerous criminal in you. But we'll keep our distance. We won't jeopardize you."

"How will you know whether you're jeopardizing me or not?"

"A signal," Gomez suggested. "Wait." Frowning. "Let's say that when Hamlin is threatening you, you clap your right hand to your left shoulder. So."

"So." Clap.

"That'll tell us to back off, so we don't provoke him. And when you want us to withdraw from the vicinity entirely, that is, when you feel that you're in extreme danger, you also clap your left hand to your right shoulder. So."

"So." Clap. Clap. Idiocy. "How about a secret password, too?"

"I'm trying to help you, Macy. Don't be clever."

"Is there anything else you want to tell me, or can I get back to my work now?"

"One more signal, if you don't mind."

"The one that I use in asking for permission to take a crap?"

"The one to tell us that Hamlin is dormant and that it would be safe for us to seize you. Do you agree that it's possible such a situation might arise? All right, then. That would be our opportunity to grab you and try to exorcise him completely, fast. But only when you give the signal."

"Which is?"

Gomez thought a moment. Deep concentration. All this Boy Scout stuff must really strain his mind. Finally: "Hands locked together behind neck. Like so."

"So," Macy said, imitating. "You won't let your goons mix up the signals, will you?"

"Just keep them straight in your own head and we'll manage to look after ourselves," Gomez said. He moved toward the door. Looking back, shaking his head. "A case of demonic possession, that's what this is. Holy shit. The seventeenth century rides again! But we'll get this corrected, Macy. We owe you an uncrapped-up life, a life without these complications." Pausing by the exit. "If you want to know what's good for you, by the way, I recommend you stop screwing around with Miss Moore. You're living with her, aren't you?"

"More or less."

"You were strongly advised not to get into any entanglements linked to your body's former identity. Specifically including picking up Nat Hamlin's old mistresses, telepaths or not."

"Should I boot her out on her ass? She's a human being. She's got problems. She needs help."

"She's the cause of all your problems, too. It's about ten to one you wouldn't be saddled with Hamlin in the first place if you hadn't gotten involved with her."

"That's easy to tell me now. But I *have* Hamlin, and I feel a responsibility toward her, too. She's a wreck. She needs an anchor, Gomez, somebody to keep her from drifting away."

"What's the matter with her?"

"The ESP. It's driving her out of her mind. She picks up voices—half the time she doesn't know who she is—she has to hide from people, to shield herself—the telepathy comes and goes, random, not under her conscious control at all. It's like a curse."

"And this you need?" Gomez asked. "You're such a solidly established individual yourself that you can keep company with dynamite like this?"

"It wasn't my idea, believe me. But now that I'm involved with her, I'm not going to toss her out. I want to help her."

"How?"

"Maybe there's some way of disconnecting this ESP of hers. It's burning out her mind. What do you say, Gomez? Could it be done?"

"I don't know item one about ESP. I'm a Rehab specialist."

"Who does know?"

"I suppose I could find out if there are any hospitals in the metropolitan area with experience in this. Some neuropsychiatric division must be pissing around with ESP. If she hates it so much, why hasn't she gone in to be examined?"

"She's afraid to let anyone fool with her mind. Afraid that she'll end up losing her whole personality if they try to rip out the tele- pathy."

"Shit. You tell me you want to help her, and two seconds later you tell me she's scared of being helped. This is crazy, man. The girl is poison. Get her into a hospital."

"Tell me where to send her," Macy said. "I'll see if I want to do it. And if she does." He gave Gomez a sudden savage grin and clapped his right hand to his left shoulder. A moment afterward he put his left hand on his right shoulder. Gomez stared at him, blinking, not moving at all. "Well, dummy?" Macy asked. "You forgot your own signals? That's the one for withdrawing from the vicinity."

"Has Hamlin begun to threaten you?"

"Don't stand there asking stupid questions. You got the signal. Go. Go. I have work to do. Let me be, Gomez."

"You poor schmuck," Gomez said. "What a lousy thing this is. For all of us." And went. Macy cradled his head in his hands. An ache behind each ear. An ache in his forehead, as though the front of his brain were swollen and pushing against the bone. Practice the signals. Right hand to left shoulder. Left hand to right shoulder. Lock hands behind back of neck. Surveillance. The friendly Rehab Center haunting me too. Jesus. Jesus. Jesus. He thought he could hear Nat Hamlin's ghostly laughter reverberating through the interstices of his frazzled mind. Hey, are you awake, Nat? Did you listen to what Gomez said? Listening now? They're out to get you, Nat. Gomez is after you. To finish the job that he didn't do right the first time. Scared, Nat? I don't mind telling you I am. Because only one of us is going to come out of this whole, at the very best. At the very best, only one of us.

# 11

If they really did have him under surveillance, he wasn't aware of it. He went through his daily routines. Finished preparing the script for the charisma story on Monday. Taping on Tuesday. Everything smooth. Back and forth from apartment to the office without trouble. Hamlin, surfacing coherently early Tuesday evening for the first time since Thursday, had a pleasant little chat with him, saying nothing about his conference with Gomez or about the abortive takeover attempt of that stoned Thursday evening. Fair is fair, Macy thought You try to finesse me, I try to sandbag you, but we don't talk about such sordid things.

Hamlin chose to turn on the charm, reminiscing a bit about his life and good times. Selected segments of his autobiography come dancing along the identity interface. With subtitles.

## THE ARTIST DISCOVERS HIS GIFT

1984, Orwell's year, the global situation quite thoroughly fucked up on schedule, although not quite as fucked up as the pessimistic old bastard had imagined, and in this small town is twelve-year-old Nat Hamlin, barely pubescent, full of ungrounded wattage and churning unfocused needs. Which small town, where? Mind your own business. The boy is slim and tall for his age. Long sensitive fingers. Father wants him to be a brain surgeon. It's a good living, son, especially now, with all the psychosis flapping in the breeze. You open the skull, you see, and you stick your long sensitive fingers inside and you chop this and you splice that and you amputate this, three thousand dollars, please, and put your money in good growth stocks.

The boy isn't listening. In the attic he models little clay figurines. He has never been to a museum; he has no interest in art. But there is sensual pleasure, in squeezing and twisting the clay. He feels a lusty tickle in his crotch and a delicious tension in his jaws when he works with it. Filling the attic with grotesque little images. You sure see the world a funny way, boy. You been looking at some Pee-cas-so, hey? Pee-cas-so, who he? He that old mother from France, he make a million bucks a year turning out this junk. No shit? Where can I see some? And going to the museum, two hours away. Pee-cas-so. That's not how it's spelled. He's pretty good, yeah, yeah. But I'm just as good as he is. And I'm just starting out.

## SOLITARY PLEASURES

The first major piece now adorns the attic. Three and a half feet high. Adapted from one of Picasso's paintings: woman with two faces, body twisted weirdly on its perpendicular axis, a veritable bitch of a challenge for a fourteen-year-old boy no matter how good he is. The creator lies naked before it. Straggly mustache. Pimples on his ass. Act of homage to the muse. Seizes rising organ in left hand. Back and forth, back and forth, back and forth. Oooh and ahhh. Sixty seconds: close, to his record for speed. And accuracy of aim. He baptizes the masterpiece with jets of salty fluid. Ah. Ah. Ah.

## AN END TO SUBLIMATION

She has long straight silken golden hair in the out-of-date style favored by girls of this town. Rimless glasses, fuzzy green cashmere sweater, short skirt. They are fifteen. He has lured her to the attic after telling her, shyly, anesthetized by pot, that he is a sculptor. She is a poet whose work appears regularly in the town newspaper. Appreciates the arts. This village of philistines; the two of us against them all. Look, this I took from Picasso, and these are my early works, and here's what I'm doing now. How strange, Nat, what brilliant work. You mean nobody knows about this? Hardly anybody. Who would understand? *I* understand, Nat. I knew you would, Helene.

You know what? Never worked from a live model. An important step forward in my career. Oh, no, I couldn't, I just couldn't I mean, I'd be embarrassed to death! But why? God gave you the body. Look, all through history girls have been posing for famous artists. And I have to. How else will I grow as an artist? She hesitates. Well, maybe. Let's smoke first. He brings out the stash. She takes two puffs for every one of his. Giggling. He is deadly serious. Reminds her. Yes, yes, yes. You're sure your mother won't come upstairs? Not a chance, she doesn't give a crap what I do up here.

And then. The clothes coming off. Her incandescent body. He can barely look. Fifteen and he's never seen it. Backward for his age, too much time spent alone in the attic. Sweater, bra. Her breasts are heavy; they don't stick out straight when they're bare, they dangle a little. The nipples very tiny, not much bigger than his. Dimples in her ass. The hair down there darker than on her head, and woolier. She looks so incomplete without a prick. His cheeks are blazing. Here, stand like this. Doesn't dare to touch her. Poses her by waving his hands in air. Wishes she'd stand with her legs apart: he isn't sure what it looks like, and he can't see. But she doesn't. She's so stoned, though.

He attacks the clay. Yes. Yes. Works furiously. Meanwhile this posing is turning her on. The artist ought to be naked too, she says. It's only fair. He just laughs. An absurd idea. Couldn't concentrate if. Half an hour. Sweat running down. Tired of posing, she says. Can I stop? They stop. She comes over to him. Leads him on. Put your hand here. And here. Oh. Oh. Oh. Unzipping him. His dong will explode. Quick, on top of me. Oh. Oh, God!

### THE BIG CITY

A small apartment. Dozens of his favorite works crammed around everywhere. The famous art critic visiting him. Tall, serious, silver-haired. The artist is tall and serious too. Nineteen. Why should you go to art school, the critic asks? My boy, you are already a master! Paternal hand fondling Hamlin's shoulder. What you need now is a dealer. With the right sponsorship you could go places. And how young you are. Cheeks still downy. So saying the famous art critic rubs the downy cheek. Staring intently into young artist's eyes. You could make me the happiest man in the world tonight, says famous art critic in tender tones.

## AT THE GALLERY

Little red circles pasted on every label. Sold. Sold. Sold. Sold. An auspicious debut. All the best people buying. The dealer, fat, glorying in flesh, slapping his back. Twenty-two years old. An instant success. Now scene follows scene helter-skelter, one blurring into the next, sometimes two running at once, split-screen.

THE ADVENT OF PSYCHOSCULPTURE
UNREQUITED LOVE
THE SEDUCTIONS OF WEALTH
THE CELEBRATED ACTRESS
ALONE ON THE PINNACLE
THE TORMENTS OF FAME
THE DAY THE MUSEUM BOUGHT EVERYTHING
MEETING HELENE AGAIN, FIFTEEN
YEARS LATER
THE WORLD TRAVELER
KICKING THE HABIT
FOUR'S COMPANY,
FIVE'S A CROWD
MY NAME IS LISSA

And the camera speeding up, running wild.

THE ANTIGONE
THE HEADACHE
THE BREAKDOWN
THE FIRST RAPE

FREAKING OUT ON TERROR
THE QUARREL WITH HIS WIFE
FINISHING ANTIGONE
KNOCKING LISSA DOWNSTAIRS
OUT OF HIS MIND
RAPE UPON RAPE
CAUGHT
CONVICTED
OBLITERATED
AWAKENED

And the sequences jumbled.

ALONE ON THE PINNACLE
AN END TO SUBLIMATION
THE BIG CITY
KICKING THE HABIT
OUT OF HIS MIND
AT THE GALLERY
SOLITARY PLEASURES
THE ARTIST DISCOVERS HIS GIFT

Faster and faster. Names, dates, events, aspirations, swirling in a thick soup of memory, everything merging, all detail lost. Perhaps none of it had ever happened.

—Good night, old buddy.

Lissa was crying softly to herself when he got into bed Tuesday night. He touched her arm and she pulled away from him. Afterward she told him she was sorry for being so unfriendly.

*       *       *

On Wednesday morning, setting out for work, Macy thought he saw one of the Rehab Center minions who Gomez had said would be keeping watch over him. A squat, potbellied man standing at the entrance to the building across the street, holding a newspaper. An awkward exchange of guarded glances. From Macy a nicker of a smile. Me and my shadow. Right hand to left shoulder, hup! Left hand to right shoulder, hup! Hands clasped at back of neck, hup, hup, hup!

That night he suggested that they go downtown to a sniffer palace, but Lissa didn't want to. A quiet evening at home with Brahms and Shostakovich. Near bedtime Lissa said that she had figured out one way for him to get rid of Hamlin.

"How?"

"You could rape somebody and arrange to get caught. And blame it on him. The authorities would see to it that he was completely erased."

"He'd kill me if we were taken into custody," Macy said. A crazy idea. A crazy girl. You could rape somebody and arrange to get caught. Within him Hamlin laughed. Lissa cried again that night, and when Macy asked her if he could help her in any way she made no reply.

There wasn't much for him to do at the network on Thursday—just a half-hour patch job on a story he had taped the week before. He consumed the rest of the day in trying to look busy. Mainly, with another weekend coming up, he tried to think of things that would divert Lissa and perhaps yank her from the mood of withdrawal that was so frequently enveloping her lately.

He sensed that he was losing her. That she was losing' herself. Slipping away into some tepid shoreless sea blanketed by thick blue fog. She hadn't left his apartment in three days. He suspected that she stayed in bed until noon, one in the afternoon, then sat around smoking, playing music, turning pages, daydreaming. Drifting. Floating. She seldom spoke any more. Or even answered his questions: just a grunt or two. Last week Macy had felt hemmed in by other people, what with Lissa sharing his apartment and Hamlin sharing his brain; but now Lissa was spinning this cocoon about herself, and Hamlin too was withdrawn and remote. Macy was experienced in solitude but didn't necessarily like it.

This weekend, he decided, we will explore the wonders of the world beyond my door. Rent a car, drive up into the country, two hundred miles, three hundred, however far one must go to find uncluttered pastures. Picnic on the grass. A bosky dell. Romantic fornications beneath the boughs of murmuring fragrant pine trees. If there are any left. And we'll go to fine restaurants. I'll ask Hamlin to suggest a few. Hello, hello, are you there? And Saturday night at a Times Square sniffer palace, all glowlight and tinsel, we will inhale the most modern hallucinogens and enjoy two hours of earthy fantasy. Perhaps we will visit the aquarium so that Lissa can eavesdrop on the ponderous leathery reveries of the walruses and the whales. Oh, a fine zealous weekend! Recreation and invigoration and the restoration of our depleted souls!

But when Macy reached his apartment that evening Lissa wasn't there. A feeling of *déja vu:* she did this last Thursday too, didn't she? A week gone by and nothing altered. But there is a difference this time, as his quick search of the closets reveals. She has taken her belongings with her. Cleared out for good.

\*     \*     \*

The easiest thing now was also the hardest. To sit tight, to forget her, to make a life without her. Nothing but trouble and turmoil, wasn't she? The steamy feminine complexities, compounded and exponentialized by the inexplicabilities of telepathy. Let her go. Let her go. A high probability that she'll come back, even as last time. But he couldn't. Damnation. Must go looking for her. The most logical place. Her apartment.

A sweet soft spring night.

Stars on display beyond the towers' tips. Peddlers of blurry dreams sauntering in the streets. Down we go into the tube. Whoosh whoosh whoosh. Transfer to East Side line. Double back on tracks. Her exit. The narrow streets, the decaying buildings, survivors of all the cultural upheavals. Scaly erections protruding from the corpus of the abolished past. Which of these houses is hers? They all look alike. Mysterious figures flitting in alleyways. A visit here is like a journey backward in time. A district of shady deeds and unfathomable espionage; an Istanbul, a Lisbon of the mind, embedded in the quivering fabric of New York. This looks like the right place. I'll go in.

Directory of residents? Don't make me laugh!

Macy squinted through the Jurassic dimness of the cavernous lobby. He caught sight of a figure far away, bent and distorted, which hobbled toward him as he proceeded warily inward. And then the shock of recognition: himself approaching. What he sees is the image of Paul Macy, reflected in a cracked and warped mirror occupying the nether wall. Laughter. Applause. On six levels of this hostelry holovision sets give forth their offerings with numbing simultaneity. Lissa? Lissa? She lived on the fifth floor, didn't she? I'll go up. Knock on her door, if I can find it. Or else

429

ask the neighbors. Miss Moore, the red-haired girl, been away for a week or so? You seen her around here tonight? Not me, man, haven't seen a thing. Up the stairs. Where else could she have fled but here? Her nest. Her hermitage.

On the fourth landing he paused. Had the hirelings of Gomez followed him here? No doubt. Keeping close watch. Maybe creeping up the stairs behind him, not wanting to let him get out of sight. It was entirely possible that some orderly of the Rehab Center was at this moment a flight or two below him, frozen, waiting for him to resume his climb. And when I take a step he takes a step. And when I stop he stops. And so up and up and up. Gripping the banister, Macy swung his body halfway out over it and peered down the stairwell. In this darkness impossible to tell. Did somebody pull his head in fast, down there? Let's cheek it. Wait a minute, then pop my head out again. There. Still not sure, though. Well, fuck it. I don't care if they follow me or not. Up we go. Step. Step. *Stop.* Listen. That time I was sure I heard someone behind me. Comforting to know that they look after me where'er I go. Up.

He halted again on the fifth-floor landing. Double row of doors receding into infinity. Lissa behind one of them, maybe. Perhaps it would be best to give her some warning that he had come for her. Perhaps then she'll come out into the hall, I won't have to go knocking on doors. A deep breath. Sending forth the most intense mental signal he could manage, hoping that it would be on her wavelength. *Lissa. Lissa. It's me, Paul, out by the stairs. I came to get you, baby. You hear me, Lissa?*

No response from anywhere.

Okay. Now we look. He began strolling down the corridor, studying the faceless doors. In a hole like this you don't put nameplates out. He couldn't remember where her room was. At the far end of the hall, somewhere, away from the stairs, but there were dozens of doors down there. Here's one that looks like it might be right. He started to knock, but held back. Shyness? Fear? These strange savage slum people here. Maybe they don't even speak English. And me intruding on their shabby dinnertime. But yet if I don't I'll never find her.

Again he started to knock. No. Holovision blasting away in there. Couldn't be her. I'll move on. Here? But they're cooking something in this one. Curried squid. Spider patties. *Lissa? Lissa? Where are you?*

Footsteps in the hall behind him.

Someone running toward him.

Mugger. Slasher. The shadowy pursuer on the stairs. Macy tried to swing around to face his attacker, but before he had completed half a turn the other was upon him, seizing his arms, pulling them up, pinioning him. A big man, as big as he was. They struggled silently in the dark, grunting. A knee rose and jammed itself into the small of Macy's back. He ripped one arm free, clawed at the assailant, tried to get an ear, an eye, any kind of grip. Before the knife flashes. Before the stungun.

Lurching, Macy managed to push the other up against the hallway wall, hard, ramming him with his shoulder, but then he felt his arm, the captive one, being bent back beyond its limits. Wild burst of pain. Desperately Macy banged the other again with his shoulder. Tried to knock his head against the other, hoping to drop him with a single stony smash. No use. No use. The fierce combat raged. Pointless even to call for help; who would open a door in a place like this? Slam and slam and slam. He was fully engaged in the task of defense. Such total concentration. Both of them breathing hard. Putting up more of a fight than he expected, I am! Stalemate. Lucky thing for me there's only one of them. If I could just get my hand free, and bash his head against the hallway wall—

And then. In the most frantic moment of the struggle. An inner convulsion.

Hamlin.

Making his move.

Time fell to stasis, so that Macy could perceive each phase of the conquest in a leisurely, detached way. Hamlin, having collected his strength for some days now, was taking advantage of the hallway battle, of Macy's full absorption in his difficulties, to seize the motor centers of their shared brain. Ripping out connections with both hands, replugging them under his own administration. Macy was tumbling through a timeless abyss. And Hamlin steadily and efficiently consummating what must have been a carefully planned takeover. Right leg. Left leg. Right arm. Left arm. Paralysis setting in, an unexpected summer freeze. Macy sinking and sinking and sinking. No way to defend himself; he had left his flank unguarded, and the enemy was pouring over the palisade. Down. Down. Down. Very cold now, very still. Where was Gomez' surveillance? Right hand to left shoulder. Left hand to right shoulder. Extreme danger. Hah. Much good that would be. Macy realized that he and Gomez had completely forgotten to devise one important signal, the one that said, *Help, he's taking me over!* Not that anybody was here to help him. Right hand to left shoulder. Left hand to right shoulder. Extreme danger. Down. Down. He has me.

# 12

He was submerged in a sea of smooth green glass. Wholly engulfed, unable to break through to the surface: above his head a solid sheet, impermeable, infrangible, sealing him away from the air. Choking, lungs bursting, head throbbing. A dull pounding sensation in both his calves; swelling of the toes. Below his dangling feet a fathomless abyss, dark, dense. From far overhead came faint greenish-gold strands of light. Blurred, indistinct images of the upper world. All perceptions refracted and distorted and transformed. His hands pushing desperately at the glassy layer above him. Which would not yield. Oh, God, I must be in hell! How can I breathe? How did he do this to me? How will I get out of here? I must be sinking. Slowly down and down. Toothy fish to pick my bones. He could feel the surging of the currents, rivers in the sea buffeting him as they swept past. He shivered. Terror invaded him. So this is it. He has me. He has me. I am within him.

Macy felt a sharp pang of loss, of displacement It had been so good living in the world. The sunlight, the people, laughter, even the uncertainties, the tensions. To be alive, at least. And then to be overthrown, cast down, evicted, disinherited. He took it all away from me when I wasn't ready to go. It wasn't fair. And now? The pain of this place. The gasping. The choking. The fear.

But he survived the first lurch of terror and discovered that there was no second one. He grew calm. Gradually Macy refined and clarified his awareness of his new condition. He realized that although he could not reach the air, neither would he sink any deeper, nor was the feeling that he was about to drown to be taken literally. In fact this was no sea. All the marine imagery, he understood now, was purely metaphorical. He was indeed submerged, he did indeed dangle between somewhere and somewhere, but he had become a mere electrochemical network spread thinly through the recesses of what he was forced at this stage to regard as the brain of Nat Hamlin. Hamlin was in charge, on top. Macy occupied some indefinable cranny or series of crannies. He could not see. He could not feel. He could not speak. He could not hear. He could not move. He was nothing but an abstraction, a disembodied identity. Whether he could properly be said to exist at all was questionable.

Now that the first shock was past, he was startled that the loss of his independence brought no despair. Surprise, yes. Irritation and annoyance, yes. (How slickly Hamlin had outmaneuvered him!) Dismay, yes. (How strange it is to be trapped in here. How claustrophobic. Will I ever be able to get out again?) But not despair. Not even fear. Hamlin had once been in this very predicament himself, had he not, and he had endured it and mastered it and escaped. Then why not I?

There was of course a great temptation to accept the situation complacently and passively. Telling oneself that one had never been entitled to a real existence anyway. That it would be best for everyone concerned, now that the upheaval of selves had come about, if he sat tight in this womblike place. Placidly letting Hamlin have the body to which he held the original birthright. But the temptation did not tempt Macy greatly. Easy though it might be to take up a vegetable existence, he preferred a more active life. A body of his own. The brief taste of living that he had had left him hungry for more.

I never really began, after all, he thought. Just a few weeks on my own away from the Center. With *him* bothering me most of that. And now this. I'll fight back. I'll push him out as he pushed me. I may not have been born, but I was real and I wish to return to existence.

Patiently he sought to examine his available options. Was it possible to establish sensory input? Let us see. Let us muster our powers of concentration. If we gather our energy—so—and direct it purposefully in a single direction—so—do we make contact with anything? No. No. Glassy darkness is all. And yet. Now. What do we have here? A node, a handle. Which we can seize. To which we can apply a subtle interior pressure. Yes! And we perceive. The inward-rushing flood of sensation. But what do we perceive? Our surroundings.

Yes, just as Hamlin said, you arrive at a kind of percept-surrogate image of the brain you're in. If only you had paid more attention, at the Center, when they were trying to teach you a little structural anatomy so that they could explain what they'd been doing to your head. The synaptic vesicles. The synaptic cleft. Dendritic spine. Axon terminal. Organelles, filaments, and tubules. Neural mitochondria. Corpus callosum. Anterior commissure. Limbic cortex. Centrencephalic system. Words. Words. This baffling torrent of referentless nouns. But somehow a little comprehension slides through. You poke around, you insinuate yourself, you learn a thing or two. And the darkness clears.

Macy sent a tendril of himself down a narrow moist corridor and found, at the end of it, a pulsing pink wall on which a golden honeycomb-textured plate was mounted. The tip of the tendril went into one of the apertures of the honeycomb and a tiny explosion of light resulted. Progress, no? Now we subdivide the tendril, and poke one end of it in here, and one in here, and one in here. Flash flash and flash. Presto jingo, we get an input! A bright cluster of sensory data. As yet what comes in is undifferentiated; it might be sight, sound, touch, smell, anything. But at least there is an input. We will continue. Macy tirelessly probing. Seeking out new avenues of exploration. More honeycombs; more subdividing tendrils slipping into slots; more bursts of light.

Will any sense ever come out of this? You are trying to tap a television image, and you can succeed in making contact only with widely scattered phosphors, a dot here and a dot there. Little spiky blurts of information, not enough for comprehension. Not yet. But no one is rushing you. You have no sense of the passage of time. Take an hour, a minute, a century, a year. Sooner or later you'll have a good hookup. It's just a matter of—what was that? A flash of coherence! Here and gone, but it was a total image. Audio? Visual? You still can't tell, but you know that you had all the information, even if you weren't able to interpret it. It was, say, a complete sentence, subject predicate adverbs adjectives expletives articles punctuation dependent clauses, which Hamlin read or heard or spoke out loud. It was, say, a full sweep of Hamlin's optical reservoir, taking in the entire visual input of a fiftieth of a second. It was, say, a spear of abstract thought crossing Hamlin's consciousness from northwest to southeast. Let us now relate such random rootless inputs to our own bank of data. So that we may evaluate. So that we may interpret. So that we can tell sight from sound from cognition. Thus. And thus. We string our telegraph wire across miles and miles of desert and at last it brings us messages.

Such as:

A sense of motion. Jolt jolt jolt, stride stride stride, Hamlin is going somewhere.

A sense of position. Hamlin is standing upright.

A sense of muscular activity. Hips and thighs in action, soles of feet hitting pavement Hamlin is walking.

A sense of environment. Bright light. Sunlight? General warmth and humidity. Morning? A summer morning? Street noises. He is walking along a street.

A sense of vision, coming jerkily into focus, now clear. Office buildings, pedestrians, vehicles. A street in Old Manhattan?

Riding along as though seated on Hamlin's back, legs around his neck, Macy felt a sharp pang of discontinuity at the absence of proper transitions. At the moment of loss of consciousness this body had been grappling in a slum-building corridor with an unknown assailant, late at night. Now it was walking down a busy daytime street. How much time had passed? What was the outcome of that struggle? What injuries, if any, did the body sustain? Where is Hamlin heading now? None of these things could readily be determined with the resources presently at Macy's command. One can try to improve one's resources, though.

The logical next step, Macy told himself, is to hook into Hamlin's consciousness. So I can read him and maybe hamper him if not entirely control him. A tentacle into the cerebral cortex. But where is the cerebral cortex? Macy could only repeat his previous trial-and-error tactics, groping here, groping there. No luck, though. Impossible to grasp the handles of Hamlin's cerebration. Macy's efforts succeeded only in giving Hamlin's memory storage regions a high colonic, stirring turbid strata of ancient events. Across the screen of Macy's awareness floated a cloud of mucky particles of experience, miscellaneous rapes, seductions, artistic triumphs, investment decisions, childhood traumas, and indignations, drifting murkily about. While the sensory inputs continued to show Hamlin swinging jauntily along down the sunny street.

Now for the first time came desolate moments for Macy. A feeling of hopelessness. A realization of the reality of this unreal captivity. Admissions of defeat, the inevitability and finality of. It was to be expected that he'd catch me and lock me up in here. A stronger ego than mine. Wilier. He lived thirty-five years and I lived only four. A criminal mentality, too. He knows how to defend himself. I'll never be able to meddle with him as he did with me. I'll never get out of here.

But as he mourned for himself Macy automatically went on searching for the right place to plug in, trying this and that and this, marching into one blind alley after another, battering himself against dead ends and withdrawing to try again. And abruptly he made his connection, tapping into the line he sought and drawing a staggering numbing dizzying but ultimately satisfying current, the pure juice, the unimpeded flow, the hefty amperage of Hamlin's unfettered soul.

go to see Gargantua first almost there ten minutes more find out what's been going on the business the buying and selling my price these days it must have gone up plenty I bet they figured I'm dead the cocksuckers no more Hamlins so double the price every week well why not why not why not and then out to the studio all boarded up I bet just take a little look of course I'll have to pose as Macy that will present some problems won't even be able to let Gargan know the truth outright although I'll drop him some hints that fucking mass of meat he's clever he's clever he'll figure it out won't say a word a buck or two in it for him you bet your fat ass there is so then to the studio a sentimental journey I mean I need to go there like a shrine like my own shrine like like all dusty I bet the Goths and the Vandals fuck fuck fuck they bust everything up maybe I wasn't so pleasant a guy but I had a decent respect for property except of course all those cunts if you consider a cunt property and anyway I was crazy then much better now purified by adversity my head clear at last rid of Macy stuck him where he belongs the poor dumb shit no personality at all just a construct a plastic man well it wasn't his fault but it wasn't mine either the survival of the fittest don't you see Darwin was no dope and then I'll visit Noreen old time's sake I'll have to play it very cagy with her that bitch is perfectly capable of turning me in but maybe not after all nobody ever gave it to her in her life the way I did even if toward the end we were somewhat estranged nevertheless that's part of the normal risks of marriage especially when you marry an officially accredited genius a member of the international elite of artistic achievement high intensity sometimes boils over I'm almost at Gargantua's now I think unless he's moved the gallery four years shit the whole shitting universe changes in four years every cell in the body turns over doesn't it or is it seven years anyway we aren't the same and Gargan probably sells his schlock out of Philadelphia now Chicago Karachi who knows but we'll find out fast enough God it's good just to walk the streets again breathe the air throw my shoulders back and tonight we'll find some friendly hole for dicky dunking yes indeed four years without a piece that's quite a long time for a man of my ability artistic and physical well maybe out in Darien I'll find Noreen willing to come across or one of the others God that creepy Lissa I guess she'd do it she'd do it for anyone even Macy thinking she's really fucking me of course but I don't want her I don't want to go within a million miles of her too dangerous what a shot in the head she gave me that time I don't want her ever again ever ever I wonder what kind of work I'll turn out as soon as I'm back in the swing of things it better be good if I can't maintain quality might as well give the body back to Macy but I think I'll pick up fast enough do some small pieces first recover my grasp of perspective my perspective of grasp and then we'll see anyway the important thing is that I'm back

—But you still have me, Hamlin. Macy. Oh, shit! Macy. I didn't think I'd be hearing from you so soon.

—Sorry to disappoint you. Why don't you just erode away? Dissolve. Let yourself be absorbed by the cranial phagocytes, Hamlin suggested. You're over and done with, anyway. Your nebulous existence has ceased to be, Macy. Admit it and go.

—The Rehab Center failed to program me for auto-destruct.

*I don't need you, though.*

—But I do, Macy said.

*What good are you? What imaginable value do you have to the world? To anyone?*

—I have immense value to me. I'm the only me I have. And I want to survive. I'm going to beat you, Hamlin. I'm going to throw you out again and this time I'll abolish you. Just watch and see.

*Please. Your buzzing is giving me a headache and it's such a beautiful day.*

—I'll give you a lot more than a headache.

Noisy threats were pointless. Macy wanted to make some dramatic demonstration of his ability to harass Hamlin. Give him as good as he got when the tables were turned. Clutch his heart, grab a bundle of muscles in his cheek, shut his eyes, make him piss in his pants. Jolt him, but without, naturally, doing real harm to the body they shared. Only he couldn't. Macy's harassment quotient was close to zero. All he could do was ride again on Hamlin's sensory input and pipe messages directly into his conscious brain. Buzzing. But no control of the motor sectors whatever. No grip on the autonomic system. Merely a passenger who hasn't the foggiest where the throttle might be, or the brakes, or even the switch for the headlights. Meanwhile Hamlin, untroubled, turned a corner and entered the vestibule of a glossy-fronted shop on the smoked-glass window of which danced the words OMNIMUM GALLERIES, LTD. in free-floating globules of green capillary light. Inside, a battery of safety mechanisms bathed him in scanner-glow. An inner door finally rolled aside, and he entered the gallery, pausing not at all to inspect the treasures of contemporary art it displayed. He said to the girl at the desk, "Is Mr. Gargan here?"

"Is he expecting you, sir?"

"I don't think so. But he'll see me."

"Your name?"

Hamlin faltered at that. Macy picked up the scathing tides of chagrin. A dilemma, yes. After a moment Hamlin said, "My name is Macy, Paul Macy." With a meaningful glance at the Rehab badge in his lapel. "Tell him I used to be Nat Hamlin, though."

"Oh." A little gasp. A flutter of confusion; a pretty spasm of embarrassment that turned the girl scarlet down to her fashionably exposed breasts. A quick recovery. Jeweled finger to the intercom. "Mr. Macy to see you, Mr. Gargan. Paul Macy. Formerly Mr. Nat Hamlin."

From some inner office, a bellow of surprise that needed no amplification. Hamlin was speedily ushered in. A spherical room, dense mossy black carpet installed 360°-wise everywhere, a man of implausible corpulence lolling along the curved left wall with a meaty hand held languidly over a control panel bristling with jeweled switches. Not rising when Hamlin entered. An ocean of blubber; flesh hanging in folds over folds of flesh. The features barely discernible within that mass: piggy little eyes, puggy little nose, narrow pinched puritan lips. Out of the vastness a thin man's piping voice: "God's own cock, what are *you* doing here? You aren't supposed to be coming here, Nat!"

"Do you mind?"

"Do I mind? Do I mind? You know I love you. Only I don't follow this at all. They took you in for Rehab; I thought that was the end of you. When did you get out, anyway?"

"Early in May. I would have seen you before this but there were problems."

"You look okay. You sound okay. Just like your old self. But you've got the badge. You're somebody else now, right? What's your new name?"

"Macy. Paul Macy."

"Don't like it. It's a name without any balls."

"I didn't pick it, Gargantua."

The fat man tugged at his dewlaps. "Am I supposed to call you Nat or Paul?"

"You better call me Paul."

"Paul. Paul. Well, I'll try. Sit down, Paul. Jesus, what a fruity name! Sit down, anyway." Hamlin sat Macy, a helpless spectator within him, sat also. Listening to every word of the conversation but unable to speak. As though watching it on a screen. He had seen this fat man, this gallery owner, before, drifting around in the debris of Hamlin's memory; but he seemed much fatter now. This man and Hamlin had grown rich together on the proceeds of Hamlin's genius. Now Hamlin stretched out voluptuously. In full command of his recaptured body. The black carpeting seemed to be a foot thick: bouncy, lush. Gargan touched one of the switches on the panel in front of him and the room silently revolved, changing its axis by some 15°. Hamlin's side of the sphere went up and Gargan's descended. Macy experienced some vertigo. The fat man lay pleasantly sprawled, kneading his belly. Shortly he belched and said, "How do you like the setup here? Or don't you remember the old one?"

"I remember. This is tremendous, Gargantua. Like a fucking Babylonian palace. A gallery for sybarites, eh?"

"We get a good clientele here."

"You're prospering. And you've gained some weight, haven't you? Unless I'm mistaken, quite a lot of weight."

"Quite. Two or three hundred pounds since you last saw me."

"You're beautiful."

"I think so."

"How the crap do you have the patience to eat so much, though?"

"Oh, I don't waste time overeating," Gargan said. "I've had my lipostat surgically adjusted. My whole body-fat-and-glucose equation has been changed. I burn slowly, my friend, I burn very slowly. The eating it takes to give you an ounce gives me a pound. And I grow lovely, eh, more lovely every day. I want to weigh a thousand pounds, Nat! Paul. I must call you Paul."

"Paul, yes."

"But none of this makes any sense." Gargan stirred ever so slightly, craning his neck. "How can you remember me? Why didn't Rehab wipe you out?"

"It did."

"But you sound just like—"

"I'm a special case. Don't ask too many questions."

"I follow you, Nat."

"Paul."

"Paul."

"Be more careful about my name, will you? I'm a brand-new man. The loathsome countersocial rapist who did such grievous damage to so many innocent women has been humanely destroyed, Gargantua, and will never walk the earth again."

"I follow. Where are you living?"

"Way uptown. A temporary place. You can have the address if you want."

"Please. And the phone."

"I won't be there long. As soon as I've got some cash together I'll find something a little more suitable."

"Are you working yet?"

"As a holovision commentator," Hamlin said. "Maybe you've seen me. The late news."

"I mean *working*."

"No. I have no equipment, no studio. I haven't even had a chance to think about work in a serious way."

"But soon?"

"Soon, yes." Macy felt Hamlin's lips curve into a sly, malicious smile. "Would you like to represent me when I get started again, Gargantua?"

"Why ask? You know we have a contract."

"We don't," said Hamlin.

"I could show it to you. Wait, let me punch the retrieve." Gargan's meaty fingers hovered over the console buttons. As he started to stab a stud Hamlin reached out and stopped him.

"You had a contract with Nat Hamlin," Hamlin said. "Hamlin's dead. You can't represent his ghost. My name is Paul Macy, and I'm looking for a dealer. You interested?"

Gargan's face looked puffier. "You know I am."

"Fifteen percent."

"The old contract said thirty."

"The old contract was signed twenty years ago. The situation then doesn't apply now. Fifteen."

Lengthy tugging at dewlaps. "I never take less than thirty."

"You will if you want me to come back to you." The voice very flat now. "All Hamlin's contracts were legally dissolved when his personality underwent deconstruct. I'm not bound by anything. Also I'm without assets and I need to rebuild my capital in a hurry. Fifteen. Take it or leave it."

In Gargan's eyes a countervailing slyness. "Nat Hamlin was an established master with a line of museum credits longer than my cock. Paul—what is it, Macy?—Paul Macy is a nobody. I had a waiting list for Hamlins, for anything he'd turn out. Why should people buy you?"

"Because I'm as good as Hamlin."

"How do I know that?"

"Because I tell you so. Business may be slow at first until the word-of-mouth starts, but when the public realizes that Macy is as good as Hamlin, even better than Hamlin because he's been through an extra hell and knows how to make use of it, the public will come around and clean you out. You'll cover your nut with plenty to spare. Do we have a deal at fifteen or don't we?"

"I want to see some of Paul Macy's work," Gargan said slowly, "before I offer a contract."

"Contract first or you don't see a thing."

A tut and a tut from the narrow lips. "Artists aren't supposed to be rapacious. That's why they need dealers, to be sons of bitches on their behalf."

"I can be my own son of a bitch," Hamlin said. "Look, Gargantua, don't waltz around with me. You know who I am and you know how good I am. I've had a rough time and I need money, and anyway at this stage of my career it's crazy for me to be cutting my dealer in for thirty. Give me a contract and advance me ten thousand so I can set up a studio, and let's not crap around any more."

"And if I don't?"

"There are two dozen dealers within five blocks of here."

"Who would jump at the chance of taking on somebody named Paul Macy, I suppose?"

"They'd know who I really was."

"Would they? The Rehab process is supposed to be foolproof. Suppose this is all a clever hoax? Suppose you *are* Paul Macy, and somebody's coached you on how to sound like Nat Hamlin, and you're just trying to sweat some quick cash out of me?"

"Test me. Ask me anything about Hamlin's life." Macy sensed Hamlin's distress now. Adrenalin flooding. Pores opening: Genitals contracting.

"I don't play guessing games," said Gargan. Idly he punched a button; the room tilted the other way. Hamlin's intestines lolled. The dealer said, "You've got no leverage, friend. No reputable dealer would trust a Rehab reconstruct who says he's still got the skills of his old self. So the take-it-or-leave-it is on my side. I'll sign you, Paul, because I'm sentimental and I love you, loved you in the old days, anyway, and I'll even give you some money to start you up again. But I won't be blackjacked. Twenty-five percent and nothing lower."

"Twenty."

"Twenty-five." A gargantuan yawn. "You're starting to bore me, Paul."

"Don't get snotty. Remember who you're talking to, what kind of talent you've got sitting next to you here. A year from now you'll regret having muscled me. Twenty percent, Gargantua."

"Twenty-five."

Now Hamlin was plainly upset. The swagger was gone; his ductless glands were working overtime. Macy, who had not ceased to probe avenues of neural connections, thought he had found a good one and that this might be a suitable moment for making a try at retaking the body. He pressed hard. Lunged. Claws outstretched, attacking the cerebral switchboard. But no go. Hamlin brushed him away as though he were a mosquito and said aloud, "Let's split the difference. Twenty-two and a half and I'm yours."


An hour's smooth drive in a rented car brought Hamlin to his old Connecticut estate. The car did its best to cope with Hamlin's surprising ineptness as a driver. He handled the steering-stick crudely, overpushing it, frequently trying to override the car's gyroscopic mind, constantly messing up the delicate homeostasis that kept the vehicle in its proper lane. Macy, from his vantage-point within, monitored Hamlin's performance with mixed feelings. Obviously Hamlin, four or five years away from driving, had lost whatever skill at it he once had had, and that was worrying him, for it had occurred to him that in his absence he might have lost other skills also. Therefore he was working himself into a singleminded frenzy of concentration, gripping the stick in sweaty palm and trying to psych himself into complete mastery over the car. Macy knew he could play on Hamlin's fears, intensifying his distress. *You think you've come back to life, Nat, but nothing came back except your ego and your dirty mouth. You've lost your manual skills. You couldn't cut paper dolls now, let alone turn out museum masterpieces.* And so on. Undermining Hamlin's self-confidence, attacking his main justification for having expelled his reconstruct. Weakening his grip on the body's central nervous system, setting him up for a push. *You think you're still a great artist? Jesus, you don't even know how to drivel The Rehab Center smashed you to bits, Nat, and you won't ever be whole again.* And then, getting Hamlin fuddled and panicky, he could make a try for a takeover.

The process was already well under way. The fumes of Hamlin's tensions drifted through Macy's interior holdfast. The oily smell of fear and doubt. Go on, give him a shove, he's vulnerable now. But the scheme was futile, Macy knew. He hadn't yet found the handles with which he could flip Hamlin out of his dominant position. Even if he had, he wouldn't dare attempt a takeover at 120 miles an hour; no matter how good this car's homeostasis was supposed to be, it wasn't programmed for self-drive, and while he and Hamlin struggled for control, the auto might go over the edge of the embankment, or up a wall, or into the oncoming flow, in some wild uncorrected orgy of positive feedback.

So Macy sat passive while Hamlin shakily negotiated the highway and more capably guided the car up the winding leafy country lanes to the place where he once had lived. Parking the car perhaps a quarter of a mile away. Leaving the road, walking cautiously through the woods. Heartbreaking summeriness here. The foliage so green and new. Bright yellow and white flowers. Chipmunks and squirrels. Clumps of frondy ferns. They had held back the urban tide here, the surging sea of concrete and pollution, the onslaught of extinctions. An outpost of natural life, maintained for the very rich.

And there, beyond that blinding white stand of stunning birches, the house. Lofty walls of high-piled gray-brown boulders set in ancient gray mortar. Leaded-glass windows agleam in the noonlight. Hamlin's heart leaping and bouncing. Old memories in an agitated dance. Look, look there. The pond, the creek, the pool. Exactly as Lissa had described it, exactly as Macy had seen it through the lens of Hamlin's reminiscing mind. And the studio annex. Where so many miracles were worked.

—Why did you come here?

*A pilgrimage. A sentimental journey.*

—It's somebody else's house now.

*Why don't you go fuck yourself, Macy?*

—I have your welfare at heart. You can't just prowl around here. It may be patrolled by dogs. Scanners everywhere. You know what'll happen to you if you're caught?

Hamlin didn't reply. He edged toward the studio, and Macy picked up an inchoate scheme for forcing a window and getting inside. Hamlin seemed to expect to find his workship intact, all the elaborate psychosculpting apparatus still sitting where he had left it Folly. The studio was probably some blithery suburbanite matron's greenhouse now. Hamlin continued to slink through the copse bordering the creek. Let him try, let him just try. The alarm will go off and the place will be full of cops in ten minutes. A frantic chase through the woods. Snubnosed shiny cyberhounds snuffling on silent treads over last year's fallen leaves, homing in on the fleeing man's telltale thermals. The fugitive encircled, entrapped, seized. Identified as Paul Macy, Rehab reconstruct, but the police, checking with Gomez & Co., would swiftly discover that Macy had been plagued by a resurgence of his prior identity. And then. Swift action. Wham! Needles in his arm. Hamlin reamed out a second time.

What about his threat to destroy their shared body in case of trouble? No, Macy thought, he can't do it, not while he's up there running the conscious brain. A man can't simply shut off his own heartbeat by willing it. He could when he was down here where I am, plugged into all the neural connections, but he can't do it now. So Hamlin will die a second time, and the body will survive. For me to have. Go on, Nat, creep and creep and creep, bust into your studio, trip the alarm, summon the hounds, start me on the road back to independent life. Yes. I'll be so very grateful.

What's this rising from the pool, though? Blithery suburban matron herself! Venus on the half shell. Woman in her middle forties, tall, not exactly plump but well endowed, dark hair, long arching waist, thickish thighs, amiable vacuous face. Her snatch chastely shielded by a skimpy cache-sexe; breasts bare, full, probably not as high as they used to be. Staring in surprise at Hamlin advancing toward her.

Quick adrenal response from Hamlin, too. Pupils dilated, heartbeat accelerated, prick stiffening. No wonder he's excited. The quintessential rape situation. Daytime, suburbs, woman alone, scantily clad, man emerges out of woods. Fling her down, hand over mouth, spread the thighs, give her the ram. *Ooom.* Load the box and prance away. Another notch carved in your cock.

—Ahaha! Still at it. Your old tricks.

*Don't bother me,* Hamlin snapped. Making an effort, recovering his sexual equilibrium, his social poise. Giving her a sexosocial smile and a little genteel nod. Everything under control. "I hope I didn't startle you, ma'am." The voice unctuous.

"Not fatally." Her eyes fluttering from his face to the Rehab badge and back to face. A little confused but not alarmed. She didn't try to cover her breasts despite the potential provocativeness of the situation. The cheerful poise of the upper crust "Forgive me if I'm making a terrible mistake, but aren't you—weren't you—"

"Nat Hamlin, yes. Who used to live here. But my name is Paul Macy now."

—Liar!

"I recognized you at once. How pleasant of you to visit us!" Obviously unaware of the impropriety of a reconstruct's visiting his earlier self's old haunts. Or not caring "Lynn Bryson, by the way. We've been here two years now. My husband is a helix surgeon. Shall I get you a drink, Mr. ah Macy? Or something to smoke?"

"No, thank you, Mrs. Bryson. You bought the place from Hamlin's ah widow?"

"From Mrs. Hamlin, yes. Such a fascinating woman! Naturally she didn't care to stay here any longer, with such terrible memories on all sides. We struck up a wonderful friendship during the time when the house was changing hands."

"I've heard many fine things about her," Hamlin said. "Of course I have no recollection of her. You understand."

"Of course."

"Hamlin's past is a closed book to me. But you understand I have a certain natural curiosity about the people and places of his life. As if he were, in a sense, a famous ancestor of mine, and I felt I should know more about him."

"Of course."

"Does Mrs. Hamlin still live in this area?"

"Oh, no, she's in Westchester now. Bedford City, I believe."

"Remarried?"

"Yes, of course."

The knife turning in Hamlin's gut

"You happen to know her new husband's name?" Very carefully, concealing all traces of tension.

"I could find it," the woman said. "A Jewish name. Klein, Schmidt, Kate, something like that, a short word, Germanic. A person in the theater, a producer maybe, a very fine man." Her smile grew broader. Her eyes appraised Hamlin's body with complacent sensuality. As if she wouldn't mind some pronging. Her vicarious way of attaining intimacy with the departed great artist. She should only know. Off with that bit of plastic about her waist, down on the grass, the white fleshy thighs parting. *Ooom.* "Won't you come with me?" she said airily. "I have it in the house. And you'll want to see the house, anyway. The studio. Do you know, we've kept Mr. Hamlin's studio exactly as it was when he—before he—when his troubles started—"

"You have?" A wild interior leap. Excited. "Everything still intact?"

"Mrs. Hamlin didn't want any of his things, so they came to us with the house. And we thought, well, the way they have Rembrandt's house on display in Amsterdam, or the house of Rubens in what is it Antwerp, so we would keep Nathaniel Hamlin's studio intact here, not for public display of course, but simply as a kind of shrine, a memorial, and in case some scholar wished to see it, some great admirer of Hamlin, well, we would make it accessible. And then of course future generations. Won't you come with me?" Smiling, turning, striding across the barbered lawn. Meaty buttocks waggle waggle waggle. Hamlin, sweating, adrenalized, following. The familiar old stone house. The squat spacious annex. A cheery wave of her hand. "There's an entrance to the studio on the far side of—" Hamlin was already on his way around there. "Oh, I see you know that." But how is it that he knows it? No indication that she suspects anything. "I'll look for Mrs. Hamlin's new name, and her address too, I suppose, and I'll meet you in a couple of minutes in the—"

Studio. Exactly as he had left it. To the left of the door, the big rectangular window. Floods of light. Facing the window, the posing dais with the microphones and scanners and sensors still in place and even his last chalk-marks still on the floor. On the right-hand wall his command console, levers and knobs and studs and dials that would surely have perplexed Rembrandt or Rubens or for that matter Leonardo da Vinci. The headphones. The ionization controller. The unjacked connectors. The data-screen. The light-pen. The sonic generator. Such a tangle of apparatus. In back, the other little room, the annex of the annex, more things visible, coils of wire, metal struts, mounds of modeling clay, the big electropantograph, the photomultiplier, the image intensifier, and other things which Hamlin did not seem to recognize. Hamlin wandered numbly among it all. Macy picked up his somber thoughts. The artist was frightened, even appalled, by the complexity of the studio. Trying to adjust to the idea that he had once used all this stuff by second nature. What was this thing for? And this? And this? Shit, how does it all work? I can't remember a thing.

—Rehab wrecked you, Nat, more than you realize.

*Shut your hole. I could pick all this up again in three hours.* A note of false bravado, though. Powerful currents of uncertainty coming from him. Hamlin broke off a chunk of modeling clay and began to knead it. Stiff, after all this time. The clay. And he was too. The fingers unresponsive. Let's sculpt Mrs. Bryson. Here, we roll a long tube of clay like so, and we. No. Instantly the proportions were awry. Hamlin nibbled his lip. Correcting his intuitive beginning. She's tall, yes, and wide through the hips, and we'll need some clay here for the boobs.

—Give up, Nat, you don't have it any more.

*Piss off, Macy. What do you know?*

Yet Hamlin was unable to conceal the extent of his uneasiness from his passenger. He was fumbling with the clay, mangling it, blundering at this elementary task of modeling, straining to get the image in his mind transferred to the lump in his hands. In that tense moment Macy made new connections and for the first time gained some control over Hamlin's central nervous system. *Plink.* Strumming the neurons. Hamlin's elbow jerked. The tube of clay bent double at the sudden accidental convulsion. *Plink.* Another twitch. Hamlin shouting silently at him now, bellowing in rage. Macy was enjoying this. He continued to tug at Hamlin's synapses while the artist trembled and shivered in mounting wrath and frustration. The half-shaped model of Mrs. Bryson a ruin. Hamlin glancing around nervously at his own equipment, so alien to him, so terrifying. Telling himself that in four, four and a half years it was possible for a person to forget all sorts of superficial mechanical things, but that you never lost the real talent, the basic underlying inborn gift, the set of perceptions and insights that is the real material to which the artist applies his learned craftsmanship.

—Go on, Nat, keep saying it, you may even start to believe it soon.

*Let me alone. Let me alone. I could learn all this machinery again in half a day!*

—Sure you could, sweetheart. Who ever doubted it?

Giving Hamlin another twong in the medulla, a blork in the autonomic, a whonk in the limbic. Yes! Really learning my way around in here, now! Just as he did in me. The shoe on the other cortex, though. I'll get him. I'll get him good. Hamlin was doing a manic dance, twitching around the room as Macy toyed with him. He couldn't seem to get himself together enough to deliver a retaliatory shot; it was as if the vibrations emanated by all the psychosculpting apparatus kept him dizzy and off balance. Keep hammering away, Macy told himself. This may be your chance to get back on top. Twong and twong and twong! Arms whipping about wildly. Knees jerking. I think I could make him crap in his undies now. A nice psychological point to score, but why shit things up for myself in case I take over?

And then Hamlin began to fight back. Coldly, furiously, ramming Macy down into subservience once more. Sweeping from his mind the distractions of this dismaying studio in order to regain inner discipline. There. There. There. Macy saw that he did not yet have the power to vanquish the other, although he was constantly learning and gaining strength. Later. Another time. He has me now.

"Isn't the studio *absolutely fascinating*, Mr. Macy?"

An idiot warble, a gay contralto trill. Enter Mrs. Bryson. A slip of paper in her hand. By no accident, she has rid herself of her loincloth, and she comes jollying in, starkers, with flatfooted buoyancy. Eyes sparkling, breasts heaving expectantly. Thick curling deep-piled black triangle. Her nipples turning to turrets. The hot scent of a rutting bitch spreading in the warm air. We're very casual about nudity out here, you see, Mr. Macy. Clothes are so primitive, don't you think! And then maybe making a quick grab for his crotch, getting the pole out in the open, down on the floor amid the paraphernalia of the great artist. To be had by his simulacrum. *Ooom.* But not this time, lady. "I had some trouble finding Mrs. Hamlin's new name and address," she said. "It was with our papers on the house, you know, tucked away, but I dug everything out, and now—"

"Yes," Hamlin said. Blurted. A frantic need to get out of here. Throat dry; face flushed; eyes unfocused. Defending himself simultaneously against Macy's assaults from within and the mockeries of this equipment from without. Her black bush and hot slot of no interest to him now. The unexpectedly overbearing atmosphere of his studio had unmanned him utterly. To escape, fast. Snatching the slip of paper from her startled hand. "Thankyouverymuchgottogonow." Moving rapidly past her toward the door. Her face suddenly a rigid mask of surprise and anger: she knows she will be denied. Hell hath no fury.

She looks ten years older. Deep lines from cheeks to chin. The nipples going soft; the shoulders slumping. All her nakedness wasted on him. Her arm outstretched, the fingers working eagerly as if to pull him back. No chance. Hamlin had reached the exit. Out into the midday brightness. Pursued by phantom tendrils of feminine libido. "You needn't leave so soon!" she calls to him. Hamlin made no reply. Glancing back once, saw her outside the studio door, naked well-endowed idle-rich lass on the threshold of middle age, bewildered by his panic, astounded by his rejection of her body. His panic bewildered him too. Head awhirl. Macy did his best to make things worse, yanking on all the neural lines at once. Hamlin yelped, but stayed in control, and went on running. Running. Run. Ning.

In the car again, jouncing helter-skelter westward across several counties, Macy wondered if they were going to survive this trip. These back roads didn't have any protective strips, and thus the auto's homeostasis mechanisms were essentially cancelled out; if the car started to slide off the road, nothing would keep it from smashing into the bulky oaks that awaited it

And Hamlin was in a ghastly state. Madly gripping the stick. Eyes glazed in Dostoevskian fixity. Jaws clenched. He was driving on reflex alone, employing one tiny plaque of cerebral tissue to operate the vehicle while the rest of his mind wildly revolved the events of the past half hour. The car teetered from side to side on the narrow road, now and then crossing the center line or running onto the shoulder.

Most of Hamlin's defenses were relaxed, but as before Macy feared to make a takeover attempt in a moving car. He hunkered down inside Hamlin's brain as though it were a storm shelter and temporarily disconnected his optical hookup, for the view of the madly slewing road through Hamlin's eyes was making him seasick. Better, this way. To sit in solemn silence in a dull dark dock. About him still flashed the lightnings and eruptions of Hamlin's distress. The studio visit had really shaken him. Moving among his implements, his elaborate sculpting apparatus, Hamlin had seemed not to know what from which or up from down. Macy wondered why. Had the Rehab process done irreversible damage to the Hamlin persona? Was there actually nothing left of the original Nat Hamlin except a clutch of old memories, a cluster of attitudes and phrases, some tics and twitches of the spirit? The sculptor, the man of genius, had he been irretrievably demolished, and was this comeback merely a delusion?

On the other hand, Macy thought, it might have been the strain of maintaining control of their shared body that had so severely drained Hamlin's psychic energy. There had been definite signs all day that Hamlin's grip was none too strong and was slipping from hour to hour. In the morning, striding jauntily down the street to Gargan's gallery, presenting the contract ultimatum to the fat dealer, all that hard bargaining—Hamlin had appeared to be in full command then, but by the end of the encounter with Gargan he had started to show some fatigue, and the troubles he had had in driving from the city to his Connecticut studio had revealed a further weakening of control.

And then the disastrous studio visit. Continued slippage. The battery running down and no time for recharging. It must take a constant terrific effort for Hamlin to operate this body, injured as he had been by the Rehab obliteration experts. Macy knew that he himself was nowhere near the point where he could regain the body, but the way things were going that moment couldn't be very far away. It was coming. It was coming. Or was he fooling himself?

He reconnected the visuals. The car still careening along the suburban back roads. Hamlin sitting rigidly, lost in contemplation, paying minimal attention. Horrifying. The body wouldn't be worth shit to them if Hamlin smashed up the car. Certainly fatal to both of them. But there was nothing Macy could do about that right now. He blanked the scene again, escaping. Diving down deep, burrowing into Hamlin's memory bank. Everything there was accessible to him, all the stored scenes of his prior self's active life. Failures and triumphs, mostly triumphs. The women. The critics. The press clippings. The one-man shows. The money. The accumulation of possessions. All the surface glamour. Yet beneath the shiny shallow business of career-making Macy could see in Hamlin the authentic artistic impulse, the hunger to make his visions real. Give Hamlin credit for that. He had been a bastard, sure, still was, but he pursued a vision, he realized it, he gave it to the world. There are those who make and give, and those who take and consume, and Hamlin had been a maker and giver.

Macy envied that. Who are the real ones among us, anyway, if not those who create, who give, who enrich those about them? Regardless of their motives. Doing it for the money, for the ego trip, for whatever unworthy reason, but *doing* it. Having something worth doing and doing it. Hamlin was one of those.

I'm one of the consumers, thought Macy. Blame Gomez & Co., I guess: they could have made me someone worthwhile. Their own artistic achievement, their creative self-justification. But of course they aren't paid to do that. Just to fill up vacant bodies with reasonably functional human beings. Gomez isn't an artist, he's a doctor, and he can't transcend himself when he does a reconstruct. If I am second-rate, it's because my makers were second-raters too.

Unlike this bastard Hamlin. Whose darker side was also visible: the inner collapse, the breaking free from moorings. Roaming the quiet streets. The artist as predator. Each rape neatly labeled and catalogued in the archives. And not just mere rape, either. Not just the shoving of Blunt Object X into Unwilling Orifice Y, but also the associated stuff, the peripherals, the leering, the mocking, the capering, the perversions, the garbage. Even in a permissive age there still are such things as abominations. Hamlin must have been out of his mind. The big-eyed twelve-year-old forced to watch her pretty young blond mother blowing the famous artist: what kind of scars does that leave on an unformed psyche? And all this buggery. A trail of torn sphincters across four states. Not even greasing it first. That's sadism, Hamlin. Out of your fucking mind.

But how crazy were you, really? Didn't you have a clear conscious awareness of what was going on, and didn't you enjoy it? Yes. And wasn't all this crap latent in you all along? Yes. Okay, something brought you out. Suddenly it was Monster Time in your head, and you went forth to fulfill all the steamy dreams you had nurtured since your cramped lonely adolescence. Right? Right. And

459

filed everything away for subsequent gloating. No wonder they sentenced you to deconstruct. Jesus, I feel filthy just rummaging through this stuff. Maker of masterpieces. Giver of unique visions. And your demonic laughter underneath. Telling the court you were insane, that you were in the grip of an irresistible impulse, an obsessive compulsion, but were you? Perhaps you thought you were creating a new kind of work of art, made not out of paint or clay or plastic or bronze but out of bleeding invaded female bodies, an abstract sculpture composed of dozens of victims, forming a pattern you alone could have designed. Jesus. What a case for obliteration you were!

Macy noticed that the car no longer was moving. Hastily he plugged in the visuals again.

They were parked in the central shopping plaza of a medium-sized suburban city, with two- and three-story Westchester Tudor halftimbered shops, freshly whitewashed and their brown beams newly painted, glistening in the amber light of late afternoon. Hamlin had his head out the side door; he was asking a policeman—a *policeman!*—how to find Lotus Lane. A rapid-fire stream of instructions. Turn left at the computer stanchion, follow Colonial Avenue to Route 4480, turn right at the yellow blinker, go about ten blocks, no, twelve, you'll come to the industrial park, you turn right there past the tall building and you drive on to the sniffer palace—a grin, we've even got that stuff up here!—and make a left and that puts you on Route 519, all the cross streets there are marked, you won't miss Lotus. On the left.

Thank you, officer. And off we go. Left, right, right, left. Quiet country lanes again. Hamlin tense. No difficulty following the instructions, though. Left, right, right, left, the sniffer palace, the residential area, Cypress Walk, Red-bud Drive, Oak Pond Road, Lotus Lane. Lotus. Number 55. A trim stucco house twenty or thirty years old, with a perspex sundome and glossy oval opaquer-windows. A sign out front: THE KRAFFTS. Hamlin presented himself to the door-scanner. From within, via intercom, a warm firm sweetly modulated mezzo voice: "Who is it?"

"Paul Macy."

"Paul. Macy." Doubtfully. "Paul Macy? Oh, my God! My God, you shouldn't have come here!"

"Please," Hamlin said. "Just a few minutes. To talk."

A moment of empty humming from the intercom. Then, hesi-tantly, "Well, I suppose. All right. Although this is probably a big mistake." Two moments more; then the door began to open. In the same instant Hamlin's left hand rose toward his throat. For the purpose, Macy sensed, of ripping the telltale Rehab badge from his clothing. Macy blocked the attempt with a fierce neural jab, the accuracy of which surprised him; Hamlin, his arm arrested in midclimb, stiffened and let the arm sag to his side, while simul-taneously snapping a furious silent curse at Macy. The door was open. Framed in the vaulted entranceway stood a woman of extraordinary poise and beauty. Tall, nearly to his shoulder, but slender, fine-boned, a delicate tiny-featured face, alert ironic eyes, sleek glossy black hair in tumbling cascades, full sardonic lips, strong chin, long columnar neck. An aristocrat. Paul guessed her age at thirty-one or thirty-two. She held herself well.

"Why did you come here?" she asked.

"To see you, Noreen."

"Noreen?" The lips quirking with distaste. "Are we so intimate, then, that we use first names?"

"Formality's foolish. We were married once," Hamlin said.

"I was married to Nathaniel Hamlin, God help me." She con-spicuously eyed the Rehab badge. "Your name is Paul Macy, and I have a stack of data cubes inside containing the documents that indicate that Paul Macy is in no way an heir or assign of the former Nat Hamlin. I don't know you. I never did."

"Don't be too sure of that. Won't you ask me in?"

"My husband isn't home."

"What of it? Am I some kind of wild beast? I'm house-broken, Noreen. You can let me in."

Her invisible shrug was unmistakable. A quick grudging nod. "All right. For a few moments."

The house was small but handsomely and expensively furnished. Hamlin's gaze traveled quickly along the walls, taking in a pair of nightmarish masks from New Guinea, an African figurine, a baffling shaped painting in the form of a tesseract, and three magnificent little crystallines. Macy would have liked to linger and study the tesseract, but he was the prisoner of Hamlin's eyes, and Hamlin continued turning until he came to rest on one of his own works, an exquisite porcelain-finish image of Noreen, half life size, nude. Small high breasts, flaring waist, and, coming from the cloud of airborne speakers mounted in the dark hair, an ominously sensual viewer-responsive hundred-cycle rumble. Hamlin turned from Noreen to Noreen. "I wondered whether you'd kept it," he said.

"Why wouldn't I? It's superb." Clouds crossing her face. "You remember it?"

"I remember plenty."

"But the Rehab—"

"Let's not talk about that. Who's your new husband?"

"Sy Krafft. I don't think you knew him." Pausing. As if to run the tape of her conversation back a bit for a correction. "I don't think *Hamlin* knew him. He does floating spectaculars. A charming and cultivated person." Pausing again. "How did you find me?"

"I went to the old house. The woman who owned it gave me your name and address."

"The Rehab Center assured me that I'd never be troubled by you."

"Am I making trouble?"

"You're here," she said. "That's enough. What is it you want with me, Mr. Macy?"

"Don't call me Macy. You know who I am."

She stepped back from him, doing it artfully, so that she seemed merely to be moving about the room and not retreating. She looked like a bird thinking of taking wing. In a low voice she said, "I never expected this. They assured me you were gone forever."

"They made a mistake."

"Rehab doesn't make mistakes. I saw your body after they burned you out of it. No, you aren't Nat. You're Macy, the new one, and you're trying to play a joke on me, and I assure you it's not in the least funny."

"I'm Nat Hamlin. His ghost walks the earth."

"You're Paul Macy."

"Hamlin."

"It can't be."

"You're so fucking beautiful, Noreen. What is it, five years, and you haven't changed at all. I get hard just standing in the same room with you. Are you making any films these days?"

"I think it's time you left."

"You still love me, don't you? I know, I know, you feel uncomfortable having me here, you're edgy and tense because you think Mr. Sy Krafft is going to walk in on us, but you want me as much as ever. I could prove it. I could put my hand between your legs and it would come away wet. It was always easy for me to smell a woman in heat, Noreen."

"You're crazy, whoever you are. I want you to go."

"And I love you too, even more than before. Listen, don't play-act with me, don't give me that icy I-want-you-to-go crap. I'm *back,* Noreen. Don't ask me how I managed it. I'm back. I'll be going under the name of Macy, but it's me, the real me here, and I'm going to start working again soon. I've already seen Gargantua. He's signing me, he's giving me money to open a studio. Very quietly I'll reestablish myself. No rapes any more. None of that I'll be sedate and bourgeois, Mr. Paul Macy, Mr. Nobody, only underneath it'll be Nat Hamlin. And you'll come visit me, won't you?"

"I'll visit you in jail, yes."

"You'll visit me in my studio. We'll sit and talk about how good it was before I crapped everything up. Remember, '02, '03, when we were just starting out? Lying on the beach in Antigua, and we couldn't leave each other alone, we did it right out there. Sand in your snatch, eh, Noreen? You didn't like that so much, but even so, you loved it. And then. The other times. I've got them all up here in my head. They banged me around at Rehab, but they didn't destroy me. They tried hard enough, but they didn't destroy me." He took a step toward her. Throat dry, fingertips cold. Getting harder and harder down below. "Don't be afraid of me. I love you. *I love you.* I wouldn't hurt you for anything. Stop backing away. Listen, it'll be our secret, you and me, the world will think I'm Macy, you can go on being Mrs. Sy Krafft, this cute little house, kids—do you have kids?—whatever you want, only on the side it'll be you and me again, Nat and Noreen, at my studio.

I'll do another nude of you. Life-size. It'll be better than *The Antigone.* Remember how sore you were, because I used Lissa for *The Antigone* instead of you? But we were drifting apart then. I didn't know what was good for me. I had to go through hell to find out. But now. You'll pose. Shit, I can see it now. You standing over there. Those sweet little tits of yours. Ten electrodes on you. And I'm at the machine, swearing like a bastard. Getting you down, immortalizing your body and your soul. An hour for work, an hour for screwing, an hour for work, an hour for screwing. Oh, Jesus, Noreen, stop staring at me like that!"

"I'll call the police. When they catch you, Nat, they'll finish you for good. They won't even put you through Rehab. They'll chop you up and flush you away."

"No. A silver bullet in my head. A stake through the heart."

"I'll call them, Nat."

"Wait. Please, no. Look, I don't mean to frighten you. I came here to tell you how much I love you. I've been in hell, Noreen, literally in hell, and now I'm coming out, I'm going to live again. And I had to come to you. Why be afraid? Tell me you love me."

"I don't love you, Nat. You disgust me."

Hamlin began to shake.

"Brava!" he cried. "Brava! Bravissima!" He started to applaud. "What an actress! What fire in your reading! What steel in your voice!" Imitating her: "'I don't love you, Nat. You disgust me.'" Wildly applauding. "Curtain. End of Act Two. Now tell me the real stuff, Noreen. How much you want me. You're scared, yes, you remember me when I was crazy, when I was doing all that hideous crap, but you've got to remember the other me, too, the one you loved, the one you married, everything we did together, the places we saw, the people, the stuff in bed, remember, even the weird stuff, you and me and Donna in the same bed, and then you and me and Alex, eh, Noreen? Love. Trust Passion." He reached toward her. "Come on. Now. Where's the bedroom? Or right here on the floor. Let me prove it to you, that you still turn on for me. Okay? Why the hell not? You opened your gate for me five hundred times. Eight hundred. So one more won't cost you anything."

He was shouting now. Her cool poise was deserting her. She

looked terrified, moving away from him, stumbling over things. He lunged at her. Seizing her wrist, pulling her close. The sweet fragrance of her body mixed with fear-sweat. Her eyes glazed with fright "Noreen," he muttered. "Noreen. Noreen. Noreen." The syllables losing meaning and becoming hollow sounds. His skull aflame. His jaws aching. His hands clutching at her clothing. Ripping. The little round breasts popping into view. Oh, Christ, how tender they are! His hands on them. Squeezing. She flailed at him with her fists, clubbing him on the mouth, the nose, the ears. He had one arm locked around her waist; the other, having laid bare her bosom, went to her crotch. To see if she was wet there. To prove to her how wrong she was to refuse him. He was snorting. Like the old days, the bad old days. Hamlin the animal. Hamlin the horny Minotaur. Fragile woman struggling in his arms. A red haze before his eyes. Sweat running down his sides. Noreen kicking, screaming, clawing.

*Now,* Macy thought, and shoved with all his might Hamlin toppled from his perch. Fell moaning into the abyss. A moment of total disorientation, infinite in duration. Who am I? What am I? Where am I? He let go of the woman he held. She slumped to the floor; he lurched backward and slammed against the wall, and stood there, gasping, exhausted. Blood draining from his skull.

But it was all right. He was in charge again. He was Paul Macy, and he was back in charge.

# 13

To get away from there, fast, that was the important thing now. But first some peacemaking. Gestures of reassurance. Noreen Hamlin Krafft lay looking up dazedly at him, a dribble of bright red on her swelling lower lip, hair in disarray, angry blotches on her exposed white breasts where Hamlin had clutched her. They would be dark braises tomorrow. She didn't move. Waiting numbly for the next onslaught. Resigned to her fate. He said, his voice coming out oddly furry and unfocused, "It's okay now. I've taken control away from him. I'm Macy. I won't hurt you."

"Macy?"

"Paul Macy. The Rehab reconstruct. They did a bad deconstruct job on Hamlin and he's still loose in my head. He grabbed the body's motor and speech centers last night." Last night? Last week, last month? How long had Hamlin been running things, anyway? "But he's down underneath again, where he can't make trouble. While he was fighting with you I was able to take over." Gently helping her to her feet. He wondered if she had gone into shock. Making no attempt to cover herself. Tip of her tongue licking at the cut on her lip. He said, "I'm sorry you had to go through all this. Are you badly injured?"

"No. No." Staring at him. Trying to come to terms with his abrupt transformation. Dr. Jekyll. Mr. Hyde. "Just shaken up." With trembling fingers she concealed her bosom, tidied her hair. Staring at him. Was his face different now? The lunatic glare of Hamlin gone from his eyes? He knew it wasn't easy for her to understand any of what had taken place. These shifts of identity: he had come to accept them as part of the human condition, but to her they must be alien, incredible, bizarre. Maybe she thought he had been Macy all along, playing insane pranks on her. Or that he was still Hamlin.

He said, "It would be best if you didn't tell anyone about this. The police, your husband, anyone. I'm trying to have Hamlin permanently eradicated before he can do some real harm, but there are problems, and getting the police into things would only make it worse for me. You see, I'm in constant danger from him, and if I went to the authorities he might force the destruction of this body, so—" He stopped. She didn't seem to be comprehending. "Just don't say anything, yes? If it's at all in my power I'll see to it you never go through a scene like this again. Do you follow me?"

She nodded distantly. Pacing about, now, working off her fright. Time for him to go. At the front door he turned and said, "One last thing, though. Can you tell me today's date?"

"Today's date." She repeated it in a flat empty tone. As if he had asked her the name of the planet they were currently on.

"Yes, please. The date. It's important."

She shrugged. "The fourth of June, I think."

"Friday?"

"Friday, yes."

He thanked her gravely and went out. His body was stiff and he moved gracelessly toward the car, arms flailing spastically, shoulders ramming the air. He and Hamlin evidently had different notions of physical coordination, and his muscles, having taken orders from another mind for eighteen hours or so, were reluctant to go back to the mode he preferred. Not surprising: Hamlin's way was this body's normal way, and his own was something imposed from without. He concentrated on reimposing it. Damned good thing Hamlin had only been running the show since last night, since that takeover during the mugging in the hallway of Lissa's house. Macy had been afraid he might have been unconscious for a week or more before surfacing this morning. In which case he'd have an endless trail of Hamlin's deeds and misdeeds to trace and follow.

But no. It seemed that he had been awake for most of the period of Hamlin's dominance, missing only the first eight hours or so after the takeover. Some comfort in that. Where had Hamlin been in those eight hours? *Most likely at my place, getting some rest. And the mugging? It couldn't have been too serious.* Macy patted his pocket. Wallet gone. *Okay, so he must have collapsed at the moment of takeover, the mugger cleaned him out, then Hamlin picked himself up and left unharmed. The wallet was no big loss. Identity papers, credit cards—all replaceable, all useless to the assailant Macy didn't even need them himself, so long as he had a thumb with a fingerprint on it. Why, Hamlin had even managed to rent this car using only his thumbprint, not even his, my thumbprint. Ours, I guess. But the charge is debited to me.* Macy felt vaguely sorry for the mugger, living a squalid lower-class life on a level of society where cash still called the tune. Fine lot of good it must have been for him to lift an executive's wallet, the wallet of a thumb-tripper, five or six dollars in it at most. Oh, well.

Moving more easily now, Macy reached the car and thumbed the doorplate. The door slid open. He got behind the controls and tentatively grasped the steering-stick. The prospect of having to drive scared him. Suddenly. They had taught him how to drive at the Rehab Center, a couple of years ago, but he hadn't had much chance to practice lately; and just now there was the special risk that Hamlin might surface and screw him up on the highway. I hit him pretty hard when I grabbed control, but even so.

*Hamlin? You awake?*

No reply from the depths. Macy felt his other self's presence, though: a tinny faint reverberation out of the far-below, like the cries of an angry djinn who has been conjured back into his bottle.

*Good. Stay like that. I don't need any static from you while I'm driving.*

If only I can keep the goddam stopper in place on the bottle this time.

He put his thumb to the ignition panel, and the car, scanning the print and finding it to be that of its duly licensed present master, came to life. Warily Macy let out the brake. Cautiously he rolled forward. The car responded well, great snorting beast under harness. Which way New York, now? Long afternoon shadows. The sun halfway down the sky on his right. Pick a direction, any direction. He found his way out of the residential area, cut off two drivers as he blurted into the business road, was rudely but deservedly screeched at, and discovered a green-on-white sign directing him to the city. Onward. Homeward. A ticklish trip. He survived it.

He hoped to find Lissa waiting for him at his apartment, slouched in bed in her pleasant wanton way, music playing, her hair a tangle, the aroma of pot in the air. Throw himself wearily down on top of her, bury his aching head between her bouncy boobs. Some chance. The apartment, empty, deserted for a mere twenty-odd hours, had the forlorn and abandoned look of a fifth-rate catacomb. Off with the sweaty crumpled clothing. Shower. Shave. Vague thoughts of dinner. The last meal he remembered having eaten was lunch on Thursday. Now it was dinnertime on Friday. Had Hamlin bothered to refuel their body at all during his eighteen hours on top? Macy wasn't particularly hungry. All this shuttling about of identities. It must have wrecked my appetite. Odd. You'd think that much mental exertion would have burned up a lot of energy. A drink might be in order, though.

He poured himself a hefty bourbon and, naked, flopped down in a chair. A little of the liquor went sloshing out onto his thigh. Cold brown drops on the golden hairs. He felt not at all triumphant at having ousted Hamlin from control. What good was it, being in charge again? Who was he, anyway, that he needed so badly to live? An oppressive sense of having come to the end of the line grew in him. Paul Macy, born 1972 Idaho Falls, Idaho, father a propulsion engineer mother a school teacher, no brothers no sisters.

False. False. False shit. I wasn't born anywhere. I am a thing out of a testube: I am a golem, a dybbuk, a construct. Without friends, without family, without purpose. At least *he* was real. He'd fuck his kid sister, he'd steal toys from a baby, but he had an identity, a personality that he had earned by living. An artistic gift.

*What about it, Hamlin? You want to have it all back? Why do I insist on getting in your way? Maybe you're right: maybe I should let you win.*

Hamlin respondeth not. Only the tinny echoes, *de profundis*. He must be dormant worn out by everything he was doing. Well, fuck him. He's no good. His soul is full of poison. Damned if I'll step aside for him, genius or no genius. The world has enough great artists. It's only got one Paul Macy, for what that's worth. This would be a good moment to go to the Rehab Center, while Hamlin's groggy. Get him carved out of me for once and all. And if he surfaces? And if he gives me that coronary he's been threatening? Fuck him. If he wants to, he can. So go ahead, coronary. So we'll both be dead. *Pax vobiscum.* We shall sleep the eternal sleep, he and I. Anything would be better than this. Nodding solemnly, Macy reached for the phone to call Gomez.

The phone rang with his arm still in midstretch.

Lissa, he thought. Calling to find out where I've been, asking if she can come back!

Joy. Excitement. That startled him: the intensity of his wish that it be Lissa calling. What was all this crap about dying? He wanted to live. He had someone to look after. And to look after him. They needed each other.

"Hello?" he said eagerly.

On the green screen bloomed the swarthy face of Dr. Gomez. The angel of death himself. Speak of the devil.

"I've been phoning all day," Gomez said. "Where the fuck have you been?"

"Driving around the suburbs. Weren't you supposed to be keeping me under surveillance?"

"We lost track of you."

"Is that a fact?" Macy said harshly. "Well, let me be the first to tell you, then. Hamlin got me last night and kept control until late this afternoon."

Gomez made elaborate facial gestures of exasperation. "And did what?"

"Visited his dealer, his old studio, and his former wife. Who he was in the process of raping when I got control again."

"He's still a psychopath, you mean?"

"He still gets a kick out of manhandling women, anyway."

"All right All right. Too fucking much, Macy. Taking you over, running around the countryside. I'm having the van sent for you. Sit tight and if Hamlin makes another try at you, fight him off somehow. We'll have you safe inside the Center under sedation in an hour and a half, and then—"

"No."

"What, no?"

"Keep away from me if you want me to go on living. I tell you, Gomez, he's a wild man. If he thinks you're seriously after him he'll shut off my heart."

"That isn't a realistic fear."

"It's realistic enough for me."

"I assure you, Macy, he wouldn't do any such thing. We've let this situation drag on too long as it is. We'll come and get you, and we'll do a proper job of deconstructing Hamlin, and I assure you—"

"Shove your assurances, Gomez. We're talking about *my survival* that's being gambled with. *My survival.* I refuse to let you have me. Where's your authority for picking me up without my consent? Where's your court order? No, Gomez. No. Keep away."

Gomez was silent a moment. A crafty look flickered into his eyes; he immediately tried to hide it, but not before Macy had picked it up. At length Gomez said in his heaviest I-know-this-will-hurt-but-it's-for-the-general-welfare manner, "You realize, Macy, that your safety isn't the only thing we have to consider here. A court has ruled that society must be protected against Nat Hamlin. The moment you notified me that Hamlin wasn't entirely gone, it became my obligation to take him into custody and carry out the court's sentence the right way. Okay, so you said you felt you were in jeopardy, you asked me to leave you alone until we worked out some sure-thing way of coping, and I let you have your way. It was against every rule, but I gave in. Out of friendship for you, Macy. Will you buy that? Out of friendship. Out of concern. And we've been trying since Monday to figure out a way of handling the situation without endangering you. But now you tell me that Hamlin actually regained command of his body for a little while, for long enough to commit an assault against a human being. Okay. Friendship can go only so far. Can you guarantee Hamlin won't take you over again half an hour from now? Can you guarantee he won't be out banging housewives tomorrow? We *have* to seize him now, Macy, we *have* to finish him off."

"Even if it entails danger for me?"

"Even if it entails danger for you."

"I see," Macy said. "You figure what the hell, I'm only a construct anyway and if I get wiped out, tough shit on me. The important thing is catching Hamlin. Nothing doing, doctor. I'm not going to be the innocent bystander who gets zapped while you and Hamlin shoot it out. Keep away from me."

"Macy—"

Macy hung up. Gomez' image shrank and vanished like a photo being sucked into a whirlpool. Macy gulped the last of his drink, dropped the glass, and looked around for some clothing. He understood that his conversation with Gomez had worked a significant and perilous change in his status. The Rehab man had served notice that they were going to come after Hamlin, no matter what risks were in it for anyone else who happened to be inhabiting Hamlin's body. He could wait here meekly for the van, of course. Let himself be hauled off to the Rehab Center. Taking his chances that Gomez would be able to get Hamlin before Hamlin got *him*. But how chancy a chance that was! He knew Hamlin. They hadn't shared a brain all these weeks for nothing. And he knew that if Hamlin surfaced and found himself at the Center, being readied for a new deconstruct job, he'd explode with destructive fury. Samson pulling the pillars down around his ears. If Hamlin couldn't have the body, he'd see to it that no one would have it. So it didn't make sense to surrender to Gomez, not now. His fatalism of half an hour ago had gone from him. He didn't want to die or even to risk dying. He wasn't sure what it was he had to live for, but even so. He would have to run. He was going to have to become a fugitive.

Night had come. Everything was washed in a peculiar faded gray light. Out the side way, down the alley. Macy looked in all directions as he left the building. Feeling faintly absurd about it. This silly skulking, so melodramatic, so unreal. But what if Gomez had a man watching the main entrance? More than a touch of paranoia. They'll have hovereyes searching for me, a ten-state alarm, all the airports being watched. And where can I go? Jesus, where can I go? Macy wanted to laugh. Some fugitive. What am I going to do, camp out in Central Park? Eat squirrels and acorns?

He thought of going to the crumbling roominghouse where Lissa had lived. A double advantage to that: he might find her there, his only friend, his only ally, and in any case the place was such an armpit, such a ghastly hole, that he'd be beyond the reach of the slick computerized search processes of the contemporary age. Hiding deep down in a rotting pre-technological subterranea. But there was one huge disadvantage, too. Gomez, knowing about Lissa, knowing that her place was where he'd be most likely to go, would certainly set up a stakeout there. Waiting for him. Too risky. So where, then? He didn't know.

He walked north. Keeping close to the darkened buildings, trying to attract no attention. One shoulder higher than the other as if he might shield his face that way. Randomly north as night closed in. Or not so randomly. He realized that his feet were taking him up Broadway, across the bridge, into Manhattan North. Toward the only other point on his compass, the vicinity of the network office.

Landmarks of his slender tattered past. Here he had walked that uneasy hopeful Maytime day. One-and-two-and-one-and-two. Step. Step. Feeling clumsy and uncertain within his own body. Trying to be natural about it. This is how Paul Macy walks. Proudly down the goddam street. Shoulders square. Belly sucked in. Opportunity beckons you. A second trip, a second start The bad dream is over; now you're awake. Step. Step. Coming to an abrupt stop, he turned to his left and picked his reflection off the mirror-bright pilaster beside an office building's entrance. Wide-cheeked, thin-lipped, standard sort of Anglo-Saxon face. And the girl, coming up behind him, caught short by his sudden halt, crashing into him. Nat, she said. Nat Hamlin, for God's sake! The long cold needle slipping into his eye. Telling her politely but firmly, I'm sorry, but you're mistaken. My name's Paul Macy. People flowing smoothly around them. She was tall and slender, with long straight hair, troubled green eyes, fine features. Attractive in a tired, frayed way. Telling him not to play around with her: I know you're Nat Hamlin, she said. Leaning toward him, fingertips clutching hard into the bones of his right wrist A baffling sensation in the top of his skull. A sort of intrusion. A tickling. A mild glow of heat. Along with it a disturbing blurring of identity, a doubling of self. The first surfacing of Hamlin, only he hadn't known that then. Clinging to the side of the building with one hand and making a little shooing gesture at her with the other. Go on. Away. Out of my life. Whoever you were, there's no room now.

And he hurried on toward the network office. Block after block, and there it was. Grim black tower. Windowless walls. He didn't go in, not now, certainly not now. Fredericks. Griswold. Loftus. My colleagues. Smith or Jones. The Hamlin over there. One of my favorites, Griswold said. A gift from my first wife, ten years back, when Hamlin was still an unknown. Coughing. If you don't mind—some cold water. Forgive me. You know, it's only my first day on the outside. The strain, the tension. No, we'll keep away from the network office tonight.

And here, the corner of Broadway and 227th, northeast side. Where he met her on a Monday evening. Pacing in a taut little circle. A self-contained zone of tension on the busy street. Looking at him in mingled amazement and delight. Color stippling her cheeks. Eyes fluttering: she's scared of me, he realized. Oh, Nat, thank God you came! No, he said, let's get this established once and for all. My name's Paul Macy. What do you want? We can't talk here, she said. Not in the middle of a crowd. Where, then? Your place? He shook his head. Absolutely not. Mine, then. We can be there in fifteen minutes. But everything's filthy, she said, and he said, What about a restaurant? There's a people's restaurant two blocks from here, she said. I've been having lunch at it a lot. You know it? He didn't. We could go there, she said. Yes.

I could go there again, too. Now. Now. The sudden call of hunger. Two blocks. Macy walked quickly. One shoulder higher than the other. Reaching the restaurant. A spartan socialist front, a plain glass window. Within, a deep narrow room with tarnishing brass walls and a bunch of sputtering defective light-loops threaded through the thatchwork ceiling. All right Let's get some dinner. In here he had dinner with Lissa that night. Standing up, turning, walking away from her. And her scream. No! Come back! Paul! Paul! *Nat!* Her words leaping across the gulf between them like a flight of arrows. Six direct hits. St. Sebastian stumbling in the restaurant aisle. His brain on fire. And Hamlin's voice, quite distinct, from a point just above his left shoulder.—How could you walk out on her like that, you snotty creep.

So here is where he first manifested himself. Very well. Let's go in.


He thought he was hungry, and loaded his tray accordingly, stacking it with meat and vegetables and rolls and more. But when he had taken a seat at one of the long tables he found he had no desire for food. He nibbled a little. He let his eyes drift out of focus and disconnected himself from reality. How restful this is. I could sit here forever. But someone was touching his shoulder. A quick impertinent prod, a withdrawal, another prod. Why can't people leave me alone? One of Gomez' flunkies, maybe. If I pay no attention perhaps he'll go away. He tried to sink deeper into disconnection. Another prod, more insistent. A hoarse harsh voice. "You. Hey, you, will you look at me a second? You stoned or something?" Reluctantly Macy let himself slip back into focus. A fat, stale-smelling girl in a gray dress stood beside him. Her face was as flat as a Mongol's, but her skin was pasty white, her eyes did not slant. She said, "There's a girl upstairs needs some help from you. You're the one."

"Upstairs? Girl?"

"You, yes. I know you. You were in here two, three weeks ago with that girl, that redhead, that Lisa. You're the one who collapsed, fell flat on your sniffer, we had to carry you out, me and the redhead and the cabdriver. Lisa, her name is."

"Lissa," Macy corrected, blinking.

"Lisa, Lissa, I don't know. Look, she helped you, now you help her."

A floating film of memory. Standing by the restaurant's credit console at the end of the counter that other time, authorizing it to charge his account ten dollars for his dinner. And a fat flat-faced girl waiting behind him in line snorting contemptuously. Was he paying too much? Too little? This girl.

"Where is she?" Macy asked.

"I told you. Upstairs. She came in yesterday, she was crying a lot, a big fuss. Passed out, finally. We got her a room and she's still there. Won't eat. Won't talk. You must know her, so you go look after her."

"But where? Upstairs, you said."

"The people's co-op, moron," the fat girl said. "Where else? Where else do you think?" And strode away.

# 14

The people's co-op, moron. Where else? Leaving his laden tray, he went outside and looked around. Of course: there was a hotel associated with the restaurant. Or vice-versa. They shared the building. Stark green-tiled facade; a separate entrance for the hotel, escalator going up, the office on the second floor. In a wide low empty lobby, much too brightly lit, a directory screen offered sketchy information about the present residents of the building. Macy, frowning, checked the *M* column first. Moore, Lissa? Not there. He glanced at *L* and, yes, there was an entry for "Lisa," nothing else, no surname, checked in June 3, eleven p.m., room 1114. There's a girl upstairs needs some help from you. And how to get upstairs?

A door to his left opened and a blind man came in, moving confidently and swiftly around table and chairs and other obstacles. The sonar mounted in his headband going boing boing

boing. Tan jacket, yellow pants, fleshy face, eyes half-closed showing only the whites. "Excuse me," Macy said, "can you tell me
where the liftshaft is?" The blind man, without stopping, pointed
over his right shoulder and said. "Elevator's back there," and disappeared through a door to Macy's right. Macy went through the
other door. Elevator. Eleventh floor. Up.

Room 1114.

No fancy communication or scanning devices here, just a plain
wooden door. He knocked and got no response from within. He
knocked again. "Lissa? It's me, Paul." Knock knock. Silence. As he
stood there, puzzled, a girl stepped out of the room across the hall,
a thin bony girl, naked and casual about it, towel draped over one
shoulder, ribs prominent, hipbones sharp, small pointed breasts.

"Looking for Lisa?" she asked, and when Macy nodded the girl
said, "She's in there. Go on in."

"I knocked. She didn't answer."

"No, she won't answer. Just go on in."

"The door—"

"No locks *here,* brother." The girl winked and sauntered down
the hall. Her backbone standing sharply out against her skin.
Pushing open another door; sound of water running, from within;
the showerroom, Macy guessed. No locks here, brother. Okay. He
tried the door of room 1114 and found that it was indeed open.

"Lissa?" he said.

This was what he imagined a jail cell would be like. His room
at the Rehab Center had been palatial by comparison. A low narrow bed—a cot, really. A flimsy green plastic chair. A small squat
brown dresser. A chipped yellow-white washstand. A grimy sliver
of window. Bare flooring; cruel naked lights. Lissa was naked
too, slouched on the bed, knees up, arms locked across them.
She looked gaunt, almost frail, as if she had dropped eight or ten

pounds in the thirty-six hours since he last had seen her. Her hair was a knotted mess and her eyes were red and raw. The room reeked of sweat. Her clothes lay in a heap near the window; the closet, its door ajar, was empty; near the washstand stood the big dilapidated green suitcase that she had used in bringing her things from her apartment to his, and from his place to here. Its sides bulged: she hadn't bothered to unpack. As he entered, her head moved slowly in his direction, and she looked at him and did not look. And her head moved back so that she stared again at the brown dresser.

Macy walked past the foot of the bed and tried to open the window, but there was no way of doing it. He spoke her name again; she gave no sign of hearing him. Crouching beside her, he took one of her feet in his hand, lifted it six inches, watched it drop heavily back, and slid the hand upward to the meaty part of her calf. Her skin blazed. Fever was consuming her. His hand went to her thigh. His fingertips dug in high, just below the curling auburn thatch, but she took no notice. He shook her thigh. Nothing. He stroked her breasts, he cupped one. Nothing. He rubbed the tip of his thumb back and forth over the nipple. Zero. He fanned his fingers in front of her eyes. She blinked once, absently. "Lissa?" he said a third time. She was gone, lost, cocooned in introspection. Beyond his reach. Anyone could do anything to her now and probably she wouldn't react. How to break through? No way. No way.

He stood by the window with his back to her.

A long time later she said, voice thin and distant, "The talking in my head was driving me crazy. Bouncing off the walls. I couldn't stay."

He swung around to face her. She was wholly expressionless. Still staring at the dresser. Her words might have been those of a ventriloquist. "You didn't need to run away," he said. "I was trying to help you."

"You had no help to give. And I couldn't help you either. We were destroying each other."

"No."

"I opened you to Hamlin."

"It doesn't matter. We needed each other."

"I needed to go," she said. "I was choking there, I had to get out. So I went. So I came here."

"Why?"

"To hide. To rest." Murmured words, windsounds. "Go away, now. I have the voices again. The pressure building up. Can't you feel it? The pressure. The pressure building up."

He caught her hand in his. The fever raging. The muscles of her arm entirely limp. Like holding a length of rope. "You're ill, Lissa, physically ill. Let me get a doctor for you." He wasn't sure she heard him. Floating away from him again. "I'll call a doctor," he said. "All right."

Her eyes like glass spheres. She was adrift, heading out on the tide. He shook her, he fondled her, he talked to her. Zero. Talked *at* her. An urgent torrent. Flooding her with words, trying to talk her back into some sort of contact with him. Come on, snap out of it. Telling her of love, of need, of second starts, of new tomorrows, of shared anguishes, of an end to self-pity and vulnerability. Anything. Inspirational words. The old sunny platitudes. Why not tell her such things? To reach her. We'll go far away and try again, you and me, me and you. A whole world of happiness. Come, Lissa. Come.

Knowing that he is losing her, moment by moment. Has lost her. A million million miles away on her planetoid of ice. Yet he continued. Striving to pour his frantic energy into her, to fill her with enough stamina to return and rise. Visions of hope, day-dreams of health and joy. A shimmering rainbow curving across the room from door to window. On and on and on, his voice growing rasping and edgy and desperate, Lissa paying no attention; the ice now entombed her, she could only dimly be seen within the sparkling wall of the glacier. He was tiring. Why go on? She didn't want to hear this.

He became angry with her, hostile, irritated, begrudging her the resources of strength she was draining from him. And for what, this tremendous effort of his? What good? Everything he gave her the fever ate. She was the conduit through which his energies rushed uselessly into a shoreless sea. Now there was loud in him the voice of temptation, telling him to leave her while he still could, to forget her, to make his own difficult way through the world without dragging her on his back.

You owe her nothing. You have troubles of your own, many of them caused by her. Why this quixotic desire to rescue and repair her? Let her sink. Let her fry. Let her freeze. Let her stew. Go. She told you to go: therefore go. This shabby burned-out girl with her implausible affliction, her ESP. Her chattering angry voices. The necklace of grime on her chest. Vacant glassy eyes. Go.

To this Macy answered, not releasing Lissa's sweating palm, that he would hear no counsel of defeat, nor would he abandon her now. He went on urging her to come out of her trance; he pleaded with her not to give up. Here I am: take strength from me. Let me be your shield and your support. He conceived the notion of hauling her from the bed and carrying her out of the room, to that shower in the hall, where he would let the cool cleansing water sluice her from her lethargy. He naked beside her as the purifying deluge descended.

Up, then. To the shower. Grunting, he seized her by the shoulders, but her body was a dead weight and there was suddenly a terrific fiery bolus in his chest and a band of hot steel across his forehead, and he realized that she had already drained too much from him, that he was no longer strong enough to lift her. He let her fall back and collapsed across her, panting. His eyes were wet, he knew not whether from pain or despair or frustration or rage. Saving her was beyond him. He was too weak. He was too weary. He was too empty. He had given all he could give, and it had not been enough, and now he could give no more. *Perhaps if I rest. Perhaps in a little while.*

But he knew he was being foolish. He was drained. He would not soon recover. And now, too, he knew who it was who had tempted him to turn back before reaching this point, for he felt the presence hot within him, rising, expanding, glowing, the dark presence of his other self coming forth from his hidden lair, whispering wordlessly to him, crooning, inviting him to yield.

*Shall I fight him? Can I fight him? I must. I must.* Macy readied himself to resist Searching the corridors of his soul for forgotten reservoirs of strength. But he feared it was too late, that the takeover was already beginning. Already he felt a familiar sensation, a prickling at the back of his neck, a tingling, a mild stiffening of the skin. The unseen fingers were at work, stroking the lobes of his brain, caressing the prominences and corrugations. Inviting him to yield. *Yes. Yes. Temptation. An end to turmoil and torment No,* Macy said, *I will not let you have me.*

He attempted to get to his feet, but the best he could manage was to roll heavily free of Lissa and lie beside her. She seemed to be unconscious. *A sleep beyond all dreams. How peaceful she looks. And I could sleep that sleep. Come,* said the voiceless voice in wordless words, *let me enfold you, let me supplant you. Let* there no longer be struggle between us. Give way to me. *No! You will not have me!*

And Macy reached out toward Lissa, seeking her, asking alliance. The two of us against him. We can strike at him, we can destroy him. Lissa was a million miles away. Her planetoid of ice. The cold light of the distant sun dancing on the walls of the glacier. The tempter said, You see, there is no help to be had from her. Now is the time. Step aside for me. Be realistic, Macy, be realistic!

Macy attempted to be realistic. Where shall I go? How shall I fight? Who shall I be? And saw how little hope there was. He could not save himself. He had not been designed for this sort of stress. They had sent him on this second trip laden with an impossible burden, and was it then any surprise that the trip was a bummer? Let us end it. Let us fight no more. He would rest, he would close himself to struggling and hoping, he would surrender. The odds were too high against him. Outside waited Gomez, the van, the long cold needles, the drugs, all the machinery of deconstruction. Inside lurked Hamlin. Beside him lay this shattered girl. All right. I yield. I will fight no more.

—Then get out of the way, Hamlin said, and let me become you.

The mixing of selves was beginning. The dissolving, the blending. Paul Hamlin. Nat Macy. I am he. He is I. Maelstrom. Blinded by churning debris raining upon them out of their entangled pasts. A holocaust of dislocated events. As we dissolve into one another. Jeanie Grossman beneath the snows of Mount Rainier. And the girl with the long straight silken golden hair. Look, all through history girls have been posing for famous artists. Let me show you these charts, ma'am, explaining the special advantages of our encyclopedia. Why should you go to art school? My boy, you are already a master! Members of the class of '93, welcome to the UCLA campus. Hey, no, officer! Put that stunner down! I surrender, damn you, I surrender! I'll go peacefully! It isn't a matter of opinion, it's a matter of voltage thresholds. A voltage doesn't lie. Amperes don't have opinions. Resistances don't fuck around with you for sly tactical reasons. We're dealing in objective facts, and the objective facts tell me that Nat Hamlin has been wiped out. One-and-two-and-one-and-two. Proudly down the goddam street. Your new career. Your new life. *Shqkm. Vtpkp. Smss! Grgg!* Will the defendant please rise. Nathaniel James Hamlin you have heard the verdict of your peers. Don't play around with me. I know you're Nat Hamlin. You're looking good, Nat THE TORMENTS OF FAME. THE DAY THE MUSEUM BOUGHT EVERYTHING. MY NAME IS LISSA. No! Come back! Paul! Paul! *Nat!* Paul Hamlin. Nat Macy. We are becoming one. We are dissolving each into each. I will be you and you will be nothing. And there will be peace at last

Lissa! *LISSA!*

Abruptly the sky darkened and without warning bolts of lightning flashed and terrible thunder came and a sword swept down, trailing streamers of fire, to cleave the hemispheres of his brain one from the other. Between the two there loomed an unbridgeable gap, and on the far side of it Macy beheld Hamlin, stunned, dazed, wandering through a charred and blasted meadow as lightning struck all about him. That sudden fierce blow had severed all connection between them just at the instant of merger. I am Paul Macy. He is Nat Hamlin. And the crashing of the lightning. Blinding white streaks splitting the sky. Is that Lissa up there? Yes. Yes. Yes. Yes. She hurls the bolts. Crash! Crash! Hamlin tries to dodge. Across the great gulf drifts the scent of burning flesh. He is wounded. He moves more slowly. Crash! She has hemmed him in by a zone of fire on every side. Now Hamlin offers resistance. He shakes his fist; he shouts; he seizes her bolts and hurls them back at her. But each act of defiance brings redoubled furies out of the heavens. Her aim is deadly. Lightning spears his toes. Lightning licks at his heels. He hops. He dances. He screams in rage and then in pain. His arm is blackened by a bolt; he can no longer return her shafts. Now he writhes on the smouldering earth; now he shrieks for mercy. But there will be no mercy. Lissa is the avenging goddess. Hamlin will be destroyed.

But what's this? In the moment of triumph she tires. She weakens. The bolts lose intensity, and Hamlin still lives! He regains strength. She cries out for help. *Paul, Paul, Paul, Paul.* Yes, he replies, from his place beyond the zone of combat. Hamlin has risen. He is hideously disfigured, he is maimed and ruined, but yet there is demonic power in him, and now he lashes back at her, trying to bring her tumbling down to his own level. Crackling energies climb the sky. Help me, Paul!

And Macy opens himself to her, letting her take from him whatever she must have, and he arms her so that she can return to the attack. Again her lightnings flash. Again Hamlin howls. His thrusts are beaten back. He cannot fight on. He falls. A bolt pierces his back. He twists and coils in frightful convulsions. Lissa transfixes him again. Again. He is burning. He is dying. The odor of charred flesh on the wind. The sky is a sheet of white fire. She is spending herself, emptying herself, to eradicate him. She is cutting him to pieces.

Hamlin still moves, but now only in the random galvanic twitches of the dead. The meadow is a blazing pyre. He burns. He burns. He dwindles. He is gone. The sky grows still. Lissa can no longer be seen. A strange silence has come; a gentle cooling rain begins to fall. The air is sweet. The clouds part; the rain ends; the soft sunlight returns. There is no gulf between the regions of the brain. Macy' crosses over. He sees no trace of Hamlin but only a dark place on the ground, a blackened scar in the grass, and quickly the grass grows to hide it, tall green blades moving swiftly in, sprouting tender new shoots that rise and meet, and soon there is no sign of destruction anywhere, although Macy knows that beneath the graceful grassy carpet one might find a layer of ash, if one chose to excavate. He walks away from that place. He is utterly alone. Lissa? he calls. Lissa? But there is no reply. Silence governs. He is utterly alone.

After a time he sat up and got carefully to his feet. The sense of being alone remained with him. There was a faint throbbing in his head, of the sort one might feel if one were transported suddenly from the heart of some great city to the eerie soundless wastelands of the polar plateau, but otherwise he was aware of no aftereffects of the battle. Except one. Hamlin was gone from him. That much was certain: Hamlin was gone.

He looked at Lissa. She lay as before, limp, glassy-eyed, self-isolated. Her bare skin glistened with sweat. The feverish look had left her, and, touching her side, he found that she was indeed cooler. Not only the fever had departed from her, though. For the first time since he had known her, Macy was unable to detect that look of terrible strain in her features, that expression of barely suppressed despair. She was calm. Her inner storms, as well as his, were over. But her calmness was of a frightening sort. She seemed vacant, almost entirely absent.

"Lissa?" he said. "Can you hear me?"

"Lis—Lis"

"Lissa."

"Lis—"

"Lissa," he said. "Lissa is you."

"Lissa is you." Her voice was high, childish, fluting, toneless.

"No. No. I'm Paul. You're Lissa."

"I'm Paul. You're Lissa."

He sat beside her. He took her hands in his. Her fingers were very cold. Her eyes closed a moment; then the lids fluttered and she opened them and looked at him in a sunny, uncomprehending way, and she smiled. He said, "You've burned yourself out, haven't you? You just used up everything you had. To save me. And now there's nothing left but a husk."

"Husk."

"Is the ESP gone too, I wonder? Can you still hear the voices? Do you hear them, Lissa?"

"Voices. Do you. Hear them. Lissa."

"You don't, do you? Not any more."

"No," she said unexpectedly. "I don't hear. Anything."

Her response startled him. "You can understand me now? The voices are really gone?"

A smile. A fluttering of the eyelids. A babyish giggle. "The. Voices. Are. Really. Gone." She had slipped away from him once more.

He searched the room for a telephone. None. He went to the door and looked into the hall. A phone out there, yes. Someone using it. Chattering away. All right, I'll wait. A few minutes. And then phone Gomez. Send your van, I'll tell him. Manhattan North People's Co-op, and hurry. Not for me. For her, for Lissa. Yes. Burned out, hardly knows her own name. But there's something still intact down deep inside her. Not much, but enough, maybe, for you to work with, Gomez. No, you don't have to bother with me. I'm okay. It's over. Hamlin's gone, obliterated for keeps, gone, really gone. A total deconstruct. But the girl. Can you fix her, Gomez? Can you put her back together? It won't be like a reconstruct, exactly. You won't have to pour a new identity into an old body, just put an old identity back where it belongs. Okay, Gomez? You'll do it? Good. Good. And how long will it take? Five months, six, a year? Whatever. Just do it.

Five months. Six. November. December. Macy saw himself waiting at the main building of the Rehab Center. Snow on the ground, the branches of the trees heavy with whiteness, the sky a wintry blue. And Lissa, renewed, repaired, coming toward him out of the inner wing. No longer a telepath. A brand-new Lissa, stripped of her gift and of her torment. Uncertain of herself as she goes forth to face the world. Hello, he'll say. Hello, she'll say. An awkward little kiss. Button up, he'll tell her, it's cold. I've got a car. She'll look worried. Are we going into the city? she'll ask. My first day out. I'm nervous. You know what it's like, Paul, coming out. Sure, he'll say, I know just what it's like. But you'll be all right. New people, new lives. The second trip. Paul and Lissa, Lissa and Paul Minus our old friend Nat. A great artist has gone from the world. How quiet it is inside my head. Five months. Six. November. December. Lissa?

She was giggling softly, and her hands were exploring her body, discovering this and that as a baby might. Lightly he touched her cheek. She wriggled in pleasure. You wait, he said. Gomez will fix you better than you were before. Macy peered into the hall again. The phone still busy. Come on, get off the line, get off, get off! He didn't say it He stood in the doorway, waiting to make his call, half expecting Hamlin to rise from somewhere, but Hamlin did not arise. Gone. Gone. My other self, my dark twin. He has left the world, and I have his place. Macy almost felt guilty about it. The merest flicker of regret. Farewell to you, Nat, a long farewell to Mr. Hyde. And I will go on through life without you. Wearing your skin, wearing your face. I am you, Nat and you are nothing.

Macy looked back at Lissa. She was drooling. As I must have drooled, he thought. Four years ago when I was very new. He went to her and mopped her chin. It's all right, he said to her without bothering to speak aloud. December isn't so far away. And then hello, and then we start again. Two ordinary people. Trip two, yours, mine. The second trip. The good one, maybe. From the hall came the click of the receiver. The phone was free at last. He went out to call Gomez.

# ABOUT THE AUTHOR

Robert Silverberg is one of science fiction's most beloved writers, and the author of such contemporary classics as *Dying Inside*, *Downward to the Earth* and *Lord Valentine's Castle*. He is a past president of the Science Fiction and Fantasy Writers of America and the winner of five Nebula Awards and five Hugo Awards. In 2004 the Science Fiction and Fantasy Writers of America presented him with the Grand Master Award. Silverberg is one of twenty-nine writers to have received that distinction.

# ROBERT SILVERBERG

## FROM OPEN ROAD MEDIA

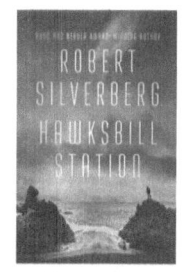

OPEN ROAD

INTEGRATED MEDIA

OPEN ROAD

INTEGRATED MEDIA

Find a full list of our authors and
titles at www.openroadmedia.com

FOLLOW US
@OpenRoadMedia

www.ingramcontent.com/pod-product-compliance
Lightning Source LLC
Chambersburg PA
CBHW032302020726

47495CB00001B/211